THE BITCH FARM

Dutch Haid

The Bitch Farm

Copyright © 2024 by Dutch Haid

All Rights Reserved

No part of this publication may be reproduced, distributed, or transmitted in any form or by any means, including photocopying, recording, or other electronic or mechanical methods, without the prior written permission of the publisher, except in the case of brief quotations embodied in critical reviews and certain other non-commercial uses permitted by copyright law.

The story, all names, characters, and incidents portrayed in this production are fictitious. No identification with actual persons (living or deceased), places, buildings, and products is intended or should be inferred.

To Janie, may this publishing justify the hours you spent being a computer widow! Your time on earth has come to an end, and so has the writing of this novel, which stole from you some of our precious time together.

May you rest in peace. I love you!

Acknowledgments

Thanks to dear friend Glenda Coursen and my loving wife, Janie, for their encouragement in completing this novel.

Table of Contents

Chapter 1 1
   Beginning "The Deed" Zac's Preparation................... 1
   James, As Zac Remembers... 6
   James, Zac, And Jessie 7
   Killing "Bitch-Mother" 11
   Gwendolyn Anne Ashley 20
Chapter 2 26
   Brad And Marci 26
   Brad And Marci Hearing Of Gwen 31
   James And The Business 37
Chapter 3 40
   Christine Lowell 40
   Brad And Marci Are Still In Vero 42
   Killing Christy 45
Chapter 4 53
   Brad Hearing Of Christy 53
   Eight Missing Women Found, Plus Christie 61
   James And Mrs. Oliver 69
Chapter 5 74
   Grotto And Task Force 74
   James Meets Carrie 77
   Brad And Marci 80
Chapter 6 83
   James And Roslyn 83

Roslyn Found	86
James Killed Instead Of Zac	91
Chapter 7	**94**
Brad's Interviews	94
Zac And Carrie	98
Brad	102
Chapter 8	**106**
Finding Gerald	106
James After Carrie	113
Brad And Jack In Jensen Beach	119
Chapter 9	**124**
Marci And Brad Seeing The Knotty Lady	124
Killing JoAnne	131
Finding Knotty Lady	137
Chapter 10	**151**
Back To James	151
Brad and Jack	153
James	155
James, Zac, And Jessie	156
Chapter 11	**161**
Brad And Marci	161
Brad And Jack	162
Jessie Comes To Life And Meets Calie	164
Brad And Marci – Mrs. O'Dell	171
Chapter 12	**173**
Zac Is Jessie	173

Marci And Brad – Jack And Sue -- Sailing 176

Chapter 13 181
Jessie and Calie 181
James and Zac meet Jessie 185
Brad and Gang and Press Release 187

Chapter 14 195
Jessie And Calie 195
Brad And The Case 199
James 202
Jack And Sue 207

Chapter 15 210
Vero Inn Party (James Uses The Alias Frank James) 210
Sue And Jack At Vero Inn 217
Back To Work 220
Jessie Switches 221

Chapter 16 225
Police Activity – Langford Murder 225
Brad And Jack – Langford Case 229
Jeffery's Report 230
Calie Brushes Off Jessie 237

Chapter 17 239
Jack And Sue – Gravedigger Theory 239
The Cemetery Questioning 241
Sue Tells Of Calie's Reported Missing 242
Sail to Daytona 245
Leave Daytona And Return To Work 253

Chapter 18 257
    Mrs. Oliver's Story 257
    Sue And Jack Discuss Jessie 263
    Franie's Plan 264
    Sue Researching James 269
    The Interview 270
    James in LA 273
    The Sale 274
Chapter 19 276
    Sue 276
    James's Plastic Surgery 277
    Boris Back At The Farm 278
Chapter 20 279
    Grotto Meeting 279

Chapter 1

Beginning "The Deed" Zac's Preparation

The light of day was gone as Zac completed removing the interior light bulbs from the rented van. He carefully placed the bulbs in the glove box for safekeeping, then opened and closed all the doors, surveying the results of his efforts. Nothing was to be left undone. The predetermined departure time drew near, and he grew antsy with the anticipation of doing 'the deed.' He rechecked the equipment neatly stowed in the oversized backpack for the third time before setting it upright on the rear center seat and snuggly securing it with the seat belt.

"I don't want my precious goodies rolling about," he mused, inspecting the backpack again.

Methodically, he retraced his steps and smiled satisfactorily at a job well done. "James was very thoughtful to rent this van for tonight, especially for this bitch," he mused. "James chose a fully loaded van with lots of room, easy access, and all of the bells and whistles, and it should be fun to drive," Zac thought. Moving to the van's rear, Zac hefted the large modified suitcase into the area between the rear seat and doors. He noticed that the case fit the space nicely, admiring James's ingenuity as he closed the doors. He was also amazed at James's ability to conceive everything needed and his conception of the meticulous details involved in doing 'the deed.'

"How James contemplates potential problems, determines the

solutions, and analyzes each precise step is far beyond me," Zac mumbled aloud.

The new large wheels he added to this new case should help. Tugging the old suitcase through the thick lawns on previous deeds was a bitch.

"Maybe that's because it was full of bitches," he snickered, "but I believe the new wheels and the moisture-proof lining will make the bitch removal portion of 'the deed' much more manageable and far less messy."

"Cleaning the trunk of those rental cars was a pain in the ass, not to mention hefting that old suitcase into the trunk of a car when it was full of a bitch. Perhaps I will call this new case a bitch-case. It will not be used as a suitcase. There sure as hell won't be any suits in it tonight," Zac chuckled. "Good old James continually devises better and easier ways to do 'the deed' even though he is not doing it."

Pausing his thoughts for a moment to review his status, Zac circled the van carefully, double-checking every detail of the plan thus far as prescribed by James. He opened the driver's door and beamed impishly, seeing no lights illuminating the interior. "Ah yes," Zac whispered, "the darkness shall remain dark, another well-done task." "The van is all set," he murmured aloud while sliding into the driver's seat, "I shall be on my joyful way." Zac fastened his seat belt, started the engine, and scanned the instrument panel, assuring himself that the gas tank was full and no warning lights were on, indicating a problem. "One thing I do not need tonight is a vehicle problem," Zac muttered as he pushed the button on the remote, opening the new garage door like magic.

"James, you certainly have made things easier for me this time. A new electric garage door, a modified bitch-case, a giant backpack with shoulder pads, and switching from a car to this neat van. What more could I ask?" He backed the van out of the barn into the seclusion of the trees and continued with his thoughts. Using the barn now to get all the gear ready is much better than trying to stay hidden under the trees, plus no more carrying things back and forth: "Damn, James, your brilliant. The new garage door has helped the farm workers as well. They can get the equipment in and out a lot easier now. Oops, sorry, James, there I go again, referring to the cemetery as a farm. I remember you cautioned me not to do that. You don't want people to think we are growing things out here. Speaking of that, I do plant some fascinating objects in the cemetery, don't I? But so far, none of their sorry asses have ever sprouted or grown," he giggled. "That would be cool, a forest full of bitch trees," he quipped. "Oh well, thanks for the improvements, James," Zac stated aloud while shifting the van into drive and edging out of the cover of the trees into the full moonlit night.

The dark-colored van motored leisurely along the back drive, winding amidst the forest of water oaks clothed in Spanish moss, then veered left onto the small dirt road parallel to the southern border along the graveyard. The sun had retired for the day, and a full moon had risen over the eastern horizon, giving Zac ample visibility to steer without using the headlights. He always tried to drive this portion of the route without lights to avoid prying eyes, but tonight, the glint of moonlight simplified his familiar trek. No houses were close to his path; however, some nosey local driving on US-1 might take note of headlights in what appeared to be an open field and disclose that to the wrong person. James cautioned Zac to take no chances, coming or going, and Zac followed James's instructions to the letter. As far as Zac is concerned, James is the boss, and James is very smart.

Zac waited patiently in the obscurity of the water oak trees lining the cemetery's southern border until all of the traffic on the highway had cleared. He then turned on the lights, progressed onto US-1, and traveled south toward Vero Beach. Zac maintained the various speed limits plus a few, attempting to be inconspicuous and not draw undue attention. Approaching his destination, he steered the van cautiously into the moderately high-priced neighborhood. He proceeded down the unlit street, beyond a group of houses, to an area of newer construction where his quarry for the evening resided. Near the far end of the road stood the remnants of a partially demolished convenience store. A trash dumpster was off the far side of the old store, out of view of the few nearby homes and hidden by the partial structure. Recalling the area vividly from his previous canvassing, Zac turned off the headlights, shifted into natural, and slowly coasted alongside the dumpster. He stopped the slow-moving van using the emergency brake, thus avoiding the flash of brake lights, which may cause the neighbors concern. Zac sat silently, taking note of the time while surveying the neighborhood. He remained there, allowing the passage of thirty minutes that James had allotted to ascertain that he was not detected.

Exiting the driver's seat, Zac walked briskly around the van. He opened the side door, removed the backpack, quickly slipped it over his shoulders, and strapped it securely across his chest. Zac retrieved the bitch-case, from the rear of the van, extended the handle, and gingerly shut all the doors with barely an auditable click. Pleased with his progress thus far, he paused, systematically re-scanning the area. Satisfied that the coast was clear, Zac stealthily slipped across the street into the seclusion of the underbrush on the vacant lot, which placed him directly behind his target's house.

Creeping closer, he noted that the backpack's weight was now barely noticed due to the new and broader padded straps and the big wheels on bitch-case rolled silently with minimal effort. Pleased with these improvements, Zac skillfully navigated the underbrush until arriving at the rear edge of the manicured yard. Again, he paused briefly in a crouching position and surveyed the local. Once satisfied, he continued, slowly but steadily, cautiously creeping through the thick, recently mowed lawn until arriving at the corner of the concrete patio extending off the house. At this point, Zac carefully positioned himself in a shadow created by a large hibiscus bush. He stashed the bitch-case out of view between the hibiscus bush and the patio, taking advantage of the darkness. Then, he took a moment to re-examine the scene, reassuring his cautious mind that his journey from the van had been undetected.

To Zac's delight, a portion of the roof jutting out over the glass sliding door cast a darkened shadow onto the patio, permitting him to proceed to the door in the provided darkness. Once there, he removed the backpack, slipped on his gloves, and removed a circular glass cutter with a suction cup attached. Zac pressed the suction cup securely against the glass adjacent to the lock. The slight sideways force of pressing the suction cup on the glass caused the door to slide ajar. The unexpected movement startled Zac and caused him to lose grip on the cutter, which fell to the patio floor with a dull clunking sound.

"Damn it. Damn it. Damn it." Zac cursed to himself. "The frigging door is unlocked. Why the hell didn't I check it before trying to cut the glass? I know it's been a month or two since I've done 'the deed,' but I didn't think I was that damn rusty. Surly, the expert I am, I haven't lost all of my sneaky-ass talents, have I?" scoffing silently to himself at his self-criticism, he retreated swiftly and blended again into the shadow of the hibiscus. Zac crouched in the darkness. His silhouette was hidden from the illuminating luster of the moon. His eyes darted with the diligence of a stalking feline, and his ears were sharply attuned for any minuscule sound that indicated his bumbled attempt had caused alarm. Remaining motionless for several minutes, which seemed like hours, he determined that the noise had gone unheard. The only sounds heard in the stillness were the chirping of crickets and the resounding thumps of his palpitating heart.

A devilish grin formed on Zac's face, realizing that the bitch had left the door unlocked. "How fucking convenient," he thought. "I don't have to waste my time breaking in. I can walk in as if being invited. That makes the score of this game Zac one and the bitch zero." The results of this incident, being in his favor, brought a sigh of relief that one step of the task would be more straightforward and that his presence remained undetected. In the shadowy dimness, he recalled the procedure James had instructed. If an error or mishap occurs, sit tight and wait ample time to assure anonymity before proceeding with "the deed." Zac was doing just that.

James, As Zac Remembers

Mental images of the past began wafting in his head as often they did, returning him to an era of uneasiness that frequently echoed through his mind. The pictures in his brain were like instant replays, bringing back the volatile world of young James. He was christened into this world as James Alfred Zachary, a bastard child born by Patsy Ann Colby, a wild she-dog. Patsy had been an atrocious mother. She treated James horribly, both physically and emotionally. With every passing day of his youthful years, James grew increasingly hostile towards her in his mind but more submissive to avoid the punishment and brutality. To this day, James cringes away from the dreadful thoughts of his battered youth. This bitch of a mother instilled a sense in him of being unwanted and rejected as her child. He cannot tolerate the slightest insinuation of being unwanted or rejected.

James was abused continuously, Zac recalled, and as a result, whenever someone causes those feelings, he withdraws to his inner self and summons me, Zac, to seek revenge.

Zac shook with sadness as he continued to ponder the story of James. The memories from that period caused James to shutter and be ill. His bitch of a mother made him feel small, she made him feel weak, and she made him wholly vulnerable to her abuse. When she chastised him and often did for little or no reason, she screamed the foulest of words in her high-pitched, snarling voice, causing young James to cringe and wet his pants in fear. The screams would be followed by the physical sting of a leather strap thrashing against his naked buttocks because he wet his pants. With his pants removed, the bitch would grab his immature penis, pinching and brutally shaking it while screaming he was a no-good 'Pee baby.' She would squeeze and yank on his small protuberance, causing it to be red and swollen while she repeated, "Pee-baby, Pee-baby, you're nothing but a Pee-baby." Then she would scream, "I never wanted you born, and I damn sure don't want your sorry ass now, so get out of here." Finally, she would tell him to take his little 'dicky-wicky' and get out of her sight.

James would quickly flee from her presence when she released her claw-like grip. James would freely permit the tears to gush from his eyes and try to soothe the painful welts on his body. Still, he could not alleviate the mental anguish pulsating through his mind. Demoralized and hatred-filled, he would retreat into his room's cramped and dusky closet, seeking solitude and safety.

"Of course, James pissed his pants during her tirades," Zac remembered, "and it was all in sheer terror of that bitch. She made him piss his pants, she caused him pain, and she is the bitch who beat him unmercifully. James did not understand the reasons for her intense hostility, nor did he ever forgive her. Frankly, she was a pure bitch. I guess that is why I was born," Zac grinned. "Brother James needed help comprehending the bitch, and he derived me from his soul and mind." Zac continued his recollection of James's past while waiting.

James, Zac, And Jessie

James cherished the shelter of his closet, as dank and dingy as it may be. It was his sanctuary and his place to escape. Zac mused quietly about the closet, for it was there and only there that he conversed with me. "I became an extraordinary person in James's life. We managed to keep our interaction private, very private. James knew if the bitch were to discover me, she would mistreat him all the more. I became a brother to James, a secret brother who would listen and comfort him just like a brother should. When James was crying, hurt, or sad, I would appear before him and be very kind and understanding. We would talk for hours and plan our future. We also contemplated seeking revenge against the bitch as soon as we were mature enough and able."

Strangely enough, though, Zac recollected, on occasion, when the bitch was at work or out boozing it up, James enjoyed what he called 'freedom time.' He would dream of frolicking and playing games like the other boys. During one of his 'freedom times,' James found an old book about a western outlaw named Jessie James. The book made it appear as though Jessie James enjoyed being an outlaw. He took no crap off anyone and seemed to relish being a badass. James surmised that since his name was James, why not be Jessie James and have fun? Whenever he had 'freedom time,' he became Jessie James, the badass. However, James possessed no characteristics or abilities to be a badass. So pretending to be Jessie eventually evolved into sessions of just having fun.

"I understood that James was fantasizing and playing this 'Jessie' game, and I didn't object," Zac remembered. "I encouraged James to have some fun. Be Jessie and shed the evil thoughts of the bitch for a while, I would tell him. Also, playing this game allowed me to relax in the quiet cells of James's brain, where I could observe him as Jessie, a different entity. However, 'Jessie' did not always prove to be a game of fun. I recall one occasion when James played Jessie on his way home from school. A female classmate noticed him role-playing and began teasing him. James became very uncomfortable, embarrassed, and disparaged, and suddenly, Jessie vanished. The girl's actions and taunting caused James to become disoriented to the point that he considered her a bitch just like his mother and, consequently, desired revenge. It was strangely weird because I also sensed the same overwhelming desire." Zac smiled as he recalled that he voluntarily stepped in to help James. "Swiftly and violently, I hammered that little bitch," he murmured. "I grabbed her from behind, cupped my hand over her screaming mouth, and pulled her into the bushes. I straddled her twitching body, pinning her tightly to the ground, reached under her dress and panties, then groped her crotch savagely. I molested her tight vagina and forced my fingers into her while staring into her eyes with such ghoulish sincerity that she became terrified. I threatened that if she ever bothered James again or told anybody what happened, I would kill her, her mother, and her little sister. I dismounted her body, and she retreated quickly, swearing never to tell. It's funny, Zac thought, but I had no idea why I did all that evil or even what I had. James also had no idea, either, but we both enjoyed it. I guess my intervention made James feel safe, and I delighted in doing so. Based on that encounter, I realized I had just become a protector of James's existence."

Staring listlessly at the moon and shaking his head at his recollections, Zac continued wondering. "Why did James have such a lousy start to life, and why did things happen the way they did? Why can't James forget those horrible feelings? Why is James, my brother? Why is James the controlling force, and why am I the protector and the avenger?" "Oh well," he murmured. "We are what we are, and enough of this asking why I need to keep my wits about me and do 'the deed' as James desires."

Regaining his presence of mind, Zac patiently waited, ensuring the coast was clear before proceeding with 'the deed.' "Yeah," he spoke under his breath, "the resplendent venture of doing away with another one of the female bitches shall be exhilarating." Relaxing on his haunches, Zac recalled how pleasant it had become since James summons him more often to help. James is Zac's big brother, and Zac appreciates that relationship. James strategizes every little move and detail to get revenge on the unsavory bitches, and in turn, Zac carries out James's strategy to the letter. "James is smart," Zac said silently, "very smart." Zac knows that James has had no encounters with ladies in the normal social world and figured it was because of his mother, the bitch. He knew James frequently seduced a few ladies at that whorehouse in Fellsmere whenever he desired feminine companionship, and those ladies treated him very well.

"Hell, they should. The money James spends in that place, they should treat him like a king," Zac snickered. "When James goes out publicly seeking a lady, I wonder why he consistently encounters a frigging bitch. Is it just his luck, or maybe he doesn't know how to choose the nice ones? However, I shouldn't complain. He finds a lady, she becomes a bitch, and he turns her over to me. I get all the fun, and I get to do 'the deed,' hell, what more could I want?" Zac again snickered quietly at his thoughts.

Still idling away time, Zac's wandering mind stirred up memories of James's father, William Alfred Zachary, better known as Billy Zac, among friends. Shortly after graduating high school, he had obtained a job on the oil rigs off Louisiana's coast and had knocked up James's mother, the sexy and lovely bitch, Patsy Ann Colby. They never married, so when James was born, she tagged him with his father's last name, Zachary. The bitch said she sure didn't want some little bastard degrading her name. At least that was the story, according to Patsy's mother, Granny Sue. Granny Sue told James stories of how his mother and father had dated while in high school and how the bitch had wrongly treated Billy Zac. Patsy threw a holy fit when she discovered she was pregnant and refused to see or talk with him. Patsy blamed the pregnancy on Billy Zac, ignoring that she willingly spread her legs.

Billy Zac tried to help and even wanted to marry Patsy, but she would have no part in getting married. She refused to let him see James when he was a baby or older. James was not permitted to ask about his father or even mention that he had one. If he did, that bitch would rant and rave and call Billy Zac vile names. Then, she would slap James across the face for mentioning his name. Granny Sue was the only person James could talk to about his father. She would tell him beautiful stories about how his dad played football and was the high school hero. Just like daddies are supposed to be, he was big and strong, and James would dream of knowing his father and yearn to be with him.

Granny Sue was nothing like Patsy Ann. She was very kind

and sweet and treated James like her own. Patsy Ann was a pure bitch, so James nicknamed her 'Bitch-Mother.' He only called her mother when she forced him to, and he would stutter and gag even then. She never called him Son or wanted him around except to do chores, and she would frequently beat him for no reason. Then, to top things off, Bitch-Mother moved to that hick town in Florida, taking James with her, and he no longer had Granny Sue to talk with or help him. James missed Granny Sue and grew to hate Bitch Mother even more. Zac shook his head in disbelief at all the vile things he remembered.

"It was in Florida, in that old shack," that James matured. He was alone most of the day while Bitch-Mother worked for pennies in the sugar cane fields. However, she was home almost every night, acting like a sloppy-ass drunken whore. Three, four, and sometimes five men a night would shuffle in and out of that shack at all hours. James would cover his head, trying to keep out the noises, the moans and groans, the squeaky bed, and all the whooping and hollering as she entertained her 'man friends,' as she called them. Bitch-Mother instructed James never to leave his room when she was entertaining, not even if he had to pee or was hungry. The few times he did sneak out and got caught, it was the traditional 'Pee-baby' and belt routine before the bitch sent him back to his room with a sore penis and a black and blue ass. "Damn," Zac thought, "why did she do those things? Why wasn't she decent like other mothers? Why was she such a bitch? Poor James, no wonder he needs me to help him." "Ah, shit," Zac mumbled. "It's those damn 'why' questions again. I must forget why and stay set on doing 'the deed.'"

Killing "Bitch-Mother"

Multitudes of memories drifted through the portals of his mind as Zac mellowed out while watching a small lazy cloud sail across the sky, creating a slow-motion shadow on the ground that aided his refuge. The one thought that gladdened him was a special memory he enjoyed reminiscing about, and that was the first time James requested his help. Zac thought, "I had voluntarily stepped in with his minor problems before, but this was the first time James purposely asked me for help." That was the most memorable day for several reasons. It was James' eighteenth birthday. The sun had just begun brightening the sky, which was already hot and humid. James was lying naked on his bed, trying to stay cool. Some pleasantly erotic thoughts entered his mind, causing him to become sexually aroused. He was tenderly stroking his erect penis, which was starting to feel very sensitive.

Unfortunately, as his feelings became more intense, Bitch-Mother, unknowing of his masturbation, burst into his room unannounced, startling James.

You could tell that the sight she beheld startled her as well. She stood speechless, peering wide-eyed at James's face, his manly chest, and ogling his nakedness, then fixed her gaze upon his enormous erection. Bitch-Mother slowly moved closer for a better view of his upright member as James attempted to conceal it with the sheet. With her still drunken voice from the previous night, she screamed, "Don't hide that gorgeous cock," and yanked the sheet from his hands. "Look at that luscious thing. Your prick stands up there tall, proud, and ready for action. No, but hell no, don't you hide that monstrous charm from me. Let me see it. I want to behold every inch of that succulent thing. I believe that Pee-baby's dicky-wicky has finally grown up."

Edging ever closer to his naked torso, she slurred, "I haven't seen a vibrant young tool like that in a long time. All the drunken dicks around here can hardly stand up anymore. I must say that you take after your father, for what it's worth. He had a big prick as well. Speaking of worth, I would estimate that yours should be worth at least eight inches of sheer lust. Not bad for a maturing Pee-baby, not bad at all. I want a closer look at that big thing. I even want to feel it and stroke it for you. Better yet, I will show you what a real woman's lips and tongue can do for your pleasure. You are eighteen now, and it's about time you know what that thing is used for." She hastily stripped off the remnants of her tattered gown while babbling, "Happy Birthday, you little bastard. Mama is going to give you a present you will never forget. I'll bet you're still a virgin. Aren't you? I bet ya never had a piece of pussy before, just your hand-jobs, huh? Well, now, birthday boy, relax. Once I go down on that delicious sausage for a minute or two, you'll be ready to enjoy the more delightful parts of a real woman."

That birthday episode was the only pleasant thing that Bitch-Mother ever did for James, Zac thought, and he recalled the event vividly. She went down on him lustfully, causing James's eyes to roll back in his head from the pleasurable sensations he was first experiencing, all the while forcing himself to ignore that it was Bitch-Mother creating such torrid desires in his loin. After several minutes of oral stimulation, bringing James to the very edge of ecstasy, she instructed him to tie her hands to the bedposts. "I love the feeling of being raped. It turns me on. Your father did that to me once, and that's how you came to be," she slurred. "Besides, the size of your shaft is bound to feel like rape. Come on now and shove it in me. I'll show you the proper way to screw. Maybe, just maybe, I can make a man out of you after all."

Zac smiled at the thought of James cunningly obeying her every wish. Tearing a pillowcase into strips, he spread her arms and tied each of her wrists to an upper bedpost. "That's good, Pee-baby," she screamed, "now rape me, and make yourself be a man." James just smirked as he tore more strips. He forcefully spread her legs and lashed them to the lower bedposts, splaying her wide open for the taking. Once she was secured to the bed, he stood back, surveyed his handy work, and smirked at seeing her vile crevice spread open. "Whoa there, Pee-baby," she murmured and cooed lustfully, "you learn fast, very, very fast. You must have read some damn good books telling you what to do if you're still a virgin. Now quit leering and pleasure me. It's been a couple of days, and I need pleasuring badly. Screw me, Pee-baby. Screw me hard with that virgin cock. Come on now, give your Mama a big birthday boy screw." James positioned himself at the mound of her crotch and thrust his engorged shaft fully into her, watching her wince and flinch with pleasurable pain. "My god, you're huge," she screamed. "Pump me full, pump and pleasure me, damn you, rape me hard, and pump me full."

Zac felt a sense of vindictive glee in his groin while recalling the remainder of that memorable day. He remembered it clearly with a vision of James pleasuring her with flurries of deep penetrating lunges until her satisfaction peaked with intensity. Seeing that look in her eyes, James withdrew his erection, dismounted the Bitch, and stood at the foot of the bed, leering at her undesirable display of femininity. "So it's some pleasure that you want, Bitch-Mother, well I'll give you pleasure, you filthy bitch," he stated as he stepped up on the bed, straddled her torso, then sat heavily upon her stomach. He slid his penis into the sweaty cleavage of her breast while squeezing them tightly together and began thrusting his prick back and forth. The throbbing end of his member pounded against her moist lips as she engulfed its sensitive head and sucked it like a lollipop. The warmth of her saliva, the tightness of her lips, and her darting tongue heightened James's urge to climax. His body arched at his waist; his eyes rolled back, and his torso quaked. With one forceful lunge and a tremendous moan of satiation, he experienced a thundering climax, showering her with a fountain of sperm. James was exhilarated by the enthralling sensation that had just spurred through him. It was a sensation that he had never before experienced. A torrid volcano had erupted from the inner depths of his testicles, causing his entire body to tremble, and James screamed with uncontrollable pleasure. He had not just climaxed. He had experienced a total orgasmic overload. Zac recalled that James had summoned him for help at that very instant while reaching the peaking ebb of his climax. "Damn," Zac thought, "I couldn't believe how revered I felt when James said," "Zac, please take over for me and do 'the deed.'" "Upon his request, I exited my mental sanctuary, and through pure instinct, my right hand grasped Bitch-Mother by her throat, and my grip began slowly tightening, and much to my enjoyment, my left hand methodically stroked my rigid member right in front of her face. This miserable excuse of a female stared at me in total disbelief as her body heaved with convulsions, her throat gurgled, her eyes bulged, and her slobbering tongue dangled from her mouth. I continued squeezing until she gasped her last wheezing breath. The bitch's body went limp as I consummated her demise with my orgasm. Neither James nor I had ever experienced such magnificent ejaculations. The climaxes arose from our intimate depths, and they were powerful and awesome, and more than that, they were harmonious with the death of a bitch. I had helped James with the schoolgirl problem, but nothing ever as profound as this. Henceforth, James and I assumed our individually defined roles. I shall never forget that fabulous moment," Zac thought. "Our first bitch was Bitch-Mother, and we had just completed 'the deed' for the first time."

Zac continued dreaming as he lulled in the shadow of the bush. Then laughing loudly at the sight of her ugly torso lying motionless on the bed, he untied the restraints, rolled her unresponsive body onto the floor, and hysterically howled as he pissed all over her nude body. He remembered James jokingly asking, Bitch-Mother, "How do you like your Pee-baby now, you old bitch? Now Bitch-

Mother, who's the Pee-baby?" "Damn," Zac muttered silently. "That was great, and it was the first time James summoned me for help, and I helped." "Yeah," Zac smiled as he repeated, "I helped, and James didn't ask me to kill her, but he asked me to do 'the deed.' I could tell he'd had enough of her crap, so I interpreted his term 'the deed' my way. James and I had invented 'the deed,' which felt great. I did it, I killed her miserable ass, and I enjoyed doing so. It made my pinus tingle and my ass quiver with delight.

Zac again snickered to himself in the darkness, recalling that first intervention, and he permitted his mind to re-live more of that day as he patiently waited. James instructed me on what to do with the body and clean up all the telltale signs left behind. I did as told. When I was done, there was no trace of Bitch-Mother's demise to be found. I washed the entire area with bleach and alcohol. I cleaned the soiled linens and burnt the ties used to restrain her. I then remade the bed and thoroughly retraced my efforts to assure myself that not one iota of evidence was remaining to be found. Nothing was left that would prove that Bitch-Mother had been the first to experience 'the deed.' I did everything exactly as James had instructed. Damn, James is smart, he's very smart, and subsequently, he and I have enjoyed a fascinating relationship. Bitch-Mother did succeed in doing one thing that birthday morning. She did make a man out of James."

Zac's concentration returned to the present as a cloud darkened the sky again, obscuring the moon's vibrant rays. "I hope Miss Ashley is wearing a skimpy nightgown," he thought, "she has nice tits and an adorable ass, so perhaps I'll get a little pussy before I send her off to the Bitch Farm. James doesn't mind if I seduce and molest the bitches. I think he enjoys that I get my rocks off before doing 'the deed.'" An imposing erection started to grow from his groin, stemming from his lustful thoughts. "Stop it now, damn it, stop this erection," Zac instructed himself. He pushed at the bulge, trying to make it go away, but it continued to rise and pulsate against the tightness of his jeans. "Don't worry, James. I can handle the job. I won't let my little head cloud my judgment."

Zac looked at the moon again and enjoyed thinking of the past. He had experienced a glorious morning killing Bitch-Mother, and even though it was James's birthday, he had gone to work as usual. "James always does the right thing," Zac mumbled and remembered that James had no more than returned home from work when a car drove up, and that lawyer-man approached the shack. After the introductions, he and James talked briefly. The lawyer-man gave James some documents, then explained that James, being eighteen now, should come down to the lawyer-man's office tomorrow where the details of the documents could be further described. Based on instructions in the papers, he advised James not to discuss anything with his Mother. James silently laughed and agreed. Once the lawyer-man left, James told me to make certain no one could see me and hide Bitch-Mother in the freezer in the back shack until he figured out how to dispose of her carcass.

Zac smiled again, recalling James getting dressed in his Sunday best and meeting with the lawyer-man. It was rare when James did himself up that way, and he looked nice. The lawyer-man informed James that his Dad, William Alan Zachary, had died in an airplane crash and had willed oodles of cold cash and a business with a large parcel of land to his only son, James Alfred Zachary. "I'm glad James is smart and that he understood all of what the lawyer-man was telling him. James said to me that he could hardly wait until he got home so he could let me out of hiding and tell me all about it."

"James was excited and started developing big plans for us, but we had to take care of Bitch-Mother's body first. James grinned as he informed me that he now knew the perfect spot to dispose of her body because, in the legal papers the lawyer-man had given to him was a property map, and we shall call our new hunk of land the Bitch Farm, mainly because Bitch-Mother will be planted there." "Oh yeah, those were good times," Zac mumbled to himself. He and James packed up what was worth taking and moved everything to the farm. Bitch-Mother made it a Bitch Farm, so a Bitch Farm it is, he snickered. "Let me think now," Zac murmured, "I have panted eight bitches on the farm so far, and the ninth one is right inside this house. I love making James happy and doing "the deed," and the disposing of Bitches makes him happy and me sexually satisfied. Damn, James is smart. He's very smart."

Zac continued rocking back and forth on his haunches, patiently dwelling on pleasant thoughts of the past. He often ignored the boredom of waiting by mentally re-visiting earlier periods, and he was off in memory land doing just that as the clouds navigated through the moonbeams. He was silently biding time until he deemed it safe to pursue this next bitch. A sudden burst of light through the window at the far end of the house shattered his mesmerizing thoughts. The frosted glow of the illuminated glass showed him that the light emanated from the bathroom adjoining the master bedroom. Having previously researched this villa's floor plan, Zac had committed the layout to memory, just as James instructed. He had trailed Miss Ashley home from the Starlite Lounge the night she rejected James, thus obtaining her address so the rest of the information was easily found. James was highly annoyed with this bitch, and Zac knew it was his job to intervene and appease James. "I do whatever James needs when it comes to bitches," Zac thought. "Now, here I am, getting ready to do 'the deed' once again," he thought, and also, once again, he noticed his flaccid penis beginning to rise, stemming from his erotic thoughts of doing 'the deed.'

Sneaking alongside the house, then crouching beneath the bathroom window, Zac arose slowly to a height that permitted him to peer through the frosted window. A slight gap between the dainty flowered curtains provided limited visibility. Moving his angle of view slightly, he saw her silhouette as she moved. She appeared to be naked and preparing for a shower. Zac pressed his body tightly against the wall, permitting him to remain in the shadow of the eave, listening to her sing as she cleaned her body. The shower's noise ceased, and he was provided fleeting silhouettes of her toweling her body dry. The bathroom light switched off, and Zac assumed she had departed for the bedroom.

"Damn," he thought, "it was good that I bumbled the glass door attempt. Hell, the bitch must have still been awake. I'll postpone 'the deed' for another half hour to ensure she has gone to sleep. Time is not the problem right now; anonymity is. I wish I could have seen what she was wearing to beddy-bye. Maybe nothing but a tee shirt. I would like that, or only panties and a crop top. I like that also, or perhaps nothing at all. I like that even better. Ah, hell, I like all that stuff. Why do I care? I shall strip her naked and then seduce her no matter what she wears." "Damn it," he snickered silently, "thinking about doing 'the deed' isn't helping this bulge in my pants," and he slipped silently back to the obscurity of the hibiscus.

Giving his next prey ample time to fall asleep, Zac mauled over in his mind what he knew about Gwendolyn Anne Ashley. His creative investigation informed him that she is 25 years of age, 5 feet, 1 inch tall, and worked for Savings and Loan as a real estate loan officer. Her parents died a few years back, leaving her and her brother Brad a small fortune, but Gwen enjoyed her job and chose to remain employed. After finishing LSU two years ago, she returned to Florida, dabbled in real estate, and is not naturally blond. "She's a poor little rich girl who turned down James's advances and pissed him off with her rejection, so James decided she should be planted at the Bitch Farm. I could care less about the bitches," Zac mused. "However, the more bitches James turns over to me, the happier I am. I get much more sex and a lot more thrills from the kills."

Zac did as James requested when investigating the bitches, and he checked this one out thoroughly, finding every detail he could about her during the past two weeks. "It's almost a shame to do 'the deed' on Gwen," thought Zac. "She's gorgeous. This broad would probably be great to spend some time with, but she didn't want to spend time with James. She is one of the hottest bitches so far, and maybe she'll at least enjoy her time with me," he mussed. "I'll try to help her enjoy it if she cooperates, but I know one thing, I'm damn sure going to enjoy doing her." "She's hot," he muttered.

Zac glanced at his watch and determined it was the right time to put 'the deed' back in motion. There had been no movement, noise, or even a late-night TV show. Zac felt confident she was asleep.

Stealthily, he moved to the patio door, slipped his gloves on, and slid the unlocked door open wide enough for his body and backpack to squeeze through. Once inside, Zac crept to the far end of the Florida room, letting the anticipation of the coming event be rekindled in his mind. "I don't mind having a hard-on right now because it will soon be used for lust," he jested quietly.

Gwendolyn Anne Ashley

The brilliance of the moonlight streaming through the window illuminated his path as he entered the hallway leading to her bedroom. Losing the moonlight in the dark hall, Zac paused momentarily, allowing his eyes to adapt. His gloved hand danced lightly along the wall, guiding him to the bedroom. Cautiously, he entered the room and inched ever closer to the sleeping beauty. A trace of moonlight bursting through the slim gap in the curtains permitted his eyes to behold her luscious body outstretched on the bed. "The bitch is sleeping soundly," he thought. "Tonight will be fun, real fun. James shall have his revenge, and I'm gonna have a fucking ball with this bitch."

Zac posed with stillness as he evaluated the situation with the poise of a stalking beast. He skillfully examined the bed placement related to his position and the other furniture while listening to the clock's rhythmic ticking. Surveying the scene, he noted that she was lying belly down on the covers, wearing only a tee shirt. The shirt loosely bloused about her hips but gathered in folds above her naked buttocks. Her nakedness glistening from the stream of moonlight emphasized the oval cheeks of her ass and the sexual crevice they created. Holy hell, Zac thought, what a stimulating sight as he edged to the window, gingerly widening the gap in the curtains. The increased light illuminated her petite derriere, making an erotic image. "It's no wonder James tried to get close to this bitch," Zac murmured as he inched closer to the bed, becoming visually enthralled with the sensual vision of her nakedness. "Indeed, this prime example of the feminine species is lovely, with a perfect ass beckoning to be molested," Zac was enthralled. Her head turned sideways, rested on a bunched-up pillow, and permitted Zac to see the faint hint of a smile formed by her arched and pouted lips as if dreaming pleasant little girl thoughts. She is indeed a thing of beauty, he thought. A pleasant aroma from her dainty body scented the air as she repositioned herself in her sleep, spreading the sexual slit between her legs to achieve more coolness. She uttered an audible sigh of contentment as her tongue moistened her seductively parted lips and comforted herself again.

Zac shook his head with a brief note of sadness, knowing what he had to do and almost reluctant to proceed. He thought what a shame as he stood silently, admiring her feminine charms and preparing his mind for the task ahead. Zac felt the throbbing sensation of licentious passion from the desire she instilled in him, causing a quake of sexual thirst to shudder through his groin. "It must be time," he murmured silently. "It must be time for me to do 'the deed.'"

Silently, he slipped the backpack from his shoulders. Each piece of equipment required to do 'the deed' was carefully positioned within the pack. James planned the utmost detail, and Zac explicitly followed the instructions. He withdrew several small rope coils, a duct tape roll, and a box cutter.

Then, he quietly cut several small pieces of duct tape, stuck them lightly on the headboard, and coiled the rope on the mattress adjacent to her lovely torso. He rapidly secured tape over her mouth, causing her to awake with a terrifying start, instinctively scrambling to escape and scream. Zac's hand and the tape muffled her scream while his powerful grip on her neck and well-placed knee pinned her tightly to the bed, preventing her escape. She gasped with fear, desperately trying to free herself from this menacing intruder who had made her a prisoner upon her bed.

"Relax," Zac whispered, lying very still. "Don't do anything unless I tell you, and you'll be fine. Do you understand me?" She nodded a silent yes as her eyes peered at the box cutter close to her throat. "Then please lay still," he repeated, "perfectly still." Holding the blade within her visibility area, he gently rolled her over, removed the tape from her mouth, and then seductively kissed her tender lips. He placed the cutter on the bed beside her and grasped her neck firmly with his right hand while his left hand slid down her quivering body, where he gently and tenderly caressed the smooth, freshly shaved mound of her vagina. Her eyes were wide with fright, and her arms and legs involuntarily retracted in self-protection. "Oh dear God," she pleaded, "please let me go. Someone, please help me!" she screamed. Zac unmercifully forced her body tight against the bed once more and muffled her pleas with a pillow. "You stupid bitch, I told you, lay still," he scolded harshly, then whispered in a lordly voice, "Tonight darling, I am your God, and only I can help you, so shut your fucking mouth and do as I say." Again, she attempted to scream, and he forcefully stifled her with another duct tape strip. "Damn, you, precious little bitch, do as you're told, or I'll cut your fucking head off. Just cooperate with me.

This portion of the fun will be over shortly, and I can go home." Gwen surmised that sex was what this monster wanted from the phrasing of that remark, and hopefully, he meant no further harm than just violating her. Based on that assumption, she obeyed his request, determining that being raped was far better than being murdered.

After seeing her resistance wane and her luscious body relaxing, Zac began concentrating on his obligated chore. With skilled precision, he sliced the tee shirt from her body. "Now, sweetness, that's much better," he whispered in a consoling voice. "See how much nicer it is when you're not fighting and fussing. I want to see the lushness of your entire body, your smooth naked skin, every sensual inch of it. Do as I say, and we will get along just fine; don't make me cut you." He removed the tape from her mouth again and gently kissed her lips. Quickly, she turned her face away.

"You're the guy who was in the Starlite, aren't you?" Gwen stammered. "Jessie, isn't that your name?" "No sweetness," Zac interrupted; "Jessie is James, and James only associates with nice girls, not bitches. My name is Zac. Once you become a bitch, Jessie retreats, and James gives you to me."

"What the hell are you talking about, and who the hell are you?" Gwen questioned loudly. "I think you're frigging nuts, whoever you are." Seeing the bewilderment in her eyes, Zac grinned broadly and re-taped her mouth, knowing she would no longer remain silent. "Listen carefully bitch, do as I tell you, and we will have a pleasant evening. Roll over on your tummy and put your hands behind your back. Do it now!" he stated sternly. Gwen, noticing the bulging erection in his jeans and the box cutter still in his hand, did as told. She quivered with fear. Her one thought was to appease this maniac, hoping he would satisfy his sexual urges and leave. She did as told.

Zac shackled her hands with plastic tie wraps, interlaced a length of rope with the wraps, and then snubbed it tightly around her waist, securing her hands in the small of her back. He could make her obey his every command by applying slight pressure on the rope. He rolled her over on her back, feasting his eyes with the visual pleasures of her charms. Her shackled hands beneath her caused her back to arch upward, creating a rather sensual and provocative pose. He stepped away from the bed and increased the opening in the curtains, permitting more of the silvery moon to glisten on her naked torso. Zac stood in reverence, enthralled with the enticing vision. Careful to avoid the possibility of a well-placed kick, Zac spread her legs wide apart and tied each ankle to a bedpost, allowing her womanhood to blossom open and present a desirable sight.

Zac removed his clothing, knelt beside the bed, and caressed her body tenderly with passionate kisses. His lips, starting at her toes, nibbled along the entire length of her body, leaving no area untouched. Caught up in his pleasure, he removed the tape from her lips and kissed them tenderly, attempting to subdue her sobs of fear. Screaming profanities, he pulled away. "You bit me, you lousy bitch. I was trying to be nice to you, and you bit me. I had thought of giving you a break and keeping you around as my private pet, but you fucked up by biting me, you dumb bitch. James was right. You're just like the rest of them, a lousy bitch."

He ruthlessly re-taped her mouth, slapping her harshly as she resisted. He tightened the ropes on her legs, spreading her sexual cavity like a hanger door. Having her secured, he mounted and seduced her multiple times during the next couple of hours until he felt satiated and his erection grew flaccid. Still furious, Zac continued to probe and abuse her with his hands until the thrill was gone. She twisted and heaved, trying unsuccessfully to scream in one desperate last attempt to live as she felt his grip tighten around her neck. She resisted until she could resist no more. Her body lay motionless, her legs and torso battered and bruised, her arms twisted grotesquely beneath her. Her eyes stared blankly in horror, her lungs no longer breathing, her heart was no longer beating, her pain was gone, her life was extinguished. Gwendolyn Anne Ashley was dead.

Zac spent the next couple of hours dismembering Gwen's body. He wrapped the severed pieces in the bed linens and plastic wrap, then used bleach and alcohol and meticulously cleansed all surfaces he may have touched. Once that task was completed, a small but powerful hand vac was used to vacuum the area thoroughly. He put on his clothes and gloves and placed her pictures and stuffed animals in various positions to suit his liking. He surveyed the scene to ensure nothing remained undone and purposely left a few distinct telltale clues for the law. Zac repacked his backpack, retrieved the bitch-case from the backyard, taking note not to disrupt other areas of the house, and stowed her severed remains carefully inside the case.

Feeling satisfied that he had completed 'the deed' with the utmost care, Zac cautiously walked around the room, taking one last look before preparing to depart the scene. Wearing the backpack with the bitch-case in tow, he exited the house and gently closed the glass sliding door. Zac remained stationary in the shadows to ensure no one was aware of his presence. Once assured, he swiftly maneuvered across the yard, retracing his steps back to the van, where he secured the backpack and bitch-case in their designated spaces. Driving home, Zac talked to himself aloud. "I did what you told me, James. I left sufficient clues to keep the long arm of the law busy and confused. The only thing they will be confident of is Jessie was here. Thank you, James; the changes helped. It was gratifying doing 'the deed' this time, she was a bitch, but she sure was a damn good bitch."

Chapter 2

Brad And Marci

The easterly breeze calmed, and the sky grew a deeper shade of blue as the sun settled lower on the western horizon. Marci commanded the helm and pointed the sloop upwind, permitting Brad to furl the genoa and drop the main before coming dockside. Marci locked the rudder, setting the boat into a leisurely crossbeam drift while assisting Brad in flaking the main and securing it to the boom. Moving forward to cleating the sheet lines, Brad couldn't help but notice her petite body as she stretched upward to reach the boom and finish lashing the main. She was a pleasant sight after a vigorous day of sailing, and those white shorts fit her firm bottom very well. With the deck clear of the lines and both sails properly stowed, Brad gave the signal from the bow, and Marci powered up the diesel slipped her into gear, and started heading toward the dock. Marci quickly discovered that instructions needed to be shouted over the wind, radio, and diesel noise but found it repulsive. She convinced Brad that a set of hand signals would be much more civilized, so they originated their unique silent communication. "The hand signals get the job done, and we are not scaring all the fish away," Brad snickered as they cruised towards home. Brad owned a condo near the Intracoastal Waterway, complete with a private slip for his forty-two-foot sloop, which he took more pride in than he did in the condo, the sports car, or any other man-toys.

The boat was his life. His parents invested wisely in Florida land in their younger years, bringing them significant wealth as property values increased. Brad and his sister, Gwendolyn, inherited a sizable bundle of cash. Unfortunately, they were both killed in a tragic auto accident three summers ago.

Gwen was not into boating, so she signed her half ownership over to Brad in exchange for a couple of pieces of property of choice. Brad was more than pleased with the deal, and he, in turn, permitted Gwen to manage the remaining property since that was more her bag, plus she was professionally involved in real estate and finance. She enjoyed her career and was doing quite well with it. Brad tried to talk her into quitting and moving to Cocoa Beach, but she was determined to stay put and remain employed in Vero Beach.

Bradford Lee Ashley, better known as Brad, was employed as an FBI Senior Special Agent and was happy and doing well with his career. He had taken some well-deserved time off and was visiting his sister in Vero Beach when he stopped for gas on the way home before turning onto I-95 north. As Brad prepared to fuel the Viper, the all too familiar sounds of gunfire rang out. Looking toward the noise, he saw a young punk fleeing the scene. The kid panicked seeing Brad and fired several rounds while running to his car. Luck was on Brad's side. If you want to call it luck, the first slug caught him in the hip, spinning him sideways, and knocked him to the ground. The next shot struck the pump right where Brad had been standing. Had he still been there, the bullet may have hit a more vital area.

Basic instinct and training kicked in. Brad quickly managed to crawl to the Viper's passenger side, retrieve his service weapon, and lay three rounds into the punk's car as it sped past him. One of the rounds hit the kid, causing him to lose control. The car veered and smashed into the trailer of a big rig parked at the far end of the lot. The impact sheared off the vehicle's top and decapitated the punk.

The station attendant had been killed, his wife seriously

wounded, and Brad's career abruptly altered, all over a paltry fifty-eight dollars the punk took from the station. If it hadn't been for Brad's quick response, the kid might have gotten away with the heist and, even worse, murder.

Brad was hospitalized for six weeks and had two operations on his hip to repair the shattered pelvic and damaged muscle. The final analysis conveyed that he would have a minor limp and a ten percent loss in using his right leg. Not being on duty at the shooting and inadvertently killing the boy brought about some investigation problems. The driver of the truck that the punk hit was an eyewitness and validated Brad's story. Not being injured in the line of duty, he was not eligible for total disability.

However, they did offer him a cushiony desk job, or he could take partial disability and early retirement. Due to his record and knowledge of various important cases, the headman of the southern division worked out an agreement with the bureau. Brad would be considered a consultant and hold a semi-retired position with pay. He could care less about the retirement funds, but this agreement let him keep his badge and weapon and assist on cases in a semi-active role, so he accepted. The benefit he liked most was the semi-retired status, providing him more leisure time aboard his boat.

Marci Allen is a beautiful and vibrant lady, 34 years old, with long reddish-brown hair. She stands five feet tall, weighs 105 pounds, has gorgeous brown eyes, and a smile that melts your heart. Not to mention, she fills out a bikini exceptionally well. Marci, living in the same condo complex and around the corner from Brad, aided them in becoming acquainted a few weeks after he retired. It was a warm sunny day, and Brad was cleaning the boat as he frequently did. Marci was casually strolling along the docks admiring the river scenery when her view was distracted by a well-tanned male physique glistening in the sun, wearing boat shoes and cut-off jeans, and aboard a beautiful sailboat. The pleasant distraction caused her to pause, admire what she saw, and initiate a conversation. She queried, "How did your boat get her name?" Glancing in the direction of a sweet-sounding voice, Brad instantly noticed the petite beauty standing on the dock. "Step aboard, fair maiden. Let me offer you a cold beer, and I will answer your question. You do drink beer, don't you?" Brad questioned as he opened the cooler without taking his eyes off her and retrieved two bottles of the chilled beverage. "Of course," she replied, "a cold beer sounds perfect right now." Marci stepped aboard with a lady's dignity and a sailor's sure-footedness. Brad intently watched her every move as she navigated around the binnacle and sat in the helmsman's seat as if in command. She was not only a beauty to behold, but to his delight, her poise reminded him very much of his mother's nautical agility. He handed her a beer and took a seat opposite her. "To answer your question, my father named the boat not after my mother but with my mother in mind. Her name was Teresa, and her favorite song was Misty; thus, Miss-T came about. Now that you know the boat's name let me tell you the captain's name. My name is Bradford Ashley, better known as Brad. Since I answered your question, what name might be associated with such a lovely lady?" "Hello, Brad, and hello, Miss-T. My name is Marci Allen. Thank you for the nice compliment. It so happens that I live around the corner from you. I've noticed you in the area and aboard Miss-T several times, but I've never had the chance to meet you until today." "I'm delighted today happened," Brad replied. He and Marci hit it off right from the beginning. Their first social outing occurred shortly after their meeting on the boat and just two days before Brad's fortieth birthday. He invited her to go with him to his sister's house for the day to attend Gwen's planned party. Brad explained to Marci that his baby sister was his one true love, sister-wise. He told her of his parent's accident and how their deaths had brought him and Gwen that much closer. Marci accepted the invitation and was delighted to meet Gwen. The two ladies shared feelings and personal stories at the party and were equally compatible. Being close to the same age gave them much in common, and they likewise clicked.

As time passed, Marci and Gwen became like sisters and

conversed over the phone frequently. During one such call, Marci had confessed to Gwen her sincere feelings for Brad and was delighted when Gwen gave her the green light to pursue her big brother, as she called him. They talked for a half-hour when Gwen excused herself and told Marci she had to run and meet some friends at the Starlite. "Kiss my big brother for me, then the rest of the night, he is all yours," Gwen snickered, "and I would love to have you for a sister-in-law." They said their goodbyes.

Brad and Marci spent much spare time together, which included time aboard Miss-T. Returning from a day of sailing, Marci gave Brad the helm, grabbed the dock hook, moved to the port side deck, and prepared to snag the dock lines as Miss-T moved slowly along her birthing position. When the lines were cleated, Brad shut down the diesel, and Marci stepped to the dock, retrieved the shore power cord, and handed it to Brad. Assured he had the cord, she jumped aboard and scurried below, signaling "the juice is on" as he plugged in the cord. Brad smiled, seeing how Marci had adapted to the world of sailing and had learned the boat easily. "An excellent first mate," he thought as she came topside, presenting him with his usual scotch. "Here is your welcome home and docking drink, Captain Sir," she said with a coy smile, "and if you don't mind, the First Mate will join you." With Miss-T secured to the dock, they relaxed in the cockpit, sipping their drinks and discussing the highlights of the sail. Brad glanced at Marci and said, "I guess we should give her a freshwater bath, then call it a day. The sun will be down in about a half-hour, and we must wrap up our chores." Marci darted for the hose and started spraying the deck, but as usual, the crew ended up as wet as the boat due to so-called accidental showers. However, they both enjoyed every minute of their little game, wet or dry.

Marci was waiting for the right moment before suggesting to Brad that the relationship be kicked up one notch higher, living together, and she felt this evening would be the right time. She was about to speak when she noticed they had company arriving.

Two men on the dock walked towards the boat as Brad managed to get the hose away from Marci and returned the accidental shower. One of the men laughing at the water play called out. "Excuse me, is Bradford Ashley on board?" "Yeah," replied Brad, "a bit wet, but I'm here." The closer of the two men approached the boat, removed a badge and ID from his pocket, and presented it to Brad. "I am Detective Cates, and this is Detective McPherson," he stated, "Cocoa Beach PD." The second man likewise held up his badge. Brad asked, "What can I do for you two Detectives?" "We need to talk, Mr. Ashley. Perhaps you could spare us a few minutes if you and the lovely lady are finished." "Sure," Brad said, "take a dry seat on the dock bench over there, and I will be right with you." Both men complied. "You gentlemen, excuse me," shouted Marci as she gathered her things. "I'm returning to the condo for a real shower and giving you some privacy. I'll be inside when you're done, Brad, and we can get a bite to eat. I'm starved." "Sounds good, Marci," he replied. "I'll see ya in a short." "Now, gentlemen, what is the nature of this visit?" he quizzed as he stepped off the boat and joined them.

Brad And Marci Hearing Of Gwen

"Nice boat," Cates responded. "Had her long?"

"She was my dad's boat," Brad answered. "She's been in the family for over twenty years, but you didn't come here to talk boat talk. What's on your mind?"

"We know of your involvement with the bureau, Brad, if I may call you that. The Vero Beach PD called us today and asked us to come and see if you have recently seen or heard from your sister, Gwendolyn, or perhaps know her whereabouts. She didn't show up for work Monday or Tuesday, nor did she call in. Her boss called her several times but received no answer, so he became concerned. A co-worker stopped by her house Tuesday evening, and she couldn't find her. Early Wednesday, when Ms. Ashley still had not shown up at work, her boss notified the police, and they dispatched a couple of Officers to do a wellness check. The Officers found no indication of her being at home. However, they saw her car was in the garage, did a quick walk around, and noticed nothing or any sign of a B and E. Looking through several windows, nothing unusual was seen except in one bedroom, assumed to be the master bedroom. A small gap in the curtain only permitted a partial view, but both officers agreed that it appeared a bit weird."

"What the hell did they mean by weird?" Brad asked. "According to Lieutenant Arendas, who called us and faxed the brief report, the officers stated the bed appeared stripped, with no sheets, pillows, blankets, Etc. The room looked empty and barren except for a few stuffed animals and pictures lined up on the floor. The report didn't go into great detail, but the bedroom had a weird and eerie look compared to what they could see in the rest of the house. Vero contacted us hoping she was with you or you knew where she might be. They said it appeared that she was cleaning and stopped right in the middle of doing so."

"Holy hell," Brad exclaimed, today is Friday. "What the fuck took them so long to get in touch with me."

"Relax, Mr. Ashley. We know how you feel, but you know the timeline before classifying someone as missing, and they didn't want false alarms."

"Ah shit," Brad said, "who is in charge of the investigation? Whom can I contact?"

"I would start with Lieutenant Arendas," replied Cates. "He is the Detective who called us. And because we know your involvement with the bureau, here's a copy of his report."

"Thanks," Brad said, "I know it's not your fault, but she's all the family I have left."

"We understand. Let us know if there is anything we can do," Cates said. "We'll be happy to help in any way we can." They departed as Brad stood motionless, staring at the report.

Brad closed and locked the companionway, bounded off the boat, and sprinted up the short length of the dock before leaping onto the patio of his condo. A quick rush of pain in his hip brought back the reality that he was semi-retired with a partial disability. "Damn, I need to remember that hip," he muttered while coming close to tripping on a patio chair.

Due to the visitors, Marci sensed something was wrong but had no idea what and was waiting inside the condo for him. She held out her arms as he halfway stumbled into her embrace. Brad began quivering all over as he repeated the story. "Give me ten minutes," Marci said. "I'll throw a few things in a bag. We can drive to Vero in a little over an hour." "Thanks," he said, "I think I need someone with me right now, and of all people, you're my first choice." She smiled and said, "I want to be your only choice." She kissed him gently and then departed for her condo. Brad went inside, quickly showered, packed a bag, and was ready to go as Marci reentered. The Viper did its job well that night, and they pulled into the Holiday Day Inn at Vero approximately 90 minutes later. Settling into the room, Brad called the local police and was informed that no additional information about Gwen was available. "I suggest that you call Lieutenant Frank Arendas tomorrow. He comes on duty at 07:00," the officer told him. "However, if it's an emergency, I can contact him." "Thanks," Brad said, "but I hope this is not an emergency and they terminated the call," Brad stated that I should have known they couldn't give out info over the phone and resolved to wait. "Let's get a bite to eat, Marci. That will allow me to think things through, and then we can stop by Gwen's place. I have a key, and we can look for ourselves."

"That sounds good," she replied, "let's do whatever we have to do or whatever you feel you need to do. I'm here for you all the way."

Following dinner, they drove to Gwen's house with guarded anticipation of what they may find. Gwen resided in a Spanish-style villa at the south end of the John's Island area, which she purchased reasonably. It was a new upscale residential area still under development and provided much privacy for the sparse residents. Numerous bushes blocked the houses' visibility, while giant water oaks canopied the streets, creating daylight shading and subdued lighting at night. The perfect setting for a peeping tom or a night stalker, Brad noted to himself; he had never thought of it that way before, but this perverted description seemed to fit for some reason. Brad slowly drove into Gwen's driveway, turned off the Viper, and he and Marci sat there momentarily, uncertain about what was happening.

The last time they parked in this driveway was a delightful occasion, but something about tonight was not right, and they both sensed it. Marci said, "Call it woman's intuition, but I'm not looking forward to this." She took Brad's hand, held it tightly as they proceeded to the front door, and slowly opened it. Brad turned on the lights, cautiously entered the room, and instructed Marci not to touch or disturb anything. He asked her to make mental notes of anything that seemed odd or out of place from what she could remember. Marci followed Brad's instructions as she ventured down the hallway to Gwen's bedroom while Brad walked toward the kitchen. A shocking chill ran goosebumps up and down Marci's spine as she approached the bedroom, turned on the light, and peered into a vista of strangeness. The room had an ungodly aroma scenting the air and appeared as the report implied, but several faint dark stains were visible, which Marci assumed were splotches of blood. Gwen's stuffed animals that once joyously decorated the bed were lined up on the floor one by one, facing the wall, except for two large monkeys in the corner, positioned together as if having intercourse, doggy style. The pictures were removed and placed on the floor, leaning against the wall but upside down.

Feeling nauseous from the odor and sights, Marci edged her way to the adjoining bathroom with the fear of becoming ill. Turning on the light, she remained frozen in the doorway, trembling and gasping for air as she gazed in total horror. Marci tried but couldn't prevent the guttural moan from her throat nor the sobbing scream that erupted loudly from her inner soul. She sank to her knees due to the ungodly sight she was seeing. Bloody towels were scattered in the tub. The toilet brush handle protruded from the blood-stained commode, remnants of a torn shower curtain clung to the remaining hooks, and spatters of blood dotted all the walls.

"No, god, no, this cannot be happening," Marci screamed. Hearing Marci's torment, Brad hurried down the hall to the bedroom, where he was also distraught by the scene and stood in total anguish. Marci melted into his arms. They both stood awkwardly entranced by the grotesque sight, unable to speak, comprehend, or believe what they saw.

Brad professionally started reviewing what he was seeing. As he surveyed the room, it became evident that anything that retained fingerprints had been cleansed: walls, doors, bed frame, dresser, mirrors, pictures, and more. The faucet knobs in the tub and sink had been wiped thoroughly. The carpet and the unstained mattress areas have been cleaned, and the dark stains, whatever caused them, were bleached. Bleach and alcohol must have been used everywhere, and the pungent odor still lingered. "What the hell happened in here?" Brad cried, "who on god's earth could have done this, and why?" Noticing the mattress was slightly askew on the bed, Brad lifted it carefully and found a lipstick tube. Raising the mattress slightly higher, the word "bitch," written in childish style letters, became visible. Half closing his eyes and fighting back the tears, he murmured, "We must get the police out here, now." He lowered the mattress and dialed the Vero PD on his cell as his professional training took over.

Returning from the room, Marci noticed Gwen's purse hanging in the back corner of her closet. Using Brad's handkerchief, she opened it and checked the contents. The bag contained everyday items: a wallet, driver's license, credit cards, cash, and a partial business card. She looked at Brad and stated,

Nothing unusual, standard lady's stuff except this partial card, possibly from one of her clients. "Here, take my card, copy down the contents of that card on the backside just for kicks, and then put everything back as you found it. We shouldn't touch anything until the forensic guys go over the place."

"Will do," Marci replied, "but I am going to the kitchen to do it. I need a change of scenery."

The police, including Lieutenant Arendas, arrived, and the area was cordoned as a crime scene. Brad introduced himself to Arendas, showed his credentials, and told him how he and Marci had come to be there. "I glad to meet you," Arendas said, "only not under these conditions. I think Marcy has seen much more than she wanted tonight, as have I. Why don't you and Miss Allen return to your room and let me finish up here? Please come to my office early tomorrow to discuss the situation further."

"Will do," replied Brad.

Back in the Viper, Brad looked at Marci and said, "That was pure hell, Babe; I am glad you were with me. I'll make phone calls tomorrow and see if some old acquaintances can pull a few strings. Now that we have seen the house, I know something's wrong. Something is very wrong, and I want to use every resource possible." They arrived at the motel, bypassed their room, and proceeded straight to the bar. For a Friday night, the place was quiet, which suited the bewildered couple immensely. "I'll have a double scotch and water," Brad requested of the bartender, "and give this lovely lady a tequila sunrise." They casually conversed while sipping their drinks, both deliberately avoiding the traumatic events of the evening. Completing the second round of drinks, they left the bar and meandered along the beach, shoes in hand and splashing quietly with their feet in the Atlantic's surf while keeping the undesirable topic on the back burner. Strolling from the beach to the motel, Marci held tightly to Brad. She silently communicated precisely how she felt about him without saying a word, and he understood every unspoken word. Unlocking the door to the room, Brad spoke his first words since leaving the beach. "I know we've been together at my place, but if staying together in a motel room makes you uncomfortable, I'll gladly get you a room." She took his hand, escorted him into the room, smiled, and said, "I am in my room and exactly where I desire to be, with you." She closed and locked the door. Brad engulfed her in his arms and kissed her gently, then more passionately as she returned his sensual caresses. Slowly, she removed his clothes and permitted him to do the same to her. They shared a warm, stimulating shower and dried each other's torsos, followed by a soothing massage with mildly aromatic bath oil. Marci took Brad's hand and coyly led him to bed, hoping to help him forget the previous event, at least for a short while. They snuggled together, letting the warmth of their naked bodies taunt the fires building within them. As their heated passion progressed, nature took its climatic course. The mutual excitement faded gently into a peaceful night of sleep.

James And The Business

James completed the business details for the day and was mentally exhausted. He encountered many business problems that needed to be solved daily. Most of the difficulties involved paperwork and concerned the cemetery's operation, but they consumed much of his time. James appreciated Mrs. Oliver's efforts, as she handled most of the clients and financial dealings and kept the business end of the cemetery running smoothly. If he had to deal with all the areas daily, he would likely have gone nuts long ago. James kept his mind right by jokingly telling himself that people were dying for his services. But he still frequently wondered why his father had ever become involved with a business of this nature, particularly after being a manual laborer on the oil rigs earlier in his life, especially here in a small town like Wabasso. Fortunately, his father got involved, and in many ways, James was grateful for this golden opportunity that his father had laid in his lap. Besides the business aspect, property in Florida of any kind usually turned out to be a good investment, and the cemetery had many acres of land not being used for interning the dead. James contemplated that he would build a beautiful home for himself and his woman out on the back acreage one day rather than live in the modest cottage on the side parcel he now occupies. If he could find a woman who was not a bitch.

James encountered difficulty comprehending portions of the business. However, he had persuaded Mrs. Oliver, his father's office manager, to remain employed and help him learn the ropes. She was a blessing in disguise and knew the details of operating the graveyard business very well. Mrs. Oliver was also instrumental in persuading the experienced staff of yard workers to remain on the job.

James was not wholly ignorant of business matters and was a quick learner, so with her knowledge and everyone's help, the transition of him taking over had gone much smoother than expected. The management and employees evolved into a family-like atmosphere, creating teamwork that caused the business to grow and become lucrative during the past several years. Lucrative enough to be in a seven-digit income bracket, which James shared by providing more than adequate salaries for the entire team. Of course, he took a sizable draw for himself, which provided his play money, as he called it, and permitted him to be a bit ostentatious. However, more than the acquired wealth, James treasured a secluded section of the property, providing the perfect location for his Bitch Farm.

James had carefully studied the property deed, the surveys, the aerial photos, and the land plots showing the burial sites after the legal transaction of the graveyard was complete. Right then, he determined that the remote area with large water oaks would be an ideal spot to plant "Bitch-Mother," and he instructed Zac to do just that. The site was dubbed the "Bitch Farm" from then on. Counting the recent bitch to be planted, Miss Gwendolyn Ashley, there were nine ungrateful bitches in various stages of decomposition at rest on the "Bitch Farm," with room for many more if necessary.

Sitting in his office, James stared out the window, letting thoughts run through his mind. "I wonder if all the freaking women in this world are bitches? There must be some nice women, so why do I find the bitches? I want them to be pleasant and friendly. Even sex is secondary if they are decent women. Women who don't treat you like a fool or make you feel unwanted and damn sure don't cheat on you. They should be yours, dedicated to you, and not be playgirls with loose morals and free sex."

James recalled the ladies in Fellsmere who provided him with sex. He muttered, "Those ladies are always nice to me, but they should be. I pay them five hundred dollars a visit and sometimes more if they are extra nice. Oh hell, that's my problem; I'm horny," he snickered. "Lucky Zac, he gets his dick well taken care of. Yes, Zac gets to have sex with all of the bitches. Then he has fun killing them.

Chapter 3

Christine Lowell

James had been in Sebastian several nights back and had spoken with a charming and petite young damsel named Christine Lowell, better known to her friends as Christy. Her father is the proprietor of a large automotive dealership in Melbourne, where she naturally works. Christy was known to frequent Ahab's Oyster Bar in Sebastian, a local hangout overlooking the Indian River, and she was pleasant and friendly to James the night they met. The Time Everlasting Cemetery is in Wabasso, approximately halfway between Vero and Sebastian, permitting a bar-to-bar booze cruise, which James frequently enjoys. He has become familiar with the area but remains unfamiliar and aloof with the locals, preferring to be a loner and remain unknown. James specializes in being one of those persons you see but never remember. On occasion, he has encountered a lady willing to provide sexual companionship with no strings attached, a one-night stand as they call them. However, James relinquished offers of a one-night stand. It was evident that these were not the type of women he sought. He prefers to hire a whore for the evening and pay for good sex rather than get it free from some one-night bar fly, who is undoubtedly a bitch.

James heeded the speed limit on US-1 heading north to Ahab's, knowing the area's law loved to give traffic tickets. The night was pleasantly warm, with a gentle breeze blowing in off the Atlantic, and the stars in the cloudless sky seemed to be dancing brightly. "Damn," James murmured to himself as he drove. "Tonight will be a perfect night for some serious romance if Christy cooperates. She was sociable the other night and did say she hoped we would meet again, so I certainly hope she was sincere," James uttered as he took note of his location. "I shall soon know; maybe she will be the woman I seek." He turned right onto the side street, heading towards the river, then left onto Old Dixie Highway for a short distance before entering Ahab's parking lot. James parked the car and strolled into the dimly lit bar, scanning the area for Christy. The dim lighting is one reason James liked this place. You must be close together to distinguish a person's features or see specific details.

Spotting her sitting in the dimness at the bar, James walked up to her side, took her hand in his, kissed it suavely while executing a partial bow, and stated, good evening, my fair maiden, tis lovely that we meet again. I have been yearning for this moment since last we parted. Taken back by his unnerved action and Shakespearian dialect, Christy leered at him and mockingly questioned in similar phraseology. "Excuse me, kind sir, but just who the hell are you?" She laughed as James explained their meeting last week, and upon their parting, she had told him that she hoped they would meet again. Last week, she bellowed laughingly. "Hell. I can't even remember the clown I took home last night, let alone meeting you last week, Sir Galahad, or whoever the hell you are. Now, if you don't mind, please go away, have a drink, and find someone who remembers you." He could hear snickers from a few of the surrounding patrons who were pretending not to eavesdrop. As a result, in anger and bewilderment, James glared embarrassingly at her for a moment, saying nothing as the snickers continued. Having been belittled, he cordially bowed at the waist while backing away.

"We shall meet again Bitch. Until then, I bid you a fond farewell, but please tell Zac hello," James coyly remarked and retreated. He could still hear her intoxicated voice echoing in his ears, along with the degrading laughter as he departed the bar. "What a Bitch, she is a frigging Bitch," James stammered. Then, he summoned Zac as he walked outside the bar. "Zac, where the hell are you, Zac," shouted James. "We need to talk, Zac, we need to talk now," James continued shouting. "She has earned 'the deed.'"

Brad And Marci Are Still In Vero

Marci awoke before Brad and, being as quiet as possible, prepared the complimentary coffee and slipped into the bathroom for the morning calls of nature, followed by an exhilarating shower. Exiting the shower, she briskly dried her torso, applied some talc to her freshened body, and put on her clothes without disturbing Brad. Marci smiled, gazing at him sleeping, wondering if he always slept that peacefully, or was it exhaustion from the stress yesterday had brought? Perhaps it was the fantastic sex we gave to each other last night that made him so content, she mused hopefully. Marci was delighted with the progression of their relationship and had no disconcerts about sleeping with Brad. She happily accepted that she was falling deeply in love with him, but in all honesty, like him, she didn't want to rush into things. Last night wasn't their first time sharing sexual bliss, but it was the first time they spent an entire night together. It was far more pleasurable than she had imagined, and as a result, she had a bright, cheery attitude this morning with a complete sense of satiation. It is a shame that the first overnight interlude came about under these circumstances, she thought, but she prayed that, in some way, her presence helped and will continue to help Brad cope.

Marci was experiencing eerie feelings concerning Gwen's disappearance and found it challenging to grasp the reality of the wretched things she had seen. Recalling those ghastly sights caused chills to scamper up and down her spine. Marci knew that feeling all too well, as it had previously happened to her. It was the feeling of sheer terror. She remembered the stalker who had harassed her a few years back and the horror she felt upon waking up with him standing beside her bed. Thank god, her frantic screams caused him to flee, but the fear remained with her. She had felt a similar fear last night at Gwen's house. The coffee was almost perked as Marci crept out of the room, gathered some donuts from the lobby, and returned just in time to see Brad arouse.

"Hi, sleepy," Marci said, pouring him a cup of java with just a dab of creamer, precisely how he liked it. She carried it to him as he sat upright in bed. Marci kissed him gently on the cheek, sat on the settee adjacent to the bed, and sipped on her cup. She said, "I brought some doughnuts from the lobby if you want one and more coffee." Brad grinned, took a sip of the coffee, climbed out of bed immodestly, and headed for the shower. "You're my kind of woman, Marci Allen," and he patted her thigh as he strolled by. "My, oh my," she mused as his naked body passed before her in unclothed review. "Not bad for a forty-year-old man. If you need help washing anything, holler." A couple of minutes later, he hollered, she stripped, and they enjoyed an early morning lather.

Following a pleasant breakfast at a local favorite, they drove straight to the police station, where Brad requested to talk with Detective Frank Arendas. Within minutes, they were taken to his office, where he greeted them and motioned them to have a seat. "First, let me say, Brad, news travels fast in this small town. The first thing this morning, I had a call from the Commissioner. He knew your father and informed me of your FBI status. He also asked that we extend you all the courtesy that we possibly can. I have no problem with that, and knowing your FBI record, I will be more than happy to have you around, but please understand this is our case, and we need to call the shots." "I fully appreciate that," replied Brad. "I do not intend to interfere with your investigation, but I will help with whatever I can." "Great," said Arendas. "Now, here's what we know so far." He presented all the facts they had established thus far, most of which Brad had already surmised. "We have no hard facts proving that Gwen is dead or alive," stated Arendas. "The evidence collected indicates a homicide, but again, I say we have no positive proof. We must remember that," Arendas continued, "we need proof. I don't think I have to tell you, Brad, it does not look good. You were at the house, and you saw firsthand what we saw. Whoever was there with your sister the other night is very disturbed. Assuming the perpetrator to be a male, he has already been designated as extremely dangerous. We found nothing indicating that more than one perp was involved. The blood found was Gwen's type, and we're running tests on everything we possibly can. Our CSI team stayed all night. Your FBI buddies were informed early today, and they will be helping with the DNA, but it takes time, as you know. We sent the samples to them already, and they assured us they would prioritize the effort. We feel confident that the lipstick used for the writing was Gwen's. A new tube of the same brand and shade was found in one of the drawers, which adds validity to that assumption. We have no idea concerning the placement of the stuffed animals or pictures. If you have any theories on that, please pass them on."

"The fingerprints we have been able to ID were Gwen's and a few of yours. We could not get a make on the others found, so he is not in any database if they are the perps. That reminds me, Miss Allen, we would like to take your prints since you were in the house." "No problem, Lieutenant, whenever you're ready," Marci answered. "Thanks, and both of you, please call me Frank. I don't have to tell you the rules, Brad. If you return to your sister's house, please don't remove anything without checking with us first. That's all I can tell you so far. I'll frequently keep you updated, and please don't hesitate to offer anything you think may help. You know the drill as well as I do, Brad, so bear with us. We will try to wrap this up as quickly as possible. My sympathy and prayers go out to both of you. Thanks for the briefing, said Brad, and I will be staying in touch."

Killing Christy

It had been less than a week since the Ahab Bar incident, and James had diligently completed his homework on Christine Lowell. The more he discovered, the more convinced he became that she was indeed a bitch. Miss Lowell was far from being the gracious lady James was first believed. She is truly a bitch. Each evening since the bar incident, James replayed his plan to Zac, and they would go over and over the data until Zac had every precise detail committed to memory. The implementation of "the deed" was now in Zac's hands, and at every possible minute, he stalked Christy and studied her movements, haunts, and habits to determine a reasonable time frame to do "the deed." Unlike Gwen, Christy was a boozer, a genuine barfly who liked the men and was free with her sexual favors. Zac determined that his appearance on the late-night scene would not shock the neighbors since men spending the night have been commonplace with this slut. However, Zac could not forget James's first rule was 'obscurity with a cloak of silence.' While pursuing feminine companionship, James only visited dimly lit establishments, and Zac understood why; 'obscurity.' Although tonight he will permit the bitch to see him because she won't be around much longer. Based on this rule, James's and Zac's identities shall remain unknown due to the cloak of silence, her silence. James did the overall planning, except for the actual method of doing "the deed." Zac was granted the pleasure of determining the precise manner in which the bitches achieved their demise. Zac took great pleasure in arriving at a proper technique by which each bitch passed on to their place on the Bitch Farm. Thus far, three have been strangled, one shot in the head, two stabbed in the heart, one's throat was slit, another one drowned in her bathtub, and the druggie bitch got overdosed on her drugs.

Thinking back on the past episodes as he prepared for the evening, Zac recalled that all of the bitches had been fun to play with while doing "the deed," so now he thought, what would be the best technique for doing this bitch? "Let me think," he muttered to himself. "She likes to live in the fast lane. Then I might kill her fast. No way, fast won't be fun. Oh, she damn sure likes to screw, so perhaps I should screw her to death?" he laughed. "Hell yeah, that at least would be fun and gratifying." He snickered, "So I'll let the night's happenings guide my decision."

Zac recalled that while investigating this bitch, he discovered that she designated every Thursday night as her stay-at-home night. Each Thursday, she would do her domestic chores, a general house cleaning, a weekly load of laundry, indulge in some self-pampering, and then attempt to get a sober night's sleep. Despite the dedication to her chores, this bitch was in no way the neatest of housekeepers, rarely ate healthily, and dined mostly on microwave dinners and fattening snacks while listening to hard-rock music. She did not have a steady boyfriend, enjoyed the carefree life that Daddy's money provided, and could not care less about the world's status or anybody else. Zac classified her as a first-class self-centered bitch.

It was late afternoon when Christy left work and stopped by the market on her way home. Arriving home, she drove her new convertible into the garage just as the sun set and the neighborhood's automatic lights blinked on. Noticing that her front yard light and the porch light remained dark, Christy made a mental note to tell the community handyman to replace the bulbs. She pressed the remote button, closed the garage door, unlocked the door leading into the kitchen, and flipped on the light switch, but the kitchen remained dark. "Damn," she cursed aloud, a bit perplexed. The freaking power must be out. Pausing for a moment, she realized that the power was on. The garage door worked. She could hear the refrigerator running and the AC blowing cool air. "Must be the wrong damn time of the month for light bulbs," she quipped. "All the fucking bulbs are on the rag," she said aloud.

She placed the groceries on the kitchen counter and proceeded towards her bedroom, shedding her clothes as she walked. When she entered her bedroom, she wore nothing but black thong panties. However, she never had a chance to see if the bedroom light worked. As she stepped through the doorway, a shadowy figure lunged from the darkness and viciously entrapped her body.

Within seconds, a rag was stuffed into her mouth, and she was thrust face down onto the bed. Her arms were pulled behind her, and her wrists were bound tightly with plastic shackles. Then, the heavy force of a knee in the small of her back pressed her firmly against the mattress. The more she struggled, the heavier the pressure, scrunching her body deeper into the bed. She felt as though her spine was about to snap. She couldn't scream, nor could she move. The pain was unbearable. She flinched as her body was flipped over like a sack of potatoes. She was now staring at the ceiling but seeing nothing. The darkness of the room and the blur of her tears restricted any possibility of sight. The rag was yanked out of her mouth and replaced immediately by a slab of duct tape brutally forced across her lips and cheeks, sealing off any attempt to make a sound. She glared in anguish at the man who was brutalizing her, unable to distinguish him. However, a brief glimpse of familiarity associated with Ahabs entered her mind. Her body was flipped over on her stomach, and once again, his knee pinned her forcibly to the bed. Grabbing her flailing legs, Zac quickly bound them together at the ankles with duct tape. She was hogtied, muffled, and under his control in less than twenty seconds.

"Just like bulldogging at the rodeo, wouldn't yeah say? I got your sweet little ass right where I want it." Zac mumbled as he screwed a low-wattage bulb onto the small lamp on the dresser.

Carefully, he placed it such that his movement around the bed would not cast a shadow on the window blinds, which may bring outside attention to his prescience. Stepping away from the bed, he watched Christy squirm and admired the slim, fully tanned body he was about to abuse. It was evident that she sunbathed in the buff. The entire surface of her luscious body was a rich, deep bronze with no bikini lines. Zac thought that her tan had to have come from the sun and not one of those yellowing tanning booths. "You must enjoy getting naked," Zac whispered, "and I bet you look pretty damn good, all oiled up and glistening in the sun."

She stared at him in total disbelief at what was happening while struggling in vain to loosen the bonds that restrained her. Encouraging her to watch him, Zac removed a long-bladed knife from his backpack and smiled at the terror flashing in her eyes as he approached the bed. With sheer malice, he visibly rubbed the flat side of the blade across her cheek for effect as his eyes leeringly scanned the entire length of her body. He smiled and spoke gently to her." Relax, sweetness; from the looks of your all-over tan, it is evident that you relish being naked. I will oblige you tonight and permit you to be naked. Unfortunately, there is no sunshine for your luscious body to soak up, so I guess you'll have to soak me up instead of Mr. Sun," he giggled. Skillfully, he slipped the blade under her panties' thin material, sliding it slowly across the upper base of her vaginal mound. Feeling the coolness of the steel against her abdomen, she froze with fear. With one swift motion, the razor-sharp blade severed the thin crotch band running between her legs, and again, Zac smiled at her terrorized reaction.

Tenderly he reached down and touched her now exposed vaginal lips, caressing them gingerly with his fingers as he watched the expressions on her face change from anguish to bewilderment. With one more rapid swipe of the blade, Zac severed the narrow waistband of the thong, releasing all the securing aspects of the garment as the material now lay loosely on her taut belly.

Grabbing her ankles, Zac pulled her to the foot of the bed, where he slowly forced his hand between the sensual curves of her thighs, spreading them apart, and removed the severed remnants of her panties. Christy suddenly shivered as she experienced a strange sensation fleeting through her mind that even though the rest of her extremities were unclothed, she now, for some reason, felt unbearably naked and highly vulnerable. Her entire body trembled as the sudden realization of what was happening crept over her. Using all her energy, she squirmed, twisted, and wiggled back to what seemed to be the security of the headboard. She curled into a fetal position, her eyes fixed on this maniac who had invaded her sanctity.

"Ok, Christy, let me ask you, do you remember James now?" Zac queried. "The other night, you claimed you didn't recognize him. James was trying to be nice to you, but no, you had to be a bitch and create a scene, didn't you? You're not only a bitch, but you're also a dumb bitch. All that was needed was for you to be pleasant to James, and none of this would be happening. He would have treated you like royalty if you had given him the slightest chance. He liked you. You could have been his queen, and he would have lavished you with pleasures far beyond your imagination. But no, you wouldn't allow yourself to be pleasant. Oh noooooo, not you. You're so freaking spoiled and such a self-centered bitch that you wouldn't let your little ass take the time to be nice to James. After studying you for the past few days, I've seen that you're only nice to a person until you get what you want from them, then you become a bitch. Well, Brother James tried, but you chose to be a bitch, so he gave your sweet little ass to me. I figure tonight that I'm going to be just like you. I will be nice to you until I get what I want," Zac stated, "and once I do, I no longer need to be nice anymore. Now, won't that be fun? You'll get a chance to see the other side of the coin. That will be the tail side, which I will do. I will get a juicy piece of your tail side."

Zac's talking caused fear and frustration in Christy. Confused and terrified, she stared at him. His dry, methodically monotone speech heightened her concern even more than his words. The unpleasantness of the encounter at the bar vividly returned to her thoughts. This guy looks very much like that man, but he was named Jessie, or that's what he said. So, who's this character? Who the hell is this guy? Could they be twin brothers or something? She could not remember much about Jessie besides his unusual actions at Ahab's, but tonight made no sense. Then her mind flashed back to the leering look on his face that night when he told her, "We shall meet again." Then he said to tell Zac hello. Is this what he meant? Oh dear god, she thought, someone, help me, please help me, this man is insane.

Zac smiled as he heard her muffled attempt to scream and asked her, "Are some memories returning?" He then laughed as she winced more vigorously with each of his touches. Zac thoroughly enjoyed playing this teasing game, and since Miss Christy had teased James, he now took great pleasure in teasing her. Again, Zac roughly yanked her away from the headboard and gropingly felt her supple breasts, kneading them like mounds of dough and enjoying her visible reactions of pain. Zac steered his hands in gliding motions up and down her nakedness, letting his fingers gently touch and feel all her feminine curves and sensual areas. He crammed his fist between her legs and watched her hips twist and roll, trying to avoid his groping hand and probing fingers as they forcibly explored her inner chamber.

After a prolonged examination, Zac leaned close to her cheek and whispered, "Ok, my little darling; you're determined to be an aggressive little bitch. So I dare not unleash your legs, even though I would love to spread them wide. And do you know what? That is a sincere shame because you might enjoy what happens next if your legs were free. However, since you insist on being a bitch, I will leave your wild ass hogtied and give you a good screwing. I will turn you over and prop your luscious ass up to ride you like a bucking bronco. A bareback bronco," he laughed as he moved from the bed.

Christy continued to spasmodically twist her torso, attempting to free her hands and legs, but to no avail. She was entirely at Zac's mercy, and he was about to do 'the deed.'

Christy watched in horror as he removed his pants, watched his every move, and saw him becoming aroused. She noticed the size of his protrusion and was tempted to cooperate for a fleeting moment. "You like what you see, don't you, bitch? I heard you were looking forward to screwing Long Dong Herold, so maybe this long dong will satisfy your snatch." Zac laughed as he grasped her body roughly, lifting her straight up, flipping her over, and tossing her face down on the bed. Lay there and don't move, he ordered as he rifled through the drawer of her nightstand. "A broad like you must have lubricant around here somewhere. Ah yeah, here it is, Slick and Smooth; that's a decent brand if I must say so." He grabbed her waist, slid her to the edge of the bed, put her knees on the floor, and bent her upper torso flat against the surface of the mattress. Her petite ass was now well exposed as he squeezed the gel from the tube, letting it puddle on her buttocks. He scooped up lubricant with his fingers and smeared it all over her vagina and anus. The worst of her fears clamored in her mind as, without compassion, he began probing her cavities with his penis. Suddenly, his fist hammered down on the back of her neck, causing excruciating pain to rumble up and down her spine. Her body went limp as she passed out from the traumatic impulse rushing to her brain. Seeing the results of his well-placed blow, Zac admired the sexual feast before him. Obtaining complete control of her body, he released her legs, spread them wide apart, and mounted her like a male dog humping a bitch. She regained her senses and tried to escape, but again, she was battered into submission. Reaching the apex of his lust, he oriented her limp body into every possible exposing position and assaulted her.

Zac violated her using every object he could find until all her invaded orifices appeared to be a mass of blood and tattered flesh. The torture continued until her agonizing demise, and she was a lifeless figure lying used and abused in front of him.

Admiring his handy work, Zac proceeded to sanitize the area and destroy the traces of his presence. Amusingly, he spoke to the battered corpse lying on the bed. "You loved to live fast and screw hard, didn't you? Well, you didn't die too fast, but I think I did screw you hard, and I screwed you to death. It serves you right, you bitch." Zac proceeded with his usual cleansing and manipulation of the pictures and stuffed animals to be appropriately placed for effect for the remainder of the evening. Once complete with 'the deed,' he rechecked his efforts. Zac removed her depleted body from the house and planted her in the Bitch Farm with the others.

Chapter 4

Brad Hearing Of Christy

The sun had not yet risen when the phone rang. Stirring from a sound sleep, Brad rolled over and peered at the clock. 5 o'clock, he mumbled as he answered the phone. "Hello," he managed to stammer. "Brad, this is Frank Arendas. Sorry to call so early, but we have a situation, and I think you need to be involved. I don't want to say much over the phone, but we have a missing woman, and there are many similarities to Gwen's case. This case may be a break we need. Can you come down here today?"

"I'll be there in a few hours," Brad responded and hung up the phone.

Marci peeked out from under her pillow, asking. "Was that good news, I hope?"

"Yes, but no," Brad replied. "They have another woman missing that might have some ties to Gwen's case. Frank wants to discuss it with me; I'm unsure what is happening, so I need to meet with him."

"Go for it!" Marci told him. "I'll head for work and catch up with you when you get home. Please, do me a favor. Should you decide to stay down there tonight, call me so I won't worry, OK?"

He pulled back the covers and patted her tenderly on the bare ass. "If there is any way possible, I'll be back tonight to pat that cute little thing again," he smilingly said. "Just remember to whom it belongs."

"You need my permission to see it, let alone pat it. Now, be on your way, Mr. Ashley, and let me get back to sleep. I don't have to get up until seven. P.S. I'll most likely give you my permission," she giggled.

The Viper came to a screeching stop at Vero Beach Police Station. Brad unbuckled his seat belt and leaped out without opening the door. After a few long bounds, he opened the lobby door, received a "wave on" from the desk sergeant, and entered Frank's office. "Not bad for a disabled Agent," he thought; "the old body still has some life left in it as long as I pamper the hip." Frank was talking on the phone and gestured for Brad to have a seat. Brad poured coffee, added his usual dab of creamer, and sat beside Frank's desk. Once the call was complete, Frank told Brad he had been talking with the Melbourne PD about a missing woman, Christine Lowell.

"One of her neighbors, who was out walking, remembered seeing a man changing light bulbs in the front yard pole lamp and the porch light at Lowell's house late in the afternoon the day of her disappearance. The guy told the neighbor the bulbs were burned out, and he was putting in new ones. However, she said the lights didn't come on that night as they should have. The homeowner's association handyman typically changes the bulbs, and she assumed this guy was a new handyman. As a result, she didn't pay any more attention to it. It's a few hundred feet from the neighbor's house to the Lowell house, so she did not get a good look at the guy. Melbourne PD said they generated a sketch from what little description she could give, but they don't place much faith in it. They also checked with the HOA and have not hired any new handymen. The neighbor also commented that men were always coming and going from Miss Lowell's house. By the way, Brad, does Lowell ring a bell with you?"

"The only Lowell I've heard of is the car dealer in Melbourne," answered Brad.

"You got it," replied Frank. "Christine is his daughter, 27 years old, petite, pretty, with no money problems, and known to live in the fast lane."

"So, what makes you think there is a connection to Gwen?" Brad asked.

"Let me give you the rest of the story," Frank answered. "The interior of the Lowell house appeared normal except for the master bedroom and bath. The Melbourne PD described the scene as similar to Gwen's room. Every touchable surface had been washed down with bleach or alcohol, bed linens were missing, pictures were off the wall, blood-soaked towels were in the tub, and the bathroom was a mess. She didn't have many stuffed animals like Gwen, but a large teddy bear, was on the bed, humped over with a curling iron stuck up its ass."

"Now, Brad, do you see why I called you? I'm afraid we have a serial wacko on our hands."

"What about the possibility of a copycat?" Brad quizzed. "I don't think so," replied Frank. "We never divulged the details of your sister's case, and I ordered all the officers involved to keep mum. To my knowledge, nothing has leaked out. I wanted the details kept quiet to be used against him, and I stressed that point with all my men."

"OK, call Melbourne back," Brad suggested, "and ask them about the mattress and the word Bitch. If that data is the same, it will confirm your serial theory."

"Good idea," replied Frank as he dialed the phone.

While Frank talked with Melbourne, Brad retreated to the waiting room. He called the Bureau and was given Jack Baird's name as the Melbourne area's FBI Special Agent. The Bureau informed Brad that Jack had a lot of pull with the Brevard County law agencies and the local politicians, so he should prove valuable on the case. As Brad completed his call, Frank stepped to his office door and gestured for Brad to come in. "I am afraid that our worst fears are founded," Frank commented. "Melbourne just confirmed the mattress and bitch data."

"I didn't want to hear that shit," Brad replied. "Let me make a phone call before we go any further."

Jack Baird answered the phone and, finding it to be Brad, gave him a heads up that the Bureau had already spoken with him about providing support. "That's great," Brad stated, "one more victim defines this perp as a serial killer, putting you on the case anyway." Brad gave Jack his and Frank's contact information and said, "I'm looking forward to meeting you, Jack; I only wish it were under better circumstances. I'll get the data we have faxed to you on the secure line ASAP." They concluded the call.

Frank and Brad looked at each other and, almost in unison, said, "We've got a sick SOB out there."

"Let me get someone started on those faxes for you," Frank said. "I know you're retired, Brad, but I could use your expertise. I think it's time you and I go for a drink and devise a plan."

Ever since Gwen disappeared, Brad had visited Vero several times a week. During those times, he obtained important information concerning Gwen's recent activities. The information he gathered was interesting but frustrating, as it led nowhere. No person on her list of acquaintances or associates was found wanting to do her harm or to be vengeful. All of her friends were deeply concerned, and each had an airtight alibi for the night of Gwen's disappearance. Brad had talked to all of them, and they all told the same basic story. She had one drink at the Starlite bar with the gang, mentioned that she had things to do, and left the bar alone, which was normal. She was in good spirits, showed no unrest, and hoped to close a big deal on some acreage near Orlando. All her contacts spoke highly of her and passed on nothing that might indicate a problem. That fact convinced Brad that the perpetrator arrived after she got home, possibly following her home or waiting for her at the house. The data provided no clues to work, except she went home from the bar alone.

Todd McAfee was the only person she associated with who was unavailable to interview. He was on vacation in Europe and had left before Gwen's disappearance, which provided him a solid alibi. Brad knew he and Gwen had dated a short time ago, and they remained close friends, so perhaps he might have info the others did not. Knowing Todd would be arriving home today, Brad arranged an interview. He stopped at the security gate for Todd's housing complex, showed his credentials, and gave the guard Todd's name and address. The guard dutifully notified Todd and waved Brad on through. The community was rather plush, with golf courses, tennis courts, swimming pools, a huge clubhouse, and all the niceties. He parked the Viper in the designated visitor's spot for Todd's townhouse, went to the door, and rang the bell. The door opened instantly. "Come in, Mr. Ashley. The guard told me you were coming, so I was expecting you. Thanks for calling earlier and requesting a meeting. It gave me an excuse to tidy up, but please excuse the musty odor. The place has not aired out yet from being closed up. You mentioned that you were Gwen's brother and wanted to talk with me, so what's up? Are you throwing a big surprise party or something? She deserves payback. She's always surprising other people."

"No, Todd, it's not quite that simple, and you, just getting home from Europe, have not heard, but Gwen is missing." Todd asked, "What do you mean, missing? Do you mean missing, like disappeared or gone, or what? No way, not Gwen."

"Unfortunately, missing is what I mean. Gwens has been missing since the tenth of this month, shortly after you left on vacation. Maybe you might remember something from your past association with her that may give us a lead. I know you two dated for a while, so perhaps you may recall someone with whom she may have had a problem?"

"Oh, shit, man," Todd stammered! "This situation isn't good. Doesn't anybody know anything? How about Jill or Freda? They are close to Gwen. How about Bill? She dated him recently."

"No luck," Brad answered. "I've talked with them all, plus several others. It appears she was solo that evening, met the gang at the Starlite, had a drink, went home, and nobody has seen or heard from her since. The police checked out all known group members, and everyone checked out. As I said, I hoped you might remember something the others didn't. Was anybody bothering her? Did she have a run-in or a business problem with someone? Is there anything of that nature that you might recall?"

"Oh hell, Brad, I want a scotch," Todd stated. "How about you?"

"Sure," Brad answered, "a scotch right now sounds excellent."

Brad and Todd conversed at length, enjoying a couple of scotches as they reminisced. Todd talked of the good times he and Gwen had, and they remained close friends and continued to date socially on occasion. "We met in the Starlite a couple of days before my trip. She wanted to hear all my plans. She was sitting at the bar when I walked in, which is acceptable in Starlite. It's a neighborhood pub in a good neighborhood, and mostly locals. Anyhow, I noticed that she was talking to some guy I didn't know, so I moseyed over to the other side of the bar, but when Gwen saw me, she nodded for me to come her way. As I started around the bar, I heard her say, 'No thanks,' the guy shook his head, shrugged his shoulders, and headed for the far corner." Hey, damn it, Brad, maybe that is useful. Gwen told me he had become a pest for the past few nights. She said he offered to buy her a drink one evening, and she declined. He offered again the next time he came in, but she refused. The next time, he offered her a drink and dinner. When she told him no thanks, he said something derogatory about her rejecting him and that she reminded him of his mother. Gwen told me that, for some reason, this guy made her feel uncomfortable.

We noticed him watching us from the booth he was sitting in, but nothing further happened. While Gwen and I talked, he must have left, but we didn't see him leave. A little later, Jill came in, and the three of us went for pizza at the Italian Village. I'm guessing it was around ten when we finished eating. I took off before the girls did and went home. But ya know, I swore as I was driving away, I saw that asshole window shopping at the store next to the restaurant. I guess I didn't think much of it then, and a couple of days later, I was off on my trip."

"Could you describe this guy," asked Brad.

"Brad, I'm sorry, but I didn't pay that much attention to him. From what I can remember, I would say he was average height, five-ten or so, with a slender build, dark hair, and nothing distinguishing about him that I noticed. I don't remember enough about his looks to describe him. I remember Gwen said she thought he was cute and that it was a shame he had no personality. Oh ya, she also said something about a big red pinky ring he wore that was expensive-looking but tacky. She never did mention his name."

"I don't know if anything I told you has helped," Todd said, "but that little episode at the Starlite is the only negative situation I can recall. Gwen is a doll, and we all love her. I genuinely hope there is no foul play involved."

"Thanks," replied Brad, "so do I, but it doesn't look good right now. Please get in touch with me if you remember anything else. Thus far, you're the first person who has given me anything of value. This guy and the ring info could be a valuable lead, and I certainly appreciate it."

"My pleasure," Todd stated. "Please call me if you hear or need anything, even if it is just another scotch; you're welcome to come back whenever."

Brad quickly walked to the Viper, retrieved Jill's phone number, and called, telling her what Todd had said. Jill commented that she did remember Gwen mentioning a man trying to buy her drinks, and she made some remarks about his ring. However, Gwen did not seem concerned about the incident but just commented about him. Unfortunately, she had not seen the guy nor knew anything about him.

"Thanks," Brad commented. "If you get a chance, ask around and see if any others are aware of this guy. I'll be back in a day or two and check in with you and the rest of the group."

Brad drove home, calling Marci to let her know he was coming. "It's nice having someone to go home to. I might keep her around for a while," he quipped to himself. Marci answered on the second ring. "Hi, Babe," he flirted. "Do you have some time for a tired old FBI has-been?"

"Well, let me check my datebook. However, if you're interested in night sailing, I might be able to give you time this evening," she jested. "That is if you like naked sailing." "Naked," he quizzed. "I didn't know clothes were required in nautical attire."

"Great," she said in a bubbly voice. "The sky is clear, the wind is perfect, and the moon is full. I'll have the boat ship shape when you arrive, and you pick up a bucket of fried chicken."

"Marci Allen, you're one hell of a woman and my kind of a woman." He clicked off the cell, goosed the Viper, and temporally forgot the problems that plagued his mind.

The sun peeked over the horizon as the sloop swung gently on its anchor in the morning breeze. Marci awoke to discover Brad was already up and about. The coffee was brewing in the galley, and Brad stood on the companionway ladder surveying the anchorage. Quietly, Marci crawled out of the bunk in the spacious aft cabin and crept along the walkthrough into the main salon. Seeing his naked torso halfway up the ladder, she could not resist sneaking up behind him, sliding her arms around his waist, and giving him a sensual good morning hug. "Wow, that was nice, and good morning to you also," Brad said. She scanned the torso standing before her. "I see you are cheerful this morning, and I can see that a certain part of you and the sun is rising." Brad descended the ladder, and they merged in a carefree nude embrace. "This naked sailing is not bad," she said. Brad commented that naked sailing is excellent, and the first mate is the best part. Her cute little butt makes me stand up and take notice.

"I see it's standing up. Oops, I mean, you're standing up," Marci said. "Oh goodness, let me freshen up, get my words together, and I will serve you a playful treat for breakfast." "Sounds good. First-Mattie, you take the forward head, and I'll take the aft. I'll take that treat you offered sunny side up, served nice and hot in the captain's quarters," Brad stated with a pirate brogue. "No problem, my captain; as long as your bacon is nice and crispy, I will make sure that the treat is sunny side up and ready to serve," she quipped.

Brad was enjoying the shower when his cell phone rang. He grabbed a towel and proceeded to the main salon to retrieve the cell. Brad questioned, "Should I answer it?"

"You better, or you'll be so antsy during our breakfast treat that you'll not enjoy the server," she replied. "However," Marci teased, "had you enabled your voice mail as I asked, you could have responded to a message after breakfast." "I hate voice mail," he interrupted. "I know you do," she sighed, "but the bad timing of this call might have been worth saving a message until afterward."

Eight Missing Women Found, Plus Christie

"Brad, Jack Baird here."

"Hello Jack, what can I do for you?" "It's more of what I'm hoping to do for you," Jack continued. "Please listen carefully. I researched missing females throughout the state occurring before Lowell's case and found nineteen unsolved. Eight of them are especially interesting. Three of the eight lived in the central Florida area, and five more are from out of state but were last seen in central Florida. The Florida women all have similar reports concerning the condition of their houses or rooms. Two out-of-state females disappeared from motels and had similar situations in their rooms.

The last three reports are sketchy, with little detail, but I think we can get clarity by talking to the local authorities. I'm afraid this is about to break into something big. It sounds like a kook on the loose.

Unfortunately, the various PDs didn't spot the commonality. However, I'll give them the benefit of the doubt. The cases have been spread over the past few years and occurred in different cities in central Florida. Each department classified its case as a runaway or domestic problem, not a missing person. When you group the cases, the coincidences can not be ignored." Jack asked, "When could you be free to look over these files?"

"I'll be at your office around noon," Brad replied. "We can hit the books all afternoon."

"See ya later," answered Jack, "and I'll have some cold beer ready."

Marci entered the solon, wearing nothing but a towel. "The call sounded urgent. Would you like a rain check on the morning treat?" Brad looked at his sailing mate and could not resist her toying smile. He took her hand, led her to the aft cabin, removed the towel, and gently placed her on the oversized bed. "Miss Allen, may I say that breakfast is the most important meal of the day, and I don't intend to miss this one." She opened her arms, bidding him a warm welcome, her hands exploring his body as she prepared to serve the morning treat. She pressed herself tightly against him, whispering in his ear, "I am all yours, Brad. Take me; please take me, now." The captain feverishly obeyed.

They pulled anchor mid-morning and departed from the protected cove, savoring the feeling of their morning treat and the warm sun on their skin. Nell chugged smoothly along as she pushed the sleek hull towards home in the morning's calm air. The dock was only a half-mile away when Brad finished enlightening Marci on the latest information. "That's scary," Marci stated. "Do you think all those cases may be related?

Damn, that means we may have," she paused and hesitatingly said, "a serial killer."

"Right now, it's hard to say," Brad answered. "We thought of the possibility when Jack became involved but was unsure. I've heard of these nuts before and studied them in training, but I was never involved with an actual case. I hope to hell; this is not one." Brad powered Miss-T to her berth and gently slid alongside the dock. Marci told Brad to go ahead and leave; she would tie the boat up and stow the gear. She kissed him on the cheek and told him to see Jack and find out what was happening. "I can tell the suspense is killing you. Now go," she commanded!

"Thanks, Marci," Brad replied. "I'll be at Jack's office most of the day and home as early as possible."

"Sounds great," she said, "now, please go so you can return here soon. I Love you, and I miss you already."

Brad parked in front of Jack's office shortly after twelve. He got with Jack, and they headed for lunch. Jack related some of the details as they ate, agreeing that there was more to this than presently known. Returning to the office, Jack couldn't stop talking about the similarities of the cases. He was amazed that no one had picked up on them before, but missing person reports are common and normally are solved quickly. Unless relatives or friends are persistent, many unsolved cases are frequently stuck in a drawer and eventually forgotten, just another cold case. "Take this case," Jack said, "Gloria Jean Hays, 24 years old, has been missing for about two years now. She is from Fort Pierce, about fifteen miles south of Vero Beach. The report says she was last seen leaving a cocktail lounge on the beach. Her house resembled Gwen's house, including the word 'bitch.' Here is another, Sandra Karnes, from Stuart, Florida. It's almost an identical report to the Hays case and another, Rene Barkowski from Jensen Beach, the same scenario."

"Those towns are within short driving distance," remarked Brad.

"Good point," Jack replied, "there's roughly a year between each of these three. However, the out-of-state cases are scattered among Florida women."

"What you're saying," remarked Brad, "is that we now have nine similar cases. All nine are within five years."

"Christine Lowell is the latest, making them approximately six months apart. What concerns me," Jack stated, "is there are only a couple of weeks between your sister and Lowell. Could that mean he is escalating his actions, or what?"

"It indicates to me that the bastard lives in the local area, and he's getting more brazen," Brad stated, "and yes, I think he's a local."

"There is a significant item of interest in several of the cases," Jack stated. "According to the victims' friends, each had encountered a man who appeared to be over-friendly, and the vics were not receptive to his aggressive approach." "Explain your opinion of his aggressive approach," Brad said. "This man consistently offered to buy them drinks, asked them to dance, or go out to dinner," Jack answered, "and he was turned down on each offer. In several instances, this guy verbally expressed his dissatisfaction with being rejected. Our few descriptions of him lack in detail and are vague yet similar. He apparently would approach the vic when she was alone, and the areas he was seen in were dimly lit, so friends could not describe him. I nicknamed him Mr. X for commonality."

Brad informed Jack of the information he had obtained from Todd McAfee, which concerned a guy who offered Gwen drinks. That coincides with the other cases. Brad stated that this guy, whoever he is, might well be the perp. "We need to talk with as many people as possible and get as much data on Mr. X as possible. I'll lay odds that he is common to all the cases."

Jack replied, "I have already contacted the local police departments and gave them this info, but I was unaware of Gwen's information. I've also initiated a joint meeting of all departments next Monday morning at 0800 in Vero Beach. Vero is a central location. Can you be there?"

"Hell, yes," Brad replied. "I hadn't mentioned Gwen and this guy because I learned about him yesterday when talking with Todd. I felt this tidbit of knowledge would benefit me, and you proved me correct. I'll tell you, Jack, I beat myself silly trying to get a lead in Vero, and I have to give you credit. You dug in and got the job done. You don't know how much I appreciate your compliment, and I'm glad to help," replied Jack. "I just mentioned that you needed this info, and I got it quickly. I know your status with the Bureau, and as a consultant, you have limitations, but your name carries a lot of weight. Maybe we can make sense of all this mess using your name and my active duty."

"Thanks, Jack," said Brad, "but let's get real. It's been over a month, and you know as well as I that the chances of finding her alive are slim to none. We're both professionals, so let's be honest with each other: She is my sister, but my eyes are dry now. The tears have been shed, and I simply want to get the son of a bitch that did it." They shook hands on that statement.

The following day, Brad decided to delve deeper into this latest disappearance and asked Marci to join him for a leisurely drive to Sebastian. The ride had been pleasant, and the scenery lush, giving them both a feeling of being in a tropical, laid-back atmosphere. They entered the parking lot of Ahab's Oyster Bar, tucked the Viper into a shady parking spot, and strolled hand in hand into the restaurant. The hostess showed them to a table overlooking the water and the docked boats dancing at the pier. "Very lovely," commented Marci. "This place could make you go bohemian very quickly."

Brad smiled and observed the local scenery, including the number of apparently single women sitting at the bar. "I must confess why we are here. This bar is the last place that Christy Lowell was seen before disappearing.

I had an ulterior motive in bringing you here. The first was to enjoy your company, but the second was to see if we could casually probe some locals and maybe acquire more information about Mr. X." Marci replied, "You are not using me for bait, are you?" "No way, sweetness, I would not place you in that position, but perhaps after we eat, we can sit at the bar with all those ladies, and you can help get some clues. You being with me, they might be more receptive to talking, and I would not object if you ask them a few questions." "OK," she stated, "I get to play FBI." He joked, "You certainly do, and we'll call you Agent Marci. You might ask them if they know a man who comes on strong, asking to buy drinks and go to dinner. Females talk more freely to other females than to men. So yes, please play a sexy FBI agent."

Thoroughly enjoying the fresh seafood dinners cooked perfectly to their liking, Brad and Marci proceeded to the bar for an after-dinner drink and to converse with the clientele. Marci was the first to establish social discourse with the young woman next to her, who introduced herself as Cathy Owens. Marci felt like Sherlock Holmes when she discovered that Cathy knew Christy and was here when she encountered Mr. X. Giddy with her good news. She got Brad's attention and introduced him to her new acquaintance. Brad showed Cathy his ID and explained his association with the case and his position as Gwen's brother. Cathy told him she willfully talked with the local police and would gladly help the FBI. She introduced them to three other women who also knew Christy. Brad asked the women to join him and Marci at a table to talk easier and have less confusion. He ordered a round of drinks and began questioning.

Cathy started telling her story. "Christy and I were sitting at the bar as we frequently do on a Friday night. Not being engaged, committed, or dating anyone steady, we meet here and check out the male population. Noticing this man walking in, Christy said, 'Oh hell, here comes that pest. I think his name is Jessie.' Glancing his way, I couldn't see his face well in the dim light, but I noticed he was well dressed, looked like money, and headed our way. Christy said he came on real strong the first time she met him, and he did not impress her, but she was courteous, and ever since then, he has pestered her to go out. She said that if he started that crap tonight, she would have to put an end to it. She predicted his actions well. He came on like gangbusters, reciting gibberish from my fair lady or some theatrical terms. I had turned away from him as he approached, trying to stay uninvolved. I could hear what he said and tell Christy wanted no part of his BS. She verbally laid into him and made some wisecracks about not being able to remember him. I could hear him stammer when Christy shouted that she couldn't even remember who the hell she was with last night, let alone remember an asshole like him. Christy could use some four-letter words when she wanted to, and she interjected a few appropriate ones just for the shock effect. You could tell he was taken aback and belittled by her verbal abuse. It didn't help matters when all of us seated close by started laughing. This poor guy was not amused. He threw his hands in the air and stormed away. He headed out the door, spouting some verbal tirade about her ruining his evening and that she would pay for it. Henry, the bouncer, came over a little later and said that the guy was out in the parking lot ranting and raving like a madman and trying to find someone named Zac. Christy left alone around 11:30, and we all told her to be careful."

The other ladies concurred with Cathy's story, added a few minor enhancements, and agreed to call Brad should they see him again. However, none of the women could provide Jessie's description.

They openly admitted they were trying to avoid the situation and avoided eye contact with him. Not to mention the facts of having a few pina coladas, the dark atmosphere in the club, and their general difference of opinions on him, all of which clouded their memories. As he looked around, Brad noticed the visibility was hampered due to the dim lighting. Based on that, he thought it best not to suggest a sketch artist. Even Marci admitted that the ladies were pleasant, on the flakey side, and maybe drank too much, but they were friendly. She told Brad that playing agent was fun but not as much fun as playing with one. They headed for home.

The meeting with the law enforcement agencies started promptly at eight o'clock a.m. All of the law agencies involved were represented. Jack requested that each department describe its case and divulge any pertinent evidence not documented in its reports. The attending officers quickly noted the similarities between all the cases. The essential items showing similarity were the bedrooms, the pictures, the stuffed animals, the cleaning, and the word 'bitch.' There also appeared to be a non-descriptive male, referred to as Jessie, and a bar or cocktail lounge scene in every case. Even the cases involving the visiting out-of-state women included similarities to the local victims.

Jack stepped to the podium and gave a brief synopsis of what had just been disclosed. He introduced Brad and explained his involvement and the theory of a serial killer in east-central Florida. "I am asking Lieutenant Frank Arendas of the Vero Beach PD to establish a Task Force and a central base of operations in this area. I also request that each department assign at least one investigator who will be a member of this Task Force to work with the central base. This investigator will keep their departments abreast of the latest data and coordinate their department's investigative efforts with the Task Force. Being the assigned lead FBI Agent, I will alert the other Federal Agents in your jurisdictions to assist as needed. I will coordinate the overall activity, and Frank Arendas will take charge of the central base.

We will closely manage all press releases, so Frank will also place that responsibility under central base control. When you return to your respective departments, please advise Frank ASAP who your representative will be. Being a member will not require relocation, but attendance at Task Force meetings and physically working out of the central base as much as possible is. Each rep will also be bound by an oath of silence regarding all case data. We will issue our first press release later this week, informing the public that this Task Force has been created to investigate missing-person cases. We can assume we have a serial killer, but I am not sure we want to go public with that data. Our goal is to find Mr. X, who, due to the latest information, we shall refer to as 'Jessie.' We need to apprehend this individual before he kills again. Several of us are confident that he will kill again, possibly soon."

After adjourning the meeting, Jack, Brad, and Frank discussed various issues of the session. Jack informed both that he had contacted the Bureau and obtained permission to have Brad officially assigned to the case as a consultant. By doing this, Brad could assist Jack and the Task Force with whatever was needed. Jack told him there is an extra desk and plenty of space in my office, so move in. "Thanks," replied Brad, and they departed for home.

James And Mrs. Oliver

Five elderly souls and two younger individuals who passed from natural causes were laid to rest this week and created mounds of paper to be organized, properly registered, and signed. Paperwork was one function of the responsibilities that James found tedious. However, to stay in business, it must be done. James took a break from the reams of paper involved with the death ritual and relaxed in his office. A picture flashed on the TV, catching his eye and directing his attention to the breaking news.

"We have a missing person report," the newscaster stated. "Local authorities and the family of Christine Lowell have requested that anyone who knows her whereabouts or has information concerning Christine please get in touch with your local police or sheriff's department. Christy, as she is known, was last seen on Friday. The cause of her disappearance is unknown at this time." James hit the mute button when he noticed Mrs. Oliver watching the TV from the doorway. "What a shame," she said, "such a pretty girl. I'll bet some weird asshole did the poor girl harm."

"Poor girl?" James questioned in an unusually high-pitched voice but quickly regained self-control to subdue his reaction. "What makes you think she was a poor girl, Mrs. Oliver?" James always addressed her as Mrs. Oliver since she was his elder, and he had much respect for her, but her current reaction and language caught him by surprise. "Should I tell her Christy was a bitch and where she is planted? No, I best not," he thought, "and I best not tell her I was the person she called a weird asshole." "Oh please, excuse my language, James," she begged. "I am letting my mind think negatively instead of positively concerning young ladies' well-being. The area has had several missing women cases lately, and I think I am assuming the worst. She carefully scanned James's reaction to her comment, all the while thinking that one day she would tell him a fascinating story when she deemed he was ready, but not until then."

"I'll be willing to bet you, Mrs. Oliver," James stated, "if this lady were as lovely of a lady as you are, she would not be missing today. However, one day, they will probably find her. Perhaps in 2121, an archeologist exploring an ancient burial site will find her remains." "Gracious," Mrs. Oliver replied, "what an odd thing to say, but I do believe I understand your thoughts."

James felt it best to end this discussion as he started craving female companionship. He asked Mrs. Oliver, "Would you mind closing the office today? I have a few items that I need to take care of, and I am finished here. You may likewise leave before time if you wish." Knowing that he was going to Fellsmere and visit his favorite house of ill repute. She could see that wanton look in his eye, much like his father looked on occasion. She knew about the Fellsmere activity and other things he had done but never divulged her knowledge. The more she got to know James, the more confident she was that he was a young version of his Father. "I was hoping he would find the right woman and settle down one day," Mrs. Oliver said as she watched him drive away. "Have a nice day, James, my boy. Your future will soon enough be changing, so enjoy the present."

James arrived at the Old Florida Inn just before dark, following a rapid journey on Fellsmere Road, where he ignored the speed limit and threw caution to the wind. Hurriedly, he entered the quaint establishment and approached the desk. "Good evening, Mr. Zachary. The madam said we haven't seen you for a while. You haven't found another hostel with better accommodations, have you?"

"Goodness, no, Miss Phyllis, this place is the best in the south, and you are the most beautiful." "Oh, James, you never change, and please don't; you're perfect for my morale. Now, love, would you like your usual room for the night, or would you like to try something different?"

"You know, Miss Phyllis, I think I'll try the room in the southeast corner on the third floor. I understand you can see the whole way around the world from there."

"Excellent choice, my dear; I am sure that accommodation will give you a night of utter pleasure and comfort. You appear a bit troubled," she continued. Drinks are currently being served in the lounge. Why don't you take a moment or two and relax? A succulent surf and turf will be served at seven, breakfast will be as usual, and that is whenever you should awaken and partake of a consumable substance." He slid five crisp one-hundred dollar bills across the counter as she handed him the key to his chosen chamber. James proceeded to the lounge and ordered his usual brandy in an extra-large sniffer, filled just shy of the brim, allowing him to inhale the delectable aroma.

Savoring the brandy, James thought of Old Joe at the Cemetery. Old Joe had coyly given him a subtle tip about this place, and now James owed him an outstanding debt of gratitude. It's not as good as having your own woman, but Old Joe said sex is the next best thing, and he was right, James admitted while sipping his brandy. "It is the next best thing for taking the edge off my tensions. I sure as hell have had some stress recently."

James finished his brandy and rode the mid-century elevator

to the third floor. Exiting the lift, he turned and strolled down the hall to his chosen room. To his pleasure, the door opened as he approached, and he was greeted by a stunning redhead wearing sheer white lounging attire, which displayed lustful hints of her feminine nakedness beneath. "The name is Marsha," she purred. "Miss Phyllis advised me that you are a very special patron, so Mr. Zachary, please enter and join me for the night. Now, kind sir, if you permit me, I have drawn you a warm bath and will lavishly bathe every inch of your manly physique. Tonight, you shall be treated to a world full of outstanding and enticing experiences which will bring you the utmost sensations of gratification. Once I have bathed you, we shall go downstairs, where I shall pamper you with our delicious feast. Then, I shall glide you around the dance floor until our mutual vibrations encourage us to return to your nest of sheer passion for the night."

She systematically stripped him of his clothing and led him to a bubbling Jacuzzi, where she immersed him in the warm, gently pulsating fluid. Her fingers pranced gingerly about his body, tantalizing his entire torso and erasing the hassles of the day from his thoughts. She supported him caringly as he emerged from the liquid, engulfing his moist frame with a large heated towel. Tenderly, she dried every inch of his nude and reinvigorated body, then led him to a sizeable, overstuffed lounging chair where she joined him in its lavish comforts. Softly, she guided her supple lips, kissed and engulfed his male protrusion, and successfully released his tensions, letting him fully relax.

Marsha anointed his freshly bathed skin with warm, scented oils that seeped into his thirsting pores, making him feel pliable and full of youth.

"Now, my sweet," she sexually murmured, "slip these lounging pajamas on, and we shall enjoy a delicious lobster and steak feast. The meal shall permit you time to re-energize and regain your stamina for the remainder of your magnificent night. Your usual private dining area awaits us, where we can dine alone and enjoy intimate consumption. Following our feast, we shall snuggle and dance until you desire to retire to an incredible night of satiating dessert."

Chapter 5

Grotto And Task Force

The Task Force was becoming well organized, and all the members consistently brought in data. Frank had confiscated an older building that the motor pool once used for storage, which proved ideal for the Task Force to set up shop. There was ample space to house everyone, and the maintenance department spruced it up with cubicles, providing each investigator with his workspace. The large section in the center was partitioned as the briefing room. This Task Force was the first time a joint effort of this magnitude had ever been established to Frank's knowledge, so he wanted it to be perfect. To help ensure success, he had the building thoroughly secured. Authorized personnel were issued photo IDs, and guards were on duty around the clock.

Phone lines and computer connections were placed in each cubical for communications and data sharing. The DA and the State Attorney's offices were consulted to establish the correct data handling procedures. Frank wanted to ensure there would be no technical loopholes from something new he created when the perp was brought to trial. Frank personally contacted each Task Force member, informed them of the new headquarters, and advised them to come in to get their access badge and organize their cubical. The structure was appropriately nicknamed the Grotto. It soon proved a significant asset to the members' and Frank's planning.

It was midsummer, and the tropical heat had set in for the duration. Brad and Marci had been spending as much free time as possible sailing. However, Brad's free time was relatively scant as he spent several days a week working on Gwen's case. Marci understood and shared his devotion but missed him being present every day, and she missed their playtime aboard Miss-T. She had just fixed him a scotch as he relaxed in the shade of the bimini top when his cell rang. "Hi Brad," Frank Arendas said, "I was speaking with Jack, and he asked me to call you since he will be out of town for a few days. The Grotto is up and running in first-class condition now. I knew you requested a few days' liberty before returning to the working world, so I arranged your cubical alongside Jack's so the two of you could be close. About ninety percent of the gathered evidence and related data has been turned in, and on average, there are at least six detectives here at all times, so the briefing room has a lot of data posted. I would appreciate it if you would come and review the info if you're ready. Your expertise would be beneficial. I hope you may want to get a Bureau profiler down here once you absorb all this information. This Mr. X, now known as Jessie, is a frigging nut."

"Thanks for the input, Frank. I will be there first thing in the morning," Brad replied.

At 0800 the following day, Brad arrived at the Grotto. He introduced himself and presented his FBI credentials. "We were expecting you," the guard stated. "Please proceed to the main station and get your badge."

"Yes, sir," Brad replied as he obeyed the instructions. After obtaining his ID, he returned and entered the Grotto, where three other detectives were already working. Heeding Frank's suggestion, he made minor alterations in his cubical and then examined the vast array of data posted in the briefing room. Brad had reviewed the clues by noontime, but calling him Jessie didn't settle right. Could it be Jessie is an alias?

One of the other detectives showed Brad the 'Effort Board' that Frank established to inform each other which detective was investigating what case. Frank was listed under Gwen's case. Jack, Brad, and the other FBI Agents were listed as "Feds" assigned to all cases. Also, the board had an area for the investigators to note operational issues they were working on. Brad added that he was reviewing the perp's description and the associated names, Jessie and Zac. He posted copies of several reports referring to those names, then went to his cubical to examine the data he acquired from the board.

Completing his reviews, Brad left the Grotto and walked across the parking area to the central station. Frank told him to come in when he saw Brad approaching. "How's the world treating you?"

"The world's OK, Frank. It's the people in it that you have to watch out for."

Frank snickered, "I guess you're right on that one. I see you have been to the Grotto."

"That I have," Brad answered, and you did an excellent job setting it up."

"Thanks," Frank replied. "I was hoping you would give me your thoughts concerning the duties of the Feds."

Brad answered, "The Feds, as you named us, should assist the individual cases as needed and dig into items relevant to all cases. That is why I am looking into various cases. There is one exception: I want to stay abreast of Gwen's case."

"I see no problem with that, and I understand," Frank replied. "I also agree with you, Feds, for helping with the general aspects. By the way, I requested another Vero detective to work closely with you and Jack. She and I will be the only ones authorized to make media releases. Her name is Susan Gunther, and she will be assigned to the Grotto soon."

"Sounds good, Frank; let me know when she arrives. In the meantime, I'm heading home; call if you need anything."

James Meets Carrie

Several days had passed since James was pleasantly entertained at the Old Florida Inn, and he well recalled the interlude. He was highly satisfied and departed from the Inn following a delectable breakfast served in bed by his lovely lady of the night. She dished him his favorite, eggs benedict with extra muffins, four lean, crisp bacon slices, and hot tea, topped off with a sensual serving of her charms. James was wholly satiated and utterly pleased with Marsha. He extended his compliments on her behalf to Miss Phyllis and presented Marsha with a well-earned three hundred dollar tip for her devoted service. She invited him to frequent her boudoir again and hopefully very soon. During his trip home, he exuded a highly relaxed and satiated demeanor from the pleasant encounter.

James sat at his desk, with elbows propped and hands under his chin supporting his head as he idly gazed out the window, watching the Spanish moss dangling from the water oaks swing gently from the warm breeze blowing through the Bitch Farm. The moss gently swaying inspired some sexual desires in his groin as he replayed recent experiences with Marsha in his mind. She was delightful, extremely sexual, and quite attractive, but she was not what was truly desired in a woman. "I don't believe that she would be a loving and caring wife," he told himself. "No, she is not the woman I would desire as a permanent mate. I'll save Marsha for those lonely nights when I ache for pure sexual pleasure and nothing more until I can find the perfect female." James knew he wanted a woman who would nurture him, cuddle him, share things, work with him, and, even more importantly, she would be loyal to him and only him. Most of the bitches out there will seduce any man that pays attention to them, just like 'Bitch-Mother' did. Marsha is at least an honest whore, and pretends to be nothing more. He said aloud that he would keep her on my list of desirable encounters.

Mrs. Oliver interrupted his thoughts as she entered his office and placed several burial certificates on his desk for him to sign.

"Daydreaming," she asked in a chipper voice. "It's a lovely day for dreaming, but you should be chasing some cute young lady across the sand at the beach." "You are so right, Mrs. Oliver, and as soon as I sign these things, I think I shall do just that. Would you mind locking up when you leave?" "My pleasure," she answered, "providing that you don't care if I sneak out a tad early myself." "Be my guest, Mrs. Oliver," James replied. "You are correct; it is a lovely day, and neither you nor I deserve to be pent up in the office. Hang up the sign that tells the world, should they stop by, that we are out of the office until tomorrow, then have fun yourself." "Thank you, James," she replied, "I will do that and enjoy your day."

James left the office, stopped by his house, and re-dressed appropriately for the beach. He quickly gathered a towel along with his swim trunks and exited through the door when he heard the siren of a police car in the distance. "Where were you cops when Christy the bitch needed you," he thought? "Not that you could have helped her because I took good care of that damn bitch." Suddenly, he noticed that he was sporting a bulging erection. "Wait a minute," he thought, "why am I having erotic sexy thoughts? I must be horny again. Should I masturbate and get rid of it, or should I keep those thoughts out of my mind?" He then realized that he wasn't thinking of sex. He was thinking of killing, murder, and mayhem, and those particular subjects were arousing him for some reason. "What the hell is happening to me?" He asked himself. "These types of feelings happen to Zac, not me. Zac gets all excited about those things, not me. What the hell?" he asked. Searching for an answer, he recalled that he had thought about the bitches in the Bitch Farm, and remembering what Zac had done to the bitches, caused him to become aroused. Why did horrid kinds of thoughts give him an erection? "I don't get turned on by doing 'the deed,' Zac does," James murmured. "What the hell is happening to me?" He wondered as he proceeded to the car.

James parked the Mercedes, entered the bathhouse, and

changed into his swimsuit. He returned his other clothes to the car, locked them in the trunk, stuck the keys and money into the small pocket of his suit, wrapped the towel around his neck, and jogged slowly towards the beach. He dropped the towel in the soft sand at the edge of the surf and splashed into the Atlantic, jumping the waves and becoming refreshed. A beachside resort had recently been built just a short distance south of the parking area, and James noticed several young women sunning themselves in the lounge chairs sprinkled around the resort. Emerging from the rolling surf, he surmised that he could use a cool drink. James grabbed his towel and strolled to the resort's tiki bar, ordering a cold beer. Leaning against a palm, he noticed an attractive lady heading his way. He smiled, and she smiled back while walking towards him. James snapped a mental picture, developed it, and stowed it away in his brain. He thought she was almost perfect, with Auburn hair, mid-length down her back, green eyes, five one or two, a hundred and five pounds at the most. She was exceptionally well built and wore a thong bikini, which left little to the imagination. "May I buy you a drink?" He asked as she approached. "Sure," she replied, "I'll have a vodka-Collins with a twist. Any particular brand," he asked. "I prefer Sky Vodka if they have it. Otherwise, Absolute," she answered.

Returning from the bar, he handed her the drink, saying, "Absolute it is. They have Sky vodka at the main bar but not out here, and the name is Jessie." "Thank you, Jessie," she replied, taking a sip of the cocktail. "My name is Carrie, Carrie LaPort. Do you live around here?"

"Yes," James answered, "on the mainland, and you?" She replied, "I am visiting from Virginia, the Portsmouth, Norfolk area, and I'll be here another two weeks."

"Ah yes, the 'land of the Navy,' James responded, and may I ask, are you single, or is that being too forward? Yes, I'm single, and no, I don't consider that forward," answered Carrie. "We should know those things, so how about you?" "Likewise," answered James, "single, that is."

"Great," she replied. "However, I must leave shortly. I expect a call from my sister, but I understand the Holiday Inn on the beach in Vero has an excellent lounge and happy hour. I was planning on checking it out later. Why don't you meet me there?"

"I would love to," James told her. "I know the place, and I look forward to meeting you. I should be there around seven."

"Fine, see ya later," she said and gave him a pleasant smile as she walked towards her poolside room. James watched the sensual movement of her lower extremity and the perky bounce in her stride. From this angle, the thong bikini exposed her buttocks, and he admired her firm curvature and graceful sway as she pranced away.

The bulge returned to his groin, and this time, he knew the reason and glanced around with a trace of embarrassment as he noticed a couple of older women coyly ogling his protruding crotch and giggling among themselves. Hearing the giggles, James became aware that his bulge was evident. He walked towards them, smiled, and said, "Excuse me, ladies, I guess I was daydreaming." They giggled and glanced again at his crotch before turning the other way. He stepped up behind them and said, "Ladies, has it been long since you've seen one, or have you forgotten its purpose? Such a shame wasting your time peeking and giggling at a cock you could be fucking one. He patted them both on the ass and walked away, leaving them with their mouths agape, eyes wide, and staring in shock as he departed."

Changing his clothes in the bathhouse, it dawned on James what he had just done. "Whoa," he said, "that was not me. James would not have commented about his erection or stunned those women in such a manner. What the hell is going on with me today?"

Brad And Marci

Marci was rinsing the salt spray from the decks and rigging on Miss-T when a distant sound caught her attention. She heard the deep-throated roar of the engine as Brad geared down the Viper in the corners over a mile away. Marci knew he must be happy about something. Brad loves to drive that car, but he puts that V-10 power plant through its paces when he's in a good mood. She could visualize the smile on his face as the car squatted into the corners and leaped down the straightaways. Marci knew he enjoyed the sound and the speed of his car almost as much as he loved the silent slowness of his sailboat. She watched as he parked the car and headed for the dock. "I'm falling in love with this guy," she said and turned off the hose, jumped onto the dock, and rushed into his arms.

"Hi, Babe," he said. "I hoped you would be here but didn't expect you to clean the boat." "Why not?" she asked, "do you think you own the market on loving Miss-T?"

"No, ma'am," he replied, "but I hope I own the market on loving you." "Whoa, wait a minute, mister," Marci stated, "that's the first time you have ever mentioned love. Would you like to explain yourself?"

"You caught me red-handed, Marci. I guess I'll have to confess. Why do you think I was in such a hurry to get home? I believe I have fallen in love with you, Ms. Allen. When I'm with you, I'm happy. When you're not here, I miss you. I want you with me all the time. I have resolved myself to the fact that I love you, Marci."

"And I love you, Brad," she answered. Boarding the boat together, they disappeared below deck.

Lying next to her in the aft cabin, fully satiated after sharing some meaningful moments, he enlightened her about the Grotto and that he had decided to concentrate harder on finding this mystery man. Brad said, "This guy we call Jessie has my attention, and I feel he is involved with Gwen's case and the others. I am confident it will be a major break for everyone if I get a good lead on him. However, my dear, if you remain to lie there naked, with that lustful look on your face, I will not find anything but you."

"That's my plan, sir; I'm your duty as long as you are not on duty. I want you all to myself, which means I want you all over me. Now, FBI Agent, does that give you a good lead on the Marci case?"

"A lead hell," he said, "that pretty well tells the whole story, no pun intended." She cocked her head, smiled seductively, then whispered the whole story in his ear. The sun was setting when they departed from the boat. Arm in arm, they strolled to the condo, prepared a steak on the grill, and enjoyed a glass of wine. "This relationship is becoming fantastic, Marci said. I only wish Gwen was here so that I could tell her how great her brother is."

Chapter 6

James And Roslyn

Freshly showered and shaved, James stood naked in front of his full-length mirror. "Not bad," he mused. The few rays of sunshine I soaked up today give my body a seductive glow. A body like mine should impress Miss Carrie tonight. Now, what shall I wear that will make me even more appealing?" He couldn't stop thinking of this lady. Every time he closed his eyes, the image of her cute ass, the sun glistening in her long auburn hair, the smoothness of her skin, and the vividly pronounced breast flashed before his eyes. "More than just her female appeal, she was friendly, polite, and sounded wholesome and honest. I've been searching for a woman like this for years. God, I hope I have found her," he murmured aloud. He selected a slender-cut pair of khakis, a crisply starched navy blue shirt, his favorite oxblood loafers, and navy blue socks, and just for fun, he chose low-cut bikini underwear.

Admiring his clothed image in the mirror, he told himself how it would be impossible for her to resist such a perfect specimen. "There is no way. I know she won't resist; tonight, she shall be mine."

A few minutes past seven, the Mercedes stopped in front of the Holiday Inn. James slid the valet a fiver, then proceeded to the lounge. Scanning the area and the moderate crowd hanging around the bar, he was disappointed not to see Carrie. He thought perhaps she had not yet arrived as he meandered to the bar, found a vacant barstool, and ordered his usual brandy. A somewhat older and marginally attractive woman sitting on the stool beside him looked his way several times, trying to gain his attention. James avoided eye contact and continued surveillance, hoping to see Carrie arrive. Ignoring that his attention was elsewhere, the older woman lightly tapped James on the arm and asked, "Are you alone?" Perturbed by the interruption, James said, "Can't you see I am waiting on someone?"

"Sorry," she said and turned back to her drink. "I didn't mean to be rude, ma'am," James said. "It's just that she is late, and I am a little worried."

"That's quite all right," the lady replied. "I was looking for some company for the evening, someone with whom to socialize."

"OK," he snickered at her persistence. "Please, talk your little heart out until my lady friend arrives. Talking may help pass the time. My name is Jessie. What's yours?"

"Hi Jessie, my name is Roslyn."

After three hours of continuous conversation, James was agitated that Carrie had not shown up. I don't understand. He thought to himself as Roslyn maintained her damnable yakking. Carrie did not seem to be that type of a person, but I should have known she was a bitch. Wearing that revealing thong, damn it all, she's just a bitch, raced through his mind.

"Jessie, oh Jessie," Roslyn said, trying to get his attention. Hearing his name shook him out of his mental detour and returned him to the current world. "Oh, sorry, I guess I am a bit concerned about my un-present companion. It seems rather apparent that I have been stood up," Jessie replied. "I have been stood up before," stated Roslyn. "I know the feeling, but perhaps it's for the best. Otherwise, we would have never met. It's up to you, but I greatly enjoyed your company tonight. Therefore, if you are willing, can we find a more intimate place for the remainder of the evening?"

"You're right," answered James. "What do you have in mind, my lovely lady?"

"We could go to my condo and have a nightcap." She teasingly commented while her ogling eyes traced up and down his torso. "The view from my front overlooks the beach, and you can see the twisting path of the Indian River from my rear." He jokingly answered, "We are on the beach now, and it's a lovely view, but your rearview sounds very enticing."

"Naughty boy," she said with a grin, "but I feel it will be interesting to show you my views and complete landscape. I suggest you follow me in your car, that is, if you're ready to give up this unrewarding vigilance." Jessie nodded and escorted her to the door.

James parked the Mercedes in the back of the condo's lot, somewhat hiding it from view. He met Roslyn by the outside elevator. Her condo was on the sixth floor, at the south end of the building. It was also a considerable distance away from the elevator. His watch indicated 10:15, and he noticed that most units they walked past were dark. Either nobody is home, or they are in bed already. James wondered why he was so observant but chalked it up to his regular habit of noting details.

Roslyn unlocked the door, bid his entrance, and turned on soft lighting over the wet bar. She scooped some cubes from the ice maker and poured brandy on the rocks in a large sniffer. "If I remember correctly, this should be just how you like your brandy, my dear," she stated. "Thank you," he said. "You have a sharp eye to have noticed my drink. Let's say I appreciate a good man," she answered. "Most high-caliber men like brandy and prefer a large sniffer so that they may savor the aroma." "Have you appreciated many men?" James quizzed. "That is somewhat personal, my love," she replied. "Let's say, at my age, I am not a virgin." She gently kissed him, took his hand, and led him to the bedroom. She dimmed the bedroom light, creating a seductive ambiance, and with a few simplistic alterations to her attire, she stood before him, alluringly naked. James was in awe of the youthful condition of her mid-aged body. The mounds of her buttocks were well-shaped and toned. Her ample breast rose proud and perky, with just the slightest bounce as she approached him. James admired her flat tummy and firm thighs as she moved closer, and he became very aroused. All in all, she was sensually enticing, regardless of her age.

Sexually, she slinked up in front of James, stripped him gently of his clothes, and whispered for him to lay face-up on the bed, where she seductively kissed him all over and pleasured his throbbing erection. With both participants now lusting for satisfaction, she straddled his hips and rode his upright member.

James had heard women moan and scream with pleasure before, but they were whores, and he had paid them to do that. "Is this woman a whore?" James asked himself as he listened to her express her genuine desires while achieving multiple orgasms. "Decent women don't say those things. Decent women don't do the things she is doing. Decent women don't fuck the way this woman is fucking, raced through James's mind as he reached a pulsating climax."

"Oh Jessie, my dear Jessie," she screamed. "I can feel you erupting inside me. You're the best man that I have ever had. I have had dozens and dozens of men, but you are the best. Do me again, Jessie. Please do me again and again." "Dozens and dozens of men," James shouted, with a questioning air, as he lurched upward and threw her down on the bed.

Roslyn Found

Marci and Brad had planned on sailing for the entire weekend. In fact, they had stretched it a day by her calling in sick Friday morning so that they could leave early. "That's not nice to fake a sick day," Brad said teasingly. "Why did you enjoy your naked breakfast so much if the sick day wasn't nice?" she questioned. "Besides, I have many sick days built up and have only been out twice in the past five years."

"That's not bad. Not bad at all," Brad remarked, "but you shouldn't fib. I think I'll have to spank you."

"No way," she replied, "you'll put me over your knee, pull my pants down, forget what you were mad about, and I would have to fib again on Monday," she giggled. "You're right, but wouldn't it be fun? Now the heck with the spanking, come over here, sit on my lap while I stay on course, and let's see what subject comes up."

Just as things began to be interesting, Brad's phone sounded. Marci just smiled, arose from his lap, and went to the aft cabin to retrieve his phone. She partially came up the ladder and smugly looked at Brad behind the wheel as she answered his phone. "Hello, Brad's office. May we help you?" "Sorry, it sounds like I am interrupting a pleasant voyage. It's Jack here, and unfortunately, I need to talk to Brad." She handed Brad the phone and took over his seat behind the wheel while he answered his call. Instinctively, she fired up Nel, relaxed the sails, and headed the boat toward home. "How did you know I needed to go in," Brad asked. "Well," she said, "the only times you haven't been on that phone since we left was when you were sleeping or making love, plus that look in your eye, and the tone of Jack's voice gave me the clues. I guess I'm getting used to you, Brad, and that's scary."

"Scary, I don't mind," Brad said, "but you are getting used to my job and my thoughts; that has got to go. It indicates that in your book, I am becoming old hat."

"There are no old hats in your closet," Marci replied. "When I notice the old in you, I'll let you know."

"Thanks, Babe," he continued. "Jack couldn't tell me much over the phone. He thinks Jessie has struck again. Only we have a body this time. I'm already steering toward the dock," she replied. Marcie docked Miss-T, and Brad headed to see Jack.

Brad and Jack exited the elevator on the sixth floor and proceeded toward the southernmost condo. Showing their badges, the patrolman at the door admitted them. He told them Lieutenant Arendas would be there shortly and instructed them to be careful as the forensic team was not finished. "This one has a little different MO," Jack said. "Let me tell you what I know so far. The victim's name is Roslyn Conti. A friend of hers, Alice Thornton, was to meet her this morning for breakfast and a shopping spree, but Conti didn't show. Ms. Thornton called her several times, but no answer, so she decided to swing by her condo. Conti's car was in its designated parking spot. Thornton went to her condo, thinking Conti had just overslept. Getting no answer at the door, she became worried and persuaded the manager to open the door. They found her just the way you're going to see her. I asked CSI and the Medical Examiner to leave everything intact until you arrived. They weren't happy but agreed.

The only area altered is where poor Ms. Thornton got sick. It must have been a hell of a shock for her to find her friend like that," Jack said as he led Brad across the vastness of the living area. Noting that nothing appeared out of place, they proceeded toward the bedroom, encompassing the unit's southern half. They noticed it was lavishly plush, expensively decorated for a one-bedroom condo, and had a sizable wet bar off the side. Moving through the front room, they entered the bedroom, which was déjà vu for Brad. All of the pictures and stuffed animals were arranged similarly to previous cases. Her body was sitting with her back tightly against the headboard. Her neck was broken, her head twisted halfway around, and her chin resting on her left shoulder. Her arms were tied to the headboard with silk scarves, and her legs spread ungodly wide and tied to the bedposts with electrical cords. A stuffed gator had been forcibly crammed with its snout between her legs, completing the grotesque scene. Jack motioned to the bed linens, which had been taken off the bed and neatly stacked in a corner. "That is one of the differences in the M.O. There are no visible traces of blood on the linens, so he must have removed them before the mutilation."

"Mutilation, what mutilation?" Brad asked. Jack asked the medical examiner to remove the stuffed gator. Brad's stomach did flip-flops. Her entire crotch had been cut out. There was a large gaping hole from which various parts of her innards protruded. "Oh God, what kind of a sick bastard is he?" Brad asked. "Sick bastard is right," replied Jack. The prick must have taken her vagina as a souvenir of his conquest. Brad walked into the adjoining bath, where writing was on the wall. The childish lettering appeared similar to the other cases. "Here are more M.O. differences," Brad remarked. This message has more to say than just bitch, and he read it aloud. 'She was an old whore, who screwed a dozen or more, but when my cock made her twitch, she became a real bitch. So to hell with her soul, I took her hole.'

"And look," he continued, there are crudely drawn arrows pointing from the limerick to the top of the commode. "The remaining portion of the lipstick tube is standing upright. Make sure the lipstick tube is checked for prints," Brad stated and continued surveying the scene. "By the looks of it, the shower is where most of the butchery took place. Dried blood is pooled around the drain, and there are also small chunks of flesh and pubic hair present. Bloodstained towels and a large carving knife, probably his surgical instrument, are stacked up in the corner. Sure as hell, he left evidence this time but was not as prepared for this attack as he was with the others."

"I agree," Jack stated. "It looks more spontaneous, and the knife is from a set of knives in the kitchen. Let's get out of here and let CSI do its job. We need as much data as possible, and they are patiently waiting."

"What are your thoughts so far," Jack asked. "It's hard to say until the lab boys get done," Brad answered. "But I am surmising they had sex, after which he broke her neck, drug her into the shower, dissected her crotch, and then posed her on the bed with the gator positioned for effect. He didn't take her body because getting her out of there would have been difficult. This killing was not as well planned as the others, and perhaps she was in the wrong place at the wrong time. It could have been a chance meeting, she offered to give him sex, and for some reason, he considered her a bitch, thus the limerick. Ms. Conti appears slightly older than his previous choices, indicating a chance meeting. It's horrible to say, but at least we have a corpse. Let's hope some forensic clues will be found and help nail this bastard. Maybe this spontaneous act will be his first big mistake."

Frank Arendas and Jack called an emergency meeting of the Task Force at the Grotto later that morning to share all the latest developments. "Can I have your attention?" asked Frank. "There are too many similarities between this case and our other cases not to involve the same perp. The prime difference is we have a body this time. Let's hope forensics can help. The latest victim is Roslyn May Conti, AKA Patella, Wallenberg, Brinson, and Salvicto. Her maiden is Conti, which she reclaimed following each divorce. She was 52 years old and moderately wealthy. She spent five to six months here in Vero at her condo and traveled the rest of the time. She has one sister, Grace Cosentino, in Patterson, New Jersey. Parents are deceased, no children, and ex-husbands are out of state and currently being notified. Her known friends in the area are listed in your handouts. See me after the meeting if anyone knows one or more of them. Detective Sue Gunther has been assigned to this case, and she is the newest member of our Task Force, so I'm asking you to make her welcome. The handout has as much info as is currently known about this victim. Updates will be distributed ASAP. I don't need to tell you that this guy must be caught quickly. He's smart, he's cautious, and we believe he's a local. He will make a mistake, so let's be there when he does. Better yet, let's find one that he has already made. There is no way of keeping this homicide hidden from the press, but I see no reason to expose links to other cases until we are certain. We don't want a serial murderer story hitting the news on top of everything else. Detective Gunther will also be our media contact for the entire Task Force on all cases. She has a lot of experience handling the press, so I don't want to see anything released to the public unless she or I have approved it. I believe the FBI will back me on that statement." Jack and Brad both nodded their consent. "Thank you for coming, and I am asking all of you to join Brad, Jack, and me in a brainstorming session right after lunch."

James Killed Instead Of Zac

James awoke with a dizzy head; he had overslept his usual time, and his head pounded and throbbed. It felt like he was hungover from too much brandy, but he knew that was not the problem. James rolled over and sat on the edge of the bed, talking to himself and trying to recall the previous night. He had to force himself to concentrate. Slowly, the events of the last evening began drifting back. "That bitch Carrie stood me up, and that old broad talked my ear off all night and wanted to take me home with her. Holy shit, I went home with her. I remember I went home with that old broad, and she turned out to be a bitch. Who else but a bitch would tell you that she had fucked dozens of men while fucking you? She even said that I was the best. What kind of shit talk was that? Did she think telling me I was the best would make me feel good? What a scuzzy slut, what a bitch, what a lousy damn bitch. But when did Zac get there? Strange, I don't remember Zac being there at all."

In all his naked glory, James stumbled across the room, grabbed a towel from the rack, and prepared to shower, hoping it would make him feel better. "It's a good thing this is Saturday," he thought. "Mrs. Oliver would be upset if I came into work in this shape. She would preach to me for hours about getting married and settling down. I sure as hell don't need preaching this morning." As he entered the shower, he stepped on something slippery and almost lost footing. Regaining his composure, he bent over and examined the object lying there. Picking it up, he said, "What the hell? It's a hunk of raw meat, and it looks like a woman's pussy. Holy shit," he screamed. His hands flew in the air, and his evening trophy went flying. "My God, Zac, what have you done? You did this, didn't you? You did this, and I didn't tell you to do it, Zac, Zac, where the hell are you, Zac?"

"Come on, James, get a hold of yourself, think man, think it through; what happened last night? Think, damn it, think," he stammered. Permitting the water to help return his senses, he remembered going to the old broad's condo. "What was her name?" He questioned himself. "Damn it, think. What the hell was her name? I remember that we made love, hell no, not love. I screwed her. I damn sure didn't make love to her. After the crap she told me, the old bitch didn't deserve love, but she enjoyed every position I could remember. At least she did enjoy it until she kept talking about doing all the other men, dozens of men. Can you imagine? That old bitch screwed dozens of men.

I have to get her washed off of me. I need to scrub my entire body. Every place that bitch touched me needs scrubbing." Turning the water on hotter, he called for Zac. "Did you kill her, Zac? Did you bring home that hunk of meat, Zac? Answer me, Zac. Tell your brother James what you did last night. You did "the deed" without letting me plan it. Didn't you, Zac? You can tell me. I won't get mad. I just hope you cleaned up afterward and planted the bitch. Answer me, Zac. Please answer me." Zac remained silent.

Somewhat refreshed from his shower, James shaved and dressed casually for the day. "Saturdays were days for fun; if he could get the queasy feeling to go away, he could have some fun. Maybe Zac will tell me what happened, but I must discard that gross vaginal thing. Zac takes care of these tasks, not me, but I best do it and protect Zac." James put the oozing flesh into a freeze-lock baggie and drove to the Bitch Farm. Ensuring no one could see him, he dug a deep hole near Granny Sue's daughter and buried the baggie. James smiled and told himself, "We not only have bitches planted here, we now have a pussy. Maybe that's where pussy willows come from," he chuckled.

Arriving at the house, he turned on the TV, flipping the channels until he found the local news. He poured a brandy, sat down to relax, and watched last night's coverage, hoping for a hint to what Zac had done. "Good afternoon. We have breaking news. A woman was found murdered early this morning. Her name is being withheld pending notification of next of kin. It has been determined that she was killed late Friday night. This morning, a friend became concerned when the victim did not show up for a planned outing and went to her condo, where she and the manager discovered the body. Anyone living at the Gentle Sea's condominium who may have seen or heard anything or has information about this crime is asked to contact Detective Susan Gunther of the Vero Beach PD. That's all the information we have on this horrible crime, and we will keep you informed as details are released."

James bolted upright in his plush recliner, a look of panic and shock on his face. "My God," he muttered in a raspy voice. "Zac didn't kill that woman. I did. What the hell is happening to me? It is Zac who does the killing, the raping, and the mutilation, not me? I'm the lover, not the killer. Zac is the killer, and he does it, not me. It can't be me." He recoiled back in the chair, drawing into a fetal position, and cried like a baby. He looked at his hands, shaking uncontrollably. He felt the pulsating bulge rising in his pants, the lustful sensation in his groin, the desirable urge for gratification, and that's when James was confident he had killed that bitch, not Zac. "That's why they found the body, he stammered. I killed that frigging bitch, I did it, and I didn't wait for Zac, but why did I do it? This killing is not good. Last night was not good. Zac, we need to talk; maybe we need a rest or more killing. Oh shit, what am I saying, and why am I thinking this way? What has happened to me, Zac? What has happened to us?"

Chapter 7

Brad's Interviews

Reviewing the Task Force meeting in his brain, Brad left his condo early Monday morning. He had previously contacted several of the witnesses on cases who had witnessed the existence of this man named Jessie and was able to make an appointment to talk with one of them. Marci had fixed him a he-man-style breakfast and passionately kissed him goodbye as a reminder to come home as soon as possible. As a result, he was very upbeat with a festive mood, steering the Viper south on I-95 towards Stuart. Entering the city limits, he called Jackie Williams, a friend of Sandra Karnes, one of the victims. Jackie informed him that she had invited another lady friend to their meeting who had likewise been with Sandra the night of her disappearance. That news gave him an even better feeling about the day's success.

Brad had barely pushed the doorbell when Jackie opened the door wide and invited him in. Brad asked, "Don't you want to see some identification?" "Oh, sure," she replied, "but I know you're Brad Ashley, the FBI Agent who called me, right?" "Yes, you're right. I am Brad Ashley," he answered as he presented his ID, "but I suggest you obtain that information before opening the door. I'm not trying to scare you, Ms. Williams, or sound authoritative. It's just that there are some strange people out there, and I suggest you be a bit more cautious."

"Sorry," she said, "and you're right, I usually am not that

accommodating, but since you had just called, I assumed it was you, and I will be more careful, I promise." "Good," he replied. "Now, please introduce me to your friend so we can start."

"Brad, this is Estelle Dwyer. Both of us were with Sandra that night."

"How can we help you, Mr. Ashley?"

"First, call me Brad, then tell me all you can remember about that night and this man you called Jessie. Even the slightest detail that you may think unnecessary. Jackie, you start, and Estelle, you fill in with information she might omit, OK?"

"Of course," replied Jackie, "I'll be happy to start," and she did.

"Sandra was an old college bud of mine. She came down here several times a year from Atlanta to hang out and have fun. She frequently rented an apartment or condo for a few weeks while here rather than staying with me. We got along great, but a little privacy is sometimes needed if you understand. Sandra was very outgoing, petite, and pretty, so she had no problems getting attention from the masculine gender. Her job was with a big marketing firm that did promos for a major beer company. Her job required her to travel frequently, and she loved it. On this visit, she rented a condo near Sand Point Park, not far from our favorite watering hole, the Sandpiper. It's a singles bar but not a meat market. There are a lot of locals and classy types who hang out there. Sandra had mentioned this guy she referred to as Jessie was becoming a pain in the posterior. He kept buying her drinks and insisted she go to dinner with him.

However, we were there a few nights before she disappeared, and he showed up. We were unaware of his arrival until Shelia, our waitress, brought us a round of drinks and a note for Sandra. I remember Sandra reading the message and getting a little pissed. She commented that she had had enough of this prick and asked Shelia to wait a minute until she answered the dude."

Brad asked, "Did either of you read her answer to him?" "No," answered Estelle. "I sat closer to Sandra than Jackie, but she didn't show it. Come to think of it," Estelle stated, "I don't recall her saying what was in the message or what she wrote back."

"That's a shame," Brad commented. "Her words may have been valuable data." Jackie continued, "After Shelia returned the note to him, we could tell he was pissed, so Sandra decided it would be best to say it in person. She walked over to him and returned quickly with a look of disgust. Sandra told us that the ass just called her a bitch, then said we were all bitches, and that we should get to know Zac. None of us have any idea who Zac is. Sandra mentioned that Jessie also told her he was conducting a funeral in the morning, and she should be happy it wasn't hers. I remember her saying that Estelle chimed in. I believe that statement frightened her, even making me uneasy as well. Jackie stated likewise, but what bothered me more was when he stormed out, pulled his cap down to shield his face, and gave us the finger."

Brad said, 'I take it then that neither of you got a good look at him."

"I didn't," Estelle replied, "most of the time, his back was to me."

"Nor did I," replied Jackie. "They keep it dark in most singles bars, and he stayed in that far dark corner. But perhaps if I saw him again in there, I might recognize him. Sandra and Shelia are the only ones I know who saw his face. He had an athletic build, was approximately six feet tall, clean-shaven, and had no beard or mustache. I estimate him to be in his mid to late thirties. His clothes appeared neat and a little higher priced than average. Unfortunately, Shelia was killed in a car wreck shortly after all this happened. We don't know the other servers, but you may want to question them."

Jackie continued, "A few days later, Sandra didn't attend our usual tennis game. I couldn't contact her, so I drove to her rental to check on her. Her car was there, and looking through the window, I could see no sign of her inside. I went to the beach area, and she was not there either, nor was she in the laundry or social room, which bothered me. I located the manager and sweet-talked him into helping me. We searched everywhere possible, and he finally agreed to open her door, and you know the rest of the story. I try not to remember how awful that place looked. I still have bad dreams."

"Did you tell this story to the local police?" Brad asked. "Yes," Jackie replied, "but they didn't think much of it. The local law around here tends to believe that we singles are just jet-set brats. In my opinion, they tend to favor the more influential locals."

"Let me say this, Jackie, and you also, Estelle," Brad stated on behalf of the FBI, "we do care, and I think your local police care. Please understand that they have all kinds of situations to deal with, often involving young people with relatively free lifestyles like yours. As all cases are, Sandra and her case are important, so bear with us. We'll find out what happened and see that justice is done. At least one of your local detectives is a member of our Task Force, as am I, and our goal is to catch this bastard. Excuse my language." "You're right, Brad. We probably ignore what the cops have to go through daily, many of which come from people like us who are not thinking."

"I didn't come here to preach," Brad said. "I want you to understand that we are working on this case, and Sandra has not been forgotten. I can tell you that a significant Task Force has been organized to deal with this case and a few similar ones. As I mentioned, your local police have a member assigned to the Task Force, and we are all working together. Thanks for your information, ladies; it has been beneficial, and if you think of anything else, no matter how trivial, please call me." Brad gave both of them his card and bid them a good day.

One part of Jackie's story rattled around in Brad's mind: Jessie's comment about conducting a funeral. The term funeral was a new piece of data, but how did a funeral fit into the picture?

Could he be a man of the cloth, a minister, a priest, or maybe Jessie is an undertaker? One thing was for sure: Brad was determined to check out the scheduled funerals for the day following Sandra's disappearance. "This word may be the first break we've received," Brad thought. He entered the Stuart PD and talked with Leon Sharps, the detective assigned to the Karnes case and the Task Force. Brad informed him of the story Miss Williams told. Sharps immediately opened his case report and started scanning through it. "The story she told you sounds very similar to the story the original detectives documented, except for the funeral. I don't see any reference to it here. The comment has significance, and I'll have it checked out and sent to the Grotto."

"Thanks," Brad said, "and I look forward to hearing from you soon. I'll have the Task Force research the other cases."

Zac And Carrie

Zac had been secretly stalking Carrie LaPort for several days, studying her every move while memorizing the resort's layout and the staff's routine. It became apparent to him that Miss LaPort was a real prick teaser, and not only stood up James, but she has stood up three other men since he started the vigilance. According to the resort's help, Carrie is looking for a rich husband, so if you're an average Joe, Carrie teases and forgets. No matter how Zac or James rearranged the facts, she proved to be a bitch, which is all the data James needed to turn Zac loose.

Zac reported every detail back to James for his planning involved with 'the deed.' James was contemplating a different strategy with this bitch since she not only stood him up but also caused him to lose control and whack the Conti bitch. Those issues pissed James off, and he told Zac he wanted to do 'the deed' on her in some out-of-the-way motel and have another man involved. Due to this, Zac found himself becoming anxious to do 'the deed.' Zac knew it would be exciting, it would be revenge for James, plus this bitch had a scorching hot body.

Carrie drove her rental car from the resort entrance to A1A

and turned north. Zac knew she was on her way to the Beach Club as expected. He accelerated past her, permitting him to enter the club's parking lot several minutes before her, and parked in the seclusion of the pines at the far end. Zac knew parking spots were at a premium at this time of night and chose one where she would park. After parking, Zac ducked behind the adjacent vehicle, waiting for her to arrive. This area has the closest spots available, and if I judge her correctly, she will park here, he said to himself. Within minutes, her car entered the lot, and as Zac predicted, she drove down the first and second rows, finding no spaces, and finally down the third row where Zac was hiding.

Zac quickly scanned the area to ensure there were no nearby persons to witness her abduction. All was clear as she exited the car, and he forcibly hammered the blackjack down on the back of her head, rendering her uncautious. He shut her car door and laid her prone between the vehicles. Again surveying the area for privacy, he duct-taped her mouth, bound her legs and hands, picked up her purse, and retrieved the few things that had fallen out. He hefted her limp body over his shoulder, trudged swiftly to his car, dumped her and her purse into the trunk, and covered her with an old throw rug.

Zac cautiously returned to Carrie's car, locked the doors, and rescanned the ground for additional items he may have missed and any other tell-tale signs. Satisfied all was well, he returned to his car. He left the parking lot, steered north to Wabasso Causeway, turned east to US-1, and then drove south past Vero to the Pleasant View Inn, a small Mom and Pop motel. Earlier in the day, Zac had paid a vagrant $50 to rent a room using the vagrant's name. He was not worried about the vagrant identifying him because his body lay in the trunk with Carrie. Mr. Gerald Cozzy, the vagrant, did his part and was already dead.

"Thus far, this has been very exciting," Zac whispered. "It is my first double homicide and my first male victim. Exciting, yes, very exciting indeed. It's also unusual, one bitch and one bastard with a strange last name. James precisely planned each detail so the results of this escapade would throw the cops for a loop once they got on board," he snickered. The vagrant, as instructed, rented a room on the far side of the motel, opposite the highway. Being the only room rented in this section and just three rooms in the front section, Zac felt confident there would be sufficient privacy to do 'the deed.' This location allowed Zac to bypass the front entrance, proceed to the next building, and back the car trunk first into the slot in front of the room.

Zac lifted Carrie from the trunk, put her in the room, and laid her on the bed. "That, my dear, is the end of your gentle treatment," he told her, noticing the trace movement of her eyes as she began to regain conscience, "so just lay there Bitch, and behave yourself." He returned to the car, slung Gerald's torso over his shoulder, totted him into the room, and propped him up in the corner. "There you go, Gerald, old boy, you sit still and watch the fun. I'll put on a little show and leave you here for the cops to find. You will be the only witness ever to see me do 'the deed.' But no worries, you can't tell them, can you?" Zac snickered as he pictured the cop's reaction to seeing Gerald in the corner.

Coming out of her stupor from the blow on the head, Carrie began to realize her situation as she struggled to release the bindings. The blur in her eyes cleared as she opened them in terror and focused on Zac standing beside Gerald's slumped body. Lying on her stomach, she attempted in vain to free herself while holding her head up to see all she could. Zac grinned broadly as he roughly rolled her onto her back. He verbally explained that James had called him and was unhappy about her standing him up last weekend. "You said you would meet him, and then you deliberately stood him up," Zac shouted. "That was the worst thing to do, and it was downright stupid on your part. When bitches do dumb things, James calls me, and I take cure of the situation. You screwed up good, Carrie, because James actually liked you. He thought you might be the one he's been looking for, and then you go and fuck with his mind. James was so pissed his anger killed that old bitch Roslyn Conti." Zac sensed she had heard about Conti and watched her eyes sharpen with fear as he spoke. "Yeah, damn your hide; the same night you stood him up, he sliced up that old bitch. Did you hear about it? It was all over the fringing news, did you listen to it? Damn it, Carrie, it was you that caused that fucking mess. Yes, you caused it. Nod, or do something, you dumb bitch." Carrie finally nodded her head, and Zac smiled. Well, your sweet little ass is about to discover how much fucking trouble you caused.

He removed the surgical scalpel from his backpack and slashed it at her, making quick slices barely above her face in the air. Tears welled in her eyes as she watched him place it gingerly on the nightstand beside the bed. He then removed a large pair of scissors, and panic set in as she tried desperately to move away, kicking furiously at him as she coiled tightly into a fetal position. Zac laughed loudly at her useless struggle. He retrieved some lengths of rope and tied her hands to the headboard. "There now, that should keep you confined until later." Using the scissors, he proceeded to cut off her clothing. "Hold still, or I might snip something you don't want to be snipped," he jested. He first cut her blouse into several strips, which he tore away from her body and placed in a trash bag.

Then, with a couple of well-placed cuts, her upper body was fully exposed as her bra fell to the bed. Zac paused momentarily to admire the lushness of her perky breast, heaving with desperation as she tried in vain to shriek. Zac could no longer resist the temptation. He caressed her breasts gently and suckled on them until she squirmed loose from his grasp. Aggravated by her resistance, Zac unmercifully grabbed both boobs and squeezed painfully hard. He pinched the nipples while powerfully twisting them with his fingers before mashing his course palms into the tender mounds, causing Carrie excruciating pain.

Zac sheared the seam on each side of her tight shorts, grabbed them by the crotch, and pulled the severed pieces forcibly from between her legs. The abrasiveness of the denim chafed the tender skin of her inner thighs as he ripped the cloth away. Once again, she winced in pain, making her more easily subdued. Zac retrieved the scalpel and methodically sliced her bikini panties, exposing her vagina's sensual mound of lust.

He tied ropes to each ankle, looped the loose ends around each lower bedpost, and severed the tape binding her legs. With one quick tug on both lines, her legs spread wide apart. Zac knotted the rope with her hands tied to the headboard and her legs secured to the bedposts, exposing her charms.

Zac stepped back and admired her exposed beauty. Carrie defiantly twisted and squirmed, anticipating what would happen as she watched him slowly strip off his clothing.

Zac inflicted his sexual prowess on her several times during the next few hours, and in between the torturous seductions, he groped, fondled, and molested her entire body. Being fully satiated, he injected large syringes of embalming fluid into her veins and giggled as her body went into convulsions from the fluid flowing through her. The look in her eyes, the grimacing, and the screams excited him immensely as her death concluded 'the deed.' Zac placed her in the rust-stained bathtub, letting her blood ooze down the drain as he surgically extracted her sexual playground. Since James taught me how to do this, he mused, it's fun to take a pussy souvenir. Stowing her body in the car and thoroughly cleaning the scene, Zac looked at Gerald, quietly sitting in the corner, and laughingly remarked, I hope you enjoyed the show, old boy, but do not tell anyone who took part in this saga.

Brad

Brad was interviewing Nancy Brendon, another witness who came forward in Jack's office. She had been a close friend of Lenora Sanchez, who disappeared two years ago. Nancy and Lenora were flight attendants who had frequent layovers in

Orlando and often came to the coast for a day or two when their schedule permitted. Nancy told of a man they met named Jessie. She didn't know his last name and was uncertain that he had mentioned it. Her general description was like the others and was not enough for an artist to create a facial sketch. She explained that they first met him in the Mouse Trap Lounge on Cocoa Beach. "Since he appeared attracted to Lenora, bought her drinks, and tried to get a date with her," she stated, "I paid him little attention. The jerk was very persistent. Lenora finally told him she would go to dinner on her next layover to get him off her back. She figured it unlikely ever to see him again."

Starting to become emotional, Nancy continued. "However, the weekend Lenora disappeared, I got slammed with back-to-back flights and had to return to Atlanta. Lenora left Orlando and went on to the coast. She called me that night and teasingly rubbed in the pleasant weather I was missing.

Lenora also mentioned that 'Jessie, the jerk,' somehow knew her schedule and waited outside the Hilton, where we always stayed. She told me she had to get rude to get rid of him. Lenora told her the ass flew off the handle, called her a bitch, started ranting and raving, then stormed to his car. That was the last I heard from her. I'll bet the jerk had something to do with it. The local police refused to tell me much other than her room was a mess." Brad explained that many details are not public knowledge, but Jessie is a definite person of interest. "Did he mention anything about a funeral, someone named Zac, or refer to bitches?" Brad asked. She thoughtfully replied, "I was only around him that night, but he casually mentioned a funeral and a bitchy woman. He also mentioned 'Zac,' but I am unsure about the entire remark. The only thing I am certain of is he is one strange dude."

"Thanks for coming in, Nancy. Brad said you were a big help. I'll keep you informed if we find anything further." "Great," Nancy said, "if I think of anything, I'll call you, and don't hesitate to contact me if you have more questions or need anything."

Marci walked into the office as the interview was concluding. She had the day off work and dropped Brad off at Jack's office to conduct interviews. "Oh, goodness, who was that charming lady?" Marci teasingly asked. "She's pretty and discreetly requested that you call her if you need anything. Is she the type of work you do around here?"

"Of course," Brad snickered. "My specialty is in lovely ladies, and he quickly ducked as Marci threw a wad of paper." He laughed and said, "Those are my notes you're pitching. I guess I'll have to occupy the rest of the day with the lovely lady retaking the notes."

"I can straighten out your crumpled notes," Marci replied, "and I know I can keep you well occupied the rest of the day, so drop that thought."

"Oh," Brad said, "what do you have in that pretty mind of yours?"

"That's better," Marci chirped. "I'll gladly take you home and show you if you've finished your work here." Jack entered the office just as the banter started. "I have, but one thing to say," Jack quipped, "if you don't go home with her right now, you're a blooming idiot."

"You're right," Brad answered. "I shall accompany this lady and enjoy the fringe benefits of being in love."

"Love?" questioned Jack.

"That's right," said Brad." I have fallen in love with this delectable woman and don't mind admitting it." "Congratulations," replied Jack. "Since I first met you both, I have pictured you were a chosen pair. I guess my first hunch was correct. You two go home; I'll cover the FBI activity for the rest of the day, but leave me your notes on that lovely interview."

Brad and Marci left the office and stopped at the Surf, a local eatery that had been in business since before the space race. Brad delightfully admired Marci. "You're the greatest," he said. "How do I deserve you?"

"You probably don't," she replied, "but I am not complaining. Now, back to the problem: What did you find out about our friend Jessie?"

"Well, most of it, you already know. Brad proceeded to tell her Nancy's story. The name 'Zac' keeps popping up and references to funerals and bitchy women. Beyond that, Jessie is still a mystery."

"A question," said Marci, "could he have schizophrenia?"

"What makes you think that?" Brad asked.

"Think about it," she replied, "he is Mr. Nice Guy one moment, but when spurned, he does a one-eighty, a real Jekyll and Hyde personality."

"You may have hit upon something, Marci. Let me ponder that and present the Grotto with that prospect."

"Enough of this cop talk, Miss Marci; you said you would keep me occupied. Now tell me, what's on your mind? I'm hoping you will talk dirty to me," Brad jested. "Perhaps," she said with a glint in her eye, "now let's finish eating, and I'll take you home and show you what's on my mind." They did, and she did.

Chapter 8

Finding Gerald

Brad entered Jack's office with a bounce in his step. Jack noted and said, "Good morning; you appear chipper this morning. However, I won't ask why, but I'm glad you're here. We have a strangesituation. I just spoke with Frank, and he faxed this data to me. I'll tell you in general what it says."

The owners of the Pleasant View Inn, south of Vero, reported a dead body yesterday morning. At firstglance, Frank thought this report was unrelated to the Grotto, but he and Detective Gunther got involvedafter further review. "There are many similarities, pictures off the wall, blood in the bathtub, the word bitch, and the cleaning. The one main exception is that the body found at the scene is a male, but there is evidence of a missing female.

The owners, Mr. and Mrs. Tennyson, are pretty shaken. They told Gunther that the dead guy registered around 2:30 p.m. signed the register as Gerold Cozzy, paid by credit card, and requested aquiet room in the back so he could retire early due to driving to Key Wes in the morning. The vehicle was a dark blue sedan, and the tag number is being run as we speak.

The sign-in data indicated Little Rock, AK, and Mrs. Tennyson recorded the tag on the car. All seemed normal, except he looked a bitshoddy to Mrs. Tennyson. She thought she noticed another person in the car when he drove to his room, but she couldn't be sure. She was certain that there was only one person when it drove out a while later. The Tennysons do not recall the time when the car returned or when it left.

The male's correct name is Gerald Cozzy, and he was 50 years old. The cause of death is a broken neck, plus he had blunt force trauma to the back of his head. He may be a vagrant. His record indicates a couple of drunk and disorderly, but nothing more. There was some loose change, no bills in his pockets, and no driver's license, but he had a Florida State ID. Frank assumes the perp whacked him with a small bat or blackjack after they were in the room, then broke his neck. The Medical Examiner determined the time of death close to the check-in time. Mrs. Tennyson was correct; he was not alone when he went to the room. Cozzy's body was propped up in a corner, with his pecker super-glued to his hand. Here's the real kicker: the CSI crew found additional evidence, some long hair and a broken fingernail that are not Cozzy's, and indicates a female in the room. Otherwise, the room resembled the bedrooms of the previous vics except for no stuffed toys or pictures. Jack said that if this was Jessie, his MO certainly changed for this case."

"I know this has been thrown at you quickly, Brad, but what is your opinion," Jack asked. "I'm trying to decipher all of this," Brad stated, "but so far. I would say Jessie picked up Cozzy somewhere.He persuaded him to rent the room with the premise of buying him dinner, a place to sleep, some cash, and maybe a ride to Key West. That's why Cozzy seemed sincere to the Tennysons at check-in. Cozzy was no longer needed once the registration was complete, so break his neck, and presto, no witness. We will also find the car, and the tag was stolen.

Jessie wouldn't use his car or a rental to be traced. Most people know motels record a vehicle's makeand tag number, and Jessie is too damn smart to let something simple link him to this. Regarding the female aspect, I surmise that Jessie left the motel after killing Cozzy and went wherever to grab the lady involved. He brought her to the motel late after the owners retired for the night, did his thing, packed up her body, and left before they opened for business. Thus, he wasn't seen returning or leaving. I'll lay odds that we get a missing person on a female within a day or two. Let's sit tight until we hear more from Vero, but we need local police checking on a missing vagrant, a stolen credit card, and a stolen car. Jessie left us the clues he wanted us to have and nothing more." Jack agreed and contacted Sue Gunther to get help.

"Why did you call Sue and not Frank?" Brad questioned. Jack answered, Sue is designated as Frank's assistant, and she is a very intriguing lady. "Ah ha," snickered Brad, "an ulterior motive, and I think it's great, but for now, let's get back to work. What, if any," Brad asked, "are the new developments in the other cases?" Jack replied, "We have the lab reports, additional evidence, and the usual modus operandi. The powder found at the scenes comes from commercial-grade latex gloves. The brands of bleach and alcohol used are the same. They, too, are used commercially and in the medical field.

However, the general public can obtain these brands from warehouse stores, so they are little help. Finding a buyer would be difficult or almost impossible.

The handwriting experts indicate the scribbling was written by the same person, most likely a right-handed male. What I just told you isn't much, but it's at least new data. Jessie leaves the scene toosterile. Nothing left behind points directly to him. Even the few stray hairs we found were from the victims. This new DNA testing is incomplete, so we have very little data to use. Plus, nothing shows his DNA on file. Even the fingerprints we found are not on file. If they are Jessie's, he is not in any known file. There is just nothing firm to give us a clue to his identity. We don't have the foggiest," Jacksighed. "Somehow, he will fuck up, and we better be on top of it when he does."

Brad enlightened Jack on the findings of his recent interviews. "There was commonality concerning funerals, bitches, and Jessie and Zac's names, but all the leads were dead-end. No funerals are associated, no ideas about who Jessie or Zac might be, nor any ideas why the victims have been considered bitches. I plan on going to the Grotto and researching these subjects further. Marci brought up an interesting point, though. She said maybe he has schizophrenia. That would explain his changes in temperament, and perhaps one personality is Jessie, and the other is Zac."

"That is an interesting point," Jack replied. Let me maul that over a little while, but it sounds like a real possibility.

Brad organized his notes and called it a day. He couldn't help but think about the recent possibility of another missing woman. Thus far, there is no positive indication of there being one, except for a feeling deep inside. I-95 was almost deserted at this time of day, so he took advantage of it to blow out the cylinders' cobwebs. His enthusiastic driving continued the rest of the way home. Marci was sitting in the boat's cockpit, soaking up some of the late afternoon rays, when she heard the Viper's distinctive sound and the pitch change as Brad downshifted the gears through the turns leading to the condo's parking lot. She could tell he enjoyed his ride and knew it would put him in an upbeat mood for the evening. Brad had been uptight lately, and Marci knew that the gruesome killings, including his sister, had stressed him. She knew it was toying on his mind. Hearing the Viper enter the parking area meant Brad was close to home, so Marci descended below deck, poured his favorite scotch on the rocks, and eagerly awaited his arrival. "Hi, handsome," she said, then kissed him with profound feelings and presented him with the scotch as he boarded the boat. "Sit by me in the cockpit and relax for a few minutes," she said, "you look like you need a break, then tell me how things went today."

Brad explained the day's events and that they possibly had another missing woman, but not confirmed. "Oh hell," said Marci, "doesn't this bastard ever give up. He will create total panic in the area if the story ever breaks, and you know the press will let it out sooner or later." "Yeah, I know, Marci. I only hope the Grotto breaks the news right after we catch him. If he knows things too soon, I feel he will disappear, and we may never get him." They finished their drinks silently while watching the sun fall from the sky. "Are you ready for dinner?" Marci asked. "I fixed a pot of spaghetti with thick sauce andchunks of pork and steak, just as my man likes." "You're spoiling me," Brad quipped, "but don't you dare stop." They walked hand in hand back to the condo.

Brad was savoring his last bite of breakfast, and Marci was pouring more coffee when the phone rang. "Oh hell, there goes another gourmet breakfast," he stated. "I was ready to take advantageof the fringe benefits," and he ogled her bare butt. "Should we answer it?" Brad asked. "Unfortunately," Marci moaned, "you best do so. I need to go to work on time." "Okay, but since breakfast was interrupted," he said, "I propose we try a nude dinner tonight." "You're on," she replied, retreating to the bedroom with her coffee, letting Brad answer the phone.

"Brad, this is Jack. You were right with your predictions. We have a missing woman this morning in the Vero area. The car tag was a duplicate, so it was undoubtedly a fake. No info on the car yet;it might have been stolen. Will you be coming in today?" "I'll be in there in about an hour," Brad replied.Hanging up, he joined Marci for what was becoming a routine shower for two. He said I'd wash yours if you wash mine, entering the shower and telling her the bad news. "That's awful," she said. "However,let's give each other a real wash this morning to leave here on time. You guys need to catch this bastard, and if we keep playing in soap suds, he's not getting caught. Besides that, I'll be late for my morning meeting." Brad said, "You're right, sweetness; save it for tonight when we have more time for playtime." "You're becoming a horny "old man," but I love it," Marci quipped. "It's all your fault. Just look in the mirror," Brad retorted. "You're hard to resist, and being a horny "old man" is far better than beinga senior citizen any day." They dressed for work, parted with a kiss, and headed to their business-oriented day.

Jack rode with Brad in the Viper, and they headed south on I-95 to the Sebastian exit, turned east to US-1, and south to the

Wabasso causeway, went across to the beach, and pulled into the parking lot at the Times Resort in less than an hour. "That was quite a ride," Jack said as they approached the lobby where Arendas was waiting. "Hello Jack," hi Brad, good to see both of you again," he stated, "only not under these circumstances. Follow me, and I'll show you what we have. The condo is registered in the name of Carrie LaPort from Norfolk, VA. To our knowledge, no one accompanies her, so she is assumed to be a solo occupant." They entered through the front door into a large room with a poolside view, and all appeared normal.

Moving to the bedroom, they saw the dresser drawers emptied and the contents neatly placed. Twelve panties lay on the bed, forming a circle, each with the crotch cut out. Six bras formed a smaller circle inside the panties. Each bra cup had the nipple end cut off, and on the nightstand, twelve plastic cups were lined up in two rows of six each. Brad said, "This arrangement doesn't appear to be Jessie's MO." "I didn't think so either," replied Frank, "but look here." He turned the pillows over, the number 12 was on one pillow, and the word bitches on the other, written in lipstick. "What's with this crap?" Jack asked. "The number 12 has some significance," Brad answered. "Why only six bras?" Jack again asked. "Six bras with two cups per bra equals 12," Brad answered. "I'm guessing this lady is his twelfth victim. I didn't think of that," Jack stated. "We interpret the reference to twelve the same way," Frank commented. "Although the Grotto data only reflects eleven. There must be one we are unawareof. Look in the bathroom, and you'll see more references to twelve bitches," Frank continued. "This guy is one sick bastard."

"We found a room key for number 158 at the Pleasant View Inn. That key ties Cozzy and the evidenceof a female being in that room to Ms. LaPort. He deviated from his MO with Cozzy and is now deviating again. We need to find out why he classifies her as his twelfth bitch. We have 12 vics if you count Cozzy, but not 12 bitches as he calls them. He went to her condo simply to leave clues because all signs are he killed her at the motel," Brad said, "and again, we do not have a body." "You are right," said Frank, "Jessie is one sick bastard."

Brad and Jack contemplated the latest developments on their way home. The discussion was sparse, but the concentration was immense. Jack finally broke the silence. "Was it Jessie, or do we have a copycat?" "We do not have a copycat," answered Brad. "It is all the work of the one man playing with us. Why else would he leave obvious and repetitive clues? The press has helped keep it quiet and only printed Sue's approved releases. There is not enough info for a copycat to find and repeat. I believe it is Jessie in all the cases," Brad stated. "He used Cozzy to cover up killing Ms. LaPort and thenkilled Cozzy to eliminate the witness. I also figure Conti's body was left at the scene because of her condo location and the closeness of neighbors. He left Cozzy's body at the motel since he was a man and thought it funny for us to find him with his dick in his hand. The more I think about it, the more Ibelieve Marci's theory of him having schizophrenia may be correct. That's a valid theory; unfortunately, Jack commented, we have nothing to base it on besides Marci's intuition."

"Think about this," Brad said. "Jessie goes into a bar, trying to pick up a woman. He is polite, easy-going, and somewhat shy but pleasant until he gets rejected. He suddenly becomes obnoxious and brazen and classifies the female as a bitch. We've been told that when rejected, Jessie calls outto someone named Zac, as in Sebastian, where he was heard in the parking lot calling for Zac.

From what little I understand, dual personalities can be extreme opposites. I worked a case once where we dealt with a bipolar female, and when she switched roles, you damn sure knew it." "You're indicating a Jekyll and Hyde," Jack commented. "Exactly," replied Brad, "with an undeniable mental transformation. Possibly stemming from being rejected by a woman in his youth. That rejection setsoff the change, and Jessie becomes Zac, a homicidal maniac who hates women. In Jessie's mind, these women are bitches, and Zac, his altered personality, solves the problem by killing them.

Chances are he had a dominating and abusive Mother who rejected his existence. She abused him mentally, physically, and possibly sexually during his younger years. She's his bitch, and he is now taking his aggression out on any female that reminds him of her. If that is the case, his mother maybe the bitch number twelve we have not accounted for at the Grotto." "Holly hell," Jack stammered, "that's an elaborate theory you developed from Marci's input. I remember you mentioned it once before, but not with such detail. I must say, it makes sense."

"Write up that theory and elaborate on those thoughts, and I will send this theory and all the background data on Jessie to the Bureau. We'll request them to assign a Profiler with schizoid knowledge to review it and prepare a profile. I'm betting it will agree with yours. Likewise, let's transmit your thoughts to the Task Force so they can look for telltale signs. I believe we are far beyond Marci's intuition. Maybe this will give us the lead and remind me to thank Marci for starting you on this track, Jack concluded. Not to worry, I'll thank her for you tonight," Brad snickered.

James After Carrie

James was busy in the barn at the cemetery, removing the tag from the stolen car and putting the correct one back on. Knowing that he took a bus to Orlando, where he had stolen the car from long-term parking, he was not concerned about it being reported. Moreover, his initial investigation indicated that the owners would not return for several more days, thus permitting him ample time to accomplish his task.

The chore now was to put the car somewhere it wouldn't be found quickly, if at all. He had rented a truck out of Jacksonville with a large, enclosed bed and ramps, which permitted hauing a car without being visible. As night approached, James secured the car in the truck, drove to a secluded road west of Melbourne, unloaded the car, wiped it clean of prints, and rolled it into a deep canal behind a rarelyused roadside park. He then blotted out the tire tracks and evidence indicating a car had entered the water. A few hours in that murky water, any possible trace of me in the car should be gone, James laughingly told himself. Satisfied with his efforts, he climbed into the truck and drove towards the main road. James discarded the duplicate tag in another canal approximately five miles from the car.

Determining that this portion of his task was complete, he drove north to St. Augustine, where he spent the night in a motel and resumed the Jacksonville leg the next morning. After returning the truck to the rental company, he took a taxi to the airport, where his Mercedes was parked, and he returnedhome.

The following morning, James entered the office looking rather chipper. Opening the door, he startledMrs. Oliver, who looked up quickly from the computer. "Oh, James, I didn't hear you drive up. I didn't mean to surprise you," he replied. "Unfortunately, I am running late this morning. However, I need to run a few errands. Would you tend to the office today?" "Go right ahead," she answered. "Have a good time running your errands, and I'll be fine and close up at 5 o'clock as usual." "Thanks," James said, "and please take off early if you like. It's a lovely day outside."

James had no errands to run. In reality, he had nothing to do and needed time to contemplate the development of James killing a bitch. James felt that something had changed since the Roslyn incident but was unsure. He knew he killed Roslyn, but why, he asked himself. "Why did I do it, and where was Zac? Why didn't I call Zac to do "the deed"? Why the hell didn't I, and why did I lose control? I can't let this bother me," he muttered. "I must stay focused. "The cops and FBI are searchingfor me, although I am unsure who "me" is. That's weird. I must stay focused." He muttered to himself repeatedly while driving.

Yearning for a beverage and mental relaxation, James drove into the Halfway House parking lot, a friendly little tavern frequented by locals. He strolled in, sat on a bar stool, and ordered a brandy just as the news came on the TV. "We have breaking news," the reporter stated as a picture flashed on thescreen. "A lady named Carrie LaPort has been reported missing. She is registered at the Times Resort and not scheduled to leave until Tuesday, but she has not been seen for two days. No further details are available. Any person who has seen or knows her whereabouts is requested to contact Sue Gunther of the Vero Beach PD. The Police also indicated no additional clues had been found in the case of the vagrant man found murdered at the Pleasant View Inn last Friday night. They ask anyone with information regarding him to likewise contact Detective Gunther. From this reporter's eyes, we have had several missing persons recently and now a murder in the area. I believe it is time forlaw enforcement to give us more information on what was happening. Do we have a serial killer lurking inthe area, or what? Could the murder at the Pleasant View Inn be connected with the several missing women? This reporter would like to know! I believe the public is entitled to know the full story. Now, let's move on to sports and weather."

    James ordered another brandy and noticed that most patrons in the bar were watching the news. Thetwo men beside him said they believed there was a serial killer, and the guy doing this must be a realnut case. James joined in on the conversation, agreeing with their deductions. "Yes," James stated, "I think we have a nut in the area, and we should band together and try to find the bastard." James enjoyed having this discourse with the semi-sober locals about his escapades. However, the patron'sactions caused him uneasy feelings, and he was cautious not to divulge that it was he who they werediscussing. "That asshole needs to be caught," one man stated. "They should take him out and hang him by his balls." James found it all quite amusing, getting caught up in the local gibberish, and laughed as he raised his glass in a toast to find the bastard and cut his balls off. He ordered another brandy, cautioning himself not to overindulge. "What would these people do if they had to live with Bitch-Mother," he thought. "I bet they would have Zac kill her just like I did and would have killed all those other bitches as well. These poor souls never had it as bad as I did. No wonder they don't understand that Zac and I are trying to eradicate the world of bitches. That's our worldly duty," he saidsilently with a big grin. "Getting rid of bitches, that's our domestic duty to humanity and the world."

A charming lady near him noticed his uneasy feelings and started a conversation. "Excuse me, sir," shestated. 'I believe I know you from the cemetery." This fact disturbed James profoundly and further accentuated his uneasiness as he attempted to ignore her. He didn't like people knowing him.

However, regaining his wits, he apologized to her and quietly explained that he had sipped a few too many brandies. With some relief, he noted that none of the other locals were aware of their social exchange. "Oh goodness," she said, "please relax. We all over imbibe occasionally, but I will happily drive you home if you permit me." "Thank you," James replied, "but I think I can manage. I really must begoing now, and please have a pleasant evening."

He left the bar noticeably staggering and realized he had a few too many as he weaved conspicuously towards his car. "I had fun, but I certainly drank too much," he blabbered aloud while struggling to open the car door and sit down. Unable to buckle his seatbelt, he turned on the key, rolled the windows down, and inhaled the fresh evening air as he noticed the lovely lady leaving the bar and proceeding toward him. I doubt that she told anyone she knew me. Besides, she only knows me from the cemetery, which should not be a problem. "Excuse me, madam," he said somewhat coherently as she passed alongside his car. "You made an offer to drive me home. If I may be so bold,does that offer still stand?" "Of course," she said, laughing, "I buried my father at your cemetery last month, and you were so polite and cordial that driving you home is the least I can do." James handed her his keys and said, "In that case, I have a bottle under my seat. May I have another toddy before we leave?" "Be my guest," she said, "and I will join you in a toast to your brilliant decision with this soda I have here." James replied, "Gracious and sober, you're the kind of driver I like."

"My name is JoAnne Rollins, and you perhaps don't remember me since your secretary handled most of the arrangements, but I did meet you briefly on the day of the burial. If you give me directions, we will be on our way." Arriving at his house, James asked, "Won't you come in for a minute? The least I can do is fix you a thank-you drink for your safe driving." "Perhaps you didn't notice," she answered, "I don't drink. I only go into the Halfway to converse with friends and to get out of the house. However, Iwill come in for a second and wait for a taxi to return to my car." "My pleasure," he replied as he unlocked the door and bid her enter. The room was dark, except for the dim glow of the street light squinting through the window. James reached for the light switch and brushed the front of JoAnne, making full-body contact. "Excuse me," he stammered. "I missed the light switch, but that brief encounter was most enjoyable." "Yes, it was lovely," she replied, and they merged in an incredibly profound kiss. "I'm sorry," James said. "I didn't mean to take advantage of the situation, but you are a beautiful woman, and I enjoyed the warmth of your body and the passion of your lips. I did." "Likewise," she answered and returned the kiss, along with several more.

The sun was rising as James stirred. His head was pounding, and his stomach was a bit queasy. A puzzled look appeared on his face, realizing he was not alone in the bed. "There's a woman in bed with me," he told himself. "Now, don't panic. It must be OK. Zac is not here. It's just me, James. But who is she? How did she get here? He glanced at her cautiously as if his peering eyes would awakenher. My god," he thought. "Who is she? I have seen her before. I know I have, but I don't know her. Sheis lying naked in my bed and looks pretty damn good, but who the hell is she?" He suddenly realized that although he was flaccid, he wore a condom. "Oh shit, did I fuck her? Damn, I must have. Did she like it? She must have, or Zac would have taken care of her. Shit, if Zac isn't here, she must be decent. God help me remember, nice or not nice? Was she OK? Oh, hell, I hope so. Wait a minute, I remember. At least, I think I do. She was at the Halfway Bar last night. Ya, that's it; she talked to me, her dad died, and she drove me home because I was drunk. Oh yes, she is a nice woman, I remember now." His memory gradually returned as he sat upright in bed, covered only by a sheet across his groin. Visually captivating her nakedness caused his penis to protrude upward and the urges within him to stir. She was a portrait of sexual desire, lying seductively on her back, her petite taut breast rising from her chest, her shapely legs slightly agape, providing a glimpse of her sensual crevasse. His lusting eyes seduced all of her charms as she awoke. "Good morning," she groggily saidwith a beaming and satiated smile. "I hope you are feeling better this morning." "Yes, ma'am, I certainly am, and I want to thank you." "No," she said, touching his lips in a hushing gesture. "I should be thankingyou." She stated as she surveyed his manly torso and admired the noticeably large protrusion rising under the sheet.

You are a charming, passionate lover, and you must be the most prolific man in Indian River County since you can perform that well while under the influence. You must be a sex God when you're sober.She reached beneath the sheet, gently stroked his rigid penis, and massaged his tingling testicles.

"You are nice," he said. "Thank god I have found a nice woman." She removed the used condom. "We don't need those things," she said as she rolled him over and pulled him down on her, letting his aroused member find a home. They proceeded with a morning delight that drove them both to utterecstasy.

"You are lovely," James said. "I have never had a lady treat me like this, and all I know is your name. Who are you, lovely lady? I need to know. I need to have more of you. For now, James, let's leave it to JoAnne; perhaps soon, we can elaborate on the subject and agree on a relationship that will benefit both of us. In the meantime, you may have all of me again and again, so he did."

James drove JoAnne back to the Halfway House to get her car.

She kissed him deeply and promised to meet him there later tonight. She commented that I had many things to do today, but I would be here tonight, and maybe we could enjoy tonight as we did last night. James agreed but was a little concerned. He had been this route before, but he liked JoAnne. So far, she had been nice, and perhaps she would stay that way. However, he had a gut feeling something was wrong with this lady, but right now, she wasn't a bitch.

Brad And Jack In Jensen Beach

"It's been a couple of weeks, Brad. Is there anything new on the cases?" Marci asked. "No, sugar, nothing at all, and that scares the hell out of me. So either he is gone or is holding up somewhere, letting things calm. I want to think that he quit or something happened to him, but I can't believe that. The bastard is still out there and biding time until a woman pisses him off, and he strikes again." "He must know you are after him," she stated. "Sure, he knows, and he knows we won't quit. He'll screw upone day, and we will catch his ass. Until then, it's a case of cat and mouse. I talked to Jack the other day; all areas report peace and quiet. They are getting piecemeal evidence on past cases, but thank God there is no new case."

"It never fails," when Brad starts to relax, the phone rings. "Brad, this is Jack. We should ride to Jensen Beach to see Sergeant Tisdale. He recently became aware of our Task Force. I'm not sure where this guy has been, not to have heard or seen any of the data we've put out, but then, Jensen is a small town. Anyway, a woman from his area named Rene Barkowski disappeared a few years ago, and her case looks similar to ours. He has some reports we should see. Are you able to go down there today?" "I can make it," Brad stated. "Pick you up in thirty minutes, and I'll treat you to another ride in the Viper." "Great," Jack replied. "I'll be waiting with my crash helmet." "See ya shortly, wise guy," Brad retorted.

"Sorry, Marci, but I need to go with Jack to Jensen Beach. I probably won't be back in time to go to dinner as we had planned." "Don't worry about it," Marci said. "I'll probably enjoy a day to myself."

Brad picked up Jack and headed south. Jack stated, "We have info about the car tag recorded at the Pleasant View Inn. It is registered to a pickup truck in Little Rock. The man who owns it works for the school system as a maintenance man. His tag is still on his pickup, so the motel tag must have been a fake. The owner has not been out of Little Rock in over a year. It's beginning to look like Jessie is a real pro. He's either a skilled pro or lucky enough to stay ahead of us. I hope it has been luck, and it will soon run out."

They arrived in Jensen Beach and met with Sergeant Tisdale at Poor Bob's Tavern. Tisdale greeted them and explained that he was off duty but was happy to meet with them. Tisdale was in his early sixties but still in decent shape for his age. He said, "I'm sorry you guys didn't get this info sooner. Most officers who worked the case have moved on to better-paying jobs or retired. Jensen is just a small town, and the pay is not great, but after going through the hell I went through on the NYPD, this job was like paradise. I've been here nineteen years and plan on bailing out in another year, but enough about me. Let me give you this data and tell you a story.

I was on the late shift the night Rene disappeared. Friday night is party time here at Poor Bob's; that's why I had you meet me here, so you could see where it started. Rene was partying with some friends, and I stopped by to check things out as usual. I saw Rene and spoke with her briefly. She mentioned a man was giving her a hard time and pointed him out to me. I asked her if she wanted me to speak to him. She said it was not bad; he was just a pest and wanted to know if she ever slept in a casket. I figured he was simply a wise ass. So I told her I would oblige her if she needed a ride home to call me at the station. She mentioned his name was Jessie, and he was from the Vero Beach area. She said he kept talking about a place he called the bitch farm and called her a bitch. I couldn't see him that well across the dance floor, so I wouldn't be able to identify him, but he had an average build, 5 foot 10 or so, and was neatly dressed. They keep it too dark here to get a better look, so that's all I can remember about him.

Upon leaving, I checked for Indian River County cars; that's where Vero is, but I didn't see any. I thought that was strange. If he were a Vero guy, his car would likely have tags from there or one of those dealer decals, but I could find none. All the vehicles were local, except for one from Arkansas. We don't see many Razorbacks in this area, so that got my attention. I don't recall the number, but it'sin my report. About then, I got a call about an accident on US-1, so I left. There are many similarities here, and I figured you should know about them. As I said, I got the tag number, but the accident was nasty, and I forgot to run the tag that night.

Rene's mother, Helena, went by Rene's townhouse and found the mess the following morning. We haven't seen or heard anything from Rene since. I figure that asshole killed her and done away with her body. Luther, Rene's Dad, called me and asked me to investigate the situation. I didn't get hometill around 3:00 am and was pretty damn tired, but I went to the townhouse anyway after he called.

The duty officer had cordoned off the area, and the lab boys from West Palm were on their way. We are a small town, so we asked the West Palm PD for help. They sent up a forensic team and took her house apart, looking for clues. The reports give you all the details, so I do not need to talk about them.I ran that tag just out of curiosity and found it was legit. It belonged to a farmer in Arkansas. He was here on vacation, so I didn't go further with it. I hope I've been some help to you."

"You've been a big help," said Brad. "Please don't hesitate to call if you remember anything more aboutthis Jessie character. He appears to be our primary perp, and any info on him is vital."
"Like I said," Calvin replied, "I didn't see him very well, and all I remember is what Rene said to me about the casket, the bitch

farm, the fact that he was pissed off, plus being a pest." "Whoa," said Brad, "you didn't mention him being pissed off before. I missed that part, but when she said she wouldn't dance with him, he got pissed. That's when the casket and the bitch farm came up, and, oh yeah, she said that he mentioned something about a friend, but I don't remember the name." "Wow," Brad stated, "casket, friend, pissed off, and bitch farm all tie into our info. Can you remember any more? Well, she did say that after he got mad, he was like a different guy. I told her that it frequently happens when guys drinktoo much. Damn, I wish I could remember word for word what she said, but the old brain isn't what it used to be."

"Don't sweat it," said Jack. "You've given us more than we thought we would get, and your informationis appreciated. If you would like, come up to Vero and see Lieutenant Frank Arendas; here's his card and ours. I'll give him your name. You're welcome to sit in on the Task Force with us." "Hay shit, that's great," Calvin said, "I'll do that, and thanks, maybe this old cop can be of some help. You've already helped, and if you should remember anything else, call Brad or me immediately." Brad and Jack looked around the bar, "A neat little place," Jack remarked. "It seems like it might have been a jumping club back in its day." "It was and still is," replied Calvin, "one of the local's favorites, and it's off the beaten track for the tourist, so I guess that's why it has hung on this long."

Jack sat back for an exhilarating ride as Brad steered the Viper on the narrow two-lane Indian River Drive heading north. "What's on your mind?" Jack questioned. "Links," Brad said, "I'm thinking about the connections. This Barkowski case gives us new links to Jessie. We have similar crime scenes, the word bitch, stuffed animals, etc., that are current links, but we now have more. Referring to a casket ties him to funerals, Jessie ties bitch with bitch farm, changes moods when angry, mentions a friend who could be Zac and was a pest to the girls. We also need to check into the Arkansas tag further. Allthose items bring a lot of old and new links together.

Jackie Williams said that Jessie mentioned conducting a funeral. Maybe he has something to do with funeral parlors or is an undertaker. All these links seem to point at him dealing with death other than being a murderer, of course. We need to figure out how he's connected to funerals." "Great catches," said Jack. "I missed those links altogether. Why don't we stop by Vero on the way back and pass this data to the Task Force? Maybe some of their brains can expound on your ideas and develop different theories. We may be too deep in the woods to see the trees, and fresh brains can find something we have overlooked." "Informing the force is a good idea," Brad said as he nursed the Viper through the tricky curves, enjoying the car's response and performance.

Chapter 9

Marci And Brad Seeing The Knotty Lady

Thus far, things have been going well between James and JoAnne. They had been together a few times, and she convinced him to go on a fishing trip aboard her boat. James relaxed in the fighting chair on the aft deck of the 32-foot "sports fish." He was apprehensive about a lady owning such a craft but kept it to himself. JoAnne adjusted the trim tabs, set the autopilot, and decreased the throttles to a comfortable trolling speed. "You have the right idea, Stud," she said. "Relax while you can. According to the reports, the Wahoo should be running heavily in this area, and you may be in for a few good catches." She wasn't sure why, but she had sensed when they met that a sexual relationship with him would be sensational, and thus far, it certainly was. She knew she should tell him she was married but was unsure when or how. Introducing him to the boat was tricky enough, and she did not want to push things.

JoAnne descended from the bridge and let her eyes devour his lavish body. She repeatedly told herself I don't want to lose this gorgeous hunk. He's nice-looking, not hurting for money and a fantastic lover. "How am I going to inform him?" She asked herself. She scanned his snug pair of white shorts, mannish chest, muscular legs, and arms, and that enticing bulge in his groin convinced her that she would not tell him, at least not today. "So far, he hasn't asked, so why ruin a good thing?" She thought, "numb-nuts," her husband, was only home a couple of days every six months, so keeping her play toy a secret should be easy. "I need to keep James happy, which keeps me happy, so I will keep my private life private." The sight of him glistening in the sun heightened the lust inside her. She moved to his side, unzipped his shorts, and let nature take its course.

Marci was at the helm as the Miss-T cruised briskly on the first leg of their long weekend round-robin from Port Canaveral to Ft. Pierce. The wind held steady offshore at 12 knots, providing a spirited starboard tack through a gently rolling sea. Marci noticed a fishing boat trolling off her bow heading in a northern direction and became slightly concerned with their heading. She called out, "Brad, we need to alter the course a few degrees. A sport fisher is heading this way, and it looks as if we may pass a little too close for comfort."

"Do whatever you think best," Brad shouted from below. "I'm in the process of checking out all of the electronics and the diesel as well. You have a whole ocean, so we should have plenty of room." Marci re-set Tilley the autopilot easterly five more degrees and adjusted the sails accordingly. She watched through the binoculars to see if the merging angle of the two boats increased. However, the closer the vessels came to each other, the more Marci became anxious, and she could see no one on the bridge steering the sports fish. "Again," she called out, "hey, Brad. I can't see anybody on board that darn stinkpot, and no one is on the bridge steering."

"We are also getting a bit too close for me." This exchange sparked Brad's interest, and he scampered top side, disengaged Tilley, and took the helm. He told Marci to grab the binoculars and keep scanning the boat for people. "I hope the captain wasn't out here alone and went overboard or that he isn't having trouble." Handling the helm, Brad carefully nudged Miss-T closer to the sport fish, overseeing her movements to prevent a collision should the sea or a gust cause her to alter course. They silently sailed past the vessel's port side as Brad concentrated on the helm, maintaining a close but safe distance. Suddenly, Marci began to giggle. It became very apparent to her why no one had been seen on the bridge. "It is not an abandoned ship," Marci snickered.

"Maintain your course, Brad, and let's sail on." Brad looked at her and asked, what's going on? "From what I can see," Marci replied, "two naked bodies are involved in sexual bliss on the aft deck settee." Brad quipped they must be deeply involved not to have noticed us sailing past them, or they didn't care. "I guess powerboaters are entitled to act like us sailors occasionally," he snickered. "Here, Marci, take the helm back. I'm finishing my chores below before one of us gets similar ideas." She smiled and asked, "Well, sailor, how much longer will you be down there? That particular style of boating looked rather interesting."

Glancing back with the binoculars, she said, "You best hurry. Those fishermen are giving me all kinds of ideas." "Hold those thoughts," Brad replied. "I am almost finished with my nautical chores, and my next tour of duty is topside." Marci again looked back and read the name on the stern. "The name of that boat is 'Knotty Lady,' that is somewhat apropos, wouldn't you say?" "Yes, it is," replied Brad, "but then I guess it depends on one's definition of naughty." "It didn't look naughty to me," Marci answered, "but when you come topside, bring me a cold beer, please, and perhaps we'll find out what you think is naughty." "Strip down," he said, "and I'll be there in a short, with your beer, El Captain." Marci re-engaged Tillie and giggled. The rest of the day was a pleasant sail in more ways than one, with Tilley tending the helm as they cruised southward along the eastern coastline of Florida.

Shortly after docking at the city marina in Ft. Pierce, Brad called to let Jack know they had arrived and all was well. Jack asked, "Give me your thoughts on something, Brad. One of our new members on the Task Force from the Indian River Sheriff's Department left me a message earlier today. Buried in one of the Leslie Braswell reports is a reference to the term 'bitch farm.' He mentioned that after we sent Tisdale's info to the Task Force, the phrase "bitch farm" rang a bell, so he searched back through his data and found it. A friend of Braswell's seemed to briefly mention the term during her interrogation. Her case would be number three in chronological order. She said the guy in the bar told her that she and Leslie belonged on his 'bitch farm.'

There is no more about it in the report, so I want to drive down there and re-question her. I think she might have more info than she initially gave. That makes three references to that term now."

"Sounds interesting, and we are defining links," said Brad. "Follow up on it and let me know ASAP. I wish I could go with you, but I won't be home until late Sunday evening." "Don't sweat it, Brad. I'll take Sue Gunther with me since it's in her area. I'll meet you at my office Monday morning with the details."

"Sounds good, Jack. Besides, you have hinted that you want to get to know Sue better. That is if I read the signs correctly."

"Yeah," Jack replied, "you read correctly. She's an attractive lady, and I think we have some chemistry. I need to get up the nerve to ask her out. Maybe getting together on this issue will break the ice." "Lots of luck in both matters," Brad joked. "I'll see ya Monday morning," and he turned off his cell. "Come on, Marci," Brad said, "there is a neat tiki bar up by the office, and I'll treat you to a cold Pina Colada and a juicy burger." "I'm with you," she replied, "I don't feel like cooking tonight anyway."

"Besides, I'm worn out from that wild style of boating we discovered," she giggled.

Monday morning came faster than Brad or Marci desired, and they found themselves back at the condo. They enjoyed the weekend cruise, and getting away helped clear their minds. "The change of pace this weekend put a sexy bounce in your step," Brad told Marci, watching her cute little rear-end wiggle as she pranced around the kitchen preparing breakfast. "Well, it was much more than the change of pace that got me bouncing," she replied. "Those naughty chores, a handsome captain assigned to me, and all of the powerboating we did had a lot to do with it, but I think sailboating is just as good." "Thanks for the compliment," he said. "However, if I sit here much longer watching you, I won't be on time to meet with Jack."

"Business before pleasure, sailor," Marci chimed. "Take a cold shower and shave. By the time you're finished, I'll have breakfast ready. I'll also put some clothes on, creating less of an enticement on your uncontrollable soul."

"It's not my soul that is uncontrollable, he joyfully retorted, and if you don't quit teasing my uncontrollable object, we will have breakfast in bed." "Bye," she said as she headed for the bedroom, "I'm going to get dressed, and you need a cold shower."

"By the way," Brad stated, "since we agreed not to talk shop this weekend, I can tell you now that your schizoid theory may be a fact. However, don't let it go to your head and become a Sherlock Holmes on me." "Why," she asked, "is it because I am not a cop that I can't be right? Well, let me tell you, this little lady is not just your playmate. I have a brain; if you forget, things may get cool around here." "I'll commit that info to memory," he shouted from the shower. "There is no way that I want this heatwave to cool down."

Brad arrived at Jack's office with a colossal smile beaming on his face. He had difficulty forgetting the fabulous weekend and the social discourse he and Marci enjoyed at breakfast. "Good morning," Brad said. "How was your weekend?" Jack replied, "Not bad, not bad at all, and I can see by your expression that you and Marci must have enjoyed sailing immensely." "That we did, ole boy, but I guess it's time to get back to the crap at hand. I must admit it was a pure pleasure not to think about this asshole for three whole days, and I must add, Marci managed very well to keep my mind on other things." Jack laughed. "I dare not ask what, but I can guess." "Enough about me and my weekend," Brad retorted.

"How did it go with you and Sue Friday? I am not referring to the case." "As I said," Jack replied, "not bad, not bad at all. We went to dinner after the interrogation, and it proved very interesting. We have much in common, and I believe mutual attraction is possible. We planned to spend more time together this weekend, and the potential interest might become a definite attraction." "That's great," Brad stated. "Sue appears to be a charming lady, and I thought you two clicked the first time you met. I could see it in your eyes. If things work out, maybe you and Sue could join Marci and me for the Fourth of July weekend. We plan to sail up to St. Augustine." "They have a huge fireworks show; the city is enjoyable to see and a fun town to party in," Jack replied. "Let me see how things progress by then, but I don't want to rush. I did that once, and it backfired in a divorce." "Good thinking," Brad commented. "Now, unfortunately, we should get our asses to work. What did you find out Friday?"

"I'll start at the beginning. I picked up Sue at the Grotto. She had completed a lot of the preliminary work before I got there. She had the addresses we needed and set up all of our appointments. Not only is she a good-looking lady, but she's also as efficient as hell. Our first meeting was with Alicia James. She met Leslie Braswell on the beach in the summer of 98 and became good friends. Her knowledge was very enlightening. Leslie rented a beach house from some friends of Alicia's family while attending her last year at the local college. However, she was enjoying her newfound freedom and being away from home. Thus, she was not diligent with her education. Leslie was a party girl, an avid surfer, enjoyed boats, and was an outdoors type involved with several male friends. According to the reports, they all had airtight alibis for the night she disappeared. Her beach house's condition was damn similar to our other vic's, the pictures, the stuffed animals, bed linens, the word bitch, and the whole general scenario. Leslie's blood was spattered about the scene, and the cleanup involved bleach and alcohol. The only thing that differed from the other MOs was finding a disposable razor with female pubic hair. She was maybe shaving when he came in, or he did the shaving. My bet is on him doing it since the razor had no fingerprints. It was found on the floor, behind the commode, so it's possible that he dropped it and overlooked it during his cleanup.

The Jessie portion of the story sounds like a re-run. He tried buying drinks, came on strong, got rejected, and no one could give a decent description. The bar encounter occurred three nights before Leslie's disappearance, and Alicia recalled that the term *Bitch Farm* came up. Alicia couldn't remember the exact conversation, but Jessie was bugging Leslie almost to the point of tears, and Alicia stepped in and told him to fuck off. He became outraged and said she was overstepping her boundaries and should mind her business. She just laughed and gave him the finger. That's when he sneered and said she might just become a member of his Bitch Farm if she were not careful. Leslie then told him to get out and leave them alone. He stepped back and glared at them even in the dim lights. He told them both that they were bitches, then he stomped out. They didn't see him for the next few nights and thought the problem was cured. Alicia thought the Bitch Farm comment was weird but shrugged it off. She gave the same basic physical description, but the facial detail was vague due to the lighting and his obscurity."

"Damn," Brad said, "you need to go with Sue more often. You could write a book with that pile of info. Jack stated that Sue's presence helped Alicia relax and remember things that she didn't in the original report. She gave us much more background on Leslie than on the police reports. We now know her boyfriends, school subjects, and even her favorite underwear type. Alicia was a walking fountain of information and very willing to help. Sue and I updated our report and passed it on to the Grotto and the local sheriff. I consider the day a success in more ways than one."
"You damn sure should consider it successful," Brad remarked. "You hit a home run with the interrogation, and it looks like you're on first base with Sue. As I see it, that's not a bad day at all."

Killing JoAnne

It was getting late, and James was becoming frustrated. He had tried all day to contact JoAnne, but her cell was turned off, and her voicemail was full. She had always called him if she was running late on prior engagements, so not hearing from her for a few days was troubling James. On Saturday, he waited in the park as planned, the grocery store parking lot on Sunday, the library on Monday, and now he was parked by the south jetty at Sebastian inlet. He was at all the chosen meeting places on time. He and JoAnne had established these times and places to meet previously while on the boat, but she had not made it to them. He was becoming curious about why none of the meeting places were at her house.

"What could be the problem," he wondered, "and why had she not met me?" He sat behind the steering wheel, muttering, watching the waves break on the jetties. "I don't understand this. I hope she is not turning into a bitch. She has been so pleasant to me, and I have treated her like a queen. We had a marvelous time last Friday on her boat, lots of sunshine, lots of sex, and he even snuck in a bit of fishing, so where the hell has she been all weekend? I don't understand it, damn it, I don't understand," he shouted and pounded on the steering wheel. With bewilderment, James realized he knew very little about JoAnne. All he knew was she treated him nicely. "She was kind, sexually fantastic, and had shown no signs of being a bitch. So why worry? It's only been a couple of days," he murmured. "I remember now; she must have been busy with her invalid mother. At least that's what she told me she would be doing if I couldn't contact her. I have no reason to doubt her. I'm just concerned; maybe I care for her, and that's not all that bad. I might even get used to it, but right now, I'm sure as hell getting pissed off," he screamed as he pounded the wheel again.

"Relax and calm down," said Zac in a soothing voice. "You're getting your balls in an uproar over a damn bitch that is not worth it. Besides, you're going to hurt your hand or damage the steering wheel, and you're beginning to blow your cool." "Holy hell, Zac, where did you come from?" What are you doing here, and why did you refer to JoAnne as a bitch?" James asked. "Easy now, my gentle brother," Zac, calmly stated, "let's lean back for a minute and have a sip of brandy. You have some in the glove compartment, as usual."

"Pour a stiff one, and let me tell you a fascinating story. It started last Friday when you returned from the fishing trip. Your mind was completely warped from the sex and the fun you were having with that bitch. Because of that, you had forgotten about the problem that arose. Look at yourself in the mirror, James. It's obvious you forgot, didn't you? Yeah, I know you did. Your little head, as usual, is still controlling your big head. Well, it's okay to forget things, James, but you should never ignore a bitch when you meet one, and you know deep inside JoAnne was a bitch. You did not want to admit it because the sex was good. So sip that brandy, James. I won't let you forget; your brother Zac won't let you down. Ole Zac takes care of you and all of your bitches. You have been out of it for a few days, so relax, James. Are you calm enough for me to tell you the details?" "Yes, I think I am," James replied, taking a deep breath. "Tell me your story, Zac." James slumped back in the seat, closed his eyes, and let Zac's story unfold.

Zac started his narration. "I title this story the Naughty Lady, a play on words, after her boat's name, so James, relax and listen. It was just becoming dark when you and JoAnne steered the Knotty Lady back to her dock. As you were tying the lines, JoAnne's cell began ringing. Go ahead and answer it. I'll finish here, stow the gear below, and meet you on the dock you told her. You busied yourself, putting the poles and lures away as she gossiped on the phone. However, you couldn't help but hear JoAnne's heightened tone. It became apparent she was having a heated discussion with someone, and it sounded like a domestic spat. Curiosity got to you, as it should have under the circumstances, so you tuned in more intently. It didn't take you long to surmise that the person she talked with was more than a friend. The boisterous debate concerned the money she spent and her lack of concern for their marriage. She emphasizes that if he wasn't gone for weeks and weeks, she might have more interest, but she couldn't tolerate being left alone so often. You heard her inform the caller that she could get laid whenever she pleased, and if he didn't like that, he should stay home and fuck her more often.

The words "left alone, stay home, and fuck her more often" echoed in your head. What the shit is going on here, you asked yourself. Just when you thought she was different, she proved to be another fucking bitch. It was then that I stepped in and brought you back to reality. You were getting rattled and unable to cope, and I sure as hell didn't want another Roslyn screw-up to contend with. You're not cut out to do 'the deed'; that's my job. Anyway, I finished stowing the gear and listening to the bitch's conversation. I tried to get your advice about concluding the date, but your head was too far gone, so I had to makeshift for myself. If I must say so, I think I did a pretty decent job without your directions and planning. I know you don't remember any of this, so let me enlighten you on the rest of the story.

Darkness set in, and the dock was deserted. A couple of men were fishing at the far end of the pier but far enough from the boat to be of no concern. I sat on the port gunwale, waiting for JoAnne to complete her call. She only talked a few more minutes, went below, and heatedly tossed the phone into the vee birth. Then she fixed a stiff drink and stomped onto the aft deck. James, she called. Where are you, sweetness? Then she saw me and, of course, thought I was you. James sugar, she sexually murmured, I'm so sorry, so very sorry that you had to hear all that bullshit, I wanted to tell you I was married long ago, but I was afraid you wouldn't want to see me again.

Every man I meet has trouble accepting that I am married. That's why I didn't tell you. I'm sorry, James; honestly, I am. However, I am married but miserable. Will you forgive me? May

The Bitch Farm

I fix you a drink? Talk to me, James, oh please talk to me, she pleaded. What a dumb bitch, I thought, so I didn't tell her I was not James. Knowing you couldn't handle this bitch in your frame of mind, I let you fade away until I decided what was to be done. I continued to let her think that she was talking with you, but it was me, Zac, who was about to have lots of fun with this two-timing unfaithful bitch. I answered, no thanks, I don't want a drink, but I will take a cold ass beer, and perhaps we should go below to discuss this situation in detail and privacy.

Certainly, sweetness, she cooed. It's not a problem; we need to talk it out. She told me to go ahead below, and I'll get you a beer. Hey, I didn't think you liked beer, she flirtingly said, coming down the ladder. I only drink beer when I'm a little pissed, I told her, and I think I am entitled to be a bit pissed right now. After all, you led James to believe you were a respectable lady. What do you mean? I led James on, she asked. She said I don't understand your phrasing of that statement and referring to James as someone else. I told her that James feels like he is someone else right now. Someone who is standing outside, looking in. He feels like he has had an out-of-body experience. However, I feel like I am sitting back watching you treat James like shit, making a fool out of him, making him feel sad and hurt, and I can't let that happen. You're a real bitch. Do you know that? I am not James, I laughingly told her, I am Zac, yeah bitch, call me Zac, that name fits my mood right now, and you will get to know me better, much better, I promise you."

James tilted his head back further and shook it in amazement at Zac's story and his unremembered escapade as Zac continued. "JoAnne stammered; okay, James, or Zac, or whoever you want to be called, please let me explain. Yes, I'm married, my husband travels continuously, and he is never romantic or desires to make love when he is home. He has a shallow sex drive, and in the three and a half years we have been married, he has only seduced me four times, once on our wedding night and once on each anniversary. I love him but need more male companionship than he can provide." Zac explained to James that he said, what a fucking shame, but if you're that damn unhappy, get divorced. "If you love him, be faithful, wives don't cheat, bitches cheat. I told her that James's mother was a first-class bitch, and her actions taught us to despise bitches. What are you saying? she asked. Who is this Zac and us, you keep mentioning? So I told her I was going for a ride to think this crap over and would be back around 9:30. Maybe then, I could figure out what I needed to do. She told me okay, she was planning on spending the night on the boat anyway, so take a ride, calm down, and think things over. Then she mentioned I was confusing her with all these first, second, and third- person references, not to mention the frigging names, and I just smiled.

Now, James, I think you'll appreciate this part of the story. I got in the Mercedes and high-tailed it to the farm. I retrieved the Bitch-bag, and the backpack with all the goodies. For caution, I removed the tag and put one of those false Arkansas plates on, just in case someone might see it. I was getting a real bang out of acting your role, James; it was enjoyable. Maybe I should get an Oscar or Emmy. I felt giddy with the ordeal and laughed about it back to the marina. I wanted it to look good, if only for a short period, until I got her below and started the fun, and you know how much I like having fun with bitches, don't you, James?

I parked the car with the rear-facing the river, so the tag was hard to see. The fishermen had left, so JoAnne and I were alone. I got the backpack and the bitch bag out of the car, then proceeded down the dock to the Knotty Lady. I'm glad you're back, JoAnne remarked, descending from the bridge.

She said she was afraid I would not return. Now, here's a cool part: she was stark-ass naked, not even earrings, and I might add, she looked enticing. I thoroughly scanned her body and told her she looked seductive, all naked and sexy. Do you have something in mind? I queried. Of course I do, she quickly answered and spread her legs wide.

She told me she surmised if I returned, all would be forgiven.

So I let her think that was the case, and she coyly suggested that we enjoy the rest of the night. What would have happened if James did not come back? I asked her. There you go again, talking as though you are someone else, she replied, but to answer you, I guess this freshly cleansed and hot body would be unused for the night unless there were some horny fishermen in the area. That's just what I figured would happen, I said. Some horny fishermen would have satisfied your whims. She giggled. Yes, but I would rather have your big rod than theirs. What's with the backpack and case, baby? JoAnne asked.

I answered that I had stopped by the house and picked up a few essential things I needed for the night. Wonderful, she remarked, then I take it I am forgiven, and you are spending the night. You could interpret it that way, I answered, trying not to laugh. JoAnne asked, shall we go below and retire in the main cabin, turn the AC on, and see what happens? Just be careful, I answered; Zac may happen. Who? She quizzed. What is it with you and this Zac thing tonight? The story gets much better from now on, and I thoroughly enjoyed it; Zac snickered.

She entered the cabin ahead of me, which allowed me to deliver one very sharp blow on the back of her head. Dropping like a rag doll to her knees, she shrieked in pain. I quickly muted her noise with a rag and duct tape, then threw her spread eagle across the bunk. Before she regained her senses, I bound her arms and legs to the rails around the bunk. In seconds, she was immobile and shrouded with fear. At that point, I stood at the foot of the bunk and ogled a few moments at her luscious torso. She was a good-looking hunk of flesh, and it was a shame she was a bitch. I removed my clothing, forced my erection deep into her vagina, and pounded heavily against her crotch. Each thrust virtually forced the air from her lungs. You are not James, she tried to murmur under the tape, and I understood her. No bitch, I commented; James is tender with his lovemaking. Isn't he? I am Zac, brother to James, and I am damn sure not being tender with you bitch. I knew by the look in her eyes that she was wise to the terror that was taking place. Finally, achieving a climax that rocked my socks, I withdrew, retrieved the colossal dildo, and molested her until she passed out from the pain.

After a few well-placed incisions to her crotch, I positioned her body over an access cover to the bilge with her legs wide open. She soon died from the loss of blood. I then surgically removed her vagina and dismembered her body. Next, I began cleaning and added graffiti while watching her last drop of blood drain from her body. I doubt the bilge of the Knotty Lady will ever come clean, but who cares? I wrapped her body parts in towels and put them in plastic containers and the bitch-bag, to leave no evidence on the dock or in the car. Finally, I sliced a hose on one of the thru-hull fittings, untied Knotty Lady from the pier, and let the outgoing tide do its job. "The deed" was a spur-of-the-moment decision, but I tried to be as thorough as you would have been. So relax, James, and rest assured the bitch is appropriately planted at the farm."

Finding Knotty Lady

Jack arrived at Sue's house for their first formal date, as he called it. Due to various Task Force investigations, they had often been together, had lunch, and met for breakfast, but this was their first actual date, and Jack was visibly nervous. Sue answered the door, adorned in a striking black dress, slightly above the knee, with a modest but enticing neckline accented by a single strand of white pearls. The form-fitting dress highlighted Sue's shapely, petite torso, and she was a stunning sight to behold. Usually seeing her in professional detective attire, her appearance tonight practically rendered Jack speechless, causing him to stammer his way through the cordial greeting he had prepared, and he nearly tripped when entering the house. Understandably, none of his opening dialogs came out well. However, the white orchid corsage matched her outfit perfectly. With trembling fingers, he helped her pin it on the accessorizing short black jacket, then escorted her to the car. "Are you always this nervous," Sue asked with a gorgeous smile. "No," was his simplistic reply. "Good," she said, "I shall take that as a compliment, and I am delighted you asked me out." They dined at a rustic but somewhat formal and romantic restaurant overlooking the ocean, then continued to the Hilton for drinks and dancing. Once the opening jitters were over, they were pleased to find many commonalities in their lives, and the conversation led to more personal issues. In general, compatibility appeared not to be a problem, and they both felt that there could be further developments in romance. They agreed to call it an evening after cocktails and several dances and head home.

Arriving at Sue's house, she invited him for coffee before departing on his trek home. Naturally, he agreed. He did not want the evening to end and sensed she felt the same. Although both of them knew tonight would go no further than a cup of coffee out of mutual respect. They sat across from each other at the kitchen table, sipping coffee and exchanging trivial data about their personal lives.

Just as Jack was about to leave, the phone rang. "Sue, this is Frank. I hate to call you this late, and I hope I am not interrupting your evening, but I think we have another Jessie situation. Can you meet me in about half an hour in Sebastian?" "Sure, Frank, I can be there, and if you don't mind, I'll bring Jack Baird with me." "Are you with Jack?" Frank questioned. "Yeah, said Sue, we were out tonight and are just having good night coffees." "Congratulations, I'm glad to hear that," replied Frank. "By all means, bring him. That saves me a phone call. By the way," Frank continued, "the Grotto has noticed you and Jack admiring each other, so I believe you will find it favorably accepted." "Thanks," Sue responded, "I think that will make us feel more comfortable, and I will relay that to Jack. Now, back to the subject at hand. Where do we meet you?"

"Meet in Sabastian at Sembler's Fishery on old US-1 just north of Ahab's on the river. It's a small fish camp with a few docks out back and a small boat launch ramp on the south side. Park your car near the ramp and walk to the northernmost slip." "I know the place," Sue replied, "we'll meet you there in thirty minutes or less." Sue relayed the info to Jack and excused herself so that she could change.

Jack said, "I keep a pair of Jeans, a polo shirt, and sneakers in my car. I told you I was a Boy Scout, always prepared. Is there a place where I might change as well?" She answered that there's a spare bedroom at the end of the hall, and I feel you might as well get used to the place. "Strictly professional," he replied. "At least we are both in the same profession," Sue giggled.

The portable light on Sue's unmarked car flashed blue as they sped toward Sebastian. Sue relayed what Frank had told her concerning them and the Grotto. "That's good to hear," said Jack. "I was a little concerned about the ramifications of our dating. Brad said I was being over-cautious about asking you out. He and Marci agreed that I should ask you, and I am delighted I did." "Me too," Sue replied.

Jack placed a call to Brad. "I just wanted to let you know that Frank Arendas thinks Jessie has struck again. Sue and I are on our way to Sebastian as we speak with an ETA of twenty minutes. Do you want me to call you when we get there?" "No," answered Brad, "I was at a Masonic meeting in Melbourne tonight. I just finished topping off the fuel before heading home. I'll turn south and be in Sebastian close to the same time. Give me directions to the meeting place, then some of the details." Jack heard the Viper's engine roar and tires squeal over the phone as he passed on the data. "I guess you heard, Sue, Brad's on his way." "That's good news, and I'd kiss you if I weren't driving and going so damn fast," she quipped. "Would you make that a promise?" He asked. "Yes, sir, that is a promise," she cooed.

Sue's car screeched into the parking lot of Sembler's just moments ahead of Brad. Jack and Sue paused for a moment while Brad parked and joined them. A local patrolman approached and recognized that they were members of the Task Force. Frank is waiting for you guys on the dock. He stated and led the way.

Briskly, they walked out on the north pier, where Frank watched the Marine Patrol securing a boat. "I'm glad you all came," Frank stated. "The towboat and the Coast Guard just left. Allow me to tell you what I know so far. This boat belongs to Donald Rollins, who keeps it docked here. It was grounded on a sandbar, and not sure for how long. They had to use pumps to get her floating high enough to tow. I hope they didn't unknowingly screw up evidence. The Coast Guard indicated it was adrift and sunk too low in the water to get over the sand bar. It could have drifted out to sea through the inlet or broken up on the jetties if it had not gone aground. They said a hose had been cut on one of the seacocks, creating the leak, and the excessive use of the bilge pumps drained the batteries. They also indicated that the dock lines were untied, not broken, cut, or chaffed. She was set adrift on purpose, but I think the sand bar was unplanned. They avoided touching anything except to close the seacock.

The Marine Patrol had secured the boat to the dock, bow in, making the stern not readily visible. They had to board her over the starboard gunwale and step carefully down to the aft deck. I'll tell you what I know so far," said Frank. "Tanya Green, an alert Marine Patrol, found her on the sand bar and boarded her. Shining her light around, she first noticed the scribbling under the bridge. Upon a closer examination, she saw nobody on board. However, it was evident that there had been. Realizing what she had found, she recalled our all-points bulletin regarding Jessie and called the Coast Guard and the local authorities for assistance.

There is no indication of the time or the day the boat was set adrift. However, we can assume it was sometime after dusk and during an outgoing tide. The patrolman escorting them shined his light on the bulkhead under the bridge to show them some of the findings. "BITCH" was printed in bold letters and appeared written in blood. It damn sure looks like our man, Brad stated as the foursome entered the main cabin. It was evident that something grotesque had taken place. Blood splatter was everywhere, along with graffiti referring to bitches and lewd sexual acts. The water that seeped into the cabin washed away part of the dreadful scene, but enough evidence remained to surmise the horror that had taken place."

"I feel confident it was Jessie," commented Brad. "He must have been pissed off at this vic. Never before has he displayed such vulgarity and descriptive accounts of his actions. This rhetoric is a first for him. We can only guess part of the past horrors, but he spelled it out for us this time. He's becoming awful brazen. I'll check for evidence at the aft end of the boat while you guys document this data. We need pictures showing all this graffiti and blood and as much detail as possible." Brad continued, "Jack, please check out the vee birth when you and Sue finish here, then let the CSI boys do their job. Frank, how about you joining me on the aft deck?" Brad and Frank thoroughly scanned the aft deck area, even lifting the engine compartment hatch cover, but found nothing besides blood in the bilge. Brad opened the aft companionway and stepped down onto the swim platform. "The boat's name is Knotty Lady," Brad screamed with utter distress. "Aw fuck, I don't believe it."

Hearing Brad's vocal outburst, the others rushed to the stern. "I bet anything it was him, damn it. I could have reached out and touched the bastard," he bellowed. "Damn, it. I know it was him." "What the hell is the uproar about?" Jack questioned. "It's this frigging boat," Brad roared in total frustration. "Marci and I sailed close by this damn boat on our way to Ft. Pierce the other day. It was about five miles offshore, trolling several fishing rigs, heading north, and was apparently on autopilot. Marci was at our helm and noticed no one was at the helm of this boat. She was getting nervous due to our headings and called for me. I took over the helm and sailed within 50 to 60 feet of her port beam. We made very little noise under sail, and due to their engines running, they didn't hear us. We soon discovered why no one was visible. A man and woman were on this aft deck, stark naked, and appeared to be having a sexual interlude. Once past them,

Marci couldn't resist a few more peeks and noticed the boat was called Knotty Lady. Of course, we made light of the name under the circumstances, but the thing is, it was probably Jessie and Ms. Rollins on this boat. Had I known, I could have collared that prick in the ocean. After seeing what went on here, I'm betting it was them. Have someone contact the owner or manager of this place and see what they can find out about Rollins," Brad requested. "I'm way ahead of you," Frank said. "I'm receiving a call as we speak, and it may be the deputies trying to contact Rollins."

"Lieutenant Arendas, this is Deputy Larry Gates calling with your info. We are at the residence of Donald Rollins. No one is home, but a neighbor, Ms. Clark, told us that Mr. Rollins travels constantly. She is confident he is out of town presently but has no idea where. According to Ms. Clark, JoAnne Rollins uses the boat frequently. She indicated that JoAnne is an avid boater. Clark says the husband is gone so often that no one knows him well. She gave me the company's name, which she thought was his employer. I have another Deputy checking on it now. Clark noticed that Mrs. Rollins was spending time on the boat and indicated that it often happens when her husband is gone. There are no reports of missing persons, so we have no more to go on right now." "That's great, Larry. Thanks for the info, and good work. I'll contact you when we get back." Frank relayed the news to the trio as they continued examining the boat.

"In the morning," Brad told Jack, "let's contact the Bureau and get help locating Donald Rollins. Lucky for us, the sand bar kept the boat from sinking. Jessie hoped it would sink and wash away the blood and evidence. I didn't notice the smell of bleach or alcohol. We may find fingerprints to compare." "Let's hope so," Frank said. "The crime scene crew is on the job, hoping they will find many goodies for us. The local police and the sheriff's department cordoned off the area as soon as they got the word, so things should be pretty much intact for the CSI. Sebastian is a small town; word travels fast, and they are not letting anyone close to this place without proper credentials." "That's what I call cooperation," said Brad. "However, it's getting late. So I will hit the road home. There's nothing more that I can do here anyway. I know Marci is going to love this story. I'll call you in the morning, Jack. We can get with Frank and get all the data. Maybe, just maybe, we will get a break." Brad strolled back to the Viper and headed north. Frank remained with the CSI crew. Jack and Sue drove towards her place in Vero.

"What do you think?" Sue asked. "I'm not sure," replied Jack, "but I agree with Brad; our boy Jessie must have been thoroughly pissed at this lady. Perhaps she was cheating on her husband, and Jessie didn't know she was married. When he found out, he freaked out and whacked her." "That theory is a perfect fit," said Sue. "You FBI guys are pretty sharp." "Not just us," Jack said, "you're beyond good, and I think you're an excellent detective." "Thanks for the confidence," Sue snickered, "but let's leave the quality level at 'good.' Either way you want to put it, I'm good." "Ah yes, I bet you are," Jack quipped.

"Perhaps one of these days, Mr. Baird, I'll let you check out the good and the bad," Sue retorted as she parked the car in her drive, "but I think we are both far too tired to check either tonight. It's getting awful late, Jack. Why don't you crash in the spare room tonight? I hate to see you driving back to Melbourne at this hour."

"Thanks, Sue. I'll take you up on that offer." Entering the house, he gently kissed her cheek. "Regardless of the official business interruption," he whispered in her ear, "I had a fantastic time earlier and enjoyed your company. I'll slip on back to your spare room and have pleasant dreams for the rest of the night." Before he could turn away, she pulled him close and feverishly placed a passionate kiss on his lips. "That was part of my good side. I also enjoyed tonight immensely," she cooed, "and I shall have intense thoughts about you for the rest of it." Spinning on her heels, she pranced down the hall to her room, leaving Jack momentarily awe-struck. Then, regaining his composure, he smiled and proceeded to the spare room.

It was late when Brad arrived home, but he knew he had to awaken Marci and tell her about the Knotty Lady. "That is so unreal," she said. "Had we known, you could have made a high seas arrest. That would be different." "I told the gang that tonight," Brad replied. "We could have saved that lady's life if I knew it was Jessie. It shows you that you never know who you might encounter or where." "Yeah, that's right," Marci quipped. "You've been gone so long today that I'm unsure who you are. Would you mind if I took a closer look? I want to ensure you're the man I think you are before I snuggle up tonight." "Be my guest, my lovely, and while you check me out, I will take a shower. Maybe you would like to scrub my back and make sure it's mine." "I will be happy to," she responded, "and if you are Brad Ashley, I might wash more than your back." The warm water pounded on both of them as Marci helped Brad cleanse away the nastiness of the last few hours.

Jack looked up from the papers on his desk as Brad entered his office. "Pour some coffee, Brad, it's good and fresh, and then pull up a seat. I'm going over a few of the reports on this Rollins case. Frank and the boys must have been busy all night. There's a ton of data here. Sue even went in early this morning. I slept in until eight and didn't get here until almost nine. I must have been bushed last night. I didn't hear her leave this morning."

"Whoa," Brad stated. "You said you didn't hear her leave this morning. That may be more info than I need to know."

"Don't let your imagination run away, Brad, old boy. Sue offered me her spare room so I didn't have to drive home that late, and I took her up on it. I can assure you, nothing more than a safe night's sleep in the spare room."

"I understand the late part. I didn't get home until after midnight," Brad interjected, "and by the time I got a shower and into bed, it was almost two." "It sounds like you took a long shower," Jack joked. "Let's say I was thoroughly washed and drop the subject," Brad retorted. "Understood," Jack chuckled. "Some guys have all the luck; now listen to this and see what you make of it.

According to the reports and neighbors, Mrs. JoAnne Rollins was a well-known lady in the area. Her husband, Donald, is the southeast representative for a major manufacturing company. He earns well into the six figures, plus expenses and other perks. I have the Bureau digging into his status and position at the company. That, plus a little IRS snooping, should tell us all we need to know. It appears to be common knowledge and not gossip that JoAnne likes to play around while hubby is out of town, which is frequent. She hangs out in a local bar named the Halfway House, not far from her.

They have been married a little less than four years. Here's a quirky tidbit. JoAnne's father passed away a short time ago, and a funeral enters the picture. I have people checking into who handled the funeral for her. The majority of the info thus far comes from David Sembler. He owns the fish camp where the boat is docked. Rollins has kept the boat there since he bought it three years ago. According to Sembler, JoAnne loves to fish and frequently entertains men by taking them out for a day of boating, fishing, and partying."

"I can vouch for the partying," said Brad. "She certainly was partying when we saw her, and according to Marci, it was a pretty kinky party. Marci saw much more of the action than I did, so I'll trust her judgment on kinky. Marci didn't see his face, but she knew he was naked. What does that tell you?" Brad joked. "However, she did say his hinny was untanned, and the tan lines indicated a speedo-type bathing suit. I asked her last night if she could identify his butt again if she saw it, and she threw the washcloth at me." "I understand now why the shower took so long," Jack quipped. "You couldn't find the washcloth." Brad answered, "Right; both of us were looking for it in all the wrong places." "At least we still have our humor," Jack stated, "and the volatility of these cases hasn't interfered with our heads so far."

"Continuing with the reports," Jack said, "no one at the fish camp knew who she took out on the boat the Friday you saw them. However, a local fisherman told Frank that he saw them playing grab-ass while offshore of Sebastian, which coincides with your sighting." Brad remarked that other boats were in the area, but Marci noticed this boat because of its closeness and the fact that there was no visible skipper. "JoAnne's car was in the fish camp's parking lot," continued Jack, "and no clothing, keys, or personal effects were found on the boat or in the car. Jessie must have cleaned up as usual, except with no bleach and alcohol this time. The lab boys did lift some prints, and they are running them through the Bureau. I called the lab and requested a priority."

"Maybe we will get results back quickly," said Jack. "They found small traces of human flesh around the bilge opening and lots of blood spatter in places the water didn't wash away. Until we hear back from the labs, we have nothing further from forensics. Frank and Sue are working with the local PD, checking for any other leads. Donald Rollins was finally located in Birmingham, and Frank indicated that he didn't sound very distraught about his wife. He thought she had been picked up on a DUI and was in jail when he couldn't contact her. They must have had a hell of a marriage. Frank said Rollins seemed more concerned about the boat than he did about her." "Well, good boats are hard to find," Brad joked, "but don't tell Marci I said that."

"My silence will cost you a beer," replied Jack. "Let's take a ride and visit the Halfway House just for fun. We may be able to dig up some info from the locals."

"I'm game," answered Brad, "and if I have to buy your silence, we might as well be doing something constructive. Besides, if I read between the lines, Sue is probably there with Frank." Jack just grinned.

The Halfway House was nothing fancy but appeared well maintained from the outside and had a huge parking area. They quickly noticed Frank's car was parked by the entrance. "Ah ha," said Brad, "I told you I could read between the lines. You knew

Frank and Sue would be here, and you just had to see Sue again, right?" "Just a calculated gamble," Jack retorted; "now, please don't embarrass me." "Not me, Jack. I wouldn't think of it, but I have something to barter with regarding the silent payment."

"Okay, wise-ass," Jack murmured, "we're even. Can we go in now?" Entering the bar, they found Sue and Frank talking with some regulars and the bartender. Jack sat beside Sue, and Brad stood behind them, surveying the room's general layout. It was large and open, with several small booths in the back, just big enough for two persons who may be seeking privacy. There was a postage-stamp dance floor in the corner with a jukebox to the side and a stage large enough for a four-piece band. It appeared to be a friendly watering hole with no apparent signs of a rough or rowdy crowd. Turning his attention back to the questioning, a matronly woman named Thelma O'Dell was informing Sue about JoAnne Rollins. Brad guessed she was in her early sixties, showed signs of having money, and had no qualms about telling it straight.

Brad listened as she spoke. "I live up the street three blocks, so I walk to and from here without fear of getting a DUI. I must admit that I am in here almost every night. I like my toddy for the old body. Being a widow in a small town like this is kind of lonely. My husband Bobby and I used to come here to play darts and socialize when he was alive. I feel kind of at home here, and I know almost everyone. As I said, JoAnne came over whenever she was alone, which wasn't too often, and we would talk for hours. She complained a lot about her husband, and after several drinks, she would tell all the details, if you know what I mean? It seems he is always gone on business, so she gets very lonely and horny, as she put it. When he was home, she said he has a low sex drive and a small driver, if you follow me. She indicated that he seldom satisfied her in the lovemaking category. I thought it saddened her to be neglected like that. A woman that age should be enjoying life and sex. I know I did when I was her age. I guess that's why I couldn't entirely blame her when I saw her with other men. Personally, I don't cater to extra-marital sex, but I believe that everyone is entitled to do as they please, as long as they don't hurt anyone else. Even at my age, with my husband gone, I wouldn't object to a roll in the hay if I had the chance."

"Excuse me, gentlemen; I didn't mean to embarrass you with old lady talk. Now, let me get back on track. I would sit with JoAnne when she wanted to and let her talk. She got it off her chest when we were together, and she knew I didn't have strong objections to what she was doing, other than the being married part. I enjoyed hearing some of her juicy tales. Some of them were triple X-rated, but I didn't care. However, if she was with a man, I said hi and continued my business. That would be the case about twice a week. However, I would hear all about it a night or two later. It's only been the past few weeks that she was with the same guy more than once or twice. They would sit in that smaller booth over there by the dance floor. The area is quite dark once the lights have been dimmed, making it difficult for people to see you. You know someone's there but can't see them clearly enough to recognize who. I guess that's why some people like that booth. Sam Long, the night bartender, turns the lights down low. He says it's good for business. I think it helps business, monkey business. JoAnne mentioned several days ago that she would be taking this guy fishing. JoAnne was fun to talk with, even though her mind was always on sex. I hate to hear that something terrible happened to her."

"Did you say this man's name was Jessie?" Sue asked. "Yeah," Thelma answered, "JoAnne referred to him several times as Jessie. I asked her if she knew him very well, and she said no, but well enough to know that he satisfied her deepest desires in bed. She accentuated deepest with some hand gestures. I didn't get too personal with her about that subject. I know she's married and unhappy, so a little fling, I understood, but this Jessie guy was turning into a full-blown affair. Can you describe him, and would you give our sketch artist a description? Body-wise, he's upper five feet tall, with an average build, looks physically fit, and has dark hair, but remember, I only saw his face once or twice in that dim light and on the far side of the room, so no facial description."

"I try not to be nosey," Thelma continued, "but maybe I should have been this time, and perhaps if I had gone fishing with them, JoAnne would still be here." Sue said, "Don't blame yourself, Mrs. O'Dell. Fate makes a passage; perhaps you might not be here had you been with her. Just be thankful that you could help as much as you have, and you have been a great help. Now, if you remember anything else or happen to see Jessie again, don't approach him, and please call us at once." "Will do, she answered, and if I see him, I will make all the mental notes I can. I'll try for a picture on my new cell phone." "Thanks," said Sue, "but don't do anything that would bring attention to yourself. If he is the man we seek, he is very dangerous. Also, please don't tell others what you told us. We appreciate all you have said, and don't forget we consider this person extremely dangerous. One of us will be back in touch with you soon to set up an appointment with our artist. May I have your phone number and address so we may contact you?" "I'll not tell anyone of our conversation," she stated and handed Sue one of her homemade business cards. If asked about this, I'll say I told you I knew JoAnne as a friend and nothing more. I don't know if it is any help, but the first time I saw him, he was wearing a large red pinky ring. It looked like a ruby and was flashy, and I didn't notice it again." "That's our boy," said Brad, "thank you, Thelma, you've been more help than you know."

Frank and Brad ordered a burger and discussed the newfound info, permitting Sue and Jack to retire to one of the dark booths to share a more private lunch. Looking at them in the booth, Frank said, "You have to mix a little pleasure with the business occasionally. I've been married so long, and I forget that too often. The wife frequently needs to remind me that I'm not on duty. I'm unsure if it's age or this damn job catching up with me." "It could be a combination of both," Brad responded, "and maybe you need a break, take a vacation, and shower the little lady with affection. Go to the islands or some getaway where you both can relax and rekindle the old flame." "Not a bad idea, Brad; I have one hell of a backlog of vacation time coming. Perhaps when this case is over, I'll do just that." "I'll hold you to that," replied Brad. "Look at them in that booth; the light does not permit a clear view of their faces. No wonder Jessie sat there. However, one of us must play the bad guy and interrupt those lovebirds. It's time we get back to work, plus I need to get home. I have a date with a beautiful lady who I have left out of things lately, and it's all due to this Jessie asshole." "Likewise," Frank agreed, "my misses thought I was a salesman and sicced the dog on me the other night. The bad part about it was the damn dog didn't remember me either."

Brad and Jack returned to the office and started discussing their findings. "We have another reference to that pinky ring," said Brad, "and I don't think there is any doubt that the same perp is responsible for all these murders, and the evidence points to a one-man show." "I believe you're right," replied Jack, "and a person with schizophrenia is a one-man show even if he doesn't know it. I'm willing to bet we are dealing with a schizoid, which was a good idea from Marci. Thousands of men meet his physical description, but I don't intend to look at their asses to see if they have speedo suntan. I'll ask Marci about that tonight," Brad laughingly said, "She might do a rear-end lineup if needed."

Chapter 10

Back To James

The day was warm, and the breeze taunted the Spanish moss draping from the trees of the bitch farm. James was idly staring out his office window as Mrs. Oliver tidied up the outer office. He had become so mesmerized by the trees' gentle movement and swaying moss that he was slightly startled when she asked him if he would like a glass of iced tea. "Oh, ah, no thanks," he replied. "I've sworn off that stuff for a while. I think the caffeine made me jittery. "I'm not sure about the caffeine," Mrs. Oliver replied, "but you have been edgy the past few days."

"Is something bothering you, or am I being a bit nosey?" "You're okay," James said, "and you've never been nosey. I am a little upset with this lady I have been seeing. It seems that she doesn't wish to see me anymore." "I'm genuinely sorry to hear that, James, honest I am. A lady was evident since you were walking on clouds; I knew a female was involved." "I guess I was in the clouds for a while," James responded. "I thought she would be the one I had been looking for, but, as usual, I guessed wrong."

"Now, now, James, don't let it get you down. It's not good for you to think like that. You need to hold your spirits up and hold them high. That way, you will cure your sadness. Many fish are in the sea, and I am sure you will find the right one soon. Hell, if I were a bit younger, I would have loved you to be my suitor." "Thanks," replied James. "I needed some encouragement, and I can always depend on you when needed. It is a shame that you're not younger, Mrs. Oliver. I would relish the idea of seeking your charms."

James left the office, arrived home shortly after dark, slipped into an old pair of shorts and a ragged t-shirt, and prepared a quick meal. Having eaten and tidied up the kitchen, he flopped into bed, turned on the TV, adjusted the volume low, and summoned Zac. "I know you're here tonight, Zac; I can sense it. I could feel your presence all day, so why don't you come out and let's talk? The JoAnne story enthralled me. I didn't realize how much I rely on you, and it's fascinating. I think you and I need to have an honest talk. I have decided that we must devise a plan to stop this killing. JoAnne was an eye-opener. I must have lost my sense of sound judgment. I completely overlooked obvious clues and allowed myself to think of her as a nice lady. I was totally out of touch until you showed up and told me what the fuck was going on. I was hoping so much for her to be the one that I ignored all the warning signs, and now, as I think back on it, there were many signs. You saw them, but I didn't. Hell, I hardly remember going out on the boat with her. All I remember is the fantastic sex. Do you think I am losing my mind, Zac? Do you know what that would mean to us if I lost my mind? It would mean you would have no one to steer or guide you. You would be all alone to fend for yourself. Listen to what I am saying, Zac. I must stay in charge. If I fall apart, our world will crumble, and "Bitch-Mother" will win. Even from the grave, that bitch would win. She always said that I was crazy when she would catch me talking to you. When I would tell her that you were my brother, she would bring up that shitty story of hers about Dad getting his rocks off three times one night, and all three got her pregnant, but only one bastard came out, so there was no way, she said, that I had a brother. But we know different, don't we, Zac? We know we're brothers, so please, Zac, help me, don't let me go crazy. Come on out; let's talk."

Brad and Jack

"Let's review these reports once again," Brad requested. "There must be something we've missed that will bring us closer to this bastard." "We can try," answered Jack, "but I am almost to the point of having this shit memorized." "I am also Jack, but humor me a little. Besides, we have updated reports on the older cases that need reviewing, plus we've had new updates almost daily. The Carla Townsend and Darlene McKenzie cases also need to be thoroughly reviewed. My god, Jack, it's hard to fathom that twelve women and one man are known so far, all within the past few years, and we are just now getting a handle on it. We have to find this guy, Jack, and do it quickly."

"Relax, Brad, sit back, and take a deep breath." "We have the best Agents and cops in the area working on these cases. The entire Task Force is set up and on duty 24/7. He is bound to fuck up sooner or later, or we'll get a good break and find him. Let's take a short break and then review the newer reports with clear minds. Don't let it get to you," Jack said. "I know you have a personal loss amid all this mess, but your professional expertise is needed now more than ever. The whole Task Force needs you. You alone have uncovered more potential clues and linked more things together than anyone has thus far. Let's have a quick scotch and clear our minds. I put a fresh bottle in the top file drawer."

Jack called Sue to whisper sweet nothings during their break while Brad sipped a scotch, trying to unwind and relax. He stared at the wall, thinking of Gwen and some of their good times growing up. She was his baby sister, and he cherished her. "If I ever get my hands on this prick," Brad thought, "I'll gladly tear him apart limb by limb. Come on, man, he said to himself, shake this crap, do as Jack said, stay focused, and don't let it get to you." He returned to his desk as Jack finished talking with Sue. "Okay, let me see," Brad said aloud. "We have Carla Townsend, age twenty-six, single, with red hair, green eyes, five foot one inch tall, and one hundred two pounds. She certainly fits his preferences, without a doubt, and she was last seen in a nightclub. Unfortunately, the scenario is all too familiar. Carla's friends spoke of a guy trying to buy drinks and pick her up, but she rejected him. No one could give a decent description of the man. Her apartment was found in disarray, similar to the other cases. The crime scene photos show the writing on the walls, and the word bitch was printed along with several four-letter words in various locations. A few close-up shots of the bath area revealed blood spatter." Look here," said Brad, "holding a magnifying glass, this spec in the corner of the photo. It's a rubber glove on the floor tucked behind the commode. We found traces of talcum powder, the type used in professional rubber gloves at most of the other scenes, but this is an actual glove in this picture. This report is from the Ft. Pierce area."

"Get them on the phone, Jack, and see if they have the glove with their evidence. If so, get our lab guys to pick it up. Lifting fingerprints from the glove may be possible, but more importantly, some DNA." "See what I mean about needing you," Jack said. "You notice things that slip by most of us."

"Several of us have looked at those photos and never saw that spec. I'll call Bob McCormick; he's the Agent for that area, and I know he'll get on it immediately. That's a great catch. Let's hope Ft Pierce didn't overlook bagging it."

"That leaves us with the McKenzie case," said Jack. "We better go over it carefully also. I reviewed it several times, so I'll give you the generalities, and you dig into the details. Darlene McKenzie, age 23, single but engaged, that's one minor difference, light brown hair, blue eyes, five foot three, and one hundred ten pounds. Once again, she meets his criteria, except for a few differences. She did not drink and was last seen at a charity social at her church, not a bar. Her friends said she had complained about a man stalking her, and they told her to go to the police, but she said she could handle it and didn't want her fiancé to become concerned. The problem started when she noticed a large red pinky ring that this guy was wearing, and she told him it was too pretty for a man. He said she could have it if she would go out with him. She declined, of course, and that's when the stalking started. Her friends never saw him and don't remember her mentioning his name.

There were no CSI photos included with this report, so I'll ask them to send up what shots they have. McKenzie lived close to Fellsmere. She had a garage apartment on her grandfather's farm. The Grandparents were in Alabama when she disappeared. Based on the written reports, the apartment scene matches descriptions in the other cases. It appears to be Jessie's MO," Jack noted. "This bastard is like that battery bunny on TV; he never runs down. The ring, the apartment, and the reaction to rejection point to him, but this is a first for church involvement. Nothing in the past indicates a religious or spiritual connection."

"I wouldn't say spiritual," Brad injected, "I would say he's satanic. Let's get an inquiry started, and canvas jewelry stores in our related cities, we might get a lead on that red ring. As described, a man's ring with a red stone can't be an average piece of jewelry. Check out purchases and repairs, then get an interview set up with the pastor of McKenzie's church. Funerals and churches are related." "Damn," said Jack, "that possibility was not thought of before. Why the hell did the Bureau ever put you out to pasture? These things should have been done when the reports first came in. I'll contact Frank and have him advise the Task Force. That will get us coverage in every city, and I'll see if Sue will help with the church angle." Brad chuckled, "you best be careful about asking your lady to check out something related to an altar." "I know all of this murder and mayhem is bothering you," Jack replied, "but at least you haven't lost your sense of humor."

James

Several days had passed since the episode with JoAnne, and James had not left the sanctity of his house except to go to work and the liquor store. The self-confinement was starting to take its toll on his mental state. Even Zac had not made an appearance since telling James the JoAnne story. "Screw it, I've got to get my mind right," James thought, "and it sure as hell isn't helping being cooped up in this house. Of course, that is preciously what "Bitch-Mother" would want. Maybe she's trying to haunt me from her grave. Well, fuck her. I'm going to work and get out of here."

"Let me think," James mumbled, "JoAnne made twelve bitches plus Roslyn's pussy planted out there under those lovely trees. Poor Roslyn, only her playpen got planted. Oh well, that was the only thing good about her anyway. It's good that bitches don't grow like the trees," he laughed aloud; "I would have a dozen bitch palms surrounding one pussy willow. It is strange, though; the old bitches seem to know when a new bitch has been planted, the whole farm gets a hush over it. Maybe it's just my imagination, but it seems that way. What's amazing is that the law has not figured out where the bitches are yet. But then, how could they? Zac only leaves minimal amounts of DNA or fingerprints, and his personal data is not on file, so they have repetitive clues leading nowhere."

"Interestingly, Zac did 'the deed' on JoAnne without my pre-planning. Zac is becoming an extrovert, and maybe that's good. He wants to come out in public occasionally, so perhaps I should let him, but I can't trust him that far yet. Hell, he would whack those bitches right there in the bar if they fucked with him. However, that would not be a good thing, would it? So maybe I should let him out for short periods occasionally. Some social activity may do him good, so I'll have to think about it," he contemplated as he parked the car.

James, Zac, And Jessie

James entered the office with a cheery smile. "Good morning, Mrs. Oliver. How are you on this fine Monday morning?" "Well, good morning, James. It's pleasant to see you in a joyful mood. You have mentally been a bit down for a few days, and I was beginning to become concerned." "Don't fret about me, my dear lady. As of this morning, I have vowed to turn over a new leaf. It's high time that James Alfred Zachary starts to live, and all the lives within him shall also live." "That's a rather profound statement, and I'm not sure what you mean," Mrs. Oliver commented, "but seeing you in better spirits is uplifting." "Speaking of spirits, Mrs. Oliver, I must go out of town. Would you make sure the ghosts and goblins buried out there behave for a few days? You may bring in your sister if you like. I need to help a friend obtain a wish that he justly deserves, and I think it will be fun to assist him in his quest. Do you mind?" "Not at all, James. I have no plans, and my sister will be happy to come and stay with me. Take some time for yourself, my dear boy. It will do you good. Run on now and leave the ghosts and goblins to me, as you call them. You and your friend have a good time, relax, and forget about the business for a while. It will do wonders for your morale."

The rented BMW slowed to a stop at the valet parking stand for the Adams Mark in Daytona Beach. "Good day, sir, and welcome to Adams Mark. May I have a man assist you with your luggage?" "Indeed," said James, "I have reservations for a three-day stay and will sometimes require using my car." "That will be fine, sir. Call approximately ten minutes ahead if possible. Please tell us the number on this ticket; your car will be waiting." James tipped the valet, checked in at the front desk, and was shown to his room. The bellman highlighted the rooms' amenities, graciously accepted a twenty-dollar tip, and informed James to ring him if he needed anything to enhance his stay. James smiled, reading between the lines, and slid open the glass door to the balcony overlooking the "world's most famous beach." "What a great view," James muttered while taking notice of all the sexy thong bikinis frolicking in the surf.

"Zac, come out, come out, wherever you are. This area is your kind of place, and as I promised, the next three days are all yours. So I shall withdraw and relax, permitting you, dear brother, to do as you please. No one here knows either of us, and we, or I should say you, are registered under the name of Thornton, Jessie J. Thornton, to be exact. I used a credit card under that name with a bogus address to register your room. However, pay cash when you leave and pay cash for everything needed here. I believe I supplied you with more than ample cash. Don't forget the name and have yourself a ball, but please don't get arrested," James quipped. "My, my," replied Zac, "I do thank you, James. You always keep your word, and this is a fabulous place. Look at all those lovelies down there on the beach. They look good enough to eat. And speaking of eating, you kick back and relax, James. I will change into shorts and a sporty shirt and try out those new sandals while searching for a beach bar to treat myself to a burger and beer. Trust me, James, I will be a good boy."

Zac strolled through the lobby area, where he came upon a unique bar, somewhat off the main path, and it exhibited an air of privacy. He drew up a stool and casually scanned his surroundings. "Wow, what a location," he thought. "Sitting here, I have a panoramic view of the lobby and the adjacent beach access, and I can watch the pretty ladies prancing in and out." Zac noticed a younger man sitting a couple of stools away. He had the unmistakable look of a surfer: baggy shorts, a muscle shirt, long sun-bleached hair, a dark tan, and flip-flops. "Excuse me," Zac said, "my name is Jessie Thornton; you appear to be a local. Would it be possible to buy you a drink in trade for some local info?" "That sounds like a fair trade, dude. My name is Chris Slade, and yes, I am a local. I've been here all my life."

"Where bouts you from, man?" "Central Florida," Zac answered. "I'm not a native, but I am Southern-born and bred. I came up this way for a few days' escape, if you know what I mean." "Hey dude, we all can use an escape," Chris answered. He gave Zac the inside scoop for the hot spots on Daytona's beachside during the next half hour. Chris said, "You'd find good food, good drinks, and friendly ladies in just about all those joints. My favorite pub is a short walk on the beach south of here, right beyond the pier. You'll find it an authentic beach bar that grooves day and night and is heavy with locals and tourists. The food's fantastic, the brewskies are cold, the women are hot, and at night, it rocks."

"What more could you want, man?" "Thanks for the info," Zac said. "I'll mosey down there and check out the daytime imbibers." "Yeah, man, have a blast, and if you see this really big-boobed blond with a super hot ass, her name's Rachel. Tell her I sent ya. If nothing else, my name should give you a curl ride into the local set. Trucks of luck to you, dude, and thanks for the booze. If you're around later, I'll probably see you. I frequently hang at the bar downstairs on the beach level. Gotta run now, dude!"

"Catch you later."

"Wow, that was an informative half-hour," Zac told the bartender. "Does he always talk non-stop like that, or is he a little high on something?" "I've known Chris for several years now, and by the way, the name is Susie, and I overheard yours, so I'll tell you, Jessie, Chris is not a druggie, but give him a Yeager Mister, and he will talk your ear off. If you are alone here for a few days, the bar he told you about south of the pier is an excellent spot to hang, and you won't find any trouble there. It's a friendly atmosphere and primarily locals."

Zac was savoring the last few sips of his beer when a strange sensation came over him. For half an hour or so, he has been Jessie, not Zac, not James. His demeanor was not that of Zac's nor James's. It was strangely different yet familiar. He felt unfamiliar but comfortable with his newly found actions and mannerisms. Zac would not have tolerated that lengthy discourse. He would have walked out less than halfway through, and James would have been polite but completely unattentive. "I feel like Jessie, but not the same Jessie who tries to find the perfect woman and keeps getting rejected, but here I am, Zac, who is on vacation pretending to be Jessie. This feeling is weird," he thought, "yet quite enjoyable. For some reason, pretending to be Jessie is like second nature." After all, he recalled that Jessie was the fun guy when James was younger and before Zac came to be. "I believe that I'm going to enjoy this," Zac thought.

Chapter 11

Brad And Marci

"What a beautiful day," remarked Marci while preparing to leave for work. "I wish I didn't have to go to work. I would take all my clothes off and persuade you to go sailing." Brad teased, "You keep talking like that, and I'll hire you away from that nine-to-five slave shop. If you worked for me, I would grant your sailing wish with pleasure." "Sounds very tempting, but no thanks," she replied. "You know me, I am 'miss-independent,' with no strings, no commitments, no one's dependent, and I never sleep with the boss." "In that case, I'd have to fire you," Brad quipped. "Speaking of cases, the way this case is going, I haven't been getting much sleep or anything else lately." "Oh, you poor baby," Marci cooed, "you're so neglected, and since when did your not getting much sleep interfere with you not getting anything else? I would venture to say that you're getting less sleep because you're getting much more of something else." "I hear ya 'miss independent,' but as soon as this Jessie bullshit is over, I may decide to take off for a few months and go cruising in the Caribbean, and I need to employ a first mate. Then we'll see how independent you are." "You got me there, Captain; that would be an extraordinary commitment, and I would gladly sacrifice some of my impendence for that job." "How about sleeping with the boss?" Brad questioned. "Oh, hush," she snickered, "based on that part of the problem, I guess I could make another exception to my virtues, and given a choice, I think I could tolerate being your dependent."

"You being my dependent is not a problem, my lovely lady. And for your information, I wish that you would seriously consider becoming my dependent." "Oh my goodness, are you proposing to me, Mr. Ashley? Take it any way you like, but since I am madly in love with you, I guess you could call it that." "I would love to call it that," she replied with an enlighted voice, "but I must go to work today, damn it. I have some critical data to process. I want to continue discussing my dependency at dinner tonight."

I've been wishing that you would consider it. This little hint of your feelings makes me extremely happy. Until then, bye-bye, lover boy; I'm off to my independent job. PS. Mr. Ashley, I am madly in love with you, which makes the dependency choice very simple." Marci waved goodbye and hurried off to work, and Brad called Jack.

Brad And Jack

"Things have been extremely quiet, Jack. What's going on with the Task Force, and have they come up with any new leads?" Brad asked. Jack replied, "We have a few new tokens to add to our trove. One of them sparks some interest. A jeweler in Vero remembers repairing the setting of a large ruby ring. He estimated a woman in her late fifties brought in a ruby ring and asked him to check the stone setting. She said the ring belonged to her employer. He adjusted the prongs of the setting and cleaned the ring for her. He stated that it was a high-quality ruby. It was large and appeared flashy, but it would be gorgeous and valuable in the proper setting. Upwards of 5k, he estimated. He figures it must be a family heirloom. Rubies of that size are somewhat rare today. An initial J was barely visible due to the age etched inside of the band. It was also made out of eighteen-karat gold, which is unusual for a ring because of its softness. He noted that the ring size was five to seven, indicating a medium-built woman or small man. I'm thinking Jessie's pinky finger size.

Unfortunately, the jeweler did not take long to do his thing, so the lady waited and paid cash. He has no name or information about her, nor has he seen her since." "Chances are it was Jessie's ring," Jack continued, "it means he possibly is an entrepreneur, manager, or supervisor and has a middle-aged woman working for him. That scenario could fit a lot of people. The woman is possibly his secretary, office manager, clerk, etc. The possibilities go on and on. Jessie might have asked her to run an errand for him to get the ring repaired. That responsibility puts her in a position of trust with him. We have started delving into various businesses in the area, but this covers a lot of ground."

"I have a hunch," Brad interjected, "that we should add entrepreneur to Jessie's profile. The woman referred to him as her employer, which made for a more personable relationship. Think about this scenario. A small, privately owned business, operated by the owner with the initial J and maybe a handful of loyal employees, one of whom is this valued and trusted woman. Perhaps she helps administer things and is his right hand. This business possibly deals with death in some aspect. Recheck those funeral parlors; maybe one of them fits the bill. So many links tie us back to funerals, and now the letter J in this ring suits Jessie's name. Have the Force also rack their brains for a woman that fits the description from their past interviews. If we find her, she could lead us to him."

"Brad, you amaze me. None of us put any credence to the word employer, but what you just said makes a hell of a lot of sense. When we're done here, I'll relay this info to our new FBI profiler and the Grotto."

"By the way, Jack, has Ft. Pierce sent the glove up yet, and has Mrs. O'Dell come in for the sketch session?" "Oh shit, Brad, I forgot to mention the glove never made it to the evidence box. They figure it was just an oversight. Their lab boys don't remember a glove, and when I told them to look at the picture, they said the same thing I just said, Oh shit! They feel bad, but nothing can be done now."

"Mrs. O'Dell suddenly had to go out of town due to a death in her family. We are hoping that she will return soon. I'll get someone to follow up on her status."

Jessie Comes To Life And Meets Calie

Zac strolled casually along the beach, soaking up the sunshine and playfully dodging the waves as they rolled onto the shore. "The ladies are lovely," he murmured, "young, tan, well stacked, and those skimpy thong bikinis drive me crazy. Oops, I shouldn't say crazy. James is becoming sensitive to that word. However, he'll get over it. I won't let him think about that for a few days, and my god, with all these heavenly bodies on the beach, how could one think of being crazy? I might be crazy about women, crazy about sex, but not insane crazy. Hell no, James, I won't let you go crazy. Damn," he thought, suddenly taking notice of the fact that he was acting strangely again. "What the fuck is going on, he asked himself? Why am I feeling so strange? Well, maybe not strange, but I feel very different. I was always a badass; I took no guff, thrived on inflicting pain, and craved the killing, but those desires are subdued for some reason. It must be this mini-vacation that James arranged that is chilling me out. Good ole James, he always knows what to do."

"Hey, asshole, watch where you're going," a young lady shouted as Zac nearly tripped over her. "Oh, excuse me, miss," he pleaded. "It was indeed my fault. I was off in never-never land, daydreaming and paying little attention to where I was going. The fact is, I must have been spaced out with the pleasantness of the day to have overlooked such exquisite beauty. That is, without a doubt, a major sin on my part," Zac continued. "Kindly forgive me. What the hell did I say? Am I losing it?" Zac asked himself. She just called me an asshole. I should have slapped the bitch aside the head a time or two just for the fun of it. Zac shook his head in disbelief at his remarkable calmness.

"It's okay, mister, honest, no damage; you just kicked a little sand on me because you were so close. Please let me apologize for cursing; I rarely curse. I guess I was not paying attention either, and you startled me as much as I startled you, but again, no damage was done." "Not to worry, miss, I accept your apology, if you'll likewise accept mine? May I ask you a question?" "Yeah, sure, I guess so," the young lady replied. "What's on your mind? Oh, nothing out of the way, I assure you, I didn't mean a personal question. It's only local knowledge that I seek. I met a surfer at the Mark, where I am staying, who said there is an excellent beachfront café or bar beyond the pier. Are you familiar with it?" "I sure am, and he must have meant the Sea Deck. It's maybe a hundred yards or so south of the pier." "That must be the place, Jessie responded, and for kicking sand on you, I will be most happy to treat you to a beverage of your choice if you care to join me." She giggled. "That is a unique pickup technique, but I'll gladly join you since you're sincere and honest. A cool drink right now sounds refreshing." Zac had to control his thoughts and the urge to ogle her luscious, well-tanned body as she arose from her beach towel. She was superb, slightly over five feet tall, with long auburn hair, a perfectly proportioned body, beautiful facial features, and packaged in a bright green bikini that left little to the imagination.

Surprisingly to Zac, Jessie acted very much like a gentleman. He offered her his hand and said, "Lead the way, madam; I am your slave." She laughed and said, "You are witty and cute, but I hardly think you're the slave type." Follow me, and I'll show you the best the beach offers." "She is right; I am not the slave type," thought Zac, "but right now, I am unsure what fucking type I am. However, I do know that being Jessie is not all that bad." She took his hand, and they strolled along the beach towards the pier. "By the way," she stated, "my name is Calie, and I was born and raised here in Daytona. How about you?" Hesitating briefly, he answered her with an ease that shocked him. "Jessie, Jessie Thornton is my name, and I am just visiting."

"Nice to meet you, Jessie, but I need to leave around three this afternoon; until then, let's enjoy a cool toddy." "Are all Daytona people this friendly?" Jessie asked. She giggled; "Maybe not all of them, but the area generally caters to out-of-town people. Many of our population work in the service or tourist industry, so it pays to be cordial." "That's what I like about the South," Jessie said; "we try to please." "Oh," said Calie, "are you a Southerner also?" "Yes, ma'am," he replied, "born in a little town outside of New Orleans and moved to Florida when I was still a young-in. I adopted Florida as my home state since I spent most of my life here."

"Welcome to the World's Most Famous Beach," she replied. "I hope you enjoy your stay." He smiled and answered, "Having met you, Calie, I am sure I will."

They continued strolling hand in hand along the beach until arriving at the Deck. "Here it is," she said, "good food and good drinks." "Well, thank you, Calie, you will join me, right?" "I said I would, and I never go back on my word," she informed him as she took a beach wrap out of her bag and slipped it on, permitting it to cover most of her exposed areas, and asked, "Shall we enter?" Taking a table with a pleasant beach view, they ordered drinks and began conversing. "Tell me about yourself, Jessie, you seem like a nice person." "Nice?" He thought, "wow, Jessie is nice, isn't he?" Damn, I'm calling myself Jessie. This role-playing is becoming weird, very weird, but enjoyable."

"Okay," he started, "how should I present this melodrama? As I said, I moved to Florida as a youngster with my mother and brother. My mother passed away on my eighteenth birthday, leaving my brother and me alone. During that time, we discovered that our father, whom we never knew, had also passed away, leaving my brother and me a reasonably secure inheritance plus a business he had started. Since then, it was diagnosed that my brother suffered from a multi-personality disorder, so it is up to me to manage the business and take care of him. He can help with some business matters and is sharp at keeping things in order, but he cannot tolerate social stress. They have found a medicine that works for him and helps control his disorder, but he will never be fully cured. Thus, I must be cautious in the tasks I give him for fear of adverse reactions. His type of disorder can bring on violent rampages, and he could harm others unknowingly. I have managed on a few occasions to go places alone, but not many. This trip has been the first time I have had a vacation alone in years. It has been fantastic thus far, and meeting you is the icing on the cake."

"That's an incredible story, Jessie, it's a melodrama. I'm not sure what to say except that I'm glad you kicked sand on me. But where is your brother now?" "Sorry again about the sand, Calie, but the accidental sandstorm did work out nicely thus far. So, to answer your question, James is staying with a very dear and close family friend who helps with the business and our problems. I am not sure I could get along without her. She has been a lifesaver for James and me. On the brighter side, she is one of the few persons for whom James does not create problems. She knows how to control him."

"You did say 'she,' didn't you?" Calie asked. "Yes, I did," he snickered. "I figured you would pick up on that. She knew my father very well and assisted him with the business. I think there may have been more intimate details in their relationship that I have not been privy to, if you get my drift, but her business knowledge has been a significant asset. Her age, however, is becoming a factor, and I am sure I will miss her deeply one of these days in the future. I hope it is not in the near future." "What type of business do you have, Jessie?" "Let me see how best to describe it to you. In simple terms, we divide large parcels of land into smaller plots where people can afford to retire." "That sounds beneficial to older adults and is very nice, and I think you're very nice, Jessie. However, the time is growing short, and I must go. Here's hoping you have a wonderful stay in Daytona," and raised her glass in a toast. "Thank you, Calie; you have played a significant role in making it that way. May I see you again while I am here?" "I have a dentist appointment today, cleaning only," she answered, "but I'll tell you what. I come in here frequently in the evenings, so meet here tonight. We can have a few drinks and get to know each other better." "Sounds like a plan," he answered. "What time? I should be here around eight. Will that be satisfactory for you?" I shall be here without fail," he stated. "I'm walking on air," Zac thought while ogling her sensual torso as she strolled away. "I haven't had this much fun in years. But wait a minute, who the hell am I? I have been so wrapped up in being Jessie that I believe I am my brother. What the fuck is going on? Oh well, whatever it is, it feels pretty damn good. Jessie is becoming a good guy."

Zac allowed his memory to wander as he left the bar. He slipped off his sandals and strolled towards the hotel. Permitting the roar of the surf to tease his thoughts while romping barefoot in the sand turned the pages back to a time of his youth. Back to the first time James had given him leave, he had ventured out alone. "James convinced me to take a break," Zac thought, "and to relax a little. It was scary at first, but it soon became enjoyable. The first few hours of freedom were exciting and gave me the feeling of being ordinary, and I remembered those feelings. I enjoyed being a natural person," Zac murmured, almost like I am feeling now, but today is different. Maybe it's an age factor," he thought.

Zac knew he didn't feel like he usually did when James brought him out. These new sensations and mannerisms are not the norm, and Zac is mainly violent. However, as he kicked the cool water, he thought, "I enjoy how I'm feeling today, so why the hell worry? Let it happen? I could rule the world, and perhaps I am ruling my world." He whispered 'hello' and waved to a pelican, gliding slowly just feet above the surf.

"The sun was warm, and the beach divine. It had been years since he could recall having this much fun without killing someone. Shoot," he said, "I might even enjoy myself with Calie tonight. But I won't judge her too soon, and I need to relax and have fun the way James does when he goes to Fellsmere. I'll enjoy some time with Calie. If she wants sex, I'll give her some; if she doesn't, I won't. Hell, that's simple, and if I keep that frame of mind, I see no reason to get mad. I must be getting the 'Jessie fever,'" Zac mused. "I don't know this lady; I have just met her and do not believe she is a virgin. A good-looking woman with a body like hers certainly has had men in her life. Realize that ole boy and no need to be jealous? She is not your wife or even your steady girl. Right now, she is nothing more than an acquaintance." Zac shook his head in awe at how he talked to himself. "I can't believe the joy I am having. I must tell James about this cool feeling; it's so cool, and I'm so in control of my emotions; it's scary. Hey, hell, being Jessie is not all bad."

Managing to brush the sand from his feet approaching the hotel, he slipped his sandals back on, strolled into the lobby, and stopped at the lobby bar while reminding himself that he was now Jessie. An attractive woman in her mid-thirties was tending the bar and asked, "What's your pleasure, sir?"

Tempted to tell her that she would be very pleasurable, he quickly thought better and said, "A Mic-light with a glass, please, and you're name if you don't mind?" "My name is Judith," she replied, "might you be staying here with us, or are you just passing through the lobby?" "I am staying here," he answered. "May I charge this beer to my room?" "Sure thing," Judith replied, "sign the tab and write your room number on the top. I must also see your room key to verify your first charge. After that, your signature and room number are sufficient." "Of course," he said, "I usually do not charge my tab, and I'm not sure why I am doing it now. I've been doing many strange things on this vacation. Strangely enough, I've been enjoying it." "That's what vacations are for," replied Judith. She asked, "Where are you from, and how long are you staying." Jessie answered, "From central Florida, and I hope to be here three days, maybe four. What are the hours of this bar?" Judith replied, "10:00 am to 2:00 am, Monday through Saturday, and 12 to 12 on Sundays. I come in at five on weekdays and occasionally on the weekends." "May I ask a question," Jessie said. "Indeed you may, but I only answer appropriate questions," she snickered.

"Understood," Jessie retorted, "but my question is strictly above board. I am curious as to why the bar area is so dark. I can see you because of the lights behind the bar, but it is difficult to see the stool beside me. Not that I am objecting, just curious." "I will be happy to answer your question," Judith replied.

"Oddly enough, you selected the bar's darkest area, and since we are an upscale establishment, our management thought it best to give our patrons a touch of privacy. Thus, only the bartenders are in the spotlight, so to speak. A lighting consultant designed the layout to provide sufficient lighting for the bartender while maintaining sparse lighting elsewhere. As you mentioned, you can see me, but it is difficult to see details about the person beside you. Likewise, I can only see a discernible image of you. Our customers tend to like the obscurity of the ambiance. Personally, I don't. I want to see my customers, but I am the bartender, not the boss." "That was an excellent answer," replied Jessie. "Being a customer, I like this atmosphere as it gives a romantic flair to the lounge and requires closeness for visibility between consenting persons. That, indeed, could lead to a warm relationship." Jessie said, "I am amazed at how warm and friendly everyone is here; it is refreshing." "Thank you, sir," Judith replied, "we aim to please." He finished the beer, signed the tab, 'Jessie Thornton,' Room 612, tipped her graciously, and departed.

Entering his room, Zac was not surprised when James appeared. "Be very careful," James warned, "people can be deceptive, and you mustn't tell things we dare not divulge. If I hear you talking out of school, so to speak, it will require me to step in and take over the situation. You know you tend to talk too much, so have fun, but please use caution." "Don't worry, James," Zac said as he looked in the mirror, shaving. "I will not divulge secrets, but I may bring a lady back tonight, so don't peek." "Enjoy yourself, Zac. You have earned it." "By the way, James, there is something that we need to discuss," Zac muttered.

"It's the name 'Jessie.' Oh, never mind, it can wait till another time when I am not on vacation. I don't want to ruin my good vibes right now." James said, "You know I'm here should you need me," and he faded away.

Brad And Marci – Mrs. O'Dell

It was late evening when Brad answered the phone and remained silent for a minute. "Oh shit," he exclaimed, "just our luck, that's a damn shame, and it knocks the hell out of our investigation. I was hoping for a break with a sketch. I suggest you contact the family and see if we can do anything besides offering our condolences." Brad hung up the phone and sadly shook his head. "What's the problem?" Marci quizzed. "That sounded like bad news." "It was," he answered. "That was Jack, and Sebastian P. D. just called him. Mrs. O'Dell was rushed to the hospital earlier today due to a heart attack. She didn't make it. Her neighbor told the paramedics Mrs. O'Dell was preparing to leave for a meeting with our sketch artist. She was telling her neighbor about it and keeled over. They listed her as DOA at the hospital. I understand she just experienced a death in the family, and I believe it was her older brother. Maybe his passing was more than she could handle," Brad surmised. "We are back to 'blind man's bluff' regarding Jessie. That's a real bummer for the cases." "Brad," Marci stated, "your luck concerning Jessie always goes wrong. Come to bed now, try to relax, and let's try a different approach."

They lay quietly in bed, coupled in each other's arms. Marci softly asked Brad if he was serious the other day when he halfway proposed. "Of course I was," he answered. "I think you and I are one hell of a team. We have a lot in common, we think a lot alike, you fill in all the gaps in my life, and I believe we can be happy together. More than that, Marci, we are friends. We care for each other in many ways, not just during intimate moments. I feel that we both care, and that is what is essential." "Are you sure it's just not our wonderful sex life?" Marci asked. "Well, now that you asked," he quipped, "our sex is the greatest, but you as a person are even better." "Okay," she happily responded. "I will marry you, Mr. Ashley, but no more sex until after the wedding. I want the first marital intercourse to be a remembered occasion." "Okay, I'll agree," he said, "but I am not making bets on this agreement lasting long. You like our sexual encounters just as much as I do, and in your words, they are wonderful."

As the evening passed, they began to set plans for the future and establish a date. They were elated over the recent decision, and an air of self-content filled the room. Brad disappeared for a moment while Marci poured some wine. When he returned, he asked her to close her eyes and hold out her hands, then gently slid a ring on her third finger, left hand. You may open your eyes now, Brad whispered as he kissed her hand and tenderly kissed the tears trickling down her cheeks. "The ring is beautiful," she exclaimed, "but when and where did you get it? You have been planning this, haven't you?" "Yes," he answered, "I have ever since I met you, and the ring was my mother's. She left it to me in her will and asked that I give it to a lady who would make me happy. That would be you, Miss Marci Allen. You are that lady." The evening was blissful, and all bets on the sexual agreement were put aside.

Chapter 12

Zac Is Jessie

Following his brief conversation with James and re-sensing the day's positive vibrations, Zac decided to refer to himself as Jessie for the remainder of his vacation. The name felt right, seemed right, and sounded right, so he made it right. Therefore, Zac is now Jessie. He arrived at the oceanfront pub precisely at eight and seated at a table alone was Calie. Once again, that strange sensation caused a twinge of pleasure to rush through him upon seeing her. "That damn sure was not a Zac sensation," he thought, "it must be Jessie's, and it felt very pleasurable."

"Good evening, Calie," he said as he approached.

"I was not sure you would be here, but I'm delighted you are. It's rare when I stand up a date," Calie replied, "especially one as nice as you." "Well, thank you, my dear. May I order us some wine, or would you prefer another beverage?" "Wine will be fine," she mused, giggling at the rhythmic verse of her answer. "Did you drive or walk from the Mark?" she questioned. "Tonight, my dear, I opted to walk. It's such a pleasant evening, and the lights and sights along the boardwalk made for an appealing stroll. I take it you drove?" "No," she replied, "I live a short distance away, so I also walked." "Well then, let us order dinner and enjoy the evening," he said serenely. He reveled in the gentle feeling and accepted that Jessie brought it forth. As time passed, Zac knew, without a doubt, Jessie was now in control.

With total tranquility and peace of mind, he permitted his newfound self to openly exchange pleasantries with Calie as they sipped their wine and enjoyed an evening meal.

"My full name is Calie Lynn Lucas," she cited while enlightening Jessie with her details. "I was born here in Daytona. However, Mother passed away when I was 12, and Pops, as I call him, traveled a lot with work, so I spent most of my teenage years living with my Grandmother in Dunedin on Florida's west coast. After high school, my boyfriend joined the Army, so I returned to Daytona, completed college, and majored in economics. Pop's had connections with a local producer of tanning products, which provided me with a little pull, and I landed a job in their accounting department. I had a steady man friend I was somewhat serious about, but it didn't work out. As a result, I've kept myself very busy in my new job and decorating my little beach cottage. The backroom is getting painted, and the place is starting to reflect my personality. It's a small, older-style house, but the term "beach cottage" fits it and sounds more sophisticated. That's my story, and now it's your turn."

Jessie hesitated a moment before starting while his mind played back the words James had spoken about some people being devious when it came to prying out information. So, with marked words, he stretched the truth a bit in his favor and revealed no significant data that exposed his actual life. He reiterated his brother's mental situation, discretely flowered his younger years and carefully avoided subjects that would disclose his story's falsehoods. Time flew by quickly, and the combo played its last set before they knew it. "We recited our life stories but have yet to dance. Would you care to join me on the floor before the music ends, Calie?" "I would love to," she answered, and they concluded the enchanting evening swaying with the music.

"I will gladly walk you home or call you a cab, Calie." "Thank you, Jessie. It is late, and I think I will take a cab. It's not too far to walk, but it may be safer to ride due to the late hour." "I agree," he said, "but the fare is my treat, and if you don't mind, I will ride along. Once you are safely home, the cabbie can drop me at the hotel." "That will be nice," she replied. "May I see you tomorrow?" Jessie asked. "Yes, you may. I would enjoy that. I have a few things to do in the morning but should be home by early afternoon. I'll call the hotel; what is your room number?" "612," he answered. "Please leave a message with the desk should I happen not to be there." They sat close in the back seat of the taxi, holding hands as she enlightened him on some of the sights along the way. When the cab stopped in front of her cottage, Jessie escorted her to the door, where she presented him with a tender goodnight kiss and bid him farewell until tomorrow. Once she was safely inside, Jessie spun on his heels and floated back to the cab. He said, "Take me to the Mark, please," and the cabbie obliged.

"James, are you here, James?" Jessie asked as he entered his room. "Yes, Zac, I am here, but I remained concealed, should you have a lady with you." "I appreciate your consideration, James. As you know, I've had girls before, but tonight was a different scenario." "That's interesting, Zac. I was hoping you would enjoy your free time." "I think I have James. I do believe I have found her." "Wow," James snickered, "whoever this lady is, she has had a calming effect on you, and your demeanor reflects it." "She does affect me, James. I have never felt such peace and tranquility in the presence of a lady before. However, one more thing: I am supposed to be Jessie Thornton while here. Please help me remember and call me Jessie. I feel like Jessie and do not feel like Zac." "Your request is even more exciting than your personality tonight," James replied. "I shall honor your request, Jessie; now get some sleep and permit me to contemplate this new development."

Jessie awoke in the morning with a smile, shaved, showered, dressed casually, and then called the valet to retrieve his car. He rode the elevator to the lobby and sundered light-heartedly to the awaiting BMW. He palmed the attendant a generous tip and requested recommendations for a breakfast establishment where the locals go. The valet said, "I like the little diner just north of here on A1A. It's on the west side of the road, all silvery and shiny, and you can't miss it. They serve a massive cup of coffee and have great food." "Thank you, my kind sir," Jessie commented and departed.

The morning was off to a pleasant start. Warm weather, sunny skies, friendly people, and a great breakfast to get things rolling. "What more could I ask for?" Jessie questioned himself. He left the diner and opted for a sightseeing trek by motoring north to Ormond Beach and Flagler. The journey was scenic along the ocean. He stopped at various locations to watch the surfers and the fishermen, along with kids playing in the sand, kites flying in the ocean breeze, bikini-clad girls bathing in the sun, and waves breaking gently on the shore. "What a fantastic day," he murmured. "If Calie calls me later, it will be perfect, most perfect indeed."

Marci And Brad – Jack And Sue -- Sailing

The sun had barely risen above the horizon when Marci and Brad put the final provisions aboard the boat and securely stowed them in preparation for a full day on the water. They had invited Jack and Sue for a day of ocean sailing to see if they enjoyed the boat before asking them to go for a long weekend voyage. Brad learned from past experiences to sea-trial all new sailors. It saves the embarrassment of all parties and provides the greenhorns with a learning curve. Nothing is worse than spending a night aboard if you're uncomfortable, seasick, or afraid. Marci and Brad had just come topside as Sue and Jack strolled onto the dock. "Good timing," Brad stated, "punctuality is one of the first signs of a good sailor. Hand me your gear and come aboard. You both must bear with me for a few minutes, but you must know a few things about a boat before leaving the dock." Brad showed them the life vest location and how to wear them, then the boat's general layout, and explained several standard nautical terms. "Now for the necessities," he said. "Marci, you take Sue, and I'll take Jack. Let's show them the heads and how to use them." Following that task, they met in the salon, where they were shown the galley and, most importantly, the cooler stocked with adult beverages.

"This introduction is why I asked you to come early. I'm a little anal about making sure my crew members know what to do and where things are," Brad explained, "and I hope you don't mind." "Not at all," Sue and Jack answered in unison, "and she is a beautiful boat," Sue chimed. "Thank you," replied Brad, "but don't try to learn it all in one day. You will learn something new on almost every sail."

Following the briefing, Marcie took the helm, powered up the faithful diesel, and eased the sloop out of her birth as Brad stowed the lines. Marci pointed Miss-T toward the Intracoastal Waterway, and the day began. Jack watched intently as Brad and Marcie worked in unison, hoisting the mainsail, adjusting the lines, and filling his memory bank as much as possible. "I can tell you two have been practicing. That looked flawless," Jack commented. "Marci is a natural," bragged Brad, "so good that she is starting to teach me." Marci blushed at the male banter. "He only requires instruction on certain things, end of the subject," she quipped. Brad told Marci to fall off the wind and steer a southern heading as he re-set the main and unfurled the genoa. Marci established a good point under sail and shut down the diesel. The peaceful silence of sailing left Jack and Sue in awe. "It's terrific," said Sue. "I have heard people talk about sailing's tranquility, and now I can see why you guys are devoted sailors." As the wind filled the sails, the Miss-T heeled to starboard about twelve degrees, increased her speed to eleven knots and almost smiled as Brad fine-tuned the sheets.

"If the rest of the day is like this, you have made a convert out of me," stated Sue. "I'll second that conversion," replied Jack. A pod of bottle-nosed dolphins inched alongside, swimming and diving in the bow wake. "They're beautiful; look at them swimming alongside the boat," Sue said, "they are playing with the boat." "We have many of them in this area," Brad explained. "They are frequently called porpoises, but they are of the dolphin family, and I understand they are one of the few mammals besides man that uses sex for social enjoyment." "Men, you're all alike," said Marci. "Take a beautiful animal and associate it with sex." "Of course, look at our two beautiful women," replied Brad. "That makes the world go around. I agree with the data exchange, but let's change subjects before Jack tries swimming with the dolphins," quipped Sue.

"Speaking of subjects," Brad said, "other than the standard safety rules, I only have six simple rules while aboard, first: no discussing politics, second: no discussing religion, third: if you go below, check to see who needs drinks and fix them, fourth: wear deck shoes while on deck, fifth: no smoking and the sixth is to avoid the work subject. Notice I used the word "avoid." As close as we are to our work, it isn't easy, but Marci and I do our best. So, for now, let's learn some sailing." Sue was instructed on handling the helm while Jack was shown the sail handling and line chores. They both adapted quickly. "I am amazed," Jack exclaimed; "sailing is total relaxation and not near as much work as I imagined." "If you think you're relaxed now, wait until we head for St. Augustine in a couple of weeks," Marci stated. "And I did say we, hoping you all will join us."

Miss-T skimmed through the water easily as Marci nursed her back into her birth. Jack and Sue handled the bow and spring lines while Brad secured the stern. "You guys are a great crew," said Marci. "Brad explained what needed to be done, and you both did it. With a crew like this, we could handle the Q-E II." "I doubt that," said Sue, "and besides, if I remember correctly, the old ocean liner doesn't have sails. You guys have spoiled me already with one sea trial. I think I'll start checking out the boat ads when I get home, and then you and Brad can teach me how to sail it." "You're on," answered Marci, "and Brad is a competent teacher. When we first met, I didn't know the bow from the stern, and with his help, I can now sail Miss-T single-handed, not that

I want to, but if necessary, I can. Brad ensured I knew how to get us home if something happened to him while we were out." "I have no doubts that you could do it," said Jack. "You handled the boat very well today, and I thank you and Brad for showing us the lines. Notice that I didn't say ropes." Jack jested. "Both of you did very well for your first time," remarked Brad. "Next week, we will introduce you all to the beautiful Atlantic." "That's a date," Jack and Sue said in unison. "What may we do to help you clean up?"

The ladies enjoyed washing down the deck while Brad and Jack stowed gear. When complete, Brad poured docking drinks and explained that his Dad had a tradition that all first-time sailors aboard Miss-T received a "Nassau Royal" drink. "So sip your beverage," Brad said, "and let's relax in the cockpit, allowing the peacefulness of the sail to soak into our minds." Marci said, "I'll drink to that," and they toasted the day.

"Since we are back at the dock," Jack said, "a little work chat won't hurt. We have been hunting this creep we call Jessie for close to a year. The problem is we have little more to go on than when we started, except for the additional cases. I am curious about your thoughts since you're personally involved due to your sister." Marci went below and brought up the cockpit serving table with snacks and more drinks. "If work is being discussed, we might as well have some booze and a snack." "In my opinion," Brad started. "This bastard is brilliant. He has made no mistakes thus far that would divulge his identity. The few prints and the DNA we found have no local matches, nor are they on file in any database. He has never been in the military, had a security clearance, been arrested, or anything else that requires an official ID. The DNA testing makes it definite that we only have one perp, Jessie, and it is proven that he is involved with four out of the twelve cases. However, I'm betting on all twelve."

"I believe he is a local guy," Brad continued, "possibly residing in the Vero vicinity and is affiliated with funerals. His quoted remarks about funerals lead me to believe he is somehow linked with death or death-associated ceremonies. Call it a gut feeling, but when we catch him, we will all find that he's been right under our noses and maybe our neighbor. He is an average citizen with a spotless record, going about his daily activities unnoticed. He's the type of guy you see, but you don't remember; he's no social butterfly nor the life of the party. He's somewhat of an introvert and has no unusual or distinguishing features. As Marcie said, we will find he has schizophrenia, and one of his personalities will eventually screw up." "I agree," said Jack. "We have lots of data but little to go on. All that the DNA and prints have done is link the same perp to several cases, plus indicate the perp to be a male. If we can find that male, we have the bastard, but we must find him first." Brad stated that as cautious as he has been, he may have deliberately planted evidence to throw us off track. "Damn, I didn't think about that, Brad, but you're right. He has been so meticulous about cleaning the scenes that I won't be surprised if he hasn't purposely left redundant clues."

"Dock or no dock, we are still on the boat." Marcie elaborated that the work subject is to be avoided. "Sorry," replied Jack. "I started it with some job-related bullshit. I believe Brad has excellent rules while on the boat," Sue stated, "and I am sure Marci will back me in saying that even though Miss-T is tied to her dock, we are still on the boat, and Brad's rules apply. Besides, the day has been far too beautiful to spoil it with a subject like that maniac. All in favor of a better topic, raise your drinks," Sue requested, "and I propose a toast to the two most excellent hosts on the waterway, Brad and Marci." "I'll drink to that," replied Jack. "Hell, you'll drink to anything," jested Brad. "Subject closed. Let's make plans for next weekend and your first long sail," Marci said. "The fourth of July will be here soon, and Brad and I hope you two will volunteer as crew for our St. Augustine cruise." The foursome relaxed in the cockpit and listened to some sea stories that Brad made comically exciting but instructive for the new crewmembers.

Chapter 13

Jessie and Calie

Jessie returned the car to valet parking and went to his room to freshen up for the evening. Entering the room, he noticed the message button was flashing, and he quickly called the front desk. "Yes, sir, Mr. Thornton, a lady named Calie called and said she was running a little late but would meet you at the lobby bar around seven o'clock this evening." "Thank you," replied Jessie and hung up the phone. "Hot damn," he shouted, "this will be a fantastic weekend; thank you, James. Thank you very much." He poured a glass of wine, retreated to the balcony of his room, and visually scanned the beach. The afternoon sun had fallen deep in the west, and the hotel cast an elongated shadow across the courtyard, which extended to the water's edge. Children actively played in the sand, adults sprawled on lounge chairs, and scantily clad young ladies played volleyball as the evening drew near. "This beach life is the life," Jessie thought, "all this luxury, incredible scenery, elegant wine, and I am meeting a beautiful woman tonight. James should try to do this and give up finding women in bars. He gets rejected, and it reminds him of Bitch-Mother. Yet, he is the smart one, and he should be able to cope and ignore rejection, but unfortunately, he can't. I must give him credit, though; he has done well with the business, doubled Dad's investment, and provided well for me. This vacation James gave me is the best, and I am enjoying being Jessie immensely."

The remainder of the afternoon quickly passed as Jessie relaxed on the balcony, watching the scenery below. The alarm on his watch beeped, reminding him to shower and shave before his evening encounter with Calie. He felt like a giddy teenager on his first date as he strutted around the room, stark naked, admiring his trim torso. "Not bad for a man my age," he murmured. "James and I have taken good care of ourselves." He boasted that pride in one's appearance pays off as he noticed his dangling penis in the mirror and vainly admired its size. Zac remembered that Granny Sue's daughter told James that it would never be big enough to use. "Well, she found out differently, didn't she? Yeah, that 'Bitch' was sexually enjoying James's eighteenth birthday until James called on me to do 'the deed.' That filthy bitch will never belittle James again." "Oh, sorry, Jessie," Zac murmured, "I got caught up in the moment and forgot. I did not mean to interrupt your holiday. I'll leave now and let you have fun tonight." "Thanks, Zac, and no problem," Jessie replied, "but I could have sworn you were not talking to me. A little confusing as to who is talking to whom."

Jessie entered the lobby and sauntered to the bar. "Good evening, Mr. Thornton. Would you like a Mic-light?" Judith asked. "I am surprised you recognized me," Jessie stated. "The lights are dim, but I can see enough to remember the silhouettes of most people," Judith replied. "I may not know you in the bright daylight if I see you, so I specialize in knowing my customers by their mannerisms, how they walk their voices, and the outline of their bodies." "Very interesting," Jessie laughed, "but no beer tonight, Judith. I will indulge in a more suitable drink for the occasion. Let me have your best single malt scotch on the rocks, please." "Yes, sir, and may I ask, what's the occasion?" "I met a sweet young lady on my trek down the beach yesterday, and we shared some wine at the Sea Deck. I asked to see her again, and she left me a message that she would meet me here this evening around seven. Therefore, I should drink a toast to the evening and thank you for being so hospitable." "Thank you, kind sir; since you'll be here for a while, the first one is on me, but be cautious;

it is only six-fifteen."

"After a couple of these scotches, you may not be awake when she gets here." "That is healthy advice, my sweet lady."

"May I request that you please restrict me to no more than two scotches before she arrives?" "No problem, Mr. Thornton, I'll ensure you're sober." "Thank you, Judith, and please call me Jessie." At five minutes after seven, Jessie sat in a darker area and conversed with a young couple on their honeymoon who were also enjoying the darkness. He had just bought them a drink in celebration when Calie came up and kissed him lightly on the cheek. "Hi," she said. "Have you been waiting long?" "All my life for someone as pleasant and lovely as you," he replied. She smiled and said, "That was a gracious thing to say, Jessie, but you certainly can't know me that well yet. I secretly could be a real bitch," she said in jest. A sudden chill ran down Jessie's spine as he jumped from his seat. "Please don't say that Calie, never say that. I don't wish to have the slightest thought of you being a bitch."

"Please tell me you're not a bitch. Relax, Jessie, I was only joking," she whispered with emphasis, "I don't think I'm a bitch, and most people who know me do not think so either, so calm down. I didn't mean to upset you."

Having noted his reaction, Judith piped in, "No problem, Jessie, I can vouch for this lady; she is no bitch. Had I known you were meeting her, I would have cut you off at one scotch instead of two. This lady is a jewel." "Thanks, Judith," Calie said, "now Jess, if you've calmed down, I'll take a drink, and you can introduce me to these lovely people." "I shall be calm, my dear," Jessie stated, "and I apologize to all for being a little sensitive. That word upsets me for some reason." Thinking quickly, he fabricated a reason. "My father constantly called my mother that when I was young, which deeply offended me."

"Please have a drink, Calie, and let's start anew."

The evening progressed much smoother; Jessie was on his best behavior, and Calie was impressed with his reestablished demeanor. They finished their drinks at the lobby bar and then went beachside to admire the beauty of the evening. Jessie asked, "May I treat you to dinner, Calie?" "That would be nice," she replied. "I know an excellent restaurant with a piano bar just a few miles north in Ormond Beach. Are you willing?" "I would be delighted," he answered. "Let's get my car out of hock and venture away." Arriving at the restaurant, Jessie could not help but notice the crowded parking area. "It must be a popular place," he said. "Yes, it is," Calie replied. "I have been coming here since they opened. The ambiance, as well as the food, is excellent, and the piano bar is fun." "Sounds like my kind of place," Jessie said, "let's go in and enjoy." The dinner was superb, and the atmosphere was very romantic.

Jessie felt ecstatic from the night's joys and was delighted to have Calie as a companion. She directed him to the beach for the drive home.

Jessie had never driven on the beach before, and the tide was low, providing a wider expanse of sand for the drive, which he found exhilarating. The ocean was highlighted by the brilliance of the rising moon glistening on the crest of the waves, and the lights from the condos and hotels illuminating the dunes gave him a feeling of peacefulness never before experienced. "The drive is fabulous and unique," he commented. "I do not remember seeing or experiencing such a thrill before." "There is a clear stretch ahead without hotels or condos," Calie stated, "why don't you park there, and we can stroll the beach for a while?" Jessie stopped the car as suggested, and they shed their shoes to walk along the surf's edge. Hand in hand, they strolled, talking and giggling like teenagers, enjoying every precious moment. "It's getting late," Calie said, "I hate to be a party pooper, but I must be getting home. I have enjoyed tonight and would like very much to see you again." "No problem, my dear," Jessie replied. "I will take you to your cottage, as you call it, and extend you an invitation. Tomorrow is Sunday, and I would like to escort you to breakfast and share the day with you." "That sounds nice, Jessie. I go to church early, but I can meet you around ten if that is not too late." "Ten will be perfect, Calie. I will attempt to survive all by myself until tomorrow."

Jessie escorted Calie to her door and told her he would impatiently wait for the morning. "You're sweet, and I must admit that I like you very much," Calie stated. She put her arms around his neck and placed a very passionate kiss on his lips. "Wow," he said, "that warmed me the whole way down to my toes, and they are tingling." "I'll take that as a compliment, Jessie, and I must admit I felt tingles also."

"Because of that, I should go into the house right now. I've enjoyed tonight and look forward to seeing you in the morning, Mr. Thornton." "It has been my pleasure, Calie. Rest well tonight, and call my room when you are free tomorrow. I shall be ready and waiting."

James and Zac meet Jessie

Jessie returned to his hotel room, showered, and dried off as James appeared. "Hi Zac, how did the date go?" "Tonight has been incredible, James, completely unbelievable, so please don't spoil it, and damn it, call me Jessie. That's who I am right now; I am not Zac." "Easy there, Zac or Jessie; whatever you say, man, it's okay. Don't get yourself all riled up. Now, kindly explain to me what you mean by "spoil it"?" "Well, darn it, James, it seems every time you get involved with a female, she ends up pissing you off, and you call on Zac to rescue your high and mighty ego. Nothing will satisfy you until Zac kills the bitch. I don't want this encounter to end like that. I don't want Zac to kill Calie. Calie is a super sweet gal. I don't think she would intentionally hurt anyone, and I believe she likes me for who I am, and I am Jessie to her. Her feelings are what counts. She likes me, Jessie, not Zac or you, James. She wants me to be Jessie." "Holy hell," stated James, "that is the most important news I have heard since Zac killed Bitch-Mother. I believe I am beginning to understand what is occurring in our relationship. I remember Bitch-Mother saying that I should have been a triplet. She told me our Dad was such a poor shot with his prick that it took him three times one night to fertilize her. I thought she was just being a bitch as usual, but thinking back on it now, with you showing up as Jessie, it's funny. That dumb bitch didn't know it, but she might have been right, and what is even more amusing is all three of Dad's shots might have worked. It was her lousy ass that didn't have enough eggs for all three of us." "What the hell are you talking about?" asked Jessie.

"Contemplate my new theory, Jessie. I have considered it since you asked me to call you Jessie. You and Zac may not fully comprehend what I am saying, but listen and think it through. We have a guy named James; he is intelligent, nice-looking, and has many good traits, except for being friendly with the ladies. He encounters nothing but trouble when he attempts to associate with the females. His ordinary advances are too strong, and their adverse reactions to his approach remind him of Bitch-Mother. He can't tolerate rejection, so he calls on his brother Zac, who has been his protector for years. James and Zac do okay with this lifestyle for a while, but something is missing in their lives. As time passes, they both realize they have a problem. One day, it becomes evident that they desire an honest and affectionate relationship with a female. James's erotic encounters with prostitutes and Zac's violent seductions do not satisfy the real inner need for love and affection. Unfortunately, the hideous need for retaliation against bitches was instilled in both of them by the actions of Bitch- Mother. Retaliation has been the dominating force thus far. James and Zac are questioning their violent urges, which have resulted in massacred women. Violence is not what they desire. Violence is a substitute for the love they can not find. I can speak for James because I am James and know deep inside what I desire, and I can't achieve it. Zac would also prefer a satisfying relationship, but his protective instinct causes him to retaliate for James's mistreatment. As a result, they are now unmasking a third personality who will provide their hidden desires. I believe we are witnessing the birth of another Zachary. That third shot of Dad's is starting to come to life. Or better yet, you're the result of our maturity and growth. A new personality is introduced into the current duo, creating a trio. Think back for a second to JoAnne Rollins. The reference to Zac kept sliding in and confused everyone, even me. Well, I think that's when Jessie started to develop. I am happy for you, Jessie, and I will do my utmost to help and guide you. I think this is going to be a very pleasant happening. Feel free to call me anytime you need. Perhaps we should let Brother Zac take a much-needed rest, so the next time I find a lady, I will call on you, Jessie, to make good things happen and avoid the violence."

"I will do my best, James, honest I will," replied Jessie. "I'm not sure I understand this as well as you do, but I'll do my best. And thanks for explaining your theory to me. It does make sense. I'm glad we had this talk, and I believe this trip will be very stimulating for all three of us. Good night, Jessie, and you too, Zac."

Brad and Gang and Press Release

Most of the Task Force was present at the Grotto meeting. "Fuck it," Brad said, addressing the Grotto, "and please forgive my language Sue, but we have not made any progress in the past few weeks."

"What the hell is going on? Are there any new leads?" The members looked at each other and shook their heads in silence. Jack finally spoke up with the latest findings from the labs at the Bureau. There was not much to go on with the Rollins case. All the blood samples from the boat were from the victim. The few pubic and body hairs found produced DNA not from the vic, thus indicating it is from the perp.

Further checking showed these hairs match previous hairs found in the Roslyn Conti case, giving us a definitive connection. However, as in the past, this DNA cannot be found in any database. As it stands right now, we need DNA from Jessie before we can test for a match. Jack concluded it would be nice if everyone had to be fingerprinted and have DNA records. "Whoa there, let's not get into constitutional rights," Frank said. "In my book, and thinking strictly like a cop, that data would be excellent, but we all have and need our rights. We don't want 'Big Brother' keeping tabs on us any more than he is already." "Frank, you're correct, but this bastard has got us in a quandary. He is smart and crazy, which is one hell of a combination to catch. We know that the name he uses is Jessie, and we don't even know if that is his real name."

"What you're saying gives me an idea," Brad injected. "Maybe we are keeping too much of a lid on this thing. What if we put out a news release to all the local papers describing this guy in detail and stating that he goes by the name of Jessie? Maybe, just maybe, someone who knows him or has seen him will come forward with information." Frank replied that it might be worth a try, and the others agreed.

Sue said, "I'll get right on it since I am in charge of publicity." Jack volunteered to assist her. The following morning, a press release was given to the public.

"Local Law authorities in Martin, St. Lucie, Indian River, and Brevard counties, along with the FBI, are desperately seeking the whereabouts or any information regarding a person meeting the following description. Anyone having information about or seeing a person answering this description is asked to call the law enforcement agency in their local area. The subject is a Caucasian male with a height of 5'10" to 6'. Weight: 180 to 200 lbs, and 35 to 45 years of age. He has dark hair, is a nice dresser, frequents nightclubs and bars, drinks brandy, likes petite women, and is presumed to go by the name of Jessie. He is a person of interest in conjunction with several missing persons. Do not attempt to apprehend or establish communication with this individual. He is to be considered extremely dangerous. All information received will be confidential, and all calls will be investigated. Your local law enforcement agencies need your help."

Marci read the news release aloud to Brad as he fixed breakfast. "Wow," she said, "Sue and Jack put together an article that gets straight to the point. Yes, they certainly did. Now we will see if it does some good," commented Brad. "No reward is offered, which should keep the bogus tips to a minimum. Let's hope that some useful info comes in quickly."

"Well, you'll have to give it time, my Captain. It's not like being on your boat, where everything happens at your command." "Yes, ma'am," he replied, "and how would the Admiral like her eggs this morning?" "Thank you," replied Marcie, "I'll take the eggs over medium and the bacon very crisp. Oh, by the way, I thought it was supposed to be a nude breakfast. After all, I came to the table in the buff and expected my cook to do the same." "Ah, I'm your cook now, am I? Well, as soon as the bacon grease quits, spattering and burning my tender parts, I shall shed this apron." "The sooner, the better," Marci giggled. "I get a strip show along with breakfast. Shall I put some music on?" "Hush and eat your breakfast before it gets cold," Brad quipped as the apron dropped to the floor.

"Much better," Marci said; "I am working up an appetite for a morning delight." "A delight following breakfast sounds good, but it will have to be an early morning delight," Brad responded. "I invited Sue and Jack up for lunch and made plans for our next voyage, so being presentable by then is recommended." "It's only 9:30, my Captain, and I believe we can appear prim and proper by lunch. In the meantime, kindly pour me another cup of coffee. I find it very enticing watching my toy bounce as you walk across the kitchen." "You're bad, Admiral; in fact, you're naughty, just the way I like you," Brad snickered.

The phone rang as Sue stepped from the shower. She quickly wrapped a towel around her body and ran to answer the call. "Hello," she said, slightly out of breath. "Goodness," Jack replied, "Did I take your breath away, or did I interrupt something?" "Neither," Sue giggled. "I just got out of the shower and ran to the phone, so don't go around bragging. However, I was thinking about you. I figured you would call as soon as I got in the shower." "Somehow, I sensed that you were thinking about me," Jack snickered, "and if I have you pictured correctly, you are dressed just the way I like you. So I'll give you a morning proposition." "You have an erotic imagination, Jack, but I am wrapped in a towel not to spoil your bare-bottomed picture. Now, just what is your proposition?" "I didn't visualize the towel, so I'll keep my original image. Now, let me proposition you. Brad invited us to lunch this afternoon to establish the itinerary for the St. Augustine trip with him and Marci. Since we passed our sea trials last week, Brad joked that we are now qualified as crew, and he would like to make plans, cook some burgers, and socialize for a while today. It was late last night when he and I talked, so I waited until this morning to call you. Can you go?" "Give me an hour to finish here," Sue answered, "then I will drive up to your place." "I should be there before noon. You can come dressed just as you are, and I won't object to the towel." "You would enjoy that, wouldn't you?" Sue asked. "I indeed would," he sighed, "and so would all the truckers on I-95. On second thought, you better cover-up. I want to make sure you get here." "See ya soon," she said.

    Marci served drinks, and Brad tended the grill as the foursome finalized their plans to sail to St. Augustine. They agreed on a minimum of five days, two up, one there, and two back, with a stop in Daytona Beach each way, and if the urge hit them, they may stay longer in St. Augustine. "Sue and I will need to schedule vacation time, but I think the Bureau will approve mine with a bit of pleading. How about you, Sue?" "I have a similar scenario," she answered, "but I'll try." "Okay," replied Brad, "we'll keep our sailing plans, only put a tentative date on them." "Now that all that is settled," Jack said, "I hate to bring up business, but we've had several calls due to our press release, one out of Ft. Pierce and one out of Melbourne that sounds promising. The Ft. Pierce and Melbourne Task Force reps are checking them out, but we have no validity of the info. The Melbourne tip may be the better of the two. The caller said she met the man in a bar in Sebastian, who fits the description. I hope we hear more on that one as soon as they finish investigating the leads she gave them." "I may know the lady from Melbourne," said Sue, "her name sounded familiar. I think I met her at a party that I attended in Sebastian. If they don't get enough info, I may contact her myself." "Wait a minute," said Jack. "Are you telling me you're a party girl?" "Don't get nosey, Mr. Baird. I did have a life before meeting the FBI, and we agreed what is in the past stays in the past, remember?" Marci said that is a good idea for everyone; the past is the past. "But after you guys catch this monster, what will our subject be?"

"Good point," Sue said. "We should invoke Brad's rules at all our social gatherings, not just on the boat," and they all agreed. "However," Brad stated, "if we don't catch this asshole before long, I may have social hours in the loony bin. The prick drives me crazy, so can we take a short break from our social life? I want to discuss some things running around in my mind briefly." "Why not?" Jack answered, "the bastard is getting to me likewise." The girls shrugged but agreed.

"Let me start this way:" Brad began: "If the DNA matches Jessie, we have enough evidence to hang him if we could find him to make the matches. This frigging Jessie character is a phantom. Maybe we are concentrating too much on finding evidence. Perhaps we should be focusing more on finding his victims. We think we know what happened to them, but what did he do with the bodies? Of these suspected murders, we only have two bodies, Roslyn Conti and the male vagrant. What the hell did he do with the rest of them? Think about it: What would you do with the body of a woman you just killed? Would you bury it? Sink it in the ocean? Dismember the corps and scatter the parts? Encase it in concrete or what?" "That is a fascinating point, Brad; if we could find the bodies," Jack stated, "they might lead us to the killer."

Brad continued, "Indeed they may. Florida is loaded with swamps, and the ocean is right there. Disposing of a body would be easy if you wanted to. If I had to do it, I would choose the ocean since I am the boating sort. However, a body without encasement buried at sea could be a problem. Parts may eventually wash ashore and be found. Encasement would make bodies much harder to handle, take time to construct, and almost surely require a sizable boat. That's why I lean more towards burying them in secluded locations here on Terra Firma. It was said that Jessie mentioned funerals several times. Generally, a funeral can refer to a grave, a funeral home, and land-type ceremonies. However, a water ceremony is called a burial at sea, not a funeral. Also, he would have left JoAnne Rollins in her boat, surmising her body would sink with the boat. Thus, she could have been buried at sea. That is one area he goofed on. He assumed the boat would float out to sea with the outgoing tide and sink, destroying all the evidence. However, it went aground on a sandbar, making it conspicuous. A person who is a boater would have known that using the bilge pumps with a slow leak would give the boat time enough to get through the inlet before sinking; thus, he would not have completely severed the tube on the thru-hull. A local boater would probably have known about the sandbar. For those reasons, I believe that Jessie is not a boater. I opt for body disposal to be dry land or swamp interments."

"Interesting," replied Sue. "Let's take what we know about JoAnne Rollins and re-evaluate it. It's surmised that Jessie previously went boating with her, and oddly enough, Brad and Marci may have seen them. The available data for the day of her demise is that her car was in the parking area, indicating that he had his car, met her at the boat, and then brutally killed her. Most likely, Jessie seduced her first; thus, pubic hair was found. Based on the blood and human tissue in the boat, he possibly cut out her vagina, as with Roslyn Conti, but why? They appeared to be enjoying the fishing trip, which Marci witnessed. So, he must have liked that portion of her body enough to keep it."

"Yes," Brad interjected, "Marci did a "peeping Tom" trick on that action. But to answer your question, Sue, why would a woman cut off a man's penis?" Brad asked. "If you cheated on me or pissed me off, I might be tempted," Marci quipped. "At least I know what not to do," laughed Brad, "but that is precisely the answer I wanted. He was pissed off and felt cheated for some reason. Removing the vagina of his victim evens the score for whatever it was the lady did. The vagina becomes a souvenir or trophy for his act of revenge. I will bet when we find him, we will discover his trophies as well." "What a gruesome thought," Marci said. "Perhaps his mother abused him, and he hates abusive or dominant women. Or maybe she cheated on his father, causing Jessie to hate cheaters," Sue injected. "I'll also bet his mother molested him, and he hates her for it, hence the word bitch. Maybe all these women reminded him of his mother, which sets him off," Brad stated. "Witnesses indicated that he changed moods and acted differently following a rejection. So once he is pissed, he becomes someone else, and that someone else is the killer, a schizoid, as Marci suggested a while back." "You've mentioned Marci's dual personality theory before," Jack said, "it is beginning to make sense." "Hey, maybe I should have been a cop," Marci quipped.

"The land burial, as surmised, is probably the better path to consider with the funeral connection," Jack agreed. "I'll get the Grotto to check out all the funeral homes in the entire area. We'll give them Jessie's description and ask them to keep an eye out during their course of business. I'll also ask the Forestry and Game Services for help on suspicious areas in the swamps or backcountry that could be graves." "That might pay off," said Sue, "and I'll do more research with the morgues for Jane Does and for anything else that might link us to him." "Just remember one thing," said Brad, "If Jessie has a dual personality, he might not be known in his regular world as Jessie, so don't concentrate on the name. His description and personality should be the key factors. Brad elaborated that this guy obviously has some real mental issues, and the only way we will catch him is to identify those issues and concentrate on them. Start with the funeral connection and go from there." "I agree," Jack said. "Let's shelve this subject for a more suitable topic during the rest of the evening." Marci and Sue fixed snacks accompanied by a round of drinks.

CHAPTER 14

Jessie And Calie

Jessie sat on the balcony of his oceanfront room, savoring the taste of the coffee that accompanied the gourmet breakfast he ordered through room service. The sun was above the horizon now, and a warm breeze danced across the water. Several catamaran sailboats raced along the shoreline, cutting through the rising surf and spewing a salty spray as the skippers skillfully maneuvered the vessels to quarter the incoming waves. "Wow," Jessie thought, "that looks like fun; perhaps if things work out with Calie as I hope they will, I shall return to Daytona more often, and I may try my hand at sailing. James had lots of fun on JoAnne's boat before things went astray, and besides, these sailboats appear much more fun than that powerboat. They say that sailing is more of a challenge than simply steering a powerboat; if there is one thing I like, it's a challenge." "That's weird," he mused; "why am I contemplating challenges? James cannot tolerate a challenge, and Zac simply eliminates challenges. So why am I considering a challenge? However, I have suggested a positive challenge, not a destructive one, such as Zac likes or a social challenge, as James hates. Oh well, the thought of a physical challenge like sailing or a relationship challenge like Calie is positive and intrigues me. I just hope the Calie challenge does not fail. I feel that I am Jessie, not James or Zac. However, I am unsure what my reaction would be if Calie disappointed me." Once again, a strange sensation ran through his body, as it frequently has done since being on vacation.

Upon hearing the phone's sound, Jessie regained composure and quickly left the balcony to answer. "Good morning," Calie chimed. "I hope I didn't wake you?" "No, I just finished an excellent breakfast and watched the activities on the beach," Jessie replied. "Oh," she said, "checking out the bikinis already." "I must be honest," Jessie said. "I noticed a few of them, but I was more enticed by the sailboats playing in the surf." "That looks like it would be fun." "It is fun, Jessie; I'll have to take you for a sail one day. My older brother taught me, and we keep our cat at a friend's house just north of Ormond." "I will hold you to that offer," Jessie stated. "Now, what is on the agenda for today?" "I have a few chores to take care of this morning," Calie answered. "I should finish around ten. How about I pick you up at eleven, and we can start with lunch? I know a neat restaurant at a marina just south of Port Orange. Wear shorts because it is an outdoor picnic table-style place with great food and a casual atmosphere. After lunch, we can head south to see our famous Ponce Inlet lighthouse, then drive the beach back up to Daytona." "It sounds like you're playing tour guide and have this all mapped out, and it sounds fabulous. I'll meet you out front at eleven," Jessie said.

The day went as planned, and Jessie became convinced that he had finally found the girl of his dreams, making James happy and keeping Zac in hiding. The sun, setting in the western sky, cast off crimson rays as they approached the hotel. Calie peered deeply into Jessie's eyes and spoke softly, "I believe that I like you, Jessie. I know there is a difference in our ages, but I don't see that as a significant problem. I would like very much to talk further with you. Could we go to the bar inside and have a cocktail?" Jessie had utterly enjoyed the entire day, and now this beautiful young lady was inferring that she was genuinely interested in him.

The valet opened Calie's door, helped her out, and escorted her around the car, where Jessie tipped him generously, took her hand in his, and waltzed on air together into the lobby. "I almost forgot that you are leaving in the morning, Jessie. I guess I secretly wished that you would stay longer." "I wish I could, Calie, and I apologize, but I have a business to tend to, and I must get back. However, I feel confident I can return next weekend if you are available." "I will be, Jessie, so please make that a definite date." "A date it is," he said.

They approached the bar area and proceeded to their favorite secluded, dimly lit table. Judith was on duty and said, "Hi. Shall I fix your usuals?" "Yes," said Jessie, but Calie replied, "No, I wish to try what Jessie is drinking. I have heard much about scotch and wish to try it." 'You're brave," said Judith. "I can't tell you what happened in mixed company the last time I had scotch. I believe I am in good company tonight," Calie said, "so bring on the scotch." Jessie laughingly said, "You may have to drive her home tonight, Judith, or call her a cab, but give the lovely lady anything she desires." "Excuse me," Calie whispered to him in a sexy voice, "but what makes you think I will be going home tonight? I may decide to spend the night with you if you don't mind." "Calie, my Dear, I not only won't mind, but that offer pleases me immensely. You have made this entire day unforgettable, and now you offer yourself to me. How could I possibly object? But please, Calie, do us both a favor and make sure you are confident about your decision. We need not rush into something uncertain."

After the drinks, Calie and Jessie took a short stroll on the beach before venturing toward his room. Jessie unlocked the door. Holding it ajar, he peered deeply into her eyes and asked. "Are you sure you have made the correct decision?" "Yes, I am sure," she answered with much certainty as she pushed the door further open. After entering the room, Calie kissed him gently, requested a nightcap, then slipped off her shoes and pranced dancingly into the bathroom. Jessie prepared the drinks as he heard the shower, followed by some refreshing murmurs as cool water trickled down her body. He let the image of her play in his mind as he finished the drinks, placed them on the balcony table, and stood by the railing, enjoying the peacefulness of the night and the thoughts of what was to come growing in his mind.

It was only a few minutes, which seemed like hours to Jessie, before she appeared beside him, adorned with only a bath towel wrapped around her, barely covering the sexual parts of her luscious torso. Gazing at the magnificence of her presence, Jessie, in total awe, whispered, "My god, Calie, you're beautiful," as he took her in his arms and kissed her passionately. Catching his breath, which she had taken away, Jessie said, "Kindly excuse me, but I, too, would like to freshen up. You smell lovely and clean, and I do not wish to present myself in any less condition. Sip on your drink, and I shall return swiftly." "I have a feeling your condition will be perfect," Calie said. "I will freshen your drink while you're gone, but please don't take long. I am becoming very aroused and want so much to enjoy you tonight." "Stay that way, my Dear. I, too, am enthralled with the anticipation of what will come." "Hurry, Jess, I get goosebumps thinking about being with you."

He returned to find her waiting on the balcony with two fresh drinks on the table and the towel draped over the back of a chair. Her nude body was a heavenly sight, partially leaning against the rail, posed like a model out of a magazine. Her silken flesh glowed in the moonlight with defining shadows accentuating the small of her back and lower extremities of her buttocks as she gazed listlessly towards the sea. Approaching her from behind, he slid his arms around her waist, securing her body tightly against him as he sensually kissed the nape of her neck. She felt his manly chest against her back, his strong arms surrounding her, and his ridged penis throbbing in the crease of her thighs. She turned to face him, pressing her breast tightly against his chest, allowing him to engulf her in his arms as they deeply and feverishly caressed each other. Gently, he picked her up and carried her to the bed, placing her gently on the mattress where he visually seduced every enchanting feature of her body before lying beside her. They kissed with emotional depth and feeling and became uncontrollably heightened with lustful desire. She seductively grasped his engorged penis in her hand, stroking it slowly as she guided him to mount her and tenderly enter her moist vagina. She devoured him entirely within her depths until their emotions were mutually satiated.

Brad And The Case

Monday morning, Brad was in Jack's office early. They were going through all the case data once again when Sue called. "Hi, you two! I updated the info on funeral homes in surrounding counties this morning. There appear to be five, possibly six, employees who could meet Jessie's description. I'm going to save the ones in the northern area till last. That way, I may have an excuse to spend the night. Think you could handle that, Jack?" "No problem, just let me know when, and I will be waiting with bated breath." She giggled. "I don't know about your breath, but just wait and don't start without me." "Not a chance of that sweetness; I'll save myself just for you."

"Excuse me for eavesdropping, but catching the end of the conversation, it sounds like you and Sue have established more than a casual relationship," Brad quipped. "Yes, we have, and this sailing trip with you and Marci may also become an engagement party. The other day, I went shopping for a ring, but she was unaware I was thinking of such a thing." "Fantastic," replied Brad. "I gave Marci hers a few weeks back, making it a doubleheader. I think it's great. Anyway, what was she saying about our boy Jessie?" Jack relayed Sue's information and explained the possibilities. "Let's hope she digs up some good data. I have a gut feeling about this funeral aspect," Brad stated. Jack replied, "Your feelings have proven to be accurate on many things. I hope your gut and Marcie's schizo theory are on the right track. We need a break."

"Mr. Lloyd, I'm Sue Gunther, Vero Beach P. D. I don't know whether you remember me. I arranged for my father's funeral with you about fourteen months ago." "I do remember, my Dear, come in and have a seat. I occasionally see your mother in the grocery store; how is she doing?" She is doing fine, Mr. Lloyd and I hope all is well with your family." "Indeed it is, Sue. Now, what can I do for you?" I'm with a special Task Force of officers from Indian River, St. Lucie, Martin, and Brevard counties, and we are in a dilemma. I'm sure you have heard or seen it in the news concerning this individual named Jessie, for whom we are searching." "Yes, I've heard about him," he answered, "but what does that have to do with me?" "Nothing directly, Mr. Lloyd; we believe this person may be connected in some fashion with a funeral parlor or mortuary. The information we have gathered indicates he may work at, be associated with, or be affiliated with funerals. Perhaps he is a mortician, a funeral director, or a general employee involved with funerals. Unfortunately, we only have a brief description of him."

"I see, said Mr. Lloyd, give me this description. I know almost everyone in this business between Jacksonville and Palm Beach." "As I said," repeated Sue, "this description is brief, but here is what we have." She repeated Jessie's description with the same detail as her newspaper release. "Well, I must say, that is brief and very general," stated Lloyd, "but the age narrows it down a bit. Let's see, Webber's funeral home in Stuart has a couple of young apprentices, and there are younger employees at the funeral parlors in Ft. Pierce, Sebastian, Melbourne, Merritt Island, and, of course, at my competitor here in Vero. None of my employees are that young. It has been six months since I saw the other owners and their employees at our annual convention. At my age, my memory is fading a bit. I am sure that if you confide with the others, they will be most cooperative. Death is our business, but we prefer to get our clients naturally."

"Thank you for the time, Mr. Lloyd," said Sue, "we appreciate your valuable input. I'll check out these recommended places, and if we find him, you will be the hero of the day." "I don't need to be a hero, missy, but if I have in some way helped to stop the violent nonsense, it will have been my pleasure. Say hello to your mother for me; she and I attended high school together here in Vero. At one time, I had a huge crush on her. She is still charming, and you have become a natural beauty." "Thank you, Mr. Lloyd; I will tell Mom hello for you. I am sure she will be pleased."

Sue opted to start with Lloyd's competitor and drove across town to Gadwin's funeral home. "I'm sorry, Detective Gunther," said the receptionist, "but Mr. Gadwin is out of town and will be gone for several weeks. However, Mr. Romane, our general manager, is here; perhaps he can help you." "That will be fine," answered Sue. "Please ask him if it would be possible to speak with him briefly." "Of course," she replied, "have a seat. I will be right back." Sue noticed the staff's photographs and their credentials on the wall but didn't see anyone resembling Jessie's description. She was scanning the photos when Bob Romane entered the room and spoke. "See anyone on your wanted list, Detective," he jested? "Oh, no," she answered, "I'm sorry, but I didn't hear you come in. I'm Detective Susan Gunther, Vero P. D. You are Mr. Romane?" "That's correct," he answered, "but please, call me Bob. Now, Detective, what may I do for you?"

Sue explained the reason for her visit and indicated the urgency of obtaining information. "I recently met a young man from Port Malabar who could fit your description. He is working on his degree and is employed part-time at the Brevard Mortuary. They sent him down here to transport a body back to Brevard County. Let me think; his name is Stokes, Marshal Stokes. He appeared to be upright, but then we never know, do we? You're welcome to interview our staff, but I know none who would meet your description. Otherwise, Detective, I am afraid I can be of no help." "Thank you, Bob; I appreciate your time. I will follow through on your information; who knows? This lead may be the one we need." "My pleasure," he stated. "Please feel free to come back and talk with Mr. Gadwin when he returns. He knows many more people in this business than I do, and I am confident he will be happy to help."

James

It was late afternoon, and James was seated in his office, gazing aimlessly out the window with a distinctive air of tranquility on his face. Mrs. Oliver entered the office carrying a stack of papers requiring his signature and noticed his serenity. "James, you look like a new man," she said, "you should take more time away from here and for yourself. Go and enjoy your life more frequently; it becomes much too short, much too quickly. You owe yourself some frivolity." "I must admit, Mrs. Oliver, I indeed feel like a new man; my inner parts have relished the freedom, and I enjoyed my mini vacation immensely. I am unsure what you mean about your inner parts, but the look of pleasure on your face indicates that the outer parts also enjoyed it." She giggled. "When I was your age, all of my parts were having fun, and I mean fun. Although we dared not discuss such things back then, we still had fun." "I guess the referral to my inner parts sounded odd," replied James. "We all have inner parts that we usually don't display, but I let my inner parts come alive this weekend. It was a pleasant experience that I shall cherish for quite some time. Now, back to reality, let me sign those burial certificates so you may mail them to the good ole state of Florida. Paperwork, paperwork, we get papers when we are born and papers when we die. Looking closely, we have papers for almost everything we do anymore."

"Indeed we do," Mrs. Oliver said, "and speaking of paper, have you read the newspaper today? They have a featured article on what they believe to be multiple murders in our area. The FBI has been brought in, and a Task Force has been organized with the various police departments. The article is vague, but I think this Task Force has existed longer than they care to divulge. They have not released any pertinent details about the cases, claiming that the evidence must remain confidential and not jeopardize future prosecution." "Do they have an actual suspect?" James asked. "It would be best if you read it, James. They indicated several possibilities, but again, the details were minor and very vague. I found it quite interesting, and I believe you will as well." She continued, "You're not a fan of the authorities, but the article is interesting and a local dilemma." "Permit me to finish this paperwork first. Then I will read the article while enjoying my evening drink," replied James, "perhaps the reading accompanied by a brandy would be relaxing." "I am not sure that you will find it relaxing," Mrs. Oliver stated. "It gave me the creeps just hearing that a monster lurks in our area." "Now, Mrs. Oliver, don't become involved with any weird strangers, and I am sure you will be perfectly safe. You are surrounded by caring and protective people here and at home." "It's not that, James; I am sure I will be very safe. This nut is looking for much younger women than me, and he likes kinky things. Something similar happened in years past, and I find it interesting that it is happening again. Good night, James, and don't work too late. I'll see you in the morning." "Good night, Mrs. Oliver. I shall not work late tonight and will call it quits very soon."

James completed his paperwork, locked the door, got in his car, and drove home. The ride was uneventful except for a couple of stops to purchase a bucket of fried chicken and a bottle of brandy. He parked the car in the garage, entered the house, placed the items on the island counter in the kitchen, and then quickly changed into a pair of shorts, a loose-fitting tropical shirt, and sandals. He opened the brandy, savored the aroma, poured a large sniffer to the proper height, and retired to enjoy his chicken dinner on the patio.

James began reading the news article titled 'The East Coast Killer.' "Wow, what a title they tagged on Zac," James stated aloud as he perused the sketchy details of the crime. He noted that only one significant clue was published, which tied the cases together. That clue was the word bitch, which indicated to the authorities that there was only one perpetrator. It further stated that the police have determined from the brutality displayed that the perpetrator dislikes women. This information caused James to laugh loudly, "Now, why would they think such a thing," he muttered. "Zac likes women. Hell, he wants to molest them, torture them, and kill them, you dumb bastards," he shouted. Sipping his brandy and giggling boisterously, James continued his reading. Local law enforcement authorities have divulged that they have little evidence to go on in these cases, nothing concrete that aids in identifying the killer. Of the ten or more suspected victims, only one body has been recovered, Roslyn Conti. All other possible victims remain missing, but authorities fear the worst due to the similarities of the crime scenes.

Once again, James laughed and spoke aloud to himself. "Missing, hell no, they are not missing. Ask Zac; he can tell where they are. Some of them are still planted out there on the Bitch Farm. The ashes of the others are scattered all over the fucking area." He again laughed boastfully. "There is no way that those asshole cops will ever find the bitches, primarily because I built the crematorium. That effort was a stroke of genius on Zac's and my part. Zac thought it would be fun to burn the bitches when he was done with them, and I determined it would also increase our legitimate business, and thus far, it has done just that. Most of the bitches are now nothing more than ashes. Ah yes, 'bust to dust and asses to ashes,'" he giggled and poured another brandy. "It has worked out fine, bitch parts mixed in with legitimate cremations, and no bitch or deceased client is any the wiser. I doubt if members of the surviving family will ever know that the urns of their dearly departed may likewise contain the residue of a bitch. Just think, tears could flow for dear old grandpa while his ashes are all snuggled up with some whore." James roared with laughter at that thought.

"However, something strange with this article," he murmured to himself. "There is no mention of poor old Gerald. They have his body. Zac left it for them purposely, but there is no mention of it, and there is no mention of the other clues left intentionally. Ah yes," he mused, "those sneaky ass cops are playing the game very coyly, aren't they? Those ass bites are only releasing what they want the public to know. Their little piggy ears will be tuned for the slightest unpublished clue, like Gerald's knowledge or any secret clues that a suspect may divulge. A slip of the tongue by a suspect concerning unpublished data could indicate your ass to be a murderer. That is if they ever find a suspect to interrogate. Those assholes will never find Zac, and even if they did, he wouldn't tell them a damn thing, and I damn sure won't." He laughed loudly and guzzled down the remainder of his brandy. The East Coast Killer saga is getting funny!

"Jessie, where are you, Jessie? It's time for you to call Calie," James stated. "Come on now. You know you call her every night around this time, so come on out and call. Come out on the patio, have a brandy, and call that Daytona beauty." "Oh yeah, thanks, James," Jessie replied. "I noticed you were deeply engrossed in the newspaper article and didn't want to disturb you during your relaxation time." "Nonsense Jess, you know that I am very happy for you, and your happiness takes priority over anything. We both know those stupid cops have nothing to indicate Zac's, yours, or my involvement with their cases. Zac or Jessie's names are the closest things that bring them our way; we know you guys don't exist. James does, but they have no idea about my involvement. Remember, there is no hard evidence to prove that you or Zac committed 'the deed.' Besides, the only substantial evidence they have is the bodies of Carrie and old Gerald. Even though they won't admit to having Gerald, neither Carriere nor Gerald can tell on us, now, can they? So relax, dear brother, savor the aroma, taste the brandy, kick back, and call your newfound playmate. Whisper sweet nothings in her ear, enjoy naughty phone sex, then go to lustful slumberland with erotic thoughts."

"Hi, Jessie," Calie answered in a bubbly voice. "I'm so glad you called. I wanted to talk with you, but then I realized that I did not have your number." "No problem, Calie; since I left you last Sunday, I have obtained a new cell with a unique number dedicated only to you, twenty-four, seven. Due to my volume of business calls, I want you to be able to contact me whenever you choose. I call it the Calie phone. I'm using it now, so use your caller ID to note the number." "Jessie, you're such a romantic fool. I guess that is why I adore you," stated Calie. "I wanted to call you because I hope nothing has changed your plans to come here in two weeks. I just found out that they are holding a street party in the old downtown section of Daytona, and it sounds like it will be fun. I also have some friends I want you to meet; they do want to meet you." "Well, well," Jessie replied, "as far as I know at this moment, I shall be there, but please allow me to check my schedule again when I get to the office Monday morning. Plus, it may be possible for me to leave here a day or two earlier than planned, giving us more time together." "Ohhh," Calie cooed. "I hope so, Jessie; no matter what happens, I want you to be here, and the earlier, the better. You have not been gone but a few days, and already I miss you." "And I miss you, Calie," Jessie replied. "The days have been long without you." "My days have been long also, Jess; however, since you will not be here this week, I will visit my Grandmother. I haven't seen her in a long time. I hope our time apart will go by quicker; nonetheless, I'll call you on our private line for private talks." The conversation continued by reminiscing pleasantries from the previous weekend and a cooing exchange of intimate words.

"Wow, Jessie, you talked to her for over an hour. What on earth is there to talk about that long?" James queried. "We spoke of many things, James, including a little verbal seduction, which aroused her very much. I could hear her heavy breathing over the phone, and I wouldn't be surprised to find that she was pleasuring herself as I told her all the sensual things I wished to do to her." "Damn, Jessie, you are a romantic devil with the ladies; perhaps we should change roles." "No way, James, you run the business and find the bitches for Zac to kill, and I shall expend my expertise in entertaining the non-bitches passionately. You know, James, as kids, you were level-headed, attended school, and kept us together. Zac was the tyrant who took on the violent role, while I was just your imaginary outlaw friend. Now that I exist, however, I am putting the civilized touch to this dynamic trio, providing us with some of the human pleasures we genuinely desire. No, I am no longer just a figment in your mind. I am here now. I am making our fantasies come true. Look at it this way, James; it all started with Calie. Zac departed from you and pretended to be me, Jessie, and he enjoyed playing that role. If we cultivate and coordinate the triple energies we possess, you shall become even more successful in business. I will lustfully pleasure the ladies, and Zac will be Zac should we ever need him. As the fairy tale states, we shall live happily ever after with a thriving business, a satiate love life, and planting a bitch or two should it become necessary. As long as the luscious Miss Calie proves sincere and does not piss me off, as she came close to doing with that Bitch comment she made. Our Daytona Beach adventure should be fine. That in itself should keep us sexually fulfilled with my weekend jaunts to visit with her between the sheets." Jessie concluded that Calie is a most satisfying seduction and knows well what to do and how to please me. "All this sounds good," James interrupted, "but getting satisfied reminded me that since you are not visiting Calie this week, there is a party at the Vero Inn tonight, and I thought I would go. You had your sexual fantasies filled last weekend. Now, I would like an evening to see if I can find a little mud for the turtle. I also could use a female encounter." "Go right ahead, James," Jessie replied. "But please remember that you are not Jessie or Zac; from here on in, you are James or some other alias if you desire, but not Jessie. Keep in mind that the paper said the cops were looking for Jessie, and right now, he only exists in Daytona, so don't give us away." "You know what, Jessie? You're becoming more level-headed than I am. I shall remember this conversation."

Jack And Sue

Jack parked the car in front of Sue's condo. He glanced around, surveying the area out of habit as he strolled up the walkway to the front door. However, before he could ring the doorbell, the door opened. "Good evening, Mr. Baird. Sue said I have been expecting you." "Oh really," he replied. "Is that why you are almost naked?" "You guessed it correctly, and on the first try," she giggled, "now, come inside before the neighbors likewise guess correctly. I must confess to you, Mr. Baird, I have been contemplating this naked act of aggression for several days. So I suggest you either enter quickly and enjoy the obvious or retreat in a hurry and glumly ponder what you missed." "I will be delighted," he answered as he leaped into her awaiting arms through the doorway. "I was under the impression that we were going to the Vero Inn party tonight," Jack said. "I had no idea that this was your definition of a night out. We shall have our night as soon as we make passionate love, if that is not too much to ask."

"Need you ask?" he stammered. "I have waited for this event since meeting you." Their bodies merged with their arms interlocking each other while their lips met, spurring the deepest sexual desires. The short black coat she had draped over her shoulders fell to the floor as Jack swept her up in his arms and carried her to her boudoir, where he laid her gently on the bed. Admiring her nude torso splayed lovingly on top of the satin sheet, he hastily became naked as she watched his every move with increased intensity. Spreading her arms and legs as an open invitation of her submittal, she bid him to join her. "Welcome to my home, Mr. Baird. I, too, have been waiting for this moment," she said as they melted into each other's pleasure zone.

"That was a beautiful experience," Sue whispered in his ear, "much better than I ever imagined. I hoped that meeting you at the door in such a provocative state was not coming on too strong. I didn't want to scare you away, but I was attracted to you at our first meeting, and the feeling has grown more profound with time. I guess I just gambled and decided tonight was the night to elevate our relationship. I hope I am not wrong." "You damn sure didn't scare me away, Sue. One look at you standing there with nothing on but that short jacket convinced me that my judgment in pursuing you was correct. I am now ever so glad that I did. Seeing you at the door took me by surprise, and your elegant presence took me to a level I had never experienced before. Lying here with you, I have never felt such unity while making love as you exhibited. I do believe our relationship has reached an exalted plateau. You're not only a great cop but a remarkable woman, and I have now found you to be a fantastic lover. What more could a man desire? I am yours for the keeping." They snuggled closely together, letting the touch of their naked flesh ignite the passion once again.

Chapter 15

Vero Inn Party (James Uses The Alias Frank James)

The party had been underway for about an hour when James strolled through the Vero Inn entrance. The band was wailing out serious blues while enthralled bodies swayed on the dance floor as others gathered in general socialization. James approached the bar, ordered a scotch and water in a tall glass instead of his usual brandy, and scanned the crowd for a prospective encounter. Jack and Sue were among the swaying bodies on the dance floor, holding each other tightly, captivated by the music's mood and the ecstasy still present from their recent interlude. The previous lust abated their sexual tensions, permitting them to enjoy the sensations of each other's movements as they flowed with the rhythm.

James sipped the scotch while glancing around the room and took notice of a familiar-looking female on the dance floor. He quickly recalled her picture from the newspaper article. "Damn," he thought, "she is one of the prime detectives trying to find Zac," he mused. "She's a hot babe with a damn nice body. Good looking, sexy, and petite, she's just how I like them. What a shame she's a cop, which makes her off-limits to me. I will say the photo in the paper does her no justice. I'll wager the guy with her is the FBI Agent they mentioned several times in the article. It appears the two of them have a little thing going. Now isn't that sweet, the local law and federal law screwing each other. Although I can't blame him, I bet she is a tiger in bed. I think I will take advantage of this situation and analyze both of them. Maybe I can figure out what makes them tick other than sex and hunting Jessie. If I can acquire insight into their thinking, it will help Zac stay ahead of them and their cronies. Man, this is cool. I'm here at a party with the frigging law. I should go over there and introduce myself." "No, James, no, damn it, don't be fucking stupid, behave yourself, and keep your ass alert. We don't need problems," Jessie whispered. "Thanks, Jessie. I didn't know you were here, but I'm glad you are. I deserved to be confronted with that thought. I'm becoming confident that you are more level-headed than I am."

"However, please stay hidden, Jess, but remain close. I may need your advice often tonight."

James watched coyly as Jack and Sue returned to their seats at the bar. "Holy shit," he thought, "if only they knew I was here. This encounter is getting very profound and exciting. I'm becoming aroused. Thank goodness it's dark here, and I am glad it is because there is only one seat between Zac's prominent adversaries and me. At least it is occupied by this charming young lady with whom I hoped to get acquainted. This situation is titillating; I feel like I am about to climax," James thought as he wiggled in his seat, trying to relieve the pressure. "Those silly cops are none the wiser that the brother of the person they seek is well within touching distance. Jessie is correct; however, I must continue being alert. Let me think: should I stay or should I go? No, I'll stay here, but I must devise a plan. I am the one who makes all of the plans, so let me think this through carefully. I must contemplate this situation; I shall use the name "Frank" and be a tourist. Also, this chick beside me is not bad. I might have fun with her and maybe get to know the two law cronies beside her simultaneously."

"Frank? Who the hell is Frank?" Jessie queried. "Frank James dummy, Jessie James's brother," Jessie answered, "now, go away and relax. I have tonight well in hand." "You're a fucking genius," Jessie replied. "I would not have thought of Frank James; that's a very clever alias, but don't screw around and get Zac caught." "Not to worry, Jessie, old boy, now please retire again, but stay tuned."

"Excuse me, sir, the young lady said, did you say something?" "Who me?" answered James, "no, I didn't say anything. I was perhaps unknowingly singing along with the music, but that's all." "Oh, I'm sorry," she replied, "it is noisy here, and I thought I heard you say something, but I guess it was just the background noise. However, could I ask you a favor?" "Ask away," James said. "It is crowded in here tonight," she stated. "Would you mind saving my seat while I powder my nose?" "It will be my pleasure," he answered, "and if I may, I would ask you the same favor when you return." "Not a problem," she quipped, "and her eyes sparkled as she flashed him a big smile and departed," James noted that she was petite, with stunning hazel eyes and dark brown shoulder-length hair. He watched as she gracefully pranced across the floor, a mid-thigh black skirt that nicely accentuated her buttocks, accompanied by a contrasting apricot blouse, and she had a very sexy walk. "This lady has class."

"Perhaps I will get as lucky as Jessie did in Daytona, and the two of us could enjoy nice ladies. But we could never double date, now, could we?" he snickered, "unless the girls were a little kinky, which might prove interesting."

Taking his turn from the bar, James stood at the urinal, laughing to himself over the unsuspected turn of events when Jack stepped up to the urinal beside him. "Nice party," Jack said. "Yeah, I hope it stays that way," James replied as he zipped up and retreated to the sinks with sudden anxiety. He washed his hands and hastily left the men's room. "Hot damn, do you believe this shit? I spoke to him. I'll bet he is the FBI Agent, and I talked to him. We were standing there, with pricks in our hands, speaking to each other. Wow, this is fucking crazy, man; I need to be extra cautious, but the ice is broken." James tapped the young lady on the arm. "I'm back," he said with a glint of laughter. He sat beside her and contemplated a conversation when Jack, avoiding the crowded dance floor, brushed by, breaking James's train of thought, and nodded hello. James grinned back in recognition and raised his drink in front of his face as a friendly gesture. Jack gestured in return, smiled, and continued to his seat beside Sue.

"This is pure insanity," thought James. "I'm glad it is dark in here. I could not see his face clearly, so hopefully, he could not see mine." He took stock of his situation and analyzed his presence for any items that might alert the two law officers. He knew he ordered scotch instead of brandy for that reason and was pretending to be Frank, not James, Jessie, or Zac, and then remembered that Jessie had not shaved since being on vacation and that he, too, had the couple weeks of facial hair which would somewhat be a disguise. He saw the red pinky ring as he raised his glass and sipped his scotch. "Oh shit," James quietly mumbled. "Did the Fed see it in the john, or did the lady cop notice it as I gestured with my drink? Damn, damn, damn," he mumbled again, quickly removed the ring, and put it in his pocket. "That ring stands out like a flashing light," he thought. "It could be used as a distinctive point of recognition." Again, he scanned for any further tale-tell signs.

Satisfied with his appearance, James regained composure, took a healthy slug of the scotch to calm his nerves, and avoided direct facial contact with the law. The young lady turned towards him and said, "I'm sorry, sir, but I didn't thank you for the favor. James smiled and said, "Turnabout is fair play. We both had our turn, thanks enough for me. The name is Frank, Frank James, but not the outlaw. Now, may I be so bold as to ask yours?" "Of course," she said, "Clara, Clara Langford, and no kin to the movie star Francis Langford." "Hi Clara, now that we know each other and are not related to anyone famous, may I buy you a drink? And you look as lovely as any movie star." "Well, thank you, kind sir." She jokingly replied, "I don't accept drinks from strangers, but since we now know each other, I'll have an extra dry Rob

Roy." "Yes, ma'am," James said with a smile, "a lady after my own heart. You have impeccable taste. Do you prefer a particular brand?" "I usually get the well brand," she replied. "Do you suggest a specific brand?" "I have recently acquired a taste for scotch," James stated, "and Chivas Regal has become one of my favorites. Allow me to order. Bartender, give this lovely lady an extra dry Chivas Rob Roy and refill mine."

Sue turned towards Clara and piped in, "Excuse me, but I couldn't help overhearing the drink order. That is a very smooth and delightful drink. I have friends in the Cape area who enjoy those frequently, as do I. But please, I didn't mean to eavesdrop or interrupt." "Not a problem," Clara said, "and no need to be excused; you did not interrupt, nor were we talking in private. This gentleman and I had just met, and we favored each other by saving seats while we took potty breaks," she giggled. "My name is Clara Langford, no kin to the movie star, and this gentleman is Frank James, but not the outlaw." Sue and Jack laughed at her references, and they likewise introduced themselves. James, trying desperately to maintain facial obscurity, said, "I am not a wild-west outlaw, perhaps a speeding ticket or two, but nothing more serious." "I didn't mean to embarrass you," Clara said. "I am joking because I recognized Ms. Gunther from her picture in the paper. Might I add the photo? It did you much disservice; you're a very attractive lady." "I'll second that," James stated while partially hidden behind Clara's head. "You are much lovelier than the paper presented."

"Well, thank you both," Sue replied. "We try to stay out of the paper, but the paparazzi are impossible, if not ruthless. If you don't give them some tidbit, they will fabricate one, which won't be good." Clara said, "I don't envy your job, but you prefer to leave the business at work if you're like me. I am sorry for bringing it up, and let's discuss that horrid subject no further." "Thanks," said Jack and Sue simultaneously. "We have been living with these cases for many months and need time." "Don't we all?" James replied with a sneaky grin. "Don't we all?" James involuntarily developed a big grin of satisfaction as he quickly faced the other direction. He now was positive of the gentleman's identity and felt a bit more confident that his cover thus far had not been blown.

James and Clara became quite friendly as the evening progressed, and minimal contact with the law had occurred. He and Clara danced, drank, laughed, and shared a few casual stories about themselves. James became very comfortable with this lady as the evening progressed. "Do you come here often?" James asked. "No," she replied. "I usually go to Lenny's for a cocktail. It is not far from home, which works since I don't particularly like driving after a couple of drinks. That is commendable on your part, but you have already had several tonight. Will you be ok driving home?" "Not a problem," she answered. "I took no chances tonight and reserved a room here at the hotel. There will be no driving for me." "Clever girl," James commented, "if I keep drinking, I should do the same." "If I am not too forward, Clara said, you already have had several drinks. There are two beds in my room, and you could use one. I would not want to read your obituary tomorrow. But please, don't take this suggestion the wrong way; I am only offering a safe place to sleep, nothing more, and the offer is because you appear to be a gentleman, which is a rare breed today." "Thank you, Clara, for the compliment and gracious offer. My better self tells me to take you up on that invitation, and I assure you that I am a gentleman. Your generosity and frankness are much appreciated. I shall fully respect your wishes, providing you allow me to pay for the room." "It's a deal," she answered.

Having eavesdropped on Clara and Frank again, Sue quietly turned to Jack and asked, "Are you ok with driving back to my place?" He answered, "Not really, and I don't think you are either." "Then we have two choices: get a room or a taxi. Which would you prefer?" Sue questioned. "I prefer a room," answered Jack, "and I think spending the night with you in this plush hotel would be fantastic." "In our condition, Jack, the fantastic part will probably have to wait until morning," Sue giggled. "You're right, my lady. We both had our fill of booze tonight, but at least we realize it." "Viva the morning," Sue said, "get us a room, and I will order us a nightcap."

Clara stirred early the following morning due to the knocking on the door and saw Frank, as she knew him, greeting a server. "Thank you, my good man. Just place it on the table, and that will be all." He tipped the young man and shut the door. "Sorry, Clara, I did not mean to awaken you, but I ordered breakfast. I do hope you like eggs benedict. That sounded like the most delicious thing on the menu." "Yes," she said, "I love eggs benedict, but please allow me a few minutes to freshen up." "The eggs will stay warm in these serving trays," he answered, "take your time. I have already taken my shower."

Clara soon joined James on the small balcony where he had moved the table for a sunrise breakfast. They dined while watching the morning activity begin on the beach. "The scenery is lovely," stated Clara, "and I appreciate you being a gentleman last night. I know I was reasonably intoxicated, and I am sure you could have taken advantage of the situation. I admire your chivalry. Not many gentlemen are left in this world, and it is a pleasure to meet one." "Thank you, Clara, but what made you trust me? After all, we only met last night." "Let's say that I am usually a good judge of character," she answered, "not always, but I will say ninety percent of the time, and you seem to fit into that percentage. Otherwise, I would have left you at the bar long before. I don't lead men on to get free drinks, and as far as my asking you to spend the night, it was strictly out of concern for your safety and nothing more. Besides, why can't a man and a woman sleep in the same room, in separate beds, without sexual innuendos?" "I agree, Clara, and if you notice, I still have my pants on. I slept in them last night. Not that you are not tempting; it was simply out of respect. However," he said jokingly, "now that we are awake, don't press your luck." They laughed, but an obvious hidden desire surfaced on both parts.

The levity hid the desire momentarily, but the glint in their eyes revealed their urge for lust. After breakfast, their bodies brushed against each other while entering the room, creating an internal spark. James stopped, took her in his arms, and kissed her tenderly. While embracing him and exchanging more kisses, she maneuvered herself next to the bed, where she coyly fell backward. Her robe opened, exposing her feminine treasures as she opened her arms, inviting him to join her. After a torrid encounter and a climactic conclusion, Clara said, "If you have no plans for the day, why don't you follow me home? We can relax by the pool, enjoy a beverage, and do whatever comes to mind."

"Lead the way," James replied.

Sue And Jack At Vero Inn

Sue rolled over in bed, groggily glancing around to find a clock. Ten minutes past eight, and the sun was well above the horizon. However, being Sunday morning, it was her day to relax. She suddenly realized that she and Jack were naked. A smile appeared as she remembered the events of last night. Even more, she savored her remembrance of earlier in the day when she willingly and lustfully had given herself to Jack. Her smile continued, recalling that they both imbibed way too much last night to partake in sexual activity, yet here they lay naked in a hotel room together. She smiled approvingly at having the forethought to get a room instead of attempting to drive home. She slid out of bed and tip-toed to the bathroom to freshen up. "Thank goodness the hotel had supplied mouthwash and various toiletries," she thought, while letting the shower run, allowing the chill to be removed from the water.

Hearing the shower, Jack instinctively awoke and paused to gain his composure while contemplating this unique situation. Slowly, he slid open the shower door, visually noting the lavish lady and her scrumptious torso as he conspicuously slipped in behind her. A smile likewise dawned on his face, realizing where he was and how he had gotten there. Sheepishly, they looked into each other's eyes, and with encouraging thoughts, they accepted the encounter of the first overnight stay as an act of normalcy for the future.

"We're a good pair," remarked Sue, "we over-indulged to the point of intoxication, and here we are, naked in a shower." "It was quite a night," Jack quipped. "It started at your house and progressed into a delightful evening, even though I don't remember much after we left the party. But I think we both needed the escape, and this shower feels excellent right now. Turn around, and I'll wash your back, then you can wash mine." "Is that something like, I'll show you mine if you show me yours?" asked Sue. "No," laughed Jack, "we've already exposed our vitals, so now it's time to figure out what to do next."

Jack lathered the cloth with soap and gently washed Sue's shoulders and back, then slid downwards to her firm, round buttocks, legs, and feet. He knelt behind her as she turned around, permitting him to work his way upward, kissing her frontal parts. Gently, he kissed the protruding mound of her crotch as he bathed her abdomen with a soothing, circular motion and cleansing lather. Chills ran the entire length of her body as she parted her thighs, permitting his darting tongue to reach its intended target. Firmly she held his head against her vaginal mound, giving her the ultimate pleasure. After exquisite elation from the oral arousal, Sue returned the favor and cleansed Jack with the same lathering and oral stimulation. Standing upright and submitting to the sensation created by the pulsating shower, they embraced each other firmly. Their nude bodies pressed tightly together, permitting the dancing streams of water to emphasize their every emotion as they shared passionate love.

Once the intimacy subsided, they departed the shower and tenderly dried each other. Jack and Sue, wrapped in towels, stood on the balcony, hand in hand, gazing at the ocean, savoring the satisfaction of their recent passion, allowing the warm breeze to revitalize their bodies. Both were treasuring the peacefulness that their submission to lust had provided as they accepted that they were now more than just working partners. A knock on the door returned them both to reality. "Ah," said Sue, "breakfast has arrived at last." She wrapped a larger towel around her body, answered the door, and took the serving cart as Jack, hiding behind the door, handed the young man a generous tip. Sue said, "You should have seen the smile on his face. It was as if he knew what was happening here. Those guys know what's going on in almost every room. But I have to admit," Sue stated, "it was a little embarrassing with nothing on but a towel and your half-naked body crouched behind the door. The poor kid, we probably made his day." "You can say that again," Jack replied. "My smallest bill was twenty, so the lad got a nice tip. Let's eat before it gets cold," Sue stated.

"Regarding bills," Jack continued, "did you notice that guy we met last night? What was his name, Frank? Yeah, Frank James and his lady friend Clara Langford. I remember the little jokes when she introduced herself and him. He had a wad of bills that would have choked a gator. I can recall that he gave the bartender at least five fifty's. I am unsure what kind of change he got back, if any, but the bartender made out very well." "It wasn't the bills that caught my eye," Sue said. "Oh, was he appealing or something?" Jack asked. "No, silly, I only had eyes for you last night," she quipped. "However, I could have sworn he wore a large red ring when I first noticed him. I can't recall if it was a pinky ring, but I thought I saw it when he first sat down. Maybe it was a reflection when he lifted his glass; the lighting was dim and had a rosy tint. If he did have a ring, he must have taken it off before we started talking. He also reminded me of Jessie's sketches, but the darkness restricted visibility. There was just something odd about his actions. He avoided looking directly at us and purposely remained partially hidden behind Clara. Why would he do that? Perhaps Frank James is Jessie; he knew who we were, and that's why he acted as he did," Sue concluded.

"I didn't notice a ring," Jack remarked. "I wish you had mentioned it earlier at the bar. I could have paid more attention.

I saw him in the restroom, but men don't stare at each other in the john." "I possibly should have mentioned it," replied Sue, "but I let it pass when I didn't see it again. Besides, Clara was between us most of the time." "I noticed," replied Jack, "he didn't look directly at you or me and tried to remain obscured by her, so I didn't see him well enough or long enough to generate a sketch." "Neither did I," Sue stated. "But we need to check this out before leaving here today. I overheard them discussing that they were spending the night here. That is what gave me the idea to do likewise."

"Remind me to thank them," Jack jested, "but I agree on checking it out. Maybe someone here at the hotel knows Frank James, but not the outlaw." "That name sounds bogus to me now," said Sue, "and it could tie in with Jessie, Jessie James, and his brother Frank."

"Ok, sweetness, I surrender," Jack stated, "now eat your breakfast, then we can get dressed and look into your idea. Maybe it's women's intuition, and perhaps you saw a ring. Either one, I feel it is worth investigating." "Thanks for your consideration," Sue injected, "but I would rather not get dressed quickly. You look cute with that tiny hand towel trying to hide your manly parts, and I'm sure another hour will not damage our investigation." "An hour?" Jack quizzed. "An hour, my lovely lady, might damage my manly parts, but if you say so, an hour it is; I'm all yours." She laughed and stroked his manly part.

Back To Work

"Hello there, nice to see you again," Brad joked. "You go to a party with Sue in Vero, and we haven't seen or heard from you for a few days. What's up? Did you two elope or something?" "Nothing that major," answered Jack, "but we had a fantastic time. I debated about coming back at all. She is one hell of a woman. What actually happened is we encountered a guy at the party who just may have been Jessie. Unfortunately, we didn't realize it until the morning after the party. Sue recalled seeing him wearing a red ring, which he must have removed before it became noticeable. Thinking about it further, we matched portions of his facial detail, as we can recall, with Jessie's description. Based on those facts, Sue and I opted to stay an extra day and check it out further. We contacted the hotel employees regarding his identity, but no breaks. Now get this, Brad; he called himself Frank James and joked about not being the outlaw. I didn't associate it until Sue mentioned the ring and that Frank James was Jessie James's brother, which adds the name Jessie into the equation. There are just too many things to be more than a coincidence. The name, mannerisms, general description, flamboyant spending, and the possibility of a red ring make too many similarities to ignore. If he was Jessie, the prick was toying with us. He knew our identities because Clara, the lady he sat with, remembered Sue from the newspaper and briefly commented on the article. We made general inquiries with the local police but turned up nothing on Frank James. Not even a driver's license or phone number was listed. Sue will dig further into locating him and Clara Langford today. The only data the desk clerk told us was that Ms. Langford had reserved the room before the party. However, the gentleman paid the room charges in cash. The clerk could not recall details about the man. The clerk stated that it is common for ladies to reserve a room and pick up a guy to pay for it on party nights. They don't record tag numbers on party nights due to the crowd and the frequency of departures and arrivals. So, in a nutshell, we know nothing about them other than she indicated she was a local. Since it's Monday, Sue hopefully will have luck contacting her. Meanwhile, I'm kicking myself in the ass for not recognizing the available clues, but I am glad Sue recalled what she did."

Jessie Switches

"James, talk to me, James. Quit staring out the damn window and speak to me. It's Monday morning," Jessie stated, where the hell have you been? I don't know what you did yesterday or last night, but you're covered in blood. What the hell is going on, man?" "Ah, shit Jessie, I'm not sure what happened," James stammered, "but I think I may have screwed up. I went to the Vero Inn party and spent the night with a broad I met. We had fantastic sex the following morning. After the sex, she asked me if I wanted to go to her house for the day and relax around her pool. She said she had plenty to eat and drink at the house, and we could enjoy some time together and get to know each other a little better, so I followed her home. She lives in Orchid Isle and has a great house on the water with a pool. Upon arriving, she practically raped me on the front room rug with a wide open door. Not that I objected because she was a real hellcat of a screw, so what the crap. I surrendered and enjoyed it. After the orgy, we stripped and jumped naked into the pool. We then proceeded to talk about various things, including each other. Clara avoided telling me much about herself, which bothered me, but then I didn't tell her much about me. Both of us being naked in the pool, one thing led to the other, and we enjoyed some water aerobics with sexual overtones. That girl did like to screw, and she was almost insatiable. Around noon, we went inside, where she fixed a gourmet lunch. We remained stark-ass naked and enjoyed playing a little grab-ass as we ate. She had a beautiful body and didn't mind showing it. She was in awe that I could recoup so quickly between our sexual encounters and remarked about it as she intently watched my unit grow into another erection as she gently stroked it. Something about her made every nerve in my body tingle with desire: I started to think that she was the lady I had been looking for, very nice, well-mannered, petite, and the looks of a model, not to mention that she was a sex fiend. I had an uncanny passion for spending more time with her and looking forward to seducing her luscious tush in the coming days. Her body's natural movements as she cleared the table caused me to crave her lustfully, and the tabletop got well used. Thank goodness it was a sturdy wooden table. Looking straight into my eyes, she told me that I was the best she had ever had, but this day was for fun and fun only. I asked her to explain, and she told me about needing to sew her wild oats before getting married next week, and I was chosen to sew them. However, it is over after our orgy today ends, and from then on, she only gives herself to her fiancé. This bitch tells me this crap while she is humping my shaft while I'm sitting on top of her dinner table. Man, I couldn't believe what I was hearing from this little bitch while fucking my brains out. She had raped me as we walked through the front door, screwed me in the pool, fed me lunch naked, munched on my woody, spread open a sexual buffet on the kitchen table, played hobby horse on my shaft, and had the female balls to tell me that she's getting married and giving herself to her fiancé. What a fucking bitch, what a real bitch, man. I couldn't control myself. I lost it. I didn't call Zac, and I didn't consult with you. I just blew my frigging cool and made that little bitch bleed profusely and beg for mercy." "Oh, mother in hell, James, you lost it again," Jessie screamed, "just like you did with that Roslyn bitch, only this time you know what you did. You didn't rely on Zac or plan things ahead of time. You just did 'The Deed' on the bitch. She probably deserved everything you did, but losing your cool without me or Zac is dangerous, James. We must work and plan on doing "The Deed" together, or things will go astray, and the law will come hard on us. I think we're getting confused with all this role-swapping taking place. No matter, man, get your ass cleaned up. We better backtrack your little spree to check the status of things. We have to make sure you didn't fuck up and leave too much evidence behind. You did pretty well the other time you blew it, but I am concerned about this time. I haven't heard anything on the news this morning. So, with luck, nobody has reported her missing yet. What's her name, James? She is missing, isn't she, James? You did plant her on the farm, didn't you?"

"Oh hell, I don't remember Jessie. I think her name was Clara. I just don't remember what the fuck I did after she told me I was just a pre-marital orgy. The last thing I clearly remember is she was riding my dong, getting her rocks off, and telling me it was all just for fun. Ok, James, it's too damn late to worry about it now. What's done is done; now get your ass in the shower and wash that blood off. Then we'll clean up this mess; you've tracked blood everywhere. Nonetheless, I am glad you got some good sex from the ordeal. Things were starting to get a little horny around here, and I thought Zac and I would have to get hold of ourselves to relieve a little tension," Jessie quipped. "She does sound like a good screw, even though she was a bitch."

Chapter 16

Police Activity – Langford Murder

"Hi, Sue, Frank Arendas here," the voice on the other end of the phone stated. A quick chill ran down her spine as she instantly received a female hunch about why Frank was calling. "Hi Frank, what's new? Although, somehow, I know the answer to that question before you tell me." "Yeah," Frank said, "you got it right. Those leads you left for the night crew to follow up on concerning Clara Langford paid off. Detective Ron Howard took the info and ran with it. As you suspected, she is renting a house in Orchid Isle. Checking the residence, he found her car and a car registered to Wesley Carter parked out front. However, Howard has not been able to establish contact with anyone inside. Based on that and your data concerning the party, Judge Thompson will grant a warrant, which should be ready shortly. Can you meet me at the station and we will ride up together?" "Give me five minutes, Frank. I just got home and must put away a few things. I'll be there ASAP."

On the way to the station, Sue called Jack and informed him of the situation. "That's everything I know right now, Jack. I'll contact you as soon as we find out what is happening. Hopefully, the two of them are off somewhere and left their cars at home. Nonetheless, I'll call you as soon as I know." "Ok, Sue, and thanks for calling. I'll contact Brad, and we will be down tonight if there is a problem. You be careful and make sure Frank is with you."

"Yes, Daddy dear, I'll be a good girl," she quipped. "I'm sorry," Jack said, "I just worry about you." "Not to worry, lover, Frank and I are riding together; he is waiting for me at the station. Talk to you later, and love you."

Frank and Sue drove towards Orchid Isle, an upscale residential area a short distance north of Vero on the Intracoastal waterway, giving it a picturesque tropical atmosphere. Frank turned onto River Drive and proceeded toward the address. It was a large house with a pool and a deck overlooking the waterway with a horseshoe drive out front. The Carter car was parked in the driveway, Clara's car was in the garage, and the garage door was open. "I'm Detective Ron Howard; you must be Arendas and Gunther. Howard said I've been here almost an hour now, and there is no sign of life in the house." "That may be a poor choice of words," replied Sue. "You're new to the Task Force, aren't you?"

"Yes, Ma'am," he answered, "I just got assigned last week." "Welcome aboard, Ron, and let's hope this is a false alarm; otherwise, you may get initiated into the Task Force in a very nasty fashion. Sue and I will take the front door," said Frank. "Ron, you and your partner take the backside and use force only if necessary. If our suspect is inside, he is one mean mother; take him alive if possible, but don't play hero with this perp, understood?" "Yes, sir," Howard replied, "we'll cover the back; just keep us informed." "We'll take it slow, Frank said. "I have dispatch trying to locate a key so we don't have to kick the door down."

Frank knocked on the door persistently and rang the bell for several minutes. "I don't see or hear a sign of life," said Sue, "and I don't particularly like using that phrase." Just then, officers Crane and Barkowski arrived; the lights from their car reassured Frank and Sue that nothing was amiss in front of the house. Crane shouted, "Hey Frank, we got the master key from the landlord. If the tenant hasn't changed the locks, we'll help you gold shields do a B and E the easy way." "Get your ass up here, Crane; we have a valid warrant. Why the hell do you think I had dispatch send you for the key? I'm trying to avoid breaking the door down if we don't need to, and if this is what I hope it isn't, I didn't want the landlord here." "Ah shucks, Frank, you're confusing, but I wanted to arrest ya and take that good-looking sidekick of yours into custody." "Thanks for the flattery," mused Sue. "Now put away your handcuffs before I claim harassment and have your butt busted." "Yes, ma'am," Crane jested. Frank stated enough frivolity, "Open the damn door and do it properly in police fashion. Our perp may be inside, and I don't want to see you get your ass blown off before Sue gets a chance to bust it!"

Crane drew his weapon and took a position at the side of the door while Barkowski, Frank, and Sue stood with guns drawn and signaled Howard that they were about to enter. The key worked, and the door opened silently, allowing Crane to charge through with the rest following. Once inside, they carefully searched and cleared the front of the house, room by room. Sue and Frank ventured towards the master bedroom while the other two officers searched the rooms on the opposite side of the house. The house was a four-bedroom split plan with a large living area in the middle. The kitchen, dining area, and great room were in the rear of the house, nearest to the waterway and the pool. Frank slowly exited the great room and crept down the short hallway to the master bedroom, with Sue following. He knocked on the bedroom door several times, receiving no response. Gently twisting the knob, Frank opened the door. The room's darkness gave him an eerie feeling, and instantly, the smell of bleach and alcohol flooded the air. I'm not too fond of this situation, he told Sue. I think our boy has found another victim. He put on his rubber gloves and felt inside for the light switch. Flipping the switch brought light into the darkness, illuminating a horror scene far beyond what they had seen before. "Oh God," Frank choked, "you don't want to see this, Sue; this is the worst," yet he gagged and puked into his handkerchief. "Excuse me," he said as he brushed past her. "I need some air." Sue stopped the others from entering the room and immediately called the crime scene investigators, then Jack.

Trying to stifle the urge to heave her guts out, Sue slowly entered the bedroom with Crane immediately behind her. "Don't touch a thing," she told him, "and if you feel sick, head for the hall." "Holly hell," Crane hoarsely said, "the smell is putrid. I read past reports and heard horror stories but never thought it would be like this. This guy is a fucking sick-o, excuse me, Sue, but there is no other way of saying it." "I think you said it adequately," she replied. "Would you get the camera out of Frank's car for me, please?" "Sure, I could use some air anyway." Frank said, "No need to; I got the camera while I was there, but you can go out for some air Crane and ask Ron to take charge of securing the entire area as a crime scene. Tape off the grounds, and please keep the nosey neighbors away." "Sure thing, Frank; call if I can help. Tonight is one time I'm glad I haven't made detective grade yet, you guys earn your pay, and I must say, you damn sure are earning it tonight."

CSI Jeffery Perillo stood in dismay after his first walkthrough, rescanning the bedroom with apprehensions about where to start his report. "It looks like a slaughterhouse in here and smells like one as well. What the hell do you make of it, Frank?" "I'm not sure," Frank answered, "other than guessing that Jessie loaded blood into one of those high-powered water guns the kids play with and used it to paint the walls." "I was hoping that you had some revelations." "Just premature surmising on my part until I get all of my data back to the lab, Jeffery Perillo, but I would venture that there is more than one blood type creating this poor excuse of a Picasso on the wall. Take close notice of the difference in the color and texture of the blood splatters. That makes me assume that some of the blood is not human. I would say it's from an animal, perhaps a dog or cat, but it is not human. The large amounts of blood in the shower stall preliminarily indicate that he butchered the vics in the shower and then laid the body parts on the bed to bleed out, thus creating the blood pools on the mattress. We will know for sure once the blood is analyzed. The graffiti on the mirrors is consistent with past scenes, and the handwriting appears to have the same childish style. I would say that all the current indications point to the same perp. I believe we have one of the worst homicidal maniacs running around out there that anyone has ever seen." "I think I have to agree with what you said, Frank."

Brad And Jack – Langford Case

The new CD player Brad installed was emitting soft background music as Brad and Marci enjoyed their wine and the serenity of the night. They both had started to relax and were exchanging small talk when Brad's cell interrupted the peacefulness. "Brad, this is Jack. I hope I am not catching you at the wrong time, but Sue just called. It looks like Jessie has struck again." "Your timing is not great, Jack, but neither is your info. Where did she call from, and what's the situation?"

"I have the address, Brad. It's in Orchid Isle, north of Vero, around the Wabasso area." "I know the area," said Brad, "I'm on my way. I'll call you for detailed instructions when I head south of Sebastian." Marci kissed him on the cheek and told him to be careful. "She is getting acclimated to this life," Brad thought.

Jack and Brad arrived simultaneously as the CSI team was wrapping up their evidence collecting. "Hi, Jeffery," Jack said, "is it looking like Jessie?" "I think I summed it up a little earlier when I told Frank it's a fucking slaughterhouse. Excuse my description. It's the worst mess I've seen so far." Frank escorted Jack and Brad into the bedroom, highlighting similarities to previous scenes and a few unique items relevant to this case. "I don't see any stuffed animals," Brad said. "However, the pictures are all arranged similarly." "I searched the entire house," Sue commented, overhearing Brad's remark. "I didn't find stuffed animals or dolls that women tend to keep. I find that strange, but some women don't save those things. I'll check it out with friends and family." "Make sure forensics dust for prints in all the rooms," Jack stated. "The prick may have left his prints in rooms other than the primary scene." Sue answered, "I already instructed them to do that, finding no stuffed animals; I assumed he might have taken them." "I hope this was Jessie," Jack commented. "I don't want to think that there is more than one maniac out there."

Days passed without new leads, even though the Task Force had worked relentlessly. Jack's cell rang. "Hello Lover," he said. "Wow, replied Sue, you have me on your caller ID already, or do you call everyone lover?" "No way, sweet thing, I have reserved that name for you. What's the latest news? It must be good for you to call me before lunch." "Well, part of it is good," she replied. "The medical examiner is ready with a presentation and summation of his report. He wants to hold a briefing in the Grotto at three this afternoon. CSI found several good fingerprints. However, they are the same as in previous cases. Jessie left prints in the other bedrooms, the kitchen, the garage, and on the pool furniture. I asked the lab boys to run them against every database again. The check is incomplete and useless thus far, except for tying cases together. Can you and Brad attend the presentation?" Jack replied, "I'll be there, and I am sure Brad will also. If Marci has no plans, she can meet us for dinner after the briefing." "It sounds good," Sue said. "I'll call Brad right now; see ya later," Jack replied.

Jeffery's Report

The room was crowded with the Task Force and other select personnel from the various law enforcement agencies along the Florida Coast. "May I have your attention, please," asked Sue. "You all know why we are here. CSI needs to report on this case, so let me turn the meeting over to Dr. Jeffery Perillo, the Chief Medical Examiner for Indian River County, assisting the Grotto Task Force. Would you please hold all questions until his presentation is complete? At that time, we will have a question-and-answer session."

"Thank you, Sue, and good afternoon, ladies and gentlemen," Perillo stated. "I wish to start by saying that I have been involved with well over a hundred homicides during my career, and this is undoubtedly the worst case of inhumane slaughter I have ever seen. You received a written copy of my report, including significant photos of crime scenes. I will remind you of the agreement you signed when becoming part of the Task Force. All information gathered and divulged within our ranks concerning our cases is highly confidential. Detective Gunther controls all press releases and public disclosures. I expect to see none of this presentation repeated outside of these walls unless duly authorized. I shall keep this briefing informal and clarify which portions are based on fact and which are strictly speculative. The subjects of this case are Clara Denise Langford and her fiancé, Wesley Stephan Carter. We have no bodies for them, so I can only assume they are the victims. Their addresses and personal specifics are noted in the report. From the evidence gathered at the scene, both subjects are presumed deceased. However, that fact cannot be validated without bodies. DNA is still being processed, and not all results are available. The families are reviewing the personal items recovered from the scene. The evidence indicates that robbery played no part in this case, with no indication of forced entry, no traces of a struggle, nor were there obvious signs of drugs other than legal alcohol involved. It can be assumed the perpetrator was known by one or possibly both victims. Like other cases, it was limited to the master bedroom and the adjoining bath. These rooms are shown in the floor plan and described in the report. Physical evidence found within these areas indicates that human body dismemberment occurred mainly in the bathtub and the sink in the master bathroom. Forensics has proven that blood and tissue recovered were from one male and one female, the two alleged victims. Multiple sets of fingerprints were found. We can assume from Langford and Carter since they were the predominant prints, but we can not substantiate this without actual records. Neither have fingerprints in any known database. The other prints can not be identified but are the same as found in our other cases. The FBI is assisting in determining DNA and has linked DNA to that of

Langford and Carter. Other DNA found can be assumed to be the perps. Lanford's vaginal fluid was found on the carpet near the front door and the kitchen table. The lab test indicates the fluid was deposited at these locations within hours of the alleged murders. There was male fluid from the unknown perp found along with Langford's, signifying that heterosexual activity between those two occurred.

Now, let's review the crime scene areas. If you refer to photos numbered one through four, they will help clarify our findings. In the master bedroom, you can see large amounts of blood splatter on all four walls and the ceiling. The spatter pattern does not relate to a high-velocity arterial spatter that one might expect to see. It is more human-made by possibly slinging around a weapon or a bloody towel. DNA verified the blood to be from both victims. However, a third blood type was found among the spatter: a K-nine. The large pool of blood shown on the floor at the bedroom door was entirely from Mr. Carter. The smaller pool found on the throw rug under the window was K-nine blood. Take note now of photos five through seven, depicting the bloodstains on the bed. My summation is that they were caused by severed body parts placed on the bed. The distance between stains made me ascertain that body parts, not entire bodies, created the stains. I surmise body parts because if you look at bathroom photos eight through twelve, you'll see the mass amounts of blood in the tub and the sink. Several quarter-size chunks of human flesh were discovered in blood pools, plus minor remnants of human tissue and clumps of hair. All of which were determined to be from a male and a female. Indications are that the bodies we placed in the tub and body parts were severed and placed in the sink. Once the sink was full, the pieces were possibly moved to the bed. Blood drippings on the floor leading from the sink to the bed substantiate this theory.

Also, note in photo nine that shower curtain rings are still on the rod, but no curtain was found. Photo ten shows the word "BITCH" printed in childish-style letters on the cabinet mirror.

You have seen that word and print style in previous cases. As I noted in the report, the known facts are duplicates of previous cases. If the evidence and theory prove out, that will make us involved with the worst crime spree in the history of our area. The worst fact is, we have no frigging idea or the slightest clue as to who this bastard is. Suppose you excuse my language and excuse me for a moment. In that case, I will ask Detective Gunther to take the floor, allowing me a short pause before presenting my theory of this case."

"Thank you, Dr. Perillo," Sue said, "you earned a break. Here are a few pertinent bits of info in the report that should be highlighted. The suspect, we call Jessie, takes every precaution to cover his tracks, and he covers them well. Our competent staff of forensic scientists has scoured the entire scene, finding very little hard evidence pointing to a perpetrator. Obviously, he was there, but even the fingerprints found cannot prove it was him without apprehending him first. In this case, he used the victim's kitchen knife rather than his knife, as in the past. We believe he purposely left the knife, clean of prints, in the bathroom; thus, we can not prove he was the butcher. He cleansed portions of the area using the victims' bleach and left us the empty bottle. He arranged the pictures as in previous cases. However, no stuffed animals were found. We do not feel that a copycat could have had enough knowledge of previous crimes to have created this similar but horrid scene. Let's take a short break before Dr. Perillo returns with his theory based on a few proven facts."

Sue, Jack, and Brad departed from the meeting, found the coffee, and motioned for Frank to join them. Jack said, "All the evidence points to Jessie, but what about the minor differences? Were they on purpose or carelessness? Do you think he could be purposely trying to throw us off course, or is he changing his MO, and if so, why?" "That's a lot of questions wrapped in one sentence," Brad replied. "But we can't be sure of his reasoning about anything at this point." "I agree," Frank chimed in, "and you guys listen carefully to the upcoming theory that the CSI crew and Perillo derived. Their supposition not only makes sense, but it also makes you nauseous just to think that this happened. If the assumptions are in any way close to correct, this guy is a damn nut case. He has to be fucking insane. Excuse my language, Sue. This prick is off his rocker."

"I think he was abused as a child and most likely at his mother's hands," Brad surmised, "in my mind, that explains the word Bitch. He hates his mother and takes it out on any woman that reminds him of her." "That's possible," remarked Sue, "but if it was Jessie that Jack and I saw the other night, Miss Langford treated him pretty damn good. They spent the night together at the Inn, and I bet she treated him to anything he wanted. Langford was hanging all over him the entire evening." "That may well be the key," Brad replied. "Perhaps she treated him too damn good and then brushed him off. She did have a fiancé. Once he found that out, that alone could have blown his mind. Let's say they spent the night at the hotel, went to her place the following day, continuing the sexual episode, and he became aware of a fiancé. In his mind, that makes her a bitch. Perhaps his mother seduced and cast aside her male friends. Hell, she possibly abused and maybe even seduced her own son. That sure as hell could give cause for his violent tendencies towards women and regarding them as bitches. That's just my theory, and it is only a theory, but it makes sense to me." "Brad may have a handle on this nut," Sue commented. "His theory makes sense. Let's listen to Perillo's theory. I'm willing to bet he and Brad have this guy pegged."

Dr. Perillo stepped behind the podium again and cleared his throat as silence fell over the room. "Allow me to start with my theorized portion," he stated. "My theory is not documented in the official report. However, it is a theory based on a few facts I have not yet disclosed. You all saw the photos of the blood spatter on the walls and ceiling. The pattern depicts a circular motion around the room as if standing in one place and spinning around, allowing the blood to spray the walls and ceiling as you turn.

A gory example would be to dismember someone's arm at the shoulder, hold it by the hand, and swing it circularly over your head. The blood spurting from the severed end would create such a pattern. We all know blood exposed to air coagulates with time. Based on this fact, the coagulation level proves Miss Langford's blood was on the walls first, followed by the dog's blood and then Mr. Carter's. This timestamp indicates that Langford's blood was the first on the bed. The blood from Carter and the dog on the bed showed a coagulation time approximately one hour later than Miss Langford's. The blood on the bed coincides with the time frame on the walls.

The coagulation time adds merit to my theory that Miss Langford was the first to be killed. Her body was dismembered when Carter, accompanied by the dog, arrived. Hearing their arrival, the assailant hid behind the bedroom door and killed Carter and then the dog, thus a surprise attack leaving no signs of a struggle. Jessie's bloody handprints were on the door's inside surface, indicating he was behind it. Carter's blood was pooled on the floor near the doorway, supporting this concept. The coagulation time indicates that Carter's body lay by the door for thirty minutes. During this time, the perp finished the dismemberment of Miss Langford. Her body parts were laid on the bed, followed by the dog's carcass. Carter's body was then dragged to the bathroom, where he was similarly dismembered and his parts placed on the bed. With both bodies cut into smaller pieces, they would be much easier to conceal and carry. The perp used the shower curtain and perhaps some towels to wrap the parts in, thus completing his ghoulish task.

Why he spattered the blood around the room is unknown. I could not fathom any apparent reason other than simply being a sadistic individual. The removal of the bodies, the blood in the bathroom, the pictures, and the word "BITCH" has become his signature. Detective Gunther mentioned that he covered his tracks well, even though this episode appears more spontaneous with much less planning than his previous episodes. The Conti case is the only case that indicated impulsive actions like this one. Perhaps we should compare these two cases extensively and see what develops. This sick individual was named Jessie based on references to that name in earlier cases, and I honestly believe, based on the facts, that this massacre is the work of Jessie. I want to thank all of you for taking the time to come to this presentation. Now, please apprehend this bastard."

"Thank you, Dr. Perillo," Sue stated. "You presented a fascinating report, and I am confident that we will read it carefully. Now, Task Force members, let me give you some general data to ensure we are all on the same page with our information. In the past, Jessie has been extremely vigilant about cleansing the scene and not leaving evidence. We believe the arrival of Mr. Carter in the middle of his goulash game disturbed his balance of thought, causing him to become bemused. Likewise, the dog could have played a role in Jessie's confusion. The neighbors noticed nothing unordinary around the Langford house and thought nothing of Carter's car being in the drive overnight. Being her fiancé's car, that was a common occurrence. No one but Mr. Price noticed a strange car parked by the vacant lot next to Langford's house. He is the neighbor to the east and swears he heard a car start up and leave just before sunrise. He thought it was Carter and was surprised to see Carter's car still in the driveway and the other car gone when he fetched his morning paper. Mr. Price's wife informed us that Miss Langford had dozens of stuffed animals, yet none were found. Jessie's work with stuffed animals in prior cases is well-known. We can only speculate that he took them for some ungodly reason. You now have Dr. Perillo's and the CSI crew's theory, based mainly on fact with limited speculation. Please read the entire report, see if you agree with the theory, or perhaps have other thoughts. The complete DNA results are still unfinished, but we doubt it will shed much more light than we now have. When finished, we will let you know. There is an artist sketch in your handouts arrived at by friends of the victims. Jack Baird and I think the drawing is a good likeness since we unknowingly associated with him briefly at a recent event. We feel he resides in the local area and is upstanding in the community. Jessie perhaps has something to do with funerals or works in a related field. Look for an average-built man in very fit condition, mid-aged or slightly younger, somewhat introverted, who secretly hates women but desires them sexually and cannot tolerate rejection. It is believed that he was possibly abused mentally, physically, and sexually as a child, raised by an overbearing mother, and may have schizophrenic tendencies. He is the type you meet on the street daily: nicely dressed, well-groomed, and pleasant-looking. However, his demeanor can change quickly. Please keep the Task Force advised of any findings. We must work together. If you see this man, proceed with caution; he is considered extremely dangerous. Good luck, guys, and let's all pray that we get this SOB before he finds another victim."

Calie Brushes Off Jessie

The Calie phone rang, startling James as he attempted to comprehend the thought of having a third personality. Realizing the "Calie phone" was ringing, he brushed his thoughts aside and summoned his third person to answer the call. "Hi, Calie," Jessie said in a musical voice, "how are you, my lovely? How was your trip to Grandma's, and when did you get home?" "Whoa there!" She stammered, "One question at a time: I'm fine, the trip was enjoyable, and I got home last night around ten. I didn't call you as I thought it might be too late. Instead, I waited until this evening to call because I needed to consider things before talking with you. I'm unsure how to say this, Jessie, but we should discontinue our daily calls. It will be best if we don't see or talk to each other anymore. I want to be honest with you, Jessie. I accidentally met that old boyfriend who joined the Army, and he now lives near Granny. For some reason, that old spark is still glowing. He and I were with each other almost every minute I was there, and he is moving to Daytona Beach. Not knowing that I lived in Daytona, he had ironically applied for a transfer and got it. Based on everything that happened while I was with him,

I am optimistic that we will rekindle our relationship as it once was, or I should say we have already rekindled it. You have been super sweet, Jessie. I think highly of you, but after much deep thought, I don't feel it would ever work out between us. I am sorry, and I hope you understand." "Of course, I understand," Jessie said in a raspy voice. "I am very sure Zac will understand as well. Zac is very familiar with such matters, and he understands them thoroughly." "I don't understand, Jessie. What on earth are you saying? Who is Zac?" Calie quizzed. Her voice echoed the questions as the 'Calie phone' went dead.

"What's wrong, Jessie? You seem very disturbed," James questioned. "When I thought things were going smoothly, and I would be the one to settle down and bring peace to you and Zac, a frigging bitch arises," Jessie answered. "You know, James, I know what needs to be done and what you would do. Hey Zac, Zac, old buddy, join us and let James devise a plan."

Chapter 17

Jack And Sue – Gravedigger Theory

When his phone rang, Jack had been busy at his desk for several hours, deeply engrossed in reviewing the various cases. "Hi, handsome." Sue said, "I am in Melbourne and have coordinated with the local law to check out the Melbourne area's funeral homes. Would you be interested in joining me?" "I'll be more than happy to," he answered. "I need to get out of here for a while," Jack replied. "My eyes are going crossed. I have too much Jessie crap on my mind." He asked, "Do you want to pick me up or meet me somewhere?" "I'll pick you up in about ten minutes," she answered." I'm at the gas station down the street from your office. Give me time to top off the tank, and I'll be there." Jack replied, "I'll be anxiously waiting, and will you be spending the night?" "Is that an invitation?" She asked. "It's a standing invitation," he replied, "and you know that you're more than welcome. Your being here makes for a highly desired situation." "Yeah, I bet you tell all the girls that, don't you?" "No," he said, "just the good-looking ones who wear a badge." Then Sue quipped, "a badge is the only thing I will wear tonight. Now that we've settled that subject, the tank is full, so get yourself ready, Mister FBI. I am heading your way as we speak." They were on their way to the first of several funeral homes in minutes.

"It's getting late in the afternoon," Sue stated. We've questioned owners and employees at every funeral home in the area and came up with nothing. "You're right, Sue. We've determined that no person in the funeral business around here fits the profile. At least we can write off the Melbourne area as Jessie's domain. That write-off is an accomplishment, plus an enjoyable afternoon with a sexy female cop makes for a productive day. I still believe that Brad is right," Jack continued, "Jessie is somehow connected with death, other than murder. But maybe the connection is not quite as evident as a funeral home. Perhaps he's a florist, a gravedigger, or something of that nature."

"Damn," interjected Sue, "you may have an idea." "Perhaps he works at a cemetery and is the groundskeeper or digs graves." Why the hell didn't I think of that?" she questioned. "That's why I'm FBI, and you're just a cop," Jack said jokingly. "Right," she sneered, "and after that remark, I think I will get a hotel room at the beach. Who are you sleeping with tonight?" "Sorry, my lady," said Jack, "I didn't mean to offend the law, and I was looking forward to seeing your badge." "Ok, smart ass, she replied, but only because I think I love ya." "Wow," Jack stammered, "your wish is my command." "Here's your first command," she ordered. "Get your hand off my leg so I can concentrate on driving, then get on the phone and see if Brad and Marci want to meet us at some romantic restaurant for dinner. If all goes well tonight, Mr. FBI, I may let you polish my badge." "I bet I can make it sparkle," he replied.

Brad suggested The Sea Room, a well-established eatery with a cozy back room that provides ambiance, service, privacy, and fantastic food. Seated in a corner booth, permitted the foursome to discuss the day's findings and Jack's new gravedigger theory. "I think you may have hit on more than a theory," commented Brad. "Jessie mentioned that he had a funeral to conduct. Maybe he was facetious and is involved with putting them into the ground, not the funeral service, as we have been thinking. Maybe, just maybe, that is why we haven't found any of the bodies. Hell, he buried them all. He might have access to burial sites and bury them himself. How much simpler can you get? You may have uncovered the answer, Jack." "Excuse me, would you all care for another round of drinks," the waiter asked. "Yes, answered Marci and Sue in unison; we need to get their minds off work for a while." "Touché," answered Brad, "we have been ignoring you, lovely ladies. Let's have a nightcap, then go to my place. We can all sit on the boat and enjoy the rest of the evening." "That sounds pleasant, but maybe next time," Jack replied. "When we finish this round, I need to return to my condo. I have to check out a badge." "A badge," asked Brad, "what's with the badge?" "Don't you dare answer that," Sue quickly stated with a reddened face. Silent smiles concluded the evening.

Sue called first thing in the morning as Jack prepared breakfast. "Listen, Frank, and think about what I am saying very carefully. We contacted every nearby funeral home and developed no leads on Jessie. The frustration caused Jack to have a brainstorm, with which Brad and I both agreed. Jessie may be involved with funerals, but not from the ceremonial end. Contemplate him as a gravedigger, florist, groundskeeper, or funerals-related job. He commented about funerals; maybe he digs graves, covers them, plants sod on the grave, places the headstone, etc. Many associated efforts could be considered part of a funeral." "I see what you're saying," replied Frank. "I'll get some of the team working on that concept today. How about you? Are you staying up there or heading back?" "I'll stay for the rest of the day and possibly tonight. While here, I'll check out our new concept in this area." "Ok," Frank said, "tell Jack and Brad hello, and call if you come up with anything; I'll do the same."

The Cemetery Questioning

"Might I help you, gentleman?" "Yes, ma'am, showing their IDs, I am Detective Morris, and this is Detective Barrett. We are with the Vero Beach Police Department and would like to ask Mr. Zachary some questions." "Oh," Mrs. Oliver replied, "I hope it is nothing serious. Mr. Zachary is out of town for a few days, visiting friends." "No, ma'am," responded Morris, "it's nothing serious." "Perhaps you could answer some of our questions?" "I'll try," she replied. "Here are some composite sketches of the man we seek. Please look at them and see if one of your employees resembles these sketches." "Indeed," she said, "but what has this person done?" "We are not at liberty to divulge the details, ma'am. He is a person of interest related to some missing-persons cases we are investigating." "I see," she murmured while looking at the sketches. "We have five employees on the grounds, none resembling the sketches. They are all older gentlemen and have been employed here for at least twelve years. This business is family-owned, and they treat their employees very well. Mr. Zachary inherited it from his father, whom most of us worked for before his accidental passing. The elder Mr. Zachary and Mr. Gibbons, a former partner, built up this business from nothing many years ago, and now, young James has done an excellent job expanding it even further." "Young James?" Asked Morris. "Yes," she answered, "he is in his thirties, and that's young to me," she snickered. "He is a delightful young man, but as I said, he is currently out of town. James is a distinguished-looking man with little to no similarity to your sketches." "We thank you for your time, Mrs. Oliver. Please call us if you encounter anyone who fits the description on these fliers. May we leave a couple of copies with you?" "Of course," she replied, "and I will call should I see him." Mrs. Oliver took the sketches into James's office and placed them in his "to-do" basket. "James will undoubtedly enjoy this, and that one sketch does resemble him somewhat. However, I wasn't about to divulge the similarity to the law. I feel it is time that James and I have a little talk when he gets home. I do believe the time has come," she murmured.

Sue Tells Of Calie's Reported Missing

Brad and Marci had just returned home from the store when Jack called. "Hi guys, are you busy?" "No, just putting the groceries away; we needed a little restocking. I was busy admiring Marci's cute butt when she bent over to put the cans on the bottom shelf." "I hate to interrupt your illicit thoughts, but if you don't mind, Sue is in town, and she has some interesting info that I think we need to discuss." "By all means, come by," Brad said. "If we are not in the house, we are on the boat. Just be advised, Marci and I grabbed a quick bite to eat while shopping, so if you're hungry, bring a take-out with you. We have plenty of beer, wine, and scotch if the topic gets serious." "Understood, we will be there in about half an hour." Brad relayed the information to Marci and went to the dock to straighten up the boat.

The doorbell rang in almost precisely thirty minutes. "Damn, you guys have good timing. Your arrival is right on the money," Marci said. "Come on in. Brad is out back with a cooler of beer, and regardless of what he said, we can light the grill if you have not eaten. I have plenty of burgers or dogs that we can fix quickly." "No thanks," said Sue, "the noble FBI man with an expense account treated me to a big burger on the way over here, and I still have gastronomical reoccurrences." "I understand," said Marci. "How about a seltzer for the tummy?" "Skip the seltzer," Sue quipped. "I'll have a nice cold beer." They settled into the boat's cockpit, enjoying the warm summer evening, cold beer, and congenial companionship. Jack stated, "Now we are all comfortable; let Sue tell you her latest tidbit concerning Jessie."

Sue stated, "The Task Force received a call from Daytona Beach P. D. today. They recalled our bulletin concerning missing women and decided to contact us. It seems that they have a woman reported missing. Her name is Calie Lucas. There appears to be some similarity to our cases. She was recently associated with a tourist in Daytona, going by Jessie, who said he was from the south-central Florida area."

"If he is our Jessie, he registered at the Adams Mark using the name Jessie Thornton. He and Miss Lucas established a brief and rather hot relationship. A bartender at the Mark, a close friend of Miss Lucas, indicated that she was very concerned about Lucas not being home or stopping by the bar frequently as she usually does. She also stated that something did not seem right about the guy Calie was seeing. According to her, he was one person one minute, then someone else the next; he was nice but aloof and weird. She remembered that he mentioned being from central Florida and alluded to a city on the coast, south of the cape, but she couldn't recall the name.

Daytona PD checked him out from the hotel registry info and found that the tag on the car he drove was traced to a John Coffee in Huntsville, Alabama. The Huntsville authorities located Mr. Coffee, who is seventy-two years old. He has not been more than fifty miles from home in years, and his alibi is rock solid: kids, family, etc. Mr. Coffee owns an older model car that still has the correct tag on it.

We can only assume that Thornton's tag was fake. With the subject turning into a dead-end, the lead on Jessie went cold. The room he stayed in was reoccupied and cleaned a few times before checking it, so there were no leads. Everyone who inner-acted with this Jessie character stated that he was very private with his personal information and avoided facial contact. Even the parking attendants don't recall getting a good look at him. It is like he was there, but he wasn't. No one can give a detailed description, just generalities that align with our current data."

"What about her house? Was that a similar scenario?" Brad asked. "No," Sue answered, "if he was our Jessie, this part is puzzling. According to the reports, her small beach house, which she recently moved into, was clean and neat, except for one room in the process of painting. There were no apparent signs of a struggle or altercation. They dusted for prints but found none that could not be verified; all prints came from Calie's friends who have alibis and are far above suspicion."

"However," Sue continued, "there is one more possible link to Jessie. The bartender, Judith, said that Calie had dozens of stuffed animals, but none were found in her house. Calie collected stuffed bears and other kinds of furry critters that you win from those game machines. Guys frequently vied for her attention by winning them for her, and she would reward them with a friendly kiss. She also mentioned that she visited Calie's new cottage, and Calie had found cozy little nooks in all the rooms for her animals. Anyway, no animals were found." Sue stated, "With Calie missing, the name Jessie, referrals to central Florida, and a fake tag indicate that the Task Force should be involved and check it out. I would say that there is a hell of a lot of similarities." Brad asked, "What does Frank think?" "He agreed," answered Jack, "and he felt as we do. It sounds like Jessie, so he would like you and me to take the lead since it is outside his jurisdiction."

Sail to Daytona

Brad said, "Jack, I hate to say it, but we should postpone our St. Augustine trip. It would require too many days out of the area and off the case. But here's a suggestion: We could sail to Daytona and spend a few days looking into this new development. I understand that Ponce Inlet is a real challenge if you have never been through it before, and the Halifax Marina is one of the nicest on the entire east coast. It will take a day to sail there, and we can rent a car." "Hold on a second," said Jack. "I would love to do that, but unfortunately, I am not half-assed retired like some people I know. However, there is nothing to say that you and Marci can't sail up. Sue and I can meet you so we won't have to rent a car. That is if Vero PD gives Sue the time off?" Sue replied, "I'm sure I can get the travel authorized based on the data." "Good," Brad said, "we can all stay aboard the Miss-T and save the Bureau and Vero PD some expense money." Jack commented, "I have a few things to clear up at the office in the morning, then Sue and I will meet you at the marina in Daytona." "It sounds like a plan," Brad replied.

"Marci and I will leave at dawn and be there mid-afternoon. Call when you guys leave Vero, and please contact the Daytona PD and let them know we are coming. I'll call first thing in the morning," Sue answered. They finished their beers and kept the rest of the evening on a more social and pleasant basis.

Brad and Marci left the dock at 4:00 a.m. Marci had grown

accustomed to early morning departures on sailing days, and this seemed like any other day except for a reason. They cleared the Canaveral locks on the first opening and headed straight out of the port. Clearing the inlet and into open water, the wind was a brisk twelve knots out of the west, reducing the wave action to a minimal offshore swell. Brad engaged Tilley, hoisted the main, and unfurled Genny. He adjusted the sail for a port beam reach, and the sleek haul heeled and settled into a comfortable eight-knot cruise.

Marci was below preparing her version of egg muffins as the sun inched above the horizon. "Is it coffee?" asked Brad. "Aye, that it tis, my illustrious captain," she replied, as she poured a steaming cup, added a dab of creamer, and handed it through the companionway. "Thank ya, Matie," he responded as he placed the cup into the holder on the binnacle and made a minor adjustment to Tilley. "Where in the hell have you been all my life?" Brad asked. "Well, it's for certain, I have not been in your galley, she replied, but I do wish I had been in the captain's quarters much sooner." "Thanks for the compliment," Brad commented, "now come on up here and enjoy the beautiful morning." "The muffins are almost done. I shall be top side shortly," she replied. The muffins outdid all the landlubber versions, the coffee was perfect, and the sail was steady and true. Much to Marcie's delight, several bottle-nosed dolphins played friskily alongside the Miss-T, adding perfection to the morning.

The breeze remained constant, and the Ponce Inlet bell buoy was off the port bow as Brad fired up the diesel. "The sailing has been great, but I prefer the added security of 'Old Nell' when entering an inlet," Brad explained to Marci, who looked disappointed at the sound of the diesel and the smell of exhaust. "You're the Captain," she sighed. "I trust your judgment." Brad noted that the elapsed time was less than expected due to the calm seas and steady wind. "I am re-calculating our ETA at the marina to be there around 1730." He called the marina on the VHF to confirm his slip and give them his ETA. Halifax responded with his confirmation and advised him to contact the evening security guard on VHF 16 when entering their channel. The guard would assist with dockage and check him in for his stay. Brad navigated the tricky waters of Ponce Inlet with Marci at his side, observing his every move.

"Just trying to learn from the pro," she stated as she kissed his cheek. "No problem," he answered. "Take the helm for a minute while I check the chart." The Miss-T cruised swiftly up the Intracoastal with the assistance of an incoming tide and the brisk wind. By 1730, they were secure at the dock and stowing the gear. "That was one fantastic sail on a beautiful day," Marci sighed as she wrapped her arms around Brad, giving him a warm hug and kiss. "Aye, 'twas a great sail," Brad voiced like a pirate, "but it was the luscious first mate, her galley preparations, frequent toddies for the body, and the occasional nude sunbathing that topped off the day for me." "Relax, El Captain; the best is yet to come," joked Marci. "Oh, by the way, I need to know the nicknames for all your boat items. You have Tilley the auto-pilot, Nell the diesel, Genny the fore-sail, Mighty the main, Sticky the anchor, and what else do you have named?"

Brad replied, "You know all the important ones, but I would like to name my first mate, Babe." "Sounds ok to me, but why, Babe?" she questioned. "Well, it's that cute butt of yours; when I see it, I would like to rub Baby oil all over it." "Goodness," she said, you've been calling me that frequently, "and now that I know your hidden meaning, please get the oil. Babe will be in the aft cabin."

Brad's cell rang as usual when things began to warm up, breaking the spell. He managed to say hello, trying not to divulge the current activity. "Hi Brad," Sue giggled, sensing her interruption. "I hope you're at the dock or at least on auto-pilot. Jack and I are in Port Orange, heading north on US1. We just passed Dunlawton Ave. How do we get to the marina?" Brad quickly gave directions, told her to call when entering the parking lot, and returned to the oiling Babe. A short while later and gratefully satiated, Marci strolled up the dock to greet Jack and Sue at the gate. Marci explained, "The guard only had one gate key for us tonight. We can get more keys in the morning. We will probably be together most of the time tonight." "Not to worry," said Sue, "we'll make due; this marina is very nice. Other than the circumstances, and regardless of them, I believe Jack and I will enjoy our stay in Daytona." "Likewise," said Marci, "but we've had a head start on you guys." "Oh, is that what you call it now?" Sue jested as they headed for the boat.

After stowing Sue and Jack's gear and settling them aboard, Brad obtained directions from the guard to the beach and the Adams Mark hotel. They were duly impressed with the hotel as the valet approached the car, opened their doors, and asked Jack if they were hotel guests. "No, just visiting for the evening, part pleasure and part business. Please park the car; we will pick it up in an hour or so." "My pleasure, sir," the valet responded, giving Jack a claim ticket. Brad handed the young man a tip, and the foursome entered the hotel. Sue paused to call Detective Don Malott of the Daytona PD to inform him of their actions. "Welcome to Daytona," he stated. "Go to the main lobby bar and talk with Judith, the bartender. She's a friend of Calie and knows much about her. I informed her earlier that you were coming, and she will keep your involvement quiet. You can trust this gal; I've known her for a long time. Give me about thirty minutes, and I will meet you there. In the meantime, feel free to talk with Judith and enjoy your first night here." Sue returned the cell to her purse and remarked that everyone seemed very friendly in Daytona. "Let's find the lobby bar."

"Hi folks, my name is Judith. What may I get for you tonight?" "Hello, Judith. Detective Malott told us to contact you; my name is Sue Gunther. I'm with the Vero Beach PD. Jack Baird and Brad Ashley are with the FBI, and our good friend Marci is Brad's significant other." Judith used her penlight to illuminate their badges and replied, "Nice to meet ya'll. Don told me you would be here. Please take a seat at the east end of the bar. It is out of the way and has a little better lighting." Once seated, Judith fixed their drinks and asked a few questions about what was happening with the investigation.

Sue answered, "We aren't at liberty to divulge much information, and we know very little about what the Daytona authorities have found. Detective Malott said he would be here shortly. Until then, may we ask you a few questions?" "Sure," Judith answered, "fire away; I want to help. Calie and I are relatively close, and I am very concerned." Brad led off the questioning, "Ok, Judith, first, tell us what you know about this guy named Jessie Thornton and Calie's involvement with him." "Wow, you're asking for a book, but there are many blank pages," Judith said and began describing Jessie. She addressed his actions, mannerisms, and even how he dressed, but very little about his facial characteristics.

"One thing I thought odd was that he never looked straight at you or made eye-to-eye contact," she said. "It seemed he tried to conceal his face as much as possible. Being in the bar business has always bothered me. This entire bar is dark for business reasons. I can barely see your faces; this is the better-lit area. However, Jessie stayed in the darker areas, and whether he was alone or with Calie didn't matter. He sat at that table in the far corner because the light was dimmer, and he was alone most of the time. I was usually busy with little time to yak with him. As a result, I didn't get to know him very well. On one occasion when he went berserk for a minute or two after Calie mentioned something about being a bitch. He was like a different person. It took Calie a few minutes to calm him down, and I even had to assure him she was not a bitch. However, Calie seemed enthralled with him, and she normally judges people well, so I accepted her judgment."

"Calie told me she had met Jessie on the beach and that he was a real southern gentleman," Judith continued. "I suspected they had one or more sexual encounters, but she never confirmed that. As far as I could tell, he regarded her highly and treated her accordingly. After he left Daytona, I know Calie kept in touch and remarked several times about talking with him. A few weeks ago, she visited her Grandmother and mentioned before she left that Jessie would be returning to Daytona as soon as she got back. Calie went to her grandma's house, and I have not seen or heard from her since, nor have I seen or heard from Jessie. That, plus I found out she did not go to work or notify them of being out, made me a little concerned. I have a key, her car is in the drive, her suitcase is in the closet, and her dresser drawers appeared full, so she has returned. Maybe she went to see Jessie, but no one heard anything, which is not her style. I did not call her Grandmother as I did not want to cause undue concern."

"If that prick did something to her, I swear, I'll kill him." "Relax," said Sue. "No one knows what has happened, but we will find out if you'll give us time." Jack brought out the sketches and asked Judith to review them. She confirmed a slight resemblance but couldn't make a positive ID. "Remember," she said, "I never got a good look at him. I mostly got glances in this dim lighting." Detective Malott approached as Judith was evaluating the sketches and finishing her story. "Hi Judith, I was hoping you could come in tomorrow and give our sketch artist a description, but that doesn't look likely from what I just overheard. Now, let me introduce myself to these fine people." Judith nodded and fixed another round of drinks as the introductions took place. The rest of the evening was spent discussing Callie's and Jessie's interaction based on Judith's knowledge and informing Malott of the Jessie scenario from the Task Force.

As the dawning sun lit the sky, the day came early for Miss T's crew and guests. "Whoa," said Brad while fixing coffee, "I sure as hell did not want to get out of that bunk after a full day of sailing and a long night of business." "I know just how you feel," replied Jack, "and I didn't sail. The girls have the right idea: stay in the bunks and sleep it off." "I'm awake," shouted Sue. "Likewise," shouted Marci from the aft cabin. "Is it coffee yet?" "It's almost done, ladies," laughed Brad. "Get dressed, have a couple of cups to wake up, and then go to a place the guard told me about for breakfast." "That's the best idea I have heard today, but then the day is merely beginning," Jack quipped, "and by the way, the vee-birth is exceptionally comfortable. I am very impressed." "Thanks," Brad said, "you guys know you're welcome." A short while later, they enjoyed a morning treat at a riverside café. The latest findings and the possible links to Jessie were the primary topics, occasionally interrupted by the tranquil view of a sailboat passing by the windows.

"Today should be interesting," remarked Sue. "Detective Malott is going to take us to Calie's beach house. Based on his verbal description, we may be able to associate something with our cases. If so, that would be a definite link to Jessie rather than just speculation. Please don't misunderstand; I would rather believe Calie has gone off somewhere for a day or two and is not another one of his victims. However, if she is a vic, Daytona Beach will be the farthest north we've known him to travel. That may mean he is letting our area cool off or changing the venue. It's also possible that he suspects we are getting close to him, and he relocated." "You may be right on all counts," Jack replied. "However, let's hope that Calie is safe somewhere."

Malott drove into the marina parking area just as they had returned from breakfast and were still by the car. "Good timing," replied Brad. "I'll ride with Malott, and you and Sue follow. That way, we won't tie up Don longer than necessary." Marci kissed Brad goodbye, waved to the others, and returned to the boat as the two cars departed. They drove to the beach, turned south on A1A for a short distance, and then into the driveway for Calie's cottage. It was a quaint little place, and Sue was eager to see the inside. "Oh boy, could a person fix this place up to be a real dollhouse," she commented, "Calie made a real deal on getting this as a singles pad." "Let's pray she is still around to enjoy it, Jack stated," breaking Sue's feminine thoughts. "It is a super beach home," Malott added. "Now let me open the door, and you can see the inside. Nothing has been touched other than forensics doing their job, which revealed nothing to indicate foul play."

Judith has been the only person to provide a potential clue from the house, which is the absence of the stuffed animals. Stepping through the front door, the three Jessie hunters noticed the distinct and familiar odors mixed in with fresh paint. "Did your CSI crew find traces of bleach or alcohol in any of the rooms?" Brad asked Malott. "Not that I recall," he stated, "but I get a faint aroma of something. They did note that it appeared that she was cleaning and painting the place." "That's possible," Brad said, "but if it isn't too much trouble, have them recheck, and if they find any traces of bleach or alcohol, have them determine the brands. You people were unaware of the cleaning chemicals from previous cases, but it is in the reports we gave you last night." "I'll contact CSI right now," replied Malott as he retrieved his cell phone and hurriedly made a call.

"CSI will be here shortly," Malott informed them. "In the meantime, let me tell you what a neighbor said." He stated, "He saw Calie taking a suitcase into the house late Saturday evening. She waved at him and remarked about the temperature. He did not notice if she stayed home or went out that evening, but he saw her Sunday morning retrieving her newspaper from the drive. Later that afternoon, while walking his dog at about 3 o'clock, a dark-colored van arrived with a man driving, but he paid no real attention to him. He also told us that the van was still there around 11:00 p.m. when he again walked his dog. The van was gone in the morning, but he had no idea when it left. Besides that, no one heard or noticed anything that would cause alarm. A few other neighbors saw the van, but they also paid little attention. Calie was new in the neighborhood, so the neighbors knew little about her habits or visitors."

The three intently perused the cottage's rooms, searching for any trace of evidence that might have been overlooked. "I have a terrible feeling," remarked Sue. "Due to painting, I understand the pictures removed from the walls, but I notice they are lined up in the hallway, on the floor, leaning against and facing the wall. That's too coincidental to ignore. There also appear to be more pictures lined up than would be in just one room." "You might be right," replied Jack from down the hall. "There are no pictures in the other bedroom. And I don't see any in the house's other rooms," remarked Malott. "I am also concerned that the room being painted was her bedroom," stated Brad. "Ask your CSI to check for blood traces under this fresh paint. Also, check out the bathroom thoroughly; it appears to have been washed down, but traces may still exist." "Damn," stated Malott, "there are similarities between what you told me, and these painted areas look scattered on the wall. It's not applied in a systematic pattern like you would usually paint. I had better brief CSI of every detail you told me and have them recheck the house." "Do that," Jack said, "and I am calling the Grotto right now to have all of our data transmitted to you. In the meantime, dig into everything you can on Calie and this Jessie Thornton character. He possibly has returned to our area, so we will head back and see if we can hopefully locate him there."

Brad requested, "Let us know what your CSI finds as soon as their new report arrives. I feel confident they will discover bleach and alcohol, and the brands will be identical to those we found. If so, the van, no stuffed animals, Jessie's name, a central Florida connection, and the pictures take away all doubt. I feel we have a link. That being the case, we want you to provide a representative to work with our Task Force and help us catch this SOB." "I'll do that, said Malott, and I will appoint myself to that position right now."

Leave Daytona And Return To Work

Brad, Sue, and Jack went to the boat, picked up Marci, and went for dinner near Ponce Inlet. With full stomachs and a couple of adult beverages, they returned to Miss-T, relaxed, and retired for the night. "Good morning, Sue. May I pour you a coffee?" Marci asked. "Yes, please, and may I say, what a fantastic weekend," Sue answered. "Regardless of the circumstances, I have thoroughly enjoyed these past few days, even though it was limited to the dock. I can understand why you and Brad love the boat so much. Speaking of the guys, where are they?"

Marcie said, "Brad heard of a donut shop nearby that bakes donuts that melt in your mouth. He and Jack left a few minutes ago to get us some." "Sounds good," Sue replied, "and since they are gone, may I ask a question?" "Sure, go ahead, but I'm noted for direct, honest answers," Marci quipped. "Well, all I want to know is this: the vee birth, as you boaters call it, is it soundproof?" Marci just laughed and told her that the noise was pretty well contained, "However, being part of a boat floating on the water, it takes very little motion to cause some rock and roll." "Oh god, I never thought of that. Now, I am embarrassed." "Don't be embarrassed. Brad and I go by an old sailor saying, 'If the boat's a rocking, don't come knocking.' Besides, we are all friends and adults, and to be truthful, the rocking generated some stimulation in the aft cabin."

"Ok, ladies," Brad shouted as he and Jack boarded the boat. "The doughnuts are hot, and we hope the coffee is too." Marci and Sue, noticing the boat's rocking motion as the men boarded, just giggled as they prepared the coffee. "What more could you ask for?" Jack asked. "Hot doughnuts, coffee, two gorgeous women, a seaworthy boat, and a picture-perfect morning. It's just a damn shame some of us must return to work." "Don't say I didn't ask you guys to sail up with us," Brad noted. "That you did," commented Sue, "but if I spent any more time in that vee-birth, I am afraid I would set up housekeeping there. I had the most pleasant night's sleep in a long time." "We noticed you enjoyed it," Brad joked, "and you both are welcome any time." "Thanks," Jack said, "we did enjoy it. However, it is Monday, and we laborers must return to work. Are you two going to sail out today or what?" "We will be cruising the ICW back, and I want to visit Titusville and see old buddy. We won't be home until Tuesday afternoon." "You have a great life, Brad; I envy you. Sue and I will brief the Grotto on our findings, and I'll contact the local Agent in the Daytona area to assist Malott. You two have a good sail home, and we'll talk later."

Later that day, Sue was in her office reviewing the various Task Force reports on the gravedigger theory. One of the reports grabbed her attention. Sergeant Morris turned it in and noted that none of Wabasso's Time Everlasting Cemetery employees fit the profile. The Office Manager, Mrs. Oliver, did not recognize any sketches, and all the employees were elderly. The new young owner, James Zachary, is out of town for several days and unavailable for questioning. The thing that heightened Sue's interest was the term 'new young owner.' That phrase and his not being available to be questioned increased her curiosity.

"Frank, all these reports look mundane, except this one concerning the Time Everlasting Cemetery," Sue remarked. "I will check that again; don't ask me why. Maybe it's just a hunch, but I feel uneasy about this 'new young owner.'" "Should I tell Jack you're looking for a younger guy?" Frank jested.

"Yeah, do that; it may keep him interested," she quipped. "It's just that this 'young guy' is in a death-related business, and I'll feel better when I can see him and talk with him myself, especially after the situation at the party." "That's a good thought," Frank stated. "Even though you and Jack didn't get a good look at the guy, seeing and talking with him may strike a familiar note."

Sue commented, "If Jessie was the person we encountered, his avoidance of facial exposure is why we could not obtain a good sketch. The Daytona people mentioned the same thing concerning his exposure." "That's entirely possible," Frank concurred, "the current drawings have slight similarities, but then, I doubt if the other ladies were paying much attention to him. I believe that women in today's world are more interested in obtaining their catch for the night than in ogling someone else's catch."

Sue replied, "You're out of sync in today's world, Frank." "Very true," he replied, "and I hope I stay out of sync from what

I have seen so far." "I hope you do, too," said Sue. "I don't think you would fit in the singles world. Besides, you and Mary are both suited for each other; enjoy it, and let us single souls rough it out." "Speaking of that, how are things going with you and the FBI?" Sue stated, "Our relationship is fine; he has not arrested me yet or made any unwanted advances." "Understood," Frank replied, "and I heard the term unwanted advances. I don't see much unwanted glowing in your eyes when he's around. Here's hoping it works for you both." "Thanks," replied Sue, "I think it will."

Chapter 18

Mrs. Oliver's Story

"James, dear boy," Mrs. Oliver said in a cheery voice as he walked into the office, "I am delighted you're home. The business has flourished just fine in your absence with no problems. However, there is a personal problem which we need to discuss, and I suggest we have a serious discussion very soon. The police are seeking someone who may have information concerning several missing women in the area. Reading between the lines, I assume their inquiries involve more than merely missing. The authorities believe the women have been murdered based on the news releases and the Christine Lowell case. Anyway, we need to talk, and I think the sooner, the better."

"My goodness, Ms. Oliver, why are you so concerned about these so-called murders?" James asked. "I'll explain later," she replied, "please allow me to continue. They left sketches of a possible suspect, which I put in your to-do file. Take a good look at the drawings, James. Then, with an open mind, look in the mirror. When you're done, perhaps we can discuss the subject one-on-one." "I will do that, Mrs. Oliver. You sound sincere and genuinely concerned. Let me look at the sketches, and we shall begin this discussion." James sat at his desk, leaned back in his chair, and perused the sketches and his mirrored reflection. Mrs. Oliver poured him a stiff scotch and water and, much to his surprise, fixed one for herself, then sat across from him at the desk. "Oh, my, Mrs. Oliver, this matter must be disturbing you. I don't think I have ever known you to imbibe, and I am surprised that you no longer speak like the prim schoolmarm you usually portray." "I'm far from a schoolmarm, James," she snickered. "I am a good old gal from the Louisiana Bayous, where you were born, and there are many other things you don't know about me. Perhaps it is time that I tell you a story. A true story, mind you, and it just may startle you a bit. Sip your scotch slowly, sit back, and relax. I shall begin by relating some facts concerning the past. Once we have acknowledged the past, we shall address the current problem." James did as told.

"Your father, William Allen Zachary, or Billy Zac, as I preferred to call him, was one sweet-talking man. He had an aura about him that swept women off their feet and, many times, right into his bed. I fell in love with him the first time I met him, even though we never hooked up. I adored him, and he was always pleasant to me. He was working the oil rigs back then and making big bucks. He was a handsome man, very mannish, with a lot of sex appeal. He had a very laid-back, easy-going personality, but don't piss him off. If you did, all hell would break loose, and he mostly came out on top. For some reason, your mother, Patsy Sue, treated him like dirt and gave him the shaft after she became pregnant with you. She blamed the pregnancy solely on him and neglected that she willingly spread her legs. Your Pa tried to do the honorable thing and marry her, but she would have no part of him or his offers of support. I believe he loved your Ma and wanted fatherhood. But she accused him of ruining her life and simply wanted him out of it. That is the first and last time I ever saw your Pa turn away from trouble, but believe me, Patsy Sue was trouble. He told me it was because of the baby, meaning you, that he didn't just do her in and solve the problem, but being a gentleman, he never did lay a hand on her. He eventually left her alone and never spoke to her again.

A good friend of your Dad's, Troy Gibbons, whom he met on the rigs, convinced your Pa to go to Florida and help him operate a cemetery he had inherited. Now, Billy Zac was the manual labor type of man and wasn't sure about running a cemetery, but Gibbons persuaded him to try it. The next thing I knew, they formed a partnership and left the Bayous. That's how your Pa came to be here at Time Everlasting. Less than a year after their move, Gibbons was killed in a car wreck right in front of the office on US-1. Some drunk tourist t-boned him as he pulled out of our drive. Because of Troy's wishes, your Dad took his body back home to Louisiana for burial.

That's when Billy Zac and I got together. I previously mentioned that I fell in love with him at first sight, so I had to chase him when I saw him back in town. After a few days and nights of being together, he asked me to come to Florida with him, and that's how I got here. If one partner died under their partnership agreement, the other partner took full possession of the business and property. Your Pa now owned this place lock, stock, and barrel, and the insurance settlement from Troy's death paid off all the indebtedness plus some. That extra money gave your father a nice nest egg and enabled him to make many improvements. It also gave him a financial pad to help the business become more profitable. Your Pa had a lot of business sense, and he quickly made this place a success. He sent me to a business school in Vero where I learned my skills and etiquette; thus, I became the prim schoolmarm you thought me to be. Billy Zac and I enjoyed living here together up until his untimely demise. That's when I got the lawyer to find you since you were the beneficiary.

Your Dad and I screwed up on one thing, to provide security for me in his will. He had his will drawn up in the early days with Troy, naming you as his heir, and we both neglected to make any changes to benefit me. I guess we both assumed that we would be here forever. That's why I gladly stayed with you when you asked, and I was praying you would ask. You did; I stayed, which covers the story's business end."

James stated, "I always thought there was more to you than

what you first told me. I just wasn't sure what it was." "Yes, ma'am," he replied and proceeded to do so. "Yes, James, and there is still much more to my story, but it's your turn to fix the scotches while I continue. Now let's uncover some of my past," Mrs. Oliver stated. "Your Dad and I had a very understanding relationship, no marriage involved, just intimate friends who worked, played, and slept together. I loved him, but I think he was hurt so badly by your mom that he wouldn't let his feelings go again. I understood that and accepted things the way they were. I had him here with me, and that mattered to me. Your Dad and I had a good thing going.

I worked hard at learning the business, developed a decent business sense, acquired enough education to handle the finances, and ran the business as I am doing for you. That left Billy Zac free to run things outside the office, which made him happy since he preferred to have little to no contact with the grieving customers. Plus, he tended to become irate if they rejected our services and chose to go elsewhere. That kind of sounds like you, James, doesn't it?"

"Usually," she continued, "your Dad and I went out together, eating and partying, but he decided to go alone one night. According to what I heard, a flirty little bitch came onto him strong, and when he was ready to take her up on it, she brushed him off. I loved your Pa very much, but he did have a wandering eye at times, and I accepted the lust he had. Well, the next thing I knew, that flirty chick made headlines as being a missing person. They never did find her, but I noticed a fresh dig by the big trees in the back part of the lot. It was an unscheduled dig that had not been entered in the books. So, I played it cool and kept my mouth shut. Besides, as I said, your Dad and I had a good thing going, so why screw it up over a few flirty bitches. Yes, I said a few. If you check the police records, you'll find six missing person reports still unsolved during that time frame. Oddly enough, six plots in the back lot are recorded as burial sites for the Oliver family. They all were relatives of mine that I never had, but since I handled the paperwork, that fact will likely never be known. Your Dad was a great guy, except when someone crossed him. If they did, he became different, and violence became his middle name. After your Dad ventured out by himself, I noticed there would soon be another night's outing, and a missing woman would make the news. The authorities never found a connection or even suspected Billy Zac, so he must have been cautious with his actions and used precise plans. Deep inside me, I somehow knew he was involved. There were just too many coincidental happenings associated with each of the women. I never questioned him about those things, and he never spoke of them. I simply accepted his extracurricular encounters for what they were: flirtations that went bad. Honestly, I won't swear to the fact that there were only six, but six is all I know."

"Holy hell, Mrs. Oliver, you're telling me that my father was a serial killer, and you knew about it all these years? Why didn't you tell me this long ago? I saw no need to bring him down off that pedestal you had him on, and I wasn't sure about your reaction, she replied. I probably should have told you since I guessed what happened to your mother. Stemming from rumors I heard from the home folk and a fresh dig about the time you became involved. I was somewhat in tune with your dilemma. I figured, like father, like son. I also perceived that the missing women in the area might relate to all the other digs. The timing was right, but I wasn't sure until I saw the police sketches. Somewhere along the line, you fucked up James. You may have become a person of interest and associated somehow with the bitches, as you call them. You allowed yourself to be seen, and people remembered you.

This association is not a good situation for either of us. Hell, since I know about you and your Dad, they can charge me for withholding information and possibly an accessory. We must convince the police that the person they pursue is not you.

Having gone through some of this with your father, I hope to give you some soulful advice that you will need to heed, and damn it, from here on in, call me Franie. The correct name is Francine, but if you call me that, I may get pissed." "Ok," James answered, "Franie it is, but if you become aware of the digs and my actions, what about Old Joe, Boris, Ted, and the other workers? Have they noticed?" "Not to worry, dear boy, those guys are relatives of mine and wouldn't dare jeopardize your position, my position, or theirs. They could also be classified as accessories since they worked and knew your Dad's story and possibly yours. I know Joe and Boris are aware of your antics but unsure of the others."

"Under the circumstances, Franie, I have no reason not to believe you, but I must say you have shocked the hell out of me. Here I was, trying to be secretive so I would not offend you, and now I find out that you know more about me than I thought. I sincerely believe that I need your advice, but first, I need to ask you, do you think Dad had an alter-personality?" "He had what he called a close friend he talked with, but I never saw this person," Franie answered. "On many occasions, I heard him talking to someone but knew he was in the office alone, so to answer your question, yes, I think he did. That could be why you have one; some ills of that nature are inheritable, and yes, I know you have one. If I have heard you correctly, you call him Zac." "What do you mean, heard me?" James questioned. "I have seen you gaze out the window in a trance, and when doing so, you mutter as though you are talking with someone. I have heard the name Zac several times, and of course, I remembered it because your father was called Billy Zac, and he would gaze out the window and mumble also, as I said, like father, like son. Now, listen carefully. I told the authorities that you were out of town for several days, and I did not say when you would return, so we only have a brief time to finalize my plan."

"I definitely need a plan, Franie. I did fuck up. I actually talked and socialized with that female cop from Vero and her FBI boyfriend at a party not long ago, and the woman I was with is now planted outback in the bitch farm. I did my best to conceal my identity and not provide them with a good look at my face, but there is the possibility that they may recognize me if we ever meet face to face. I never thought they would get this close to me, Zac, or Jessie. I guess I should have been more careful." "You certainly should have," Franie replied, "and who the hell is Jessie? Oh, hell, don't try to explain, and don't panic," she said, "we will work it out somehow. By the way, I like the name you bestowed upon the back portion of the cemetery. Let's hope no bitches grow out there," she snickered. James replied, "I have been letting Zac slip one in the crematory occasionally, so other than possible forensics in the soil, the evidence has gone up in smoke. Plus, I mixed their ashes in with legitimate cremations." "Good idea, James; I will continue that little ritual in the future until they all are gone." "Why do you say you will continue?" James asked. "Well, under the circumstances, it's going to be necessary for you to become a missing person, so to speak," Franie answered, "but not in the same manner as the bitches, of course. I have been carefully developing a plan, much like you have done with the bitches, and I will explain soon once my plan is complete."

Sue And Jack Discuss Jessie

The phone rang, but before Jack could say anything, Sue said, "Hello, how is my big brave FBI agent today?" He replied, "I'm just fine now that I have heard your voice. What's on that pretty little mind of yours? This report from the Cemetery in Wabasso is bugging me. I want to go up there and personally meet this James Zachary, who was referred to as the 'new young owner.' Also, if you recall, we have been told that Jessie referred to a person named Zac. Zac is a commonly used nickname for Zachary, and if you remember, the guy in Vero called himself Frank James. Frank James is the brother of Jessie James, and the cemetery owner is named James. Plus, do you recall the partial business card Marci found in Gwen's purse? The Wabasso cemetery is titled 'Time Everlasting.'

The partial card had the word 'Time' and the letters 'Re' under that, then the letters "Ja" under that. The cemetery card Brad got has time Everlasting; under that is Rest in Peace, and under that is his name, James A. Zachary. That all fits, plus the lady at the office could be the lady who had the ring repaired. Now, is it just me, or are there a lot of coincidences here?" "Wow, that's a lot to absorb," Jack stated. "I thought you were reciting an entire chapter from some novel. However, my pretty one, you may have found some valuable clues to open these cases, but do not go up there alone. Please sit tight and let me talk with Brad. I think it is best if all of us go together. He and Marci should be home late tomorrow, and I'll get with him on this ASAP. If I recall the report correctly, the office lady told Morris that the owner would be out of town for several days. Am I correct?" "Yes, that is correct," Sue answered. "Ok, then he is probably still out of town, so please wait until Brad returns, and you can brief him on your findings. You know he will want to be with us when we bust this guy. Promise me you won't go without us." "I promise, worrywart," Sue quipped, "but in the meantime, I'll do as much research as possible on the 'new young owner,' Mr. James Zachary."

Franie's Plan

Early the following day, Franie contacted some old acquaintances and relatives back in Louisiana whom she knew trustworthy. She had talked on the phone for nearly an hour when James walked in and overheard the conversation. "Yes, Doris," Frani said, "I am serious. I need to have Timmy come here and stay for a few weeks, possibly longer, but hopefully shorter. You mustn't tell anyone where he is going and must instruct Timmy to do everything as I say. We will pay you lavishly for his efforts; all Tim has to do is pretend to be James. He has the same build, is similar in appearance, is the same age, and has enough street smarts to make this work. I guarantee he will bring you home some nice change for your bankroll, and if all goes well, he will only be here a few days. Cousin Kurt made the driver's license, bank cards, IDs, and other necessary papers. He shipped them overnight, so I already have them for James and Timmy. The airline ticket will be waiting at the airport in Timmy's name.

When he arrives in Orlando, Boris will pick him up. Ensure Timmy has Boris's cell number and calls him when he exits the plane. Boris will be on standby and has all of Timmy's new papers. With Timmy getting here tomorrow, it will give me at least a couple of days to educate him to be James. I know Timmy, and I know I can teach him all he needs to learn quickly, and with his experience in the actors club, it will be a snap. Doris, you won't regret this and remind Timmy that the ticket is in his name, but once he is off the plane and in Florida, his name is James Alfred Zachary. I believe we have previously discussed the rest of the plan. It just recently became necessary to bring Timmy on board. I must get James out of Florida undetected quickly, and that is why Tim is needed. Ensure he studies all the data on James that I shipped out to you. That data gives the history Tim will need to know. He will be on the plane tomorrow replied Doris. Good sighed, Franie; that's what I wanted to hear. Call me when the plane leaves, and I'll call you when everything is clear. Goodbye, Doris, and thanks again."

"Holy hell, Franie, what was all that about, and who is Doris and Timmy?" James asked. "It was about my plan to save your ass, my dear boy. Doris is my sister, and Timmy is her son. They are to be trusted to the fullest. Pour us an extra big scotch, and I'll elaborate. First, it is becoming evident that the law is beginning to suspect your involvement with the murders in the area. Based on that, your presence here jeopardizes your freedom and the freedom of most of us working here since we know your involvement and have maintained silence. My plan is you will go to Louisiana, where you will be away from the local law and out of sight. I'll explain the details as soon as you get me that scotch."

Sipping her scotch, Franie proceeded with her story. "I mentioned that our yard workers are relatives. They are my cousins except for Boris, our yard foreman who handles the legal burials and the crematorium. Boris is my brother. Your Dad and Boris were close friends, and he knows about your Dad's plantings. Boris will play an essential role in my plan."

With a puzzled look, James poured the scotches and sat across from Franie. "Boris is a swell guy. I should have guessed there was a family connection, but what is his role in this plan?" "Allow me to start from the beginning," Franie stated. "I invited you to my house for more privacy and fewer interruptions than at the office. Boris is tending the shop for us today. He is very competent and helps me a lot when you're gone.

First, you will go to my sister's house in Louisiana. She lives out in the country on the north side of Lake Pontchartrain, between Slidell and Mandeville. You'll be safe there, and I doubt that anyone of importance will see you. Doris will introduce you as her cousin's boy, and your name will be Hershel Daquin from Baton Rouge. Doris will help you learn the dialect and develop the accent. You will be hiding for the first few weeks and very busy adapting to your new identity. Cousin Kurt made all the paperwork for the new you: birth certificate, driver's license, social security number, and the rest of the data to prove you are no longer James. He even has family pictures for you.

You are an only child, and the name Daquin dies with you. Kurt is a genius at creating new identities, plus Doris has some connections with a plastic surgeon who will make minor alterations to your appearance. You won't even know who you are when everyone gets done. Kurt even managed to get Hershel an excellent credit rating and several high-dollar credit cards. So Hershel Daquin will be you in your new life. Your new identity will be pleasant once you get used to it. You'll have plenty of money and no cares in the world, and the New Orleans area is a great place to live.

On the other hand, Zac is someone only you can control, and you will need to do that. If he gets out of line, it could blow your cover and your future. The same applies to Jessie. I assume Jessie is another personality of yours, similar to Zac, so James, Zac, and Jessie will now be Hershel Daquin. Hershel will remain free in the Bayous to enjoy the rest of his life; all you have to do is be willing to be him. It's up to you, James, to do it. The least I can do for your father is to keep you out of jail.

Timmy arrives tomorrow, and while here, he will be James Alfred Zachary. I shall instruct him on that task, knowing he can do it. Since he will be you, there will be no problem letting him talk with the law should they decide to return, and I feel confident they will. Several people have mentioned that the female cop you met at the party has been making inquiries. It's evident that one of your identities, or personas, has become better known than you thought, and they just may associate the serial killer they call Jessie with being you. I know that once the law sees Timmy as James Zachary, they will dismiss the thought of him being a suspect. If they request DNA or fingerprints, it will cause no problems. Tim has no DNA or fingerprints on file; he's a straight shooter.

Timmy will stay here briefly, acting as you, because the Time Ever Lasting cemetery is being sold. I used the 'power of attorney' that you gave me to have the business listed for sale. A close friend in the real estate business assisted me and made an error on the date, showing it listed on the market for the last year. Just a simple typo, but it worked, and she was well rewarded. She knows nothing besides the listing data and will not divulge the date error. That will let the police believe selling is not a spur-of-the-moment decision and that James is not panicking or running. The nice thing about it is Boris is buying the business. James Zachary is holding the mortgage and taking early retirement. Based on those facts, Timmy can act as you until Boris takes over. Once the authorities are satisfied that James is not Jessie, Timmy can return home as Timmy. We can discuss the finer details later, but that gives you a heads-up on my plan; since you leave for Orlando tonight, I need you to start preparing."

"Whoa," stammered James, "how in hell are we going to make all of this work, and how did you dream it all up?" "I have expected this day to come," Franie continued, "so I have been developing the basic plan for some time now. I had to add Timmy's role since you screwed up at the party. It would have been much more straightforward if it hadn't been for that. The timing on all this may vary slightly, depending on the cops, but as soon as they talk with Timmy, we can initiate the sale, and Tim will leave the area. In the meantime, my power of attorney gives me the authority to handle the business's sale in James's absence. I will start the preliminaries of the deal tomorrow. I am sure your cop friends will get wind of it, and that, if nothing else, should get them moving to interview James. Once they meet Timmy acting as James, the heat will be off for a while, and we can complete the sale.

All the proper paperwork will show you selling the business and its property to Boris. He will give you $250,000 down, and you will hold a note for the remaining six point five million, which is reasonable. The sale will all be legal and recorded correctly if the law decides to get nosy. All of which will permit the name James Alfred Zachary to depart from the area without suspicion. Boris and I will become partners and have a private contract between our partnership and you, providing you with a very generous monthly income. You can start a new life in a different area, and I shall remain here to run the business with Boris. We all live happily ever after, so to speak, and you and the 'Bitch Farm' will stay undetected, and James Alfred Zachary only exists on paper."

"It sounds good," James stated, "however, I should start packing for tonight's departure. By the way, am I flying, or what?" "I have booked first-class reservations in your new name, and I will give you all the necessary IDs and papers, including credit cards, so you are well-documented as Hershel Daquin. It will be best for you, Mr. Daquin, to leave your house tonight and get a motel at the Orlando airport.

That way, there can be no accidental mishaps when the new James Zachary arrives tomorrow. We wouldn't want anyone seeing both of you together now, would we? Old Joe will take you to Melbourne to rent a car to drive to Orlando." "I know I can trust you with everything, Franie," James said, "and I am glad my father had you around. It's a shame I didn't know you sooner; you would have made a fantastic mother." She replied, "We are in this together. So, as I said earlier, make the best of it for all of us."

Sue Researching James

The phone startled Sue, who was deeply engrossed in deciphering her accumulated data on James Alfred Zachary. "Hi, sweetness," Jack said. "I just finished talking with Brad. He will be a day longer than expected, but he asked that we please wait on him before going to Wabasso and interviewing Zachary. I told him you were getting anxious, but I would try to persuade you to wait. You will wait, won't you?" She replied, "One more day wouldn't hurt, but I would call and make an appointment to ensure he was there. I know this is our guy, and I hope we don't scare him off." "The thing is, Sue, we don't have enough evidence to warrant any other kind of action," Jack said. "An interview requesting information about his employees is the most we can justify right now. If he turns out to be the guy we met at the party, the DA said we could bring him in for questioning regarding the Langford case. Otherwise, we have nothing but our hunches."

"Have you turned up anything new with your snooping?" "Nothing significant," Sue said. "Zachary inherited the business several years ago from his father, who was killed in a plane crash. He took over the cemetery when he was 18 and has done well with it. Zachary has a spotless record, not even a parking ticket. He has no military history, fingerprints, girlfriends, and nothing that would provide more data. Mr. Zachary pays his bills on time, has excellent credit, files taxes quarterly, and declares an upper six-figure income. There are no complaints at the Better Business Bureau; he is a member of the Rotary Club but is not an active participant. Zachary drives a Mercedes, was paid for in cash, and is a model citizen. He almost sounds too perfect. There has to be a flaw somewhere.

Many people know of him, but no one knows him personally or has been associated with him. His assistant, Mrs. Oliver, handles 99% of the business at the cemetery and worked for his father when he was alive. He appears somewhat of a recluse and lives in a moderate house adjacent to the cemetery. I checked out most of the recent burials and cremations, but they all proved legit. I have found nothing to indicate that Zachary is our man other than my intuition. All the things we know, plus what I have just told you, make him Jessie in my mind, even though we can't prove it without DNA or fingerprints." "Hang in there, Sue, and we will let your intuition do its job. Once Brad gets back, you will get a face-to-face meeting with James Zachary."

The Interview

Franie answered the phone: "Time Everlasting Cemetery, this is Mrs. Oliver. May I help you?" "Yes, Mrs. Oliver, this is Detective Sue Gunther with the Vero Beach Police Department. A few days ago, a couple of our detectives stopped by your office and were told Mr. Zachary was out of town for a few days. I was inquiring to see if he has returned." "Yes, he has," Franie replied. "However, he has temporarily stepped out of the office. I will be happy to take a message." "Of course," said Sue, "I would appreciate it if he would call me so that I might schedule an interview with him. We hope he may supply us with the names of some individuals in your related field of business who may know about some missing persons." "I am sure Mr. Zachary will happily oblige you," Franie responded. "However, I scheduled all of his appointments. I will see if he is available if you have a date and time." "Oh, thank you," Sue stated. "Would he be available on Thursday morning at ten o'clock?"

"Let me look at the schedule. Yes, ten o'clock will be just fine. James has a nine o'clock meeting but should be available by ten." "Very good," replied Sue. "There will be two other investigators with me, and thank you. We shall see you Thursday." "You are most welcome," Franie replied and hung up the phone. Turning to the man beside her, she said, "Timmy, oops, excuse me, James, we have until Thursday morning to make sure you are prepared. We must concentrate on your indoctrination and quickly turn you into James. You, dear sir, are the prime actor in this saga, and based on your amateur theater experience, this should be a snap."

Thursday morning arrived. Franie raised her head as the door to the office opened. "May I help you?" she asked. Sue responded, "You must be Mrs. Oliver. I'm Detective Gunther with the Vero Beach PD, and these are Special Agents Brad Ashley and Jack Baird of the FBI. We have a 10 o'clock appointment with Mr. Zachary." "Yes, of course, it is almost ten. Please have a seat; James had to run home for a minute following his nine o'clock meeting but should be back momentarily. FBI, oh my," Franie stated, "you did not mention the FBI the other day. I hope this is nothing serious." "Just questions," Sue replied. "The FBI is assisting us with our investigation." "May I get you a coffee, iced tea, or water? That's about all we keep in the office," Mrs. Oliver said. "No, thank you," the trio responded in unison as they took seats in the waiting area. Just then, Boris entered the room and deposited some papers on the desk, causing curious looks to be exchanged among the three visitors.

"Oh, excuse me," Mrs. Oliver said, "allow me to introduce Boris DuBose. Mr. DuBose is negotiating to purchase this business from Mr. Zachary. He has been reviewing the books and getting to know the ins and outs of the operation." "I was not aware that a sale was pending," Sue replied. "Oh my yes," stated Mrs. Oliver. "Mr. Zachary has been trying to sell for approximately a year now." Boris remarked very dignifiedly, "My offer to purchase had been kept quiet upon my request. I have previously made similar purchases, and undo publicity can create problems. All the paperwork has been submitted to the city, county, and state to transfer the licenses and ownership.

However, we have attempted to keep it out of the press until all hurdles have been passed." Boris stated, "Your cooperation would be appreciated," as he shook their hands. "James mentioned that he had a ten o'clock appointment with local authorities, and I hope there are no problems." "No problems," replied Sue, "just questions." "You have our word on being quiet about the sale," said Brad. "When do you anticipate completing the transaction?" Boris answered, "Within days if all goes well, the lawyers are busy as we speak. If you kind people will excuse me, I must go. James has just pulled in, and I am certain you will wish to begin your meeting. I wish you all a good day and sincerely thank you, Mrs. Oliver, for your help. I shall see you later this afternoon, and please don't forget our dinner engagement." Franie allowed the quick flush of her cheeks to become apparent as she escorted Boris to the door and held it open for his departure and James's arrival.

"James, this is Detective Gunther and FBI Agents Ashley and Baird; they are your ten o'clock appointment." "Thank you, Mrs. Oliver, and let me apologize for being a few minutes late. I had an unavoidable task to attend to at home. Won't you all please come into the office and have a seat?" Sue and Jack exchanged glances as they made their way to the office. She gave Jack a facial expression indicating that this man was not the man they had met in Vero, and Brad sensed their disappointment. Timmy looked at them as they settled into their seats and asked, "How may I help?" He leaned back and smiled, seeing that his role as James was being played successfully. Feeling defeated, Sue gathered her composure and started explaining the missing persons and the funeral theory as she had with the other businesses. The general question and answer period only lasted about ten minutes. "Thank you for your time, Mr. Zachary," Brad said, "We will leave now, but may I have one of your business cards for my report?" Sensing a hunt for fingerprints, Timmy handed them all a card, knowing his prints would be on them.

The silence in the car was deafening as it left the parking area and turned onto US-1. Sue broke the ice with an unladylike comment when she said. "Oh shit!" Brad looked at her and said, "Don't let it bother you, Sue. All the indicators pointed to you being on the right track, and I'm not sure you aren't." "Thanks for the confidence, Brad, but I feel like I blew this one. However, everything did point in this direction. I find it hard to believe I was that far off base." Brad commented, "Let's not rush to conclusions, so this Mr. Zachary is not the Frank James you and Jack met in Vero, but maybe the guy we just met is not Zachary. He seemed confident and knowledgeable, but now, my intuition is kicking in. Why have we not discovered that Zachary was selling the business before now? Perhaps he has heard talk in his business community, and he senses that we are getting close and feels that he needs to make some changes." Brad continued, "That could include having a pinch hitter sit in on a meeting that concerns the law.

For some reason, I sense something to be amiss with this whole meeting scene. See if you can find someone who knows Zachary by sight, a business contact, a salesperson, or someone. Surely, as long as he has owned this business, someone has seen him and would recognize him as James Zachary. If you find this person, maybe we can somehow convince them to visually identify Zachary, even if it requires us to request another meeting. Let's turn these cards over to the CSI boys for fingerprints." "What are you saying?" Jack asked. "Do you think this guy today was a stand-in, and if so, what about the guy buying the place?" "He identified James when he arrived, and so did Mrs. Oliver. I think I understand," Sue stated anxiously. "You feel this whole scene today may have been staged, right?" "It is possible," answered Brad, "call it a gut feeling. Now, let's see if we can prove it."

James in LA

"Franie probably told you that I made you an appointment with a close friend, a plastic surgeon," Doris told James. "After looking at your pictures, Dr. Leman feels confident that a few minor alterations to your appearance and even your best friend will have difficulty recognizing you. However, he can change your prints but not your DNA, so you must be cautious. Doc wants you to come in for a consultation tonight. He will probably start on you right away. You don't mind a little transformation, do you?" "It's not a matter if I mind," James answered, "it's a matter of staying ahead of the law. If they ever catch me, I know they would love to hang me, so I gotta do what I gotta do. Did Franie tell you about my alter personalities?" "Yes, she did, and I just hope you can become Hershel while you're here. Not James or Jessie, and let's damn sure keep Zac hidden. If so, I believe all will be fine." "I'll do my best," James answered. "Hershel is distinctive sounding, and I feel I can adapt."

The Sale

The lawyers completed the paperwork and shook Boris's hand. "Congratulations, Mr. Dubose; you are now the proud owner of the Time Everlasting Cemetery." "Thank you," said Boris, "Now, if I can persuade this lovely lady to remain with the business and become my partner, things will be much smoother."

"That just might be a possibility," Mrs. Oliver stated. "I wish to thank these gentlemen for helping me and my previous employer, Mr. Zachary, complete this sale in his absence." The lead lawyer commented, "It was our pleasure and part of our job. Advise Mr. Zachary to contact us if he has any questions or problems. We know you were trying to keep this transaction low-keyed, but the press will see these records tomorrow, and the sale will become public." "Not a problem," answered Boris, "the transaction is finalized, and the publicity will not hinder anything now. Perhaps a little advertising may do the business some good, and we shall see you gentlemen again and soon to draw up some partnership papers."

Franie and Boris left the lawyer's office and drove towards Wabasso. Boris asked, "Have we forgotten anything?" "I don't think so, and I sure as hell hope not. Let's get back to the farm. Oh hell, James has me calling it a farm." Boris quipped, "Some strange things are planted there, and until I can get all those peculiar posies into the cremation oven, we need to ensure that no one gets nosey." "I agree," replied Franie. "That female cop was beginning to get on my nerves. She is nosey, so you and Timmy need to head for Louisiana at sun up tomorrow. I don't want her snooping around until after Timmy is gone.

We have been lucky that nobody who knows James has stopped by to see him. That's all we need: somebody raising a flag that Timmy is not James. Miss snoopy cop would be on that like flies on; you know what."

Chapter 19

Sue

"Wow, that was quick," Sue commented. "What are you talking about?" asked Frank. "The cemetery sale, we were just there two days ago, and yesterday, the deal was completed," Sue answered. Frank noted that a clean sale could go fast, depending on the circumstances. "Let me see what I can find in the records," Sue injected. "Yes, here it is, in the court of records report. It was a cash sale with no recorded mortgage." Frank added, "All the buyer needed was a clean title search, a survey, and a good lawyer, which he had."

"Frank, I understand what you're saying, but," Sue stated, "something about the situation that does not sit right with me. I'm beginning to agree with Brad's intuition. According to the paperwork, the business has been for sale for nearly a year. Suddenly, it is sold, just as we indicate a slight interest in this Zachary guy. I'm hoping that Gary Walton will call me today. He's had face-to-face business dealings with Zachary. Maybe I can convince him to make a personal ID and put my mind to rest." "You like that hunch of Brad's that the interview was staged, don't you?" Frank asked. "Yeah, I guess I do," she answered. "There are too many clues that point at Zachary. They are all circumstantial, but they are good leads, and we need to make them solid."

"Sue, we have dozens of top-notch cops working on these

cases, and no one has made a solid connection yet. Your clues with the business card, the Frank James outlaw thing, etc., are some of our best. Unfortunately, they are far from solid. If Zachary is our man, he has been too damn smart and cautious for firm evidence to be found. Even the fingerprints we found are not in any database, and the prints Brad got from the business card did not match any of the cases. If we had some of his DNA, we could compare it to what we found. Unfortunately, we cannot pursue a warrant for his DNA or fingerprints. If we snuck through the back door and stole his toothbrush, the DNA would probably prove our theory is correct, but the courts would throw it out, and the bastard would go free. He even burns his trash, so we can't do a dumpster dive. We cannot even justify surveillance of him. Our problem is we are behind the eight-ball on this one with no viable shot until he makes a goof or we get a break."

James's Plastic Surgery

"James, oops, I should say, Hershel, how are you feeling?" Doris asked. "Boris and Timmy are here and would like to update you on all the happenings." "I think I'm up to it," James answered. "However, I need to get used to being Hershel, and if it's not too much trouble, could you have them bring some ice water when they come in?" "Of course, Boris, you and Timmy, come on in, and I'll get the water." "Your face is puffed up like an overripe melon," Timmy joked. "Are you in much pain?" "You know the old joke; it only hurts when I laugh, but," Hershel replied, "it has not been as bad as I thought." "I'll say one thing," Boris commented, "when all that swelling goes down, I don't believe I'll recognize you or that you will recognize yourself, and that's a good thing. You will be able to come and go without a problem. Hell, nobody will know ya. How long did the Doc say it would take for the healing?" "I can venture out in public for a few weeks, but it will be a few months before the redness and scaring are gone. So I'll just be patient, but enough about me," Hershel said, "how are things on the farm?" Boris brought him up to date, and Timmy added highlights when needed. Boris said,

"I'm Glad you are making progress, but I need to be heading back to Florida and tending to business. See you again, Hershel, and good luck in your new life."

Boris Back At The Farm

Boris came into the office after working at the crematorium. "There go another couple of posies up in smoke," he said. "Not many more, and all of James's wild oats will be dug up and become dust in the wind. Once they are done, we can relax a little about possible exhumation. I got 'Bitch-Mother' and the Hays girl today, so that only leaves a few more. We have more scheduled cremations, so I should be able to get all the remaining posies mixed in with legitimate ash. I guess I didn't realize how many James planted. He sure was more active than Billy Zac was." "Yes, indeed he was, Boris, and I sure am glad you're close to completion with James's contributions," Franie replied. "We will need to weed his Dad's garden next, then we all will be safe."

"I'm happy you're back from Louisiana," Franie commented, "and Timmy has also gone. He did a fantastic job acting as James, but with him gone, James is gone. I heard today that the snoopy female cop was back asking questions again. I was casually talking with a lady who works for Gary Walton. She told me that the Vero cops had been talking with Gary. She didn't hear all the details, but she did say that Zachary's name came up several times. It seems odd that they would be talking with Walton. However, he is one of the few local persons James dealt with directly." "What will you tell this cop if she wants to meet with him again?" Boris asked. "I'll simply fabricate a little story that he is no longer in the area. We do not know his new location, and she added the last time we heard, he was visiting someone in Smithfield, VA. That should put a fly in her ointment." "Let's hope so," Boris stated. "Just remember our story should she talk with you." "No problem on my part, Sis. You have drilled the details into me so many times I feel like a sieve." "And don't call me Sis," Franie scolded. "If the female cop knew we were related, she'd get twice as nosey."

Chapter 20

Grotto Meeting

Approximately six months had slipped by with no further leads in any of the cases. Frank called a status meeting with the Task Force at the Grotto in sheer desperation and requested all members be present. Brad, Sue, and Jack were sitting in the front row, listening intently to what he had to say. "The Task Force has thirteen missing females, one missing male, and two bodies, one female and one male. That equals fourteen suspected murders and two confirmed murders, plus one missing K-9 carcass. All of which, we suspect to be associated with the same perpetrator we call 'Jessie.' In general, people, it has been over six months since the last presumed 'Jessie' victim, Calie Lucas, disappeared, and we are no closer to finding this SOB than we were when we opened the Grotto and started the Task Force. Sue Gunther has developed a concept related to a local individual named James Zachary as being Jessie. Thus far, he has been our one and only person of interest. May I ask Sue to take the floor and explain her effort to identify the perpetrator we call Jessie?"

"Certainly," said Sue as she approached the podium. "James Alfred Zachary is, or was, the owner of Time Everlasting Cemetery in Wabasso, Florida. He appears to fit most of the criteria brought forth by the Task Force via the clues and data derived from all of our cases. We have found things like his association with funerals, access to bleach, various cleaning products, the word bitch, and many others. Assuming all of our clues are accurate, Mr. Zachary could be our killer, but we have no hard evidence that legally lets us pursue him or obtain warrants. We interviewed Zachary within the limits of the law. Still, we could not ID him as a suspect, and we were uncertain that the person we interviewed was indeed Zachary and not an impersonator. A business contact was willing to help with a visual ID, but Zachary sold the business and disappeared from the area. Thus, no personal ID was made. Even the FBI has not found any trace of his whereabouts. His disappearance was not discovered until I asked Zachary's office manager to request another interview. She caught me entirely by surprise when she informed me that Zachary had an emergency arise and hurriedly left the area a few days before the completion of selling the cemetery. The lawyers handling the sale were legally authorized, and Mrs. Oliver had legal power of attorney, so the deal was legal and completed. She also stated that Zachary had packed all his belongings from the office and house. He told her that he had an acquaintance whom Mrs. Oliver did not know to load up a truck and take them. However, she claims no knowledge as to where they were taken.

She did inform me that according to the sales agreement, Mr. Dubose was to send or transfer the sales deposit to a bank account in Smithfield, Virginia. The account number she provided was a small partnership owning some Virginia rental property and other real-estate investments. We have checked every possible link that would indicate Zachary's presence in the Smithfield area or his ties to the partnership but to no avail. It's assumed that he is not physically in Smithfield and uses electronic media to access his account. We have no idea why Smithfield was established. Without warrants, we can't access records that might provide a lead regarding his location. I have some friends in the banking and computer world who could not find any data, legally or otherwise. The only data obtained was that a financial transfer was made and that the cemetery sale was complete. The individuals involved with the partnership are also unreachable, and virtually no knowledge of them is obtainable. I know that digging into this data was illegal, but I was willing to try almost anything at this stage of the game. No further missing women have been reported since Zachary left the area. That gentleman is a synopsis of my theory and investigation. I had, and still have, a gut feeling, but nothing factual to back it up."

"We are getting frustrated," said Frank, "and I agree on doing almost anything, but we must keep it legal. Should we ever be able to charge Zachary, we don't want some wise-ass lawyer getting him off on a technicality. How about the Lucas Case in Daytona, Jack?" "Nothing more on her either," Jack replied. "I talked with Malott, and they have no new leads. The cleaning fluids and bleach were the same brands as in the other cases, along with many other similarities, pointing towards Jessie, but that's all we can say. Because of the similarities, the Lucas case appears to be linked with all the others. But like the other cases, we have no hard evidence on the perp."

Just then, the door flew open, and Sergeant Fields rushed in. "Sorry to interrupt you, Lieutenant, but I have an urgent message from the Slidell, Louisiana PD that might interest you. They called for you, and I told them of your Task Force meeting. A Lieutenant out there personally faxed this to me. He remained on the phone to ensure I received it and insisted it was passed on to you, even if it interrupted your meeting." Frank read the report aloud.

"To Lieutenant Frank Arendas, Vero Beach, FL Police Department, I understand you are investigating numerous missing person cases in your general area, possibly involving murders by a serial killer.

During the past year, I have read several of your reports distributed throughout the southeastern states. We recently encountered a missing person case similar to your reported cases. We would like to ask you to compare our data against yours. Being told that you are currently holding a meeting related to these concerns, I faxed this summary. I will transmit the report disclosing complete data within the next hour. Thank you, and looking forward to hearing from you. Lieutenant Donald Carmile, Slidell LA, PD."

"Sue, since you are head of the media releases, I'll turn this document over to you. Would you please read it to the Grotto?" Sue obliged and started reading the summation.

"Case Subject: Melisa Carter reported missing for 48-plus hours. Time: 3:15 pm. Based on the following facts, they obtained a search warrant to enter and examine Melisa Carter's home. The house appeared normal except for the master bedroom and adjoining bath. The bed was stripped bare of linens. The mattress appeared stained with blood. Pictures were removed from the walls and lined up on the floor. Stuffed animals were strategically placed around the room in various obscene poses. The room reeked of bleach and alcohol, and the word BITCH was written in blood on the bathroom mirror.

Melisa Carter is considered a missing person."

The Grotto went silent. "OH MY GOD!" shrieked Sue.

About The Author

Dutch Haid was raised on the mid-east coast of Florida and is a retired Mechanical Design Engineer from the Aerospace and Defense industry. He lived aboard his sailboat for 20+ years and is an avid sailor who sailed throughout the Caribbean, the Gulf of Mexico's coastal waters, and the coastal waters, from Florida to New York, for over 30+ years. He enjoys motorcycling on the back roads of FL and in the mountain ranges of the eastern U.S. He is a 50+ yr, 32nd-degree Mason, a member of the American Legion, the Amvets, the Loyal Order of Moose, and the Fraternal Order of Eagles. Dutch currently resides in Daytona Beach, FL.

Printed in the USA
CPSIA information can be obtained
at www.ICGtesting.com
LVHW020833210724
786028LV00011B/398